FRESH SCARS

DONNA MUMMA

FIREFLY
SOUTHERN FICTION
Imprint of Iron Stream Media

Firefly Southern Fiction is an imprint of LPCBooks
a division of Iron Stream Media
100 Missionary Ridge, Birmingham, AL 35242
ShopLPC.com

Printed in the United States of America

Cover design by Elaina Lee

Library of Congress Control Number: 2021936146

ISBN-13: 978-1-64526-285-5
Ebook ISBN: 978-1-64526-286-2

PRAISE FOR *FRESH SCARS*

A powerful story about the wounds we carry, and the courage it takes to let them go.

~ Zena Dell Lowe
The Storytellers Mission

Asia and Ivy's story broke my heart, had me rooting for them, then wanting to protect them—all in the space of the first chapters. Donna Mumma's debut novel forces us to look at the possible long-term effects of childhood wounds, then give ourselves grace and time to heal, even if that healing comes in baby steps.

~ Shellie Arnold
Author of *The Barn Church Series*

Donna Mumma's debut novel, Fresh Scars, is a moving and poignant tale that shows just how strong the human spirit can be. This one touches all the emotions, and readers may very well find the courage to face a few of their own difficulties after reading it! Don't miss this well-crafted and redemptive story!

~ Jennifer Uhlarik
2020 Will Rogers Medallion Award Finalist
Sand Creek Serenade

Fresh Scars immerses readers in the skin of characters who battle the trauma of childhood abuse and discover the spiritual strength to overcome it. Author Donna Mumma crafts an authentic depiction of anxiety, sibling rivalry among survivors, and the triggers which draw each sister back to relive the past. The tangles of psychological realism weave themselves around a compelling mystery while the drama proves equally captivating. I felt entwined with the characters until reaching the perfect and satisfying ending. I couldn't recommend Mumma's novel more highly.

~ Tina Yeager
LMHC, Life Coach, Author, Speaker,
and Host of the Flourish-Meant Podcast

Donna Mumma takes readers on a thought-provoking journey into the dynamics of family history. Anyone with a long and difficult history with parents and siblings and the subsequent, "you musts" of settling an estate will relate to Fresh Scars.

~ **James Cressler**

Author of *Demimonde and Diary of an Oak Tree*

Acknowledgments

MY DADDY ALWAYS TOLD me if a person had no dreams, they had nothing. This book is the culmination of a crowd of people in my life who loved me enough to believe in my dreams.

I first want to thank my parents, John and Shirley Taylor. Through them I learned to love God, family, friends and neighbors, work hard, and adore books. They gave me the gift of growing up in a world filled with master storytellers who taught a little girl's imagination how to soar.

Writers need a great community behind them, and I am blessed with one of the best. Thank you, Word Weavers Tampa, for your abundant grace as you read all of my re-writes and restarts. You took my rough drafts and polished them until they shined.

Tina Yeager, thank you for your undying encouragement and unending patience as you read through multiple drafts of this book. Your counselor's heart and fantastic writing ability helped me fill this story with truth and make my characters breathe.

Sharron Cosby, you loved this story from the first page and never let me forget it. Thanks for sharing your writing talents, professional knowledge and for pushing me to the finish line. A good friend loveth well.

Jan Powell, you reign as the world's best accountability partner. You never ceased to amaze me with your uncanny sense of knowing when I needed a phone call. You are a perfect combination of dear friend, editor, encourager, and writer. Thanks for caring enough to always give me the unbridled truth when something was just plain bad. And for having the remedy to fix it. I needed you in my corner.

Crystal Storms, thanks for your patience in teaching me all about social media and helping me set up my marketing tools. You've encouraged me not to be so afraid of my computer. I still need to work on that.

Linda Glaz, my fabulous agent and a new writer's best friend. Thanks for taking a second look and giving me a chance to realize this dream.

Shellie Arnold, my mentor and friend, you taught me how to dig deep and search for the truth that needed to shout from every page. Thanks for helping me learn to not just put down words, but truly write.

Jessica Everson, thanks for telling me how much you loved this story while you cleaned up my manuscript. It made my day every time you sent back your edits. You have a magic touch.

To Eva Marie Everson. I walked into your fiction practicum knowing nothing, but you believed I could do this. You continue to teach me craft, make my words sing from the page, and set my writer's soul free. I am humbled to call you my editor, mentor, and friend.

Eva Marie, the team at Firefly Southern Fiction and Iron Stream Media, thank you for giving me this opportunity. You gave me a light to hold onto during a long, dark year.

To Denise. You never stopped cheering and staying interested in my writing journey. Thanks from the bottom of my orange and blue heart. Buckman rules!

To David, John Patrick, and Daniel. You hold my heart and are my forever favorites.

There are many others that I've not listed. You know who you are, know you are loved.

And lastly, I thank God for loving me more than I could ever fathom and helping me understand the true meaning of forgiveness.

Dedication

To David

You believed

CHAPTER 1

LETTERS BEARING BAD NEWS deserve fiery deaths for the trouble they bring.

Asia Butler read her landlord's one-paragraph message again, each word twisting her gut into knots. She yanked an antibacterial wipe from the package in her pocket and washed her hands.

The attack was coming.

Breathe ... relax ... breathe.

Her streak of thirty-three days free from panic attacks stood in jeopardy. She couldn't ruin her accomplishments, especially on an odd-numbered day.

Breathe ... Relax ...

According to the letter, her landlord was moving to Florida and selling the townhome. *Her* home. She had sixty days to make an offer or move. Asking price was one hundred and seventy-five thousand dollars, OBO, he'd said. Student loans, an aging car, and therapy with Dr. Prescott reduced her best offer to maybe ten thousand dollars.

She threw the used wipe away and scanned her bedroom. Cleaning solutions and twin boxes of latex-free gloves sat in order from smallest to largest. Asia bent over, inhaled the scent emanating from her freshly dusted nightstand. Lemon. The smell of peace and wooden church pews. Safety.

Moving to Florida? Florida was a rotten place to live and why anyone willingly moved there defied the mind. Nothing compared to her Tennessee sunsets. Yellow-pink skies, a glowing orange orb dipping beneath the scalloped horizon. Her heart-roots had dug deep into this neighborhood. The only other townhomes or condos her budget welcomed were of a lower quality. None offered this view.

And, in moving, she'd lose her neighbor, Russ.

Her mind switched to images of the sun baking Florida's flat-pine and oak-dotted terrain, bathing everything in choking humidity. A chill prickled her arms. *I'm fine, I'm fine.* She inched closer to her window, checked her car's alignment in her assigned spot. Not too far forward with plenty of room for the walkway.

Russ pulled in beside her, his blue truck almost filling his parking space's footprint. The lowering sun glinted off the hood, sparkled in the droplets dotting the surface. He must have just come from the car wash. She checked her own vehicle. No sunglow on its surface. She pulled her phone from her pocket, scanned her daily calendar, and added *wash car* to Saturday's to-do list.

Russ happened to see her and waved as he hurried to his front door. She waved back. Her face grew warm as she reached in her pocket and stroked the card he'd given her.

"Made this for you." Russ had handed her the note card while they sat on her couch watching college football. "I picked yellow because it's bright and cheery. I also laminated it, so you can wipe it clean." He pointed to the large, black writing on its front. "Read it."

The fear of man brings a snare; whoever trusts in the Lord is kept safe. God could help with conquering her fears, he'd said. She'd heard the same sermons in church and read the Bible passages about fear multiple times. Her pastor said God would heal her. Her therapist, Dr. Prescott, agreed.

But reality ambushed her.

She hung at the end of her mental rope, grasping fragile strands while her childhood memories sawed away her sanity one thread at a time. Her students deserved a stable teacher, so she enlisted God and Dr. Prescott in the fight. And still she walked the tightrope between staying sane or going crazy.

Breathe . . . relax . . . breathe . . .

Asia grabbed a handful of wipes from the package and washed her face. Twice. She inhaled the lemony scent, then threw the wipes away in her bathroom's trash can.

Snapshots of live oaks dripping with Spanish moss, an alligator swimming through a creek in triangular ripples, and turtles sunbathing together on a log clicked through a mental slideshow.

Florida. Again. She shook the pictures away.

Her students struggled with developmental delays, physical or emotional handicaps, and learned to conquer their challenges. She should too. And focus on their work tonight. Asia padded in sock feet to retrieve her backpack from the closet. On the way to her desk, her temples tingled.

And now a migraine threatened? She went to the bathroom and wet her hands with cold water.

Relax.

She'd stood like this once before in a bus station bathroom strewn with filthy paper towels. The stench from the unflushed toilets had curled her tongue into a gag. There she'd stared into a cloudy mirror and rinsed away blood from a cut under her left eye. If someone looked closely enough, they could spy the scar.

Asia jerked down her hands. *Don't.*

She patted her face dry with a towel. Twice. She fixed her smeared mascara.

Work. Don't think.

Once settled at her desk in the far corner of her bedroom, she put on her glasses and pulled students' papers from her backpack. Her phone buzzed. *What now?*

She checked her phone. *Russ Matthews.* He was probably calling about fixing the light by her front door. She texted her response.

Grading papers. Talk tomorrow?

Russ's answer dinged. *Perfect.*

Thank goodness Russ understood. Always.

She slid a paper from the folder, uncapped her blue pen, and read until her doorbell rang followed by four pounding knocks. "Can't a body have a quiet Friday evening?" she argued aloud as she recapped her pen. Asia checked her watch. Six thirty. Who'd come by at the supper hour?

The knocking grew louder. She hurried down the stairs, then peered out the peephole and saw a woman dressed in an express messenger's uniform outside her front door. She released the lock and cracked the door open.

The young woman held out a large envelope. "Delivery."

Asia stepped outside. "From whom?"

The woman lifted one shoulder. "It's addressed to Asia Butler. That you?"

"Yes."

"Then it's yours. Sign here." She tapped a rectangle at the base of the electronic box in her hand.

Asia complied, took the envelope. "Thank you."

The young woman stepped from the stoop. "Have a nice evening." She trotted off to her delivery truck, her red ponytail swishing across her back.

Back in the house, Asia read the sender's address on the envelope as she climbed the stairs to her bedroom.

Janice M. Browne PA, Attorney at Law

1171 CR 470

Emerson, FL 33232

Emerson.

Her birthplace. An *attorney* from her birthplace.

Her knees buckled as if unhinged. She dropped to her bed, gripped her comforter until the soft folds puffed between her fingers.

Breathe … relax … breathe …

Cotton boll dryness swelled in her throat. Her bedside clock switched to six forty-five. She ripped the envelope's cardboard tab and slid a single sheet of thick, linen stationery from within. Janice M. Browne's name emblazoned the top in dark crimson letters.

Asia's hands trembled as she read further.

My Dear Daughters,

I am in the hospital with little time left here with you.

Since you chose not to visit me through the years, I have chosen to force the opportunity to gather my sweet girls together one last time to fulfill my final wishes. You may •eci•e once again to walk away from me, but you do so to your detriment. Below are required tasks you must complete to receive a gift my attorney is holding for you. You may each claim $250,000 if all the items below are complete• to my attorney's, Ms. Browne's, satisfaction.

You must:

Clean out our house. You must •iscar• all personal property, paperwork, an• furnishings. If you fin• anything you •esire, it is yours to take. I have grante• you 30 •ays to complete this task. Go even one minute past mi•night of the •ea•line, which will be set by Ms. Browne, an• you forfeit your claim to the money.

Allow Ms. Browne to periodically check your progress.

Shoul• you not accept this challenge, the fun•s will revert to the resi•uary of my estate an• will be •esignate• to beneficiaries of my choosing. You will receive nothing from my estate or me.

You must complete these tasks together, as a unit. If one sister refuses, neither of you will receive anything.

It is my fondest dream you will both carry out Mommy's wishes. Who better to put to rest the life I carefully crafted than my dearest treasures? None but you my precious girls.

Signature lines for Asia and her older sister Ivy came next on the page, each ending with boxes to check. ACCEPT or DENY.

The bottom of the page bore a time and date designated for a mandatory meeting with Ms. Browne if Asia and Ivy agreed to Veronica's conditions. A contact number and an offer to text Ms. Browne in the off hours rounded out the letter's message. The meeting date was set for the upcoming Monday at 9 a.m. *How had they found her?*

She regarded her pasty reflection staring from the Cheval mirror by her bed. Asia curled a tendril of blonde hair behind her ear, then fluffed it back in place. Styling her hair away from her face accentuated her pointy chin and made her eyes appear too close together. She'd inherited the same blonde hair and sapphire-blue eyes as Ivy, but missed out on the high cheek bones, straight nose, and sculpted jawline that made her sister a head-turning beauty.

Asia hugged her middle. She hadn't spoken to Ivy in fifteen years. Each heartbeat knifed through her chest. Each breath grew shallower. Florida, and all that she'd run from, had found her. She dropped the letter on the bed.

I'm in Tennessee. I'm in my home. I'm safe.

But for how long? She was going to lose her home. To save it she'd have to go back to Florida. Face Ivy. And Veronica. Asia grabbed the bedpost as the world swirled around her.

Breathe … Relax … Breathe …

CHAPTER 2

Ivy Butler Morelli stuffed the letter from Veronica back into the envelope. "Well, that ruined my Friday night. Wish I'd never answered the door."

She smoothed her hair back from her face and met her husband's eyes. "A glass of wine would be so good right now." She shook her head at Denney's raised brows. "You know I won't."

Denney rubbed his hands across jean-clad legs. "That's quite a letter."

If he weren't watching, she'd tear the paper and the envelope into pieces, burn those pieces and flush them down the sewer where anything having to do with Veronica belonged.

But flushing the letter wouldn't dissolve her stress right now. Her life resembled a pressure cooker set on high, ready to blow.

Denney leaned in close to plant a kiss on her cheek, but Ivy tucked her legs into her skirt, moving out of his range. She grasped her hair and twisted the strands into a ponytail, then released. "The letter threw me for a moment." She tipped her chin and smiled at him. "I'm fine."

Denney scanned her face. He was trying to understand her mood, but his face reflected the unvoiced questions she knew were forming in his mind. "This cleanup might help to smooth things over with your sister. You can do a lot in thirty days."

"Maybe." She wasn't watering hope-seeds. The rift with Asia went deep. Ivy tried to fill in the ravine once. She wasn't repeating that mistake.

Not ever.

"What do you need me to do?" Denney's concerned gaze bore deep into her.

He knew she was hiding something. She could see through him, as if he were a freshly polished glass door. His lowered brows coupled with stooped shoulders broadcast his struggle between wanting answers and granting her space.

Ivy sat up, straightened her shoulders. "You've been going since four this morning. Instead of bags, you've got suitcases under your eyes. Go to bed."

Denney flashed a tired, half-hearted grin. His gray-peppered bangs curtained above his dark brown eyes. How many times had she pushed that hair back, experienced a fluttering stomach just from touching his forehead with her fingertips? Tonight, he pushed them away himself. "You're good?"

"Of course."

The scent of oregano and basil clouded around her as he leaned over and kissed her. "Love you." He rose from the sofa.

"Love you too."

Denney stretched, rubbed his back. Her unwavering rock. They'd made a vow on their wedding day, promised before God they would never keep secrets between them.

But she'd held back a doozy. At eighteen, being young, traumatized, and desperate, she'd run away from home. And knowingly left her younger sister in the clutches of a monster. Family reigned just below God in Denney's world. How could he understand or accept what she had done?

Ivy shoved those thoughts where all others of Veronica went to die.

On the baby grand piano, where their family photos resided, the faces of their three boys peered at her. In every shot they laughed and hugged one another. She loved this life.

Why did Veronica have to write that rotten letter and why did it have to arrive today? Furthermore, how had this Janice Browne found her? Not that it was *that* difficult to find somebody these days, but the thoughts of being investigated enough to *be* found gave her the shivers.

But this wasn't the only letter of late that had blindsided her. She'd received another earlier at work. A sweet little note from the IRS stating that her Seattle-based trucking business owed two hundred and fifty thousand dollars in payroll and income taxes. Her controller, Rae, confirmed the notice was not sent by mistake. Costs to update trucks, track driver hours, and an accident her company was held liable for had sucked too many dollars from the company coffers.

Rae cried while confessing she'd skimmed from Uncle Sam to pay employees. Ivy had given her the job because she wanted to support a single, working mom. She'd fought natural inclinations to micromanage her. And now she faced huge fines and possible time in prison. A call to her vacationing lawyer brought nothing.

Denney's voice roped her back. He'd made his way upstairs to ready for bed. "Night." He waited, so Ivy touched a finger to her lips and blew a kiss. Usually, he returned the gesture. Tonight, he walked away. The wooden planks of the landing creaked under his bare feet until he stepped into the carpeted hallway. Their bedroom door thudded closed seconds later. A long silence followed. She'd been dead set on proving to Denney and everyone else she could be independent. Now the restaurant businesses she and Denney had built together, their finances and her children's home were vulnerable to the consequences of her big, fat, failure in her first solo business venture.

And what would happen to her employees if she went under, or to jail? Many were recovering addicts and she was the only one willing to hire them. Some evaded homelessness thanks to their salaries. Others were enjoying the satisfaction of providing for their families for the first time ever. A setback like this could send them right into relapse. Thankfully, the business was listed in her name, preventing Denney and the boys from knowing. For now.

How could she have done this? Just last month her employees surprised her with a cake and a homemade certificate declaring her "Boss of the Year." Guess her certificate deserved to be sent to the sewer along with Veronica's letter.

Ivy's attention drifted to her wedding photo on the fireplace mantel. She and Denney, so young. Facing their problems, finding the solutions together.

But not tonight.

Ivy grabbed up the envelope and slid the letter out for a second read.

Two hundred and fifty thousand dollars if she and Asia cleaned out their childhood home. Together. Veronica always seemed to foresee others' bad luck. And she reveled in using that knowledge against them. Wouldn't she get a laugh knowing her nasty little proposition was her oldest daughter's saving hope?

Ivy pounded the cushy arm of the sofa. She had to take Veronica's money. There was no other way. She would go back to Florida. To Veronica.

And Asia.

Her heart went to her boys. Unlike her and Asia, they were real brothers, not simply individuals related by blood, who had shared the same childhood home.

And the same nightmare.

CHAPTER 3

JANICE M. BROWNE, ATTORNEY at Law, was making Asia wait. Chippendale furniture filled the conference room. Law degrees hung asymmetrically along the wall. The table and chairs gleamed from a fresh polishing, but a thin layer of dust powdered the frames of the diplomas and an antique wall clock. She cleaned the frames and clock with a wipe from her purse.

When she was in high school this location had been a cow pasture filled with wild phlox and holes. The local guys used to go mudding here in their four-wheel drive trucks. No bovine hooves clopped across this land now, rather some lawyer who probably wore expensive leather shoes and owned no more sense of punctuality than the cows.

She paced along lengths of the conference table. When someone made you wait, they had control over you.

"Waiting makes you stronger, Asia," Veronica said once while blocking Asia's path to the bathroom. She sat in front of the door for hours. Asia's stomach cramped and she'd begged for relief. But Veronica held firm.

In desperation, Asia ran behind the house and squatted in the dirt. Darkness hid the colony of fire ants she'd perched over. They attacked her bare feet, crawled up her legs, stung the tender skin behind her knees and inner thighs. By the time she finished, the ant bites went all the way up her back.

Now Asia's heart raced like those angry insects. Two days ago, she'd resolved to leave the comforts of home in Maryville, fly back to Emerson, and meet with Ivy and Ms. Browne. Must she *wait* too?

Simply because Janice M. Browne received a phone call. Did this woman understand professionalism at all?

The receptionist, Cara, had also performed her duties subpar. She'd simply said, "Ms. Browne is busy with a phone call. Can I show you to the conference room?"

Can? Using can and may properly were one of the first lessons Asia taught every student who sat in her classroom.

An icy chill sashayed down her back. Veronica once dated a man who used can instead of may. Her students deserved to be far better than he was.

And where was Ivy? Probably doing whatever she wanted, without thought for consequences. She should walk out. But then she'd have to reschedule and come back tomorrow. Which wouldn't work either. She had a 6 a.m. flight home.

All she could do was keep waiting, and waiting, and waiting ...

"Hello?" Her voice echoed down the hallway. The clock's ticking answered. *Tick-tock. Tick-tock.*

That clock, with its maddening, constant ticking. How satisfying to rip the timepiece from the wall and feed it into a woodchipper until nothing remained but sawdust and dented metal innards.

No more waiting. Asia settled her purse strap on her shoulder and was headed for the door when Ivy's voice filled the hallway. Asia backed up to the conference table and grabbed the edge with both hands for support. Ivy entered with her chin tipped and shoulders back. She locked eyes with Asia. Time paused. A sharp pain cut through.

Breathe ... Relax ... Breathe ...

Like everything else, her older sister defied age. Thin lines marked her forehead and her jawline had softened. Her figure remained curvy and lean in all the right places, complemented by the red silk blouse and dark skinny jeans she wore. The overhead lights gleamed in her smooth, honey-colored hair.

Cara scurried into the room. "I've told Janice you're both here."

Ivy flashed a wide smile. "Thanks. Could I get a cup of coffee? Black."

Cara nodded. "Of course. Be right back."

Ivy zeroed in on Asia. "You're so thin. Don't you eat?"

Asia's cheeks warmed. She'd spent two hours this morning choosing the white crepe blouse and black pants. Then Ivy breezed in the room dressed like a layout from a fashion magazine, co-opted Ms. Browne's receptionist into jumping and fetching for her in seconds, then dug at Asia for her appearance. She hadn't expected an apology but had hoped for acknowledgement that she seemed to be doing well. A simple "nice outfit" would have sufficed. Asia swallowed the bile of disappointment. "Nice to see you, too. You're looking well."

"Think so?" Ivy pulled out a chair and sat. The overhead lights reflected in the diamond-studded gold band on her left ring finger. She'd married well.

Asia claimed a chair opposite Ivy. She laced her fingers together on the tabletop, taking care to cover her bare ring finger. A smudge caught her attention. She took a wipe from her purse and washed the area around her.

Ivy clicked her tongue. "Still cleaning." She placed her large, designer handbag in the chair next to her.

After disposing of the wipe, Asia sat in her chair. She retrieved her phone and opened the email containing her flight information. Tomorrow. Six a.m. flight. She'd be back in Tennessee by nine and settled in her townhouse by eleven. Back to school on Wednesday. Far away from Florida. From Veronica.

And Ivy.

"This situation seems a little weird. I've never been to a lawyer's office when there wasn't a mountain of paperwork waiting for me." She leaned back in her chair, surveyed the room and smirked, acting as though the entire space was far beneath her. Like she was ignoring where she came from ... and Asia should as well.

Life seemed to have doled Ivy a silver ring enabling her to forget. "You spend a lot of time in lawyer's offices?"

A red hue colored Ivy's neck and cheeks. "For my business."

"I'm not implying anything, it just sounded—"

"It did not. I run a legitimate, well-respected business. In fact, I also co-own two others." Ivy sneered, tilted her head. "What do *you* do?"

Asia drew in a deep breath, counted to two, then exhaled. Ivy wasn't going to rattle her. She'd handled worse than Ivy's trying to be highfalutin' during parent conferences at school. "I teach high school. Special needs."

Ivy draped her wrist over the chair arm. Her gold bracelets jingled. "No surprise there. I always knew you'd be a teacher." She crossed her legs and bounced her top foot in the air. Asia couldn't miss the cherry-red, pedicured toes encased in Ivy's designer sandals.

"I guess I proved you right." Not that Ivy was so smart. She'd wasted all Asia's tutoring efforts and failed to graduate. Asia glanced at her watch. The sooner this meeting started, the sooner it ended, and she could go back to her hotel room. Dealing with Ivy might push her to lose those last few strands of her sanity.

But that was probably what Veronica desired when she concocted this scheme. She'd force her and Ivy into an emotion-charged arena, condemned to battle, to act like a couple of pit bulls in a dog fight.

Ivy chuckled. "I see you still have a thing about time."

"Time shouldn't be wasted."

"Agreed. I make the most of every second of every day."

Asia rubbed her temples. Message received. Ivy was Miss. Perfect. Everything. "I'm certain your life is wonderful."

"What's that supposed to mean?"

"Nothing. I—"

Ivy waved her off. "Forget it." She shifted in her chair. "My life *is* wonderful. How's yours?"

Fifteen years and Ivy still lived the "snap-at-me-I-snap-back" rule.

Asia paused. She inched her hand inside her pocket and rubbed the edge of Russ's card. "My life is fine."

Ivy raised one brow. "Wonderful."

A woman cradling a thick, burgundy portfolio to her chest bustled into the room with Cara in tow. "Hello ladies, I'm so sorry to have kept you waiting. I'm Janice Browne." She set a steaming mug before Ivy. "For you."

Asia's mouth fell open. She forced her jaw shut so hard her bottom teeth clacked against the top. Veronica was viciously prejudiced against anyone of color, and yet she'd chosen a Black attorney to carry out her final wishes. One look at Ivy's surprise-arched brows broadcast her shock as well.

Janice laid the portfolio down and took the chair at the head of the table. She adjusted her long gold necklace with fingernails matching the midnight blue of her blouse. "Now, let's have some sister talk."

CHAPTER 4

Ivy slapped the tabletop and her bracelets rang in protest. "I'd rather we cut to the bottom line and avoid wasting any more time."

Janice lined two pens up next to the portfolio. "Let's do that. You ladies have been estranged for several years. Veronica wanted you to use this time to reconnect."

"Which brings me to my first question," Ivy said. "How did you find us?"

"Easy enough. Your social security numbers and the right search program on any computer and I found you both within a half hour." Janice M. Browne smiled. "Or, I should say, my admin did."

Asia cleared her throat. "What else did Veronica tell you about us?"

"Ah. *Veronica.* She told me you two preferred not to call her anything maternal. I was instructed to tell you both she loved your desire to be independent and your amazing sister-bond."

"She lied to you." Ivy pointed to Asia, then back at herself. "We aren't into that whole sister-bonding thing."

Janice's expression asked Asia for confirmation.

"We're not," Asia answered.

Janice dug a set of keys from her pocket. They jingled like bells out of tune. "Then cleaning out your childhood home should be rather cathartic for you both." She placed the keys on the table.

Ivy looked at the copper-colored keys arranged on the bright green ring. The same ring Veronica hung on the hook by the front door of the house. Her stomach flipped at the sight of them. By the looks of it, they bugged Asia as well. All color had drained from her cheeks and she was green around the gills, as though she might lose her breakfast.

Janice leaned back in her chair. She crossed her legs then smoothed a wrinkle in her cream-colored pants. "I realize this situation is very unusual. Veronica wants you to take care of her home and this was the only way she saw fit to bring you back."

Asia scowled. "*Her* home? That's not true. It's a rental."

Janice tapped the portfolio. "She owns the house. I have a copy of the title."

Asia continued. "How could Veronica afford to buy that house? She never had any money, wouldn't save a penny."

"I'm not at liberty to say."

Ivy drummed her fingers on the table. She agreed with Asia; how on God's good, green earth did Veronica manage to finagle the house from the landlord's ownership? Knowing the answer would probably make her sick. But there were other details that made less sense. "That brings up another question. Where did Veronica get half a million dollars to dangle in our faces and demand we do tricks to earn it?"

An air of unease flickered about Janice. "As I said, I'm not at liberty—"

"Right. How convenient." Ivy crossed her arms on the tabletop.

If her circumstances were better, she could have shredded Veronica's flimsy bribe, thrown the pieces at the lawyer's face, and strolled out of the office with her head high, singing a victory song.

But she needed this money.

Janice unzipped her portfolio and removed two sheets of paper. She slid one to Ivy, then the other to Asia. "These are my copies of the letters you received. Veronica requested that you sign before me, and then Cara will notarize them."

"Why must they be notarized?" Asia asked.

"To ensure that the letters, her contracts with us, are executed properly and fully to her liking," Ivy said. "Standard business procedure." Asia might have come in here with the college degree, but big sis had learned plenty along the way from the school of experience, which educated a person far more than a musty classroom on some college campus.

Asia swallowed hard. "Why is Veronica in the hospital?"

Janice set a pen down by each of the letters. "She had a stroke. She's comatose."

"When?" Asia and Ivy asked in unison.

"Last Thursday. That's why you received the letters on Friday."

"She had these letters prepared *before* her stroke? How did she know?" Asia asked.

"I'm sure I have the answer to that one." Ivy eyed Janice. "You're not at liberty to say. Right?" Her question was answered by confirming silence. "How long does she have?"

Janice's face softened. "The doctors don't know." She adjusted her necklace again. "I've asked around and most cleaning companies say it takes two to three weeks to fully clear a house. Her passing and completion of this contract may coincide."

Asia brought up a calendar on her phone. "I'd like to schedule the clean-up for the beginning of June. I'm a teacher and can't return until summer break."

Janice tapped Asia's copy of Veronica's contract. "Clean-up starts today. As soon as these are signed and notarized."

Asia's face went white. "What? I can't do that. I have three weeks left in the semester. I have a flight reservation for tomorrow." She stopped talking, pulled two antibacterial wipes from her purse, and scrubbed her hands. After tossing them in the trash, she rejoined them. Her attention went straight to Ivy. "Did you know this?"

"Nope. I thought we would negotiate that today." Which would be the tenth of never-gonna-happen if she had her way. But the tax man scratched at her door, and she had no choice. She grabbed the pen closest to her, checked APPROVE, scrawled her name across the bottom of the page, then filled in the date. "Done." She pushed her contract to Janice.

Asia shook her head hard. "I can't do this now." She clasped her hands as if pleading for her life. "Can't we put this off for one month?"

Janice kept firm. "No, we can't. I thought you understood the thirty days starts as soon as you met with me."

Asia drew in a deep breath, held it for a few seconds, then exhaled. She repeated the action. "I'll make some calls. Let my principal and my paraprofessional know I'll be out. This won't sit well at all. I don't know if I can get a sub lined up at this late notice." She thrust her hand in her pocket. "This is such a mess."

Ivy silently agreed. In normal times, she'd tell Janice Browne and Veronica where she thought these contracts truly belonged. Denney often warned she jumped into fights too soon. Winning tense moments was like eating great food; you needed to let things cool a bit before you opened your mouth. Otherwise, you just ended up with a scalded tongue.

Janice set a pen by Asia's contract. "You can clean up the mess. For her."

"Veronica never did anything for us." Ivy spat the words.

Asia took the pen. Her hand shook so, it was a miracle she was able to just check the APPROVE box. After passing pen and contract to Janice, she took wipes from her purse and wiped her hands again. She held them up to her nose and breathed in and out.

Ivy watched Asia's ritual. Something was seriously wrong with her sister. When she called Denney to fill him in on the latest happenings, she'd hint that reconciling with Asia seemed improbable, maybe mention her strange behavior. She'd also tell him she planned to use the cash for business development. Wouldn't paying off taxes count as development?

Ivy's heart dropped. One lie birthed another. When would she stop?

She snapped back to the meeting. "I assume you hold onto the checks until final inspection."

"Correct." Janice passed the letters to Cara. "We'll need your driver's licenses."

In ten minutes, the contracts became official, binding agreements between Ivy, Asia, and Veronica. The means of saving everything she loved was only thirty days away. Ivy flashed a thumbs-up to Janice. "Here's to the next thirty days." She grabbed Veronica's keys and squeezed until they cut into her palm.

Janice gathered the pens and clumped them together. "You're both doing the right thing." She stood.

Asia whispered a fast thanks and good-bye, then scurried to the hallway. Ivy followed, their shoes clicking in a matched cadence as they hurried across the parking lot to their cars.

Ivy stopped short and wheeled around to Asia. "I am out of my mind to think this leads to anything but a nightmare. It's Veronica. Nothing good comes from her."

Asia stopped but said nothing.

Ivy clenched her teeth. "I swore I'd never go back to that place; never let Veronica push me—"

"Me too." Asia whispered.

"Then why are we here, doing her bidding, like always?" Ivy's voiced echoed between the parked cars. "We signed a contract with her. Why?"

Asia took sunglasses from her purse and pushed them on. "Because she always finds a way to trap us in a corner."

"Not this time. In a month, I'll be back home."

Asia readjusted her purse on her shoulder. "Why did you agree to stay?"

"I have my reasons. Four really good ones, actually."

Asia rubbed her arms as if warding off a chilled wind. "Are we really doing this, Ivy? Going back to that house?"

Ivy watched her reflection in Asia's sunglasses. "I still can't believe I'm here, agreeing to do anything for her."

Asia removed her sunglasses. "I can't either. But I think this is about more than cleaning out that house."

"What are you talking about?" Ivy unlocked the doors of her rental car by pressing the soft button on the handle.

Asia gave Ivy a long, silent look. "We're *supposed* to do this."

"What?"

"I don't know how to explain it. Ever since we signed those contracts, I got this strange feeling."

"You and your feelings. I think it's your good sense—and mine—screaming at us to run." Ivy sighed. "I'll meet you at Veronica's." The house keys felt cool against her palm. There was still time to throw them down on the pavement. Maybe drive the car over them a few times and then go home.

But she couldn't do that. She'd made a commitment. And if the boys found out, they could tally another mark on the secret score sheet they kept whenever she broke a family rule. If only that stupid list were written on paper. Then she could flush it away like their dead goldfish or send *it* through the shredder in her office.

Ivy peered over the top of her car. "Do you remember how to get to the house from here?"

"Get on 477 here, go to Highway 301, then turn left." Asia wiped the handle on her car door then swung it open. As she moved, she kept her attention on Ivy.

"Then I'll follow you."

"Oh no. We'll pass the on-ramp for I-75, and I don't trust that you wouldn't just hop on and leave this catastrophe with me. I'll follow *you.*"

The jab was not unexpected. Ivy shrugged away pricks of anger. "Suit yourself. I'll probably get lost."

Asia slid into the seat. "Then use the GPS on your phone." She started the engine.

Oven-like heat baked her cheeks as Ivy plopped into her car. If she were a cursing person, she could let loose a stream of words hot enough to peel the paint from the hood. But then she'd be breaking another home rule for controlling tempers. And if her boys found out, she'd never live that one down, either. No, Mom was going to keep her cool.

She pulled down the visor and checked her reflection in the mirror. She'd been here one day, and already the humidity had melted her hair. "I hate this place."

Was she actually going back? She'd sworn fifteen years ago she'd never set foot in Florida again. But now, here she sat, back in Sumter County headed for Veronica's.

Her hand quivered as she pressed the START button and the car purred to life.

CHAPTER 5

SUMTER COUNTY SPED PAST her windows as Asia tightened her grip on the steering wheel. The white lines dotting the middle of Highway 301 ticked off the miles to Veronica's. Each little bump in the road seemed to whisper, "Closer, closer."

Ivy had reduced her speed by five miles in the last ten minutes. Was she contemplating leaving? That would be typical. Maybe she was indeed lost. The area had changed drastically since the two of them left home. The vast acreage of old cattle ranches and Mr. Gannet's melon fields were gone. The tracts of a sprawling retirement community bearing newly built homes filled them now. Multitudes of teens had worked those lost acres to earn money for first cars. Asia had worked three seasons herself; one paid for a prom dress and the other two for college. The work was back-breaking, hot, and filthy, but worth the trouble in the end. The money she earned bankrolled her escape. Watching the "Welcome to Sumter County" sign fade into the distance from the back window of the Greyhound bus still reigned as a most-treasured memory.

Ivy stopped and Asia hit her brakes to avoid colliding. It was then she saw the weedy lot to her right and her heart pounded. Dog fennel grew waist-high in the front yard. The dingy-white, boxy house still sported avocado-green shutters. The door retained the familiar dove-gray paint.

Ivy curved into the driveway. Asia followed up the long limestone lane, then parked to the right of her sister. She hesitated. *The fear of man brings a snare.* This snare now tightened around her.

A knock on the window yanked Asia from her thoughts. Ivy glared outside the driver-side door. "I'm not going in there alone."

Asia opened the door. "I'm coming." She pulled two wipes from her pocket, washed her hands and face. Their lemony scent filled the car. Asia inhaled the aroma, but the smell failed to offer peace to quell the pounding in her ears and chest. She dropped the wipes into the trash bag on the floor and stepped outside.

A path worn through the soil once led the way to Veronica's front door, but knee-high Bahia grass covered the area now. Ivy waded through as she made her way to the steps. She brushed grass seed from her jeans and sandals. "I hate these hitchhikers."

Asia's feet cemented to the ground. Terror gripped her when she left this house, and those icy fingers caught her again. Ivy shot a silent command to join her at the stoop. Asia shuddered. The weeds crunched beneath her feet and slapped against her legs as she made her way to the steps.

Ivy used Veronica's keys, turning the lock with a loud clunk. "Are you ready?"

"No."

"Let's get this over with. Just standing outside this place gives me the creeps." The door's hinges moaned as Ivy swung it open. She grabbed Asia and led her inside the house.

Asia gasped, covered her nose and mouth. The stench of rotten food, mildew, and dust assaulted her sinuses. Stacks of garbage bags, columns of water-stained cardboard boxes, and mountains of old magazines rose to the ceiling.

Ivy released Asia and pinched her nose. "Oh my … Veronica was always a little messy, but this …"

A chill trailed down Asia's neck, as if someone blew icy breath against her skin.

A grimy white cake box from Publix sat on a table in the center of the room. A deflating silver balloon stating "Welcome Home" in faded red letters sagged above the box. A greeting from Veronica.

Bowls containing cereal lodged in black, curdled milk covered the floor to the left of the table. On the right, dishes filled with moldy macaroni and cheese sat in crooked rows on the rotting carpet. Cereal. Ivy's most hated food. And hers, mac-n-cheese. Asia swallowed against the gagging sensation in her throat. She grabbed for the wipes in her pockets. Not there. She patted both sides of her pants. No wipes. They must have fallen out when she got out of the car.

She had to get them. Now. Clean her face, hands, shoes, and then stand outside and breathe, to clear out all the dust and grime she now inhaled.

Ivy clawed Asia's wrist. "Don't you dare freak out. Get a hold of yourself."

The floor was hairy with dust, and long furry strands latticed down from the ceiling, the light fixture, and the walls.

Asia could hardly breathe now. Dust permeated the air. And that stench … filth carried dust mites, staphylococcus, and streptococcus. Each heartbeat stabbed within her chest. Sanitizing her clothes and shoes from this would take weeks. She should throw them out. And her hair … there wasn't enough shampoo in this country to wash away the putrefaction.

Ivy's grip tightened as she slunk further into the room. Dizziness clouded Asia's head. Her knees buckled and she stumbled into a stack of magazines. The tower swayed and collapsed onto the table. Roaches spilled from the cake box in a brown wave that engulfed the tabletop and skittered down one of the legs.

Asia spun for the door. Her foot caught the trash bags. She fell to her hands and knees. A roach dashed across her hand, another skittered up her arm on tiny, tickling legs. She flung the insects off, sending them both careening into a stack of yellowed newspapers. She screamed, clutched her stomach, then ran outside and vomited into a patch of pink wild phlox. She despised throwing up, such a vulgar, messy affair. And she ruined a patch of phlox. They had always been her favorite wildflower.

Wipes. Now. Clean away the grime before infections attacked her system.

Asia clutched her stomach as another round hit and then a third. Those times she took care to aim away from the phlox. Once she caught her breath, she staggered to her car and wilted onto the seat. She yanked open the glove box, tore wipes from the package and wiped her face until her skin stung.

Wipe. Wipe. Wipe. There had to be at least a foot of dust caked on her. And then her hands.

Scrub. Scrub. Scrub. Where the roaches touched her. Horrid vermin. Covered in germs. Serving no purpose other than breeding and infecting. She depleted one package of wipes, reached for another. Asia scrubbed her arm until it reddened.

"Are you okay?" Ivy called as she approached.

"No."

"I guess I shouldn't have made you go in."

"I didn't have a choice."

"Why do you keep saying that?"

Asia coughed and gagged instead of answering.

"How was *I* supposed to know it would be so bad?" Ivy crossed her arms and pivoted toward the construction site next door.

Asia held a wipe beneath her nose. The lemony scent mingled with the musty smell of dust trapped in her nose. She drew in another deep breath. "That display in there was vintage Veronica. She somehow *knew* we would come here."

"I know." Ivy rubbed the lengths of her arms.

"She left cereal, your most hated food, and mine, mac-n-cheese, right where we'd see it. She crafted that house into a hoarder's nightmare, yet she's demanding we clean it, knowing I can't stand filth and you hate cleaning."

"She planned all this to taunt us." Ivy's voice cracked. "She still has to prove we can't fight her, that she's in control, even when lying comatose in a hospital."

"It's more than that. You remember what she always said?"

Ivy flicked a fly from her sleeve. "Veronica said a lot of things."

"I'm talking about one of her favorites. 'The body heals, but scarring the mind stays fresh.' The money and that display were meant to stain our minds, torture us."

Ivy faced the house. "Too bad we can't call Ms. Browne and tell her we refuse to clean this horror-hole. I've been done with this place for years."

The unspoken *"and you"* stung. Asia grabbed another pack of wipes. "You never think about her?"

"Why would I?"

"After all that happened, it doesn't ... come back to you?"

"Nope."

Asia drew in a deep breath then dug her next words from her throat. "How did you forget everything?"

Ivy responded with a flip of her hand. "I got a life."

Her attitude made perfect sense. The one who abandoned, healed. "Tell me how."

Ivy raised her palms. "Back off, Asia. It's no great secret. I just don't think about it." She switched her stance, slid her right hip out. "After this is over, I want you to do something for me."

"What?"

"We've grown up, built good lives. Separately. Let's keep it that way."

The house called Asia. The windows watched her with wide, square lenses that dared them to enter again. Veronica perfected the same stare, used the dark expression in the rare times she or Ivy refused to obey her.

The house and Veronica remained connected in Asia's mind. Every nightmare, unwanted imagining, or recollection bore the two of them together. The house linked her and Ivy, too. They shared DNA and childhoods here. How could she promise to break contact with the one person who held the answers no therapist, self-help book, or seminar could give her? She needed to talk with Ivy, for hours, weeks, months if necessary until she understood the trick to healing the scars those memories left behind.

Ivy watched a flock of cattle egrets flying overhead. Asia studied the familiar profile of her sister's jaw and cheek, searched for signs of fear. All she saw was Ivy's brow cocked in annoyance and her fingers tapping against her arm.

"Ivy, do you believe in God?"

"I went to the same church you did." The angry flicker in her eye suggested that Asia had hit a sore spot.

"That's not what I—"

"Yes, Asia, I believe in God. Why?"

"I think He did this."

"Did what?" Ivy's face flushed. "You mean, brought us back here. That's what you think that feeling of yours was all about, isn't it?" She phooeyed Asia with both hands. "I believe God has far better things to do."

Ivy jerked her thumb in the direction of the house. "I left that behind a long time ago and I'm not going back."

How was Ivy so certain? "You've completely cleansed yourself of her? She never comes out in you, not even when you're really angry—"

"No. Never." Ivy's anger flashed bright in her red cheeks.

"Are you sure? You seem to be channeling her right now."

"Whatever. Just promise me, no contact." She swept her hands through the air in an X, as if crossing Asia off a list.

"I can't do that."

Ivy reeled back, as if she'd been slapped. "Why not?"

"I need to talk to you about what happened—"

"What's *wrong* with you? You never liked to talk about things before. Why do you want to dredge all this up now?"

"I need to talk about what happened."

Ivy held the housekeys out to Asia. "Then get yourself a good therapist."

"I need to talk to *you*," Asia pushed.

Ivy threw the keys in the grass next to Asia's open car door. "Stay here if you like. I'm going back to my hotel and taking ten hot baths." She stalked to her car.

Ivy yanked the driver-side door open. She sank into the seat and started the car. Two fishtails fountained behind her rear tires as she sped to the highway.

The yard took on a graveyard's ambience. The house leered at Asia. Veronica's voice played in her head.

We're alone again, Asia.

Ivy had left her behind once more when she needed her. She couldn't breathe.

Faint-worthy lightheadedness threatened.

Breathe ... relax ... breathe.

If she ran, she'd lose her home. She retrieved a wipe from her car and wrapped it around Veronica's keys.

As she scrubbed them a soft, serpentine voice whispered in her mind's ear. *Welcome home, my girl.*

Asia dropped Veronica's keys into the drink caddy in the console and covered them with two clean wipes.

She started her car and drove down the lane, swallowing hard to keep from vomiting again.

CHAPTER 6

Asia surveyed the arsenal of tools she'd purchased to tackle Veronica's house. After Ivy's outburst the day before, she had no idea when she'd return, but the task must get started.

Every time she threw an item of Veronica's away, she would take a little grain of control back. With her flight reservations changed and her classroom covered by a substitute plus her paraprofessional, she could now focus on her current obligations.

Asia drew in a deep breath, held for two counts, then exhaled. This could be done. Unless, of course, she had a panic attack and passed out in the yard first. She shoved her hand in her pocket and rubbed the edge of Russ's card.

Two of the largest trash cans Walmart sold stood to her left next to three cases of bleach. On her right were six boxes of rubber gloves, a dozen scrub brushes, safety masks, and a package of gauzy painter's coveralls. Two stacks of washcloths and eight plastic mop buckets filled the remaining space. Everything was lined up in categorized groups on a clear plastic painter's tarp.

She'd spent almost all her weekly budget on the items, but the expense was necessary.

And then she remembered the check waiting for her in Janice M. Browne's office. Would having that much money in the bank ease her fears over every penny she spent? Or would new fears crop up because the cash came from Veronica?

Breathe ...

In the lane, a car horn honked. Clouds of limestone dust misted around the vehicle as the driver sped toward her. She shaded her eyes from the glare of the sun's rays reflecting on the windshield.

Ivy had arrived.

Her sister maneuvered the car through a clump of thick grass and slammed to a halt several yards away. When she opened her door, the seat seemed to eject her from the car. "I'm sorry I'm late. Overslept." She slammed her door shut.

She pointed to the array of cleaning supplies. "Wow, that's a lot of stuff. You sure we'll need all that?"

Asia rubbed Russ's card again. First thing out of Ivy's mouth was a criticism. Again. "I'm thinking we may not have enough."

Ivy scowled. "Asia, I don't clean. At all. Got a cleaning service for that. Anyway ..." She gestured toward the tarp. "Even I know that is excessive."

As always, Ivy was the expert on things she didn't do. "If we don't clean the house out properly, Ms. Browne won't sign off and we don't get the money. All effort here will be wasted."

Ivy huffed. "You were always so naïve. Ms. Browne doesn't care what we do as long as the stuff is out of the house. She wants this mess out of her lap and into ours. No one expects us to be able to eat off the linoleum once we finish."

An image of the furry dust covering the floor came to Asia's mind. She shuddered. "We signed a contract, Ivy. We're bound by the law to do what Veronica wants."

Ivy smirked. "The contract also stated we were to bond again as sisters. We've already determined that isn't happening."

Asia hadn't come here expecting a BFF situation with her sister. She came to save all that was important in her life. But ... if Ivy would budge a little and share her secrets to overcoming Veronica ...

But, like a knot on a tree, Ivy never budged. "As you told Janice Browne. We aren't into that sister-bonding thing."

A not-so-satisfied look flashed at Asia. "Thanks for understanding."

"Thank you? That's a first."

Ivy locked her car doors. "You were right all those years ago.

Manners do come in handy sometimes."

"And now a compliment?" Asia lay her hand across her forehead. "I may faint."

The hardened corners of Ivy's lips softened and Asia saw glimpses of the big sister who taught her how to tie shoelaces, brush tangles from her hair, and apply mascara without stabbing herself in the eye. The person she'd longed for one black November night when a concrete floor chilled her body as she sat in the hallway of her dorm, crying over the worst decision of her life. The sister that, until three days ago, she didn't know was dead or alive.

"She really got us this time. If only…" Ivy's voice trailed.

"If only what?"

"Nothing." Ivy fanned her face. "I've been gone so long I've forgotten how this humidity sucks the breath right out of you."

What a blessed feeling that must be. To live such a wonderful life that your mind could erase all imprints of a place, time, or life and leave you with a benign hole where kinder memories took root.

Just as Ivy said. If only.

Ivy planted her hands on her hips. "This mess isn't going to clean itself. I'll bring stuff outside for you to sort. Saves you from going in there again. No way am I dealing with you passed out on the grass while I'm stuck with the filth in the house."

Asia almost swayed. Ivy's criticisms came at her like soldier bees stirred from their hive. "I'm not going to faint."

"Hard to believe when just yesterday you spit up your breakfast after being in there a grand total of five minutes."

Asia clenched her teeth. "I was in shock after seeing what Veronica had done to the house. I'm over that now."

"Uh-huh." She pointed to the tarp. "Your little collection over there screams that you aren't."

"No, those items show I'm prepared."

"That much preparation seems a bit unstable." Asia went to respond but Ivy waved her off. "I didn't mean that."

"Then why say it?"

"I'm rude when I'm irritated. Of all things, you should have remembered that."

"I remember a lot of things, Ivy." And much worthy to be forgotten.

Asia stared at the house. *Breathe ... relax ... breathe ...* She scrubbed her hands twice, then nodded to Ivy. "I'm ready."

Ivy held out her hand. "Fine. I need the keys to the house."

As Asia retrieved the keys from the cupholder in the console, sounds of buzzing wheels hummed along the highway, then slowed. A black truck sped up the driveway amidst a roar of crunching limestone.

"Who is that?" Ivy took the keys from Asia.

Asia slammed the car door. "I don't know, but they're in a giant hurry."

CHAPTER 7

Ivy stepped closer to Asia. Who would know they were here? Had Janice Browne called someone, or was this a nosy neighbor out for a look-see?

The black truck stopped halfway between their cars and the road. Ivy cast Asia a sideways glance. "Who would come here?"

"Not a clue."

The driver took his time unclasping his seat belt and removing his sunglasses.

"Oh. My. Gosh," Asia whispered.

Ivy continued to stare. "What's the matter?"

"That's Nolan Delong."

Ivy squinted. "No, it can't be."

The man opened the door and descended from the truck. He smoothed his honey-blond hair, then waved.

Ivy leaned into Asia. "*That* cannot be skinny little Nolan Delong."

"He stretched up after you left."

"Filled out nicely, too," she muttered.

Asia hooded her mouth with her hand to ensure that her words could not be discerned. "He made first string quarterback on the football team his senior year. Coach Mills had him working out with weights and running. Made him eat a high protein diet. Apparently, he kept it up."

"How do you know all that?"

"I tutored him my sophomore year. He talked about his diet and workouts endlessly. My help kept him on the team."

Ivy shifted slightly. "What's he doing here?"

Asia shrugged.

Nolan stopped and picked a beggar-tick off his pants. He wore a blue button-down Oxford shirt and khaki slacks. Fine fabric, a light weave that breathed, with the perfect crease down the front of the leg. Ivy could name the designer and store where Nolan purchased them. Denney had at least three pairs back home in their closet.

Thinking of Denney pinched her heart and she squared her shoulders. "Whatever he wants, Asia," she whispered, "let me handle it."

Asia nodded. "He's all yours."

He was almost upon them. Ivy surveyed him as he high-stepped through the waving dog fennel, his designer clothes clashing with the shoddiness of Veronica's house and yard. Must have joined Daddy's business ventures around the area. One didn't have to work too hard when Daddy owned most of the county.

Nolan flashed perfectly straight teeth. He dipped his head in greeting. "Afternoon, ladies."

Ivy suppressed a grin. Sumter County's favorite orthodontist, Dr. Mercer, must have made a mint fixing those teeth. He had a jack-rabbit overbite when he was younger. At thirteen his mouth held so much hardware that some of the kids claimed they heard him picking up radio broadcasts. She should have held more sympathy for him back then, as she and Asia both suffered with braces in middle and early high school. But she never claimed to be Little-Miss-Benevolence back then. Or now.

Ivy slid on her best first-greeting smile. "Nolan, it's nice to see you again."

He acted surprised or pretended to be. "I wasn't sure if y'all would recognize me or not. It's been a while." His drawl dripped with phony honey.

"Yes, it has."

He greeted Asia. "How are you, Asia?"

"Fine."

He flashed another sixty-watt grin. "Good, good. I heard you ended up at UF."

"I did."

"What'd you study?"

"Special Ed."

"Great calling."

One glance at Asia and Ivy had to swallow a giggle. If you could kill someone with just a sneer, a judge would slam the gavel on her.

He addressed Ivy. "And what have you been up to all these years?"

The hair on the back of her neck bristled. He kept smiling but his focus unnerved her even further. "Living. And you?"

"Pretty much the same. I ran Dad's business a few years after he died, sold it and started my own real estate development company. I built the neighborhood a couple of miles up the road."

"The retirement community where Mr. Gannet's melon fields used to be?" Asia asked.

"Yes, ma'am." He pointed to the field next door to Veronica's place. "*That* plot of land over there is slated for Phase II." He swept his hand toward the highway. "And then Phase III will be on the other side of 301. We started breaking ground next door last Monday. Once finished, all three communities will be connected. A new neighborhood."

His scheme would swallow up thousands of acres in Sumter County. No wonder he appeared so prosperous. He was sitting on Daddy's money while making a load of his own. And if Ivy knew anything about business—and she did —Veronica's house stood in his way.

"You're buying up a lot of farmland. That doesn't seem like an idea the farmers around here would go for."

"Most of them are gone or too elderly to care for their places anymore. Their children or grandchildren saw new opportunities. So, I bought the land for a fair price and developed it myself." The hunter's gleam still burned in his eyes. "Well," he droned, "sure, a lot of the folks still here resisted the plans at first, but change keeps pushing forward, right?" His brow raised a fraction. "You have to let go of the past and grow at some point."

Asia shifted and brushed against Ivy. Since when had he become so philosophical? Time to filter through the phooey. "So, you came here to talk with us about buying Veronica's place?"

Nolan clapped his hands together. "Straight to the point. I always liked that about you, Ivy."

Ivy fought to keep her face expressionless. How lovely for him, because right now, she didn't like him at all.

"I was so sorry to hear about what happened to Miss Butler. I've heard she's pretty bad off. Has there been any improvement?"

How awful would they look if she or Asia admitted they had no idea how Veronica fared? Thanks to the gossip chains, the whole county probably knew more than they did. Ivy wished she could scream.

Asia spoke up. "Still in a coma. That's all we know."

Well played, Asia. Short, simple, and move it along.

Nolan shifted. "Is there any thought as to when and if she might improve?"

"None at this time," Asia answered.

"Well, I'm not going to push any business on you right now." He reached in the breast pocket of his starched shirt and brought out two business cards. One for Asia, then Ivy. "I'm interested in the property. When the timing is better, call me. I'll pay better than market price."

He gave the house a look-over. "I'll even pay to knock the place down and haul the rubble away. The house looks pretty weathered, not one of the sturdiest in the area."

"Your father's company built it," Asia reminded him.

Ivy bit her bottom lip to prevent giggling. Touché, little sister.

Nolan scratched his head and turned back to them. "I want to be up front with you both. I know this is probably going to make my dad roll over in his grave for acting in such poor taste at a time like this. I've been right where you are, had to make the decision to sell my own home and move back in with Mother so I could care for her after Dad passed. But I'm willing to give you an offer today. Right now. I'll come in, knock the old thing down. Save you both the trouble of cleaning the place out—"

Ivy cocked her brow. "You're prepared to make an offer *and* payment? Today?"

Nolan swept his hand toward his truck. "I've got my checkbook in the glove box. I've learned over the years things happen best when you move rather than wait."

"Is that legal?" Asia piped in.

Nolan crossed his arms on his chest and shifted his legs into a wide Y. "Y'all have power of attorney for the estate, don't you?"

He persisted too much, crossed a line. "We just got in, Nolan. I think both our heads are spinning, and we couldn't make any kind of decision right now."

He placed one hand over his heart. "Ivy, I completely understand."

He touched his palms together as if praying, then pointed to Asia and Ivy. "Keep my cards and give me a call when things have settled. By the way, how long are y'all staying in town?"

Ivy paused, just to make him wait a moment. "We're not sure."

"All right then. Remember, if the cleanup gets to be too much, don't hesitate to call. I can have my crew here in less than an hour. These kinds of situations are in my wheelhouse."

"Why, thank you, Nolan." Ivy waved his card near her face. A whiff of cologne drifted to her nose. He must be one of those men who slapped on his favorite scent in the morning without wiping his hands clean afterward. Whatever and whomever he touched bore his smell for the rest of the day.

She detested men like that. "We'll keep in touch."

"Great. Have a nice day." He headed to his truck.

Nolan backed into the lane, then stopped and powered down his window. "Don't hesitate to call. We'd have this house cleared away in a couple of days."

Ivy waved but said nothing. He headed for the road, beeping his horn twice as he turned onto the highway.

Ivy brushed a no-see-um stinging her arm. "That was downright peculiar."

"In so many ways." Asia replied as she smacked a gnat on her arm. "He mentioned he'd knock Veronica's house down for us four times."

"I knew you'd catch that."

"Ivy, what's going on here?"

"Veronica wants us in there and Nolan Delong wants us gone. I'd say you and I are stuck in the middle of something like a funhouse at the fair. The kind with the distorted mirrors, that sends you in all sorts of directions."

Asia tucked a curl behind her ear. "Fun and this place were never connected."

"Speaking truth there." The morning humidity gathered around them. Ivy fanned her cheeks. "Until our little exchange with Nolan, I'd forgotten how well you back people up."

Asia tilted her head at Ivy. "Two compliments in one day. My, my." Her lips crimped into an almost pleasant expression. "We need to get this cleanup going. Thirty days comes fast."

Ivy pushed her hair back from her forehead. She needed a lifetime's worth of patience to make this work. By the end of the week she would probably be ill from nastiness she picked up in Veronica's house, or in jail for strangling her sister.

Or both. Nevertheless, she wasn't going to risk another tally mark for breaking a family rule. She'd given her word to complete this job. To. The. End. Even if the strain made eating soup for the duration to settle her stomach and a full body massage to untangle her nerves a necessity.

"Let's just get to work, and we'll stop when we can't take anymore today."

Ivy headed for the front door. The sooner they started tackling this tomb of insanity, the sooner they could go back home and be done with Veronica, her house, and each other.

Forever.

CHAPTER 8

THE MID-MORNING SUN BAKED Asia's skin as she worked in the front yard of the house. In two hours she'd managed to empty one bag. One. Of the nearly fifty Ivy found stuffed in the living room and the kitchen.

Long tremors traveled the length of her body as she untied edges of the next bag. With gloved hands she spread the opening, spied the contents and looked away, swallowed back bile boiling from her stomach.

She must do this to save her home. And maybe free herself of Veronica permanently.

Asia stepped away. She needed to desensitize herself to the filth. She glanced at her watch.

Plan. Take the task in increments, unload for five minutes ... break for five minutes. Repeat. One of the first things she learned in therapy had been that a plan made a first step doable.

Asia went back and drew out the first thing she touched. The item appeared to be a black tee, caked with some sort of hardened food stain now covered in gray fuzz. Her throat started to constrict, but she fought the gag down. She dropped the shirt on the ground.

On her second reach, she found a cracked mirror. Veronica had probably decided she hated her hair one day and smashed the glass. Some of the pieces were missing. Those shards could be troublesome while she rummaged through the remaining contents. She tightened the nose piece in her disposable mask. Who knew what smells or germs lurked within these bags?

Dizziness and a racing heart swarmed her. She checked her watch.

Three more minutes, then a rest break. Asia put the mirror in a separate place from the shirt.

She thrust her hand in again, grabbing the closest thing. Her gloved fingers sank into soft, oozing goo. She shrieked and yanked her hand free. Five minutes had to be up. She ran to a spot a few feet away.

Doubled over, she peeled off the slimy gloves and tossed them.

Breathe ... Relax ...

"Sick again?" Ivy yelled as she bounded down the front steps. She tossed two more bags into the yard, then sauntered to Asia's resting spot. "Did you get anything done?"

Asia straightened, then pointed to the mirror and shirt. "I took those out, started sorting piles."

"We don't need sorting piles."

"We need to sort things, decide what might be donated—"

Ivy huffed and stomped to the tarp. "This is how we do this, Asia." She opened the box of trash bags, stuffed one into the can. Then she yanked open the bag from the house and dug out two handfuls of junk.

"Take out Veronica's cruddy stuff, remove important papers, then shove the rest into the garbage bag. Once it's full, you tie the bag closed, stack it with the others, and start over. There is to be *no* sorting, saving, or donating. No one wants this junk." She dropped the piles into the trash can.

"But there might be—"

"No. Throw. The mess. Out."

In all their growing up years, Ivy never understood that to make things less chaotic from beginning to end one must organize. That much hadn't changed.

"If we organize—"

"Asia." Ivy stomped closer until they were nose-to-nose, then took a step back. "Where'd you get this scar?" She touched the area beneath Asia's left eye.

Asia jerked away. She yanked her mask off, pulled a wipe from her pocket, and wiped under her eye. "Veronica."

"What happened?"

"I don't want to waste time on water that's rolled down the river." She mimicked water's flow with her hands.

Ivy squinted. "Where did you get *that* saying from?"

"Nowhere. Let's get back to work." Asia retrieved a new set of gloves and a clean mask. She should get in her car, start the engine, and run away, push the memory of the scar deep in her brain. Problem was the incident wouldn't stay there. Her mind could easily transport her back to the moment. Her body would reciprocate by boiling the emotions of the moment to the surface. And she'd have an attack, right there in front of Ivy. Which would send Ivy running, leaving Asia without any hope of saving her home.

Instead, she bit her bottom lip and thrust her hands into a new pair of gloves then strapped on the clean mask. After reaching into the depths of the bag she located the blob. Ivy could watch her pull this horror out and see she wasn't overreacting by being sick again.

Asia lifted the gelatinous mass from the bag, deposited the pudding-like globule into the awaiting trash can. She squeezed her eyelids closed, avoided the chance for the image to imprint her mind and torment her into wishing there were erasers for the imagination.

The blob hit the bottom with a wet thump. She winced and shuddered at the same time. Sticky residue covered her gloves and probably everything else in the bag. Asia grabbed up the entire lot and stuffed the contents into the trash. The soiled gloves followed suit.

Ivy rushed down the steps. "You didn't check—"

Asia mimed a tossing motion. "Throw. The mess. Out. Remember?"

Ivy scrunched her face into a sneer. "Fine." She dragged another bag to Asia's workspace. "Next."

"Are you making sure there are no roaches on these?"

"Don't need to. I haven't seen any all morning. I think you scared them all away yesterday."

"That's not funny."

"Asia, I have three cans of roach spray in the house. If I see one, I'll zap the rotten critter. If one sneaks out here, it's not my fault. You left me with cleaning the inside, so give me a break." Ivy stalked back to the house.

"Fine." Asia grabbed a new pair of gloves and slipped them over her hands. She went to the bag closest to her. After untying the top, she peered inside and took out a letter. Written in a spidery, masculine hand. Years of teaching teenaged boys made her an expert at recognizing a male's handwriting. She read on.

My •earest love,

I wish I could be with you now. Every day away makes me miss you more. I'm sorry I made you angry. Please forgive me for being such a senseless jerk.

Asia crumpled the letter and tossed it in the can. Poor sap. He'd obviously been drawn in by that strange, intangible thing Veronica possessed that lured men like kids to puppies.

She gathered a handful of others, all similar in tone, yet written by different men. Each one seemed to be composed by a begging, pleading male who wanted only to be forgiven and taken back into the fold of Veronica's amazing love.

Yuck. She and Ivy probably lived through some of these winners. Veronica was always bringing some man home, drinking and laughing into the late hours of the night. Ivy coped by listening to music in her headphones. Asia tuned out the embarrassing spectacles by studying.

She removed another letter, written on thick linen paper. The words were far more legible, with nearly perfect textbook formation of the lettering. The writer didn't beg, or gush.

Veronica,

I receive• your message to•ay. Again, I must ask you to observe caution at every turn when communicating. We've been over this too many times for you to continue pushing the limits. Detection means nothing short of •isaster, for both of us. The thrill these indiscretions bring you will be short-lived if you do not heed my warnings immediately.

I will consider the new terms you have requested for our business agreement and get back with you as soon as I return.

Take care.

D

Asia searched the bag for others written on the same type of paper.

After emptying the bag, she counted an even dozen from "D."

Whoever he was, he wrote all of them in the same, forthright tone. And he certainly seemed to know Veronica well. Her love of pushing limits, her demanding nature. But how? And what kind of business did they conduct together? Veronica never had any money and jumped jobs constantly.

Did this business venture produce the money Veronica now offered her and Ivy?

Asia threw the other letters in the trash but gathered up D's and set them aside. The quality paper, the articulate wording deemed them too important to toss.

She opened the next bag. More letters from the mysterious D. They were folded into thirds and contained no messages, just a date and *Love, D* written in the bottom right-hand corner.

Asia counted a total of two hundred fifty-two. Same closing on each one. What were they, and why did Veronica keep them? The others made sense. They would stroke her ego, make her feel powerful at how she made grown men grovel and cry with their words. But why did she keep the blank ones? Maybe D's simple love declaration was the draw?

Two hundred fifty-two. What was the significance of that number? She ran through factoring formulas in her head. How could you get exactly two hundred fifty-two letters …? The factoring pairs aligned, and her pulse raced. Asia rushed to the door without entering. "Ivy, come quick."

"What's the matter?"

Asia yelled louder. "Come out here. Now."

"What for?"

Asia drew in a deep breath. "There's something you need to see. Now."

Ivy appeared, her lips curled at one corner. She leaned against the doorjamb and crossed her ankles. "You bellowed?"

Asia held up the stack of letters with both hands. "I found these, and you need to see them."

Ivy shrugged. "They're letters. So what?"

"There are two hundred and fifty-two."

"And?"

"That equals one a month, for twenty-one years. The eighteen you were here plus the additional three I lived alone with Veronica. And check the dates. They coincide with when we both lived here and stopped as soon as we were both gone."

Ivy jumped from the doorway to the ground, bypassing the steps. She snatched the letters and fanned through them. "This is weird."

"Yes, it is."

"Do you think there might be more?"

"There was a dozen from D in the other bag. In one he mentioned some business arrangement and how Veronica needed to be more careful when communicating with him."

"You think they were having an affair?"

"Looks that way."

"So, what was this business?"

Asia shook her head. "No clues to that. Whatever it was, he wanted to keep it secret, and she tried to flaunt it, which made him nervous."

"D? Do you think this guy was Dewitt the Twit?"

"No. These letters represent a man with intelligence and a strong sense of good grammar. Dewitt couldn't put a coherent sentence together. And he would never have the money or class to use high-quality linen paper."

"Whoever this guy was, the only reason she kept this secret was for her benefit."

"Let's keep these, Ivy. Maybe we'll find the answers in the midst of this chaos she created."

Ivy's lips pursed. "I think that's what she wanted."

"What do you mean?"

"Veronica junked this place on purpose. She put the important things like her file boxes way in the back of the kitchen, then piled garbage around them. There are all sorts of weird things in the house."

"How weird?"

"If you think you can stomach coming inside, I'll show you. You won't believe what she's got in there."

CHAPTER 9

If she weren't seeing all this herself, Asia would never have believed it. Ivy may have a cleaning service now, but somewhere along the way she'd actually learned how to tidy on her own. She'd opened the windows for cross ventilation, allowing the clouds of dust filling the air to drift outside. The furry cobwebs and the welcome-home disaster were gone; a narrow path now cut through the remaining piles of magazines and bags of garbage. And she'd managed the task without a single tantrum. Amazing.

Asia adjusted a mask over her nose and mouth. Too much filth remained for the house to be tolerable.

"Back here in the bathroom." Ivy clasped Asia's wrist in mom-corralling-a-toddler style. "Don't want to lose you in the mess."

Asia wriggled free. "I'm fine, thanks." The walls closed around her. Hairs on her arm stood erect, as if waiting for the floorboards, nails, and walls to reach out and grab her with germ-infested hands.

"Umm-hmm. You're fine." Ivy grasped her again. She took in Asia's mask with a wide-eyed stare. "This way, Dr. Butler." She led Asia to the bathroom.

Once they reached the door, Ivy released her grip and stepped inside. Asia peeked around the frame then gasped. Black mold covered the floor tiles. The tub and sink overflowed with empty soda cans and milk jugs.

Ivy held up a scuffed suitcase. "I found this buried under the trash in the tub." She threw the valise into the hallway. It landed with a loud thud. "And I think I saw another hidden in this cabinet under the sink."

She opened the door, swept out more cans and jugs, and stretched into its confines. "Got it." She passed the second case to Asia.

Asia recoiled and the case fell to the floor. "I can't touch that thing. I don't have gloves on."

Ivy huffed, then grabbed up both suitcases. She grimaced, then set them down again. After looking at her hands, she wiped them on her pants legs. "How many pairs of those gloves do you have?"

"Six boxes."

Ivy carried the suitcases from the bathroom using only her fingertips. "Let's open these outside." She and Asia hurried to the yard where Ivy laid them on the grass while Asia threw away her mask and retrieved fresh gloves. "Why would she hide suitcases beneath trash in the bathroom?"

Ivy smeared a quarter-sized dollop of sanitizer around her fingers. "I don't know, but she hid these back in December. All those milk jugs were dated around Christmas of last year or the week after. I think she poured the milk in the tub so she could use the jugs for cover."

"That is so bizarre."

Ivy wiggled her hands into a pair of gloves. "Yet so Veronica."

Asia spread a garbage bag on the ground next to the suitcases and knelt on the plastic. "I'll open this brown one, you take the black one." She shoved the case toward Ivy.

Asia unzipped hers while Ivy knelt beside the other.

Asia's contained women's clothing. She held up a cotton nightgown. "This couldn't be Veronica's." She held the garment for Ivy's perusal. "She'd never wear pink … or flowers. And this is extra-large. Veronica would never allow herself to go above a size six."

Ivy tsked. "She would have burned that. Covers up too much. What else is in there?"

Asia rummaged through the clothes in the case. "Underwear, socks, three pairs of pleated cotton pants and a few collared shirts. Nothing Veronica would wear." She dug in a pocket in the suitcase lid. "There's a cosmetics bag in here. Maybe we'll find the real owner's name."

Asia unzipped the bag and emptied the contents. "Powder, lipstick, deodorant, a toothbrush and toothpaste, some headache pills, hairbrush and shampoo." She studied at the brush. "This is definitely not Veronica's." She held it out to Ivy.

Ivy leaned forward. "Gray hair. She would have never allowed herself to go gray."

"Open yours."

Ivy opened the second case. "This is a man's stuff." She held up an undershirt. "And judging from the style of his clothes, he was older." She held up a pair of black pants. "Older and overweight. The waistband says size forty-eight."

"Is there anything with a name or identification?"

Ivy rifled in the case. "No, just these old clothes." She pushed her hand further into a side pocket. "Wait." She pulled out a long, yellowed envelope.

"What is it?"

Ivy opened the flap and pulled out the contents. "Plane tickets to Kansas City. Both are one-way."

"For whom?"

"Vernon Dell and Rita Robertson. Dated December 1990." Ivy glanced at Asia. "Do you recognize the names?"

"No." Asia sat back on her heels. "What was she doing with someone else's clothing and plane tickets? Did she rob these people for some sort of thrill?"

"I don't know. Makes me wonder if Nolan knew about this. Maybe that's why he's so interested in leveling this place."

"These weren't hard to find. But I don't think Nolan's been in the house," Asia said.

"How do you know that?"

"There were no footprints in the dust."

"What?"

"When we went in yesterday, there was so much dust on the floor that it looked like it was growing hair. If Nolan had been in the house, we would have seen his footprints."

"Like we would have noticed with all the other junk in there."

"*I* would. Remember, I fell on the floor. The dust was at least two inches thick. And undisturbed."

Ivy brushed away a fly that landed in the suitcase. "Your little theory isn't that convincing."

One would wonder if God himself could convince Ivy of anything. Asia sighed. "What do we do now?"

Ivy tapped the tickets against her leg. "We've got two choices. Get back in there and discover what else she's hiding or call Janice M. Browne and tell her we quit. This could all be nothing more than another of Veronica's games and we find out at the end that those checks were bogus."

Asia folded the gown and put everything in the suitcase, then closed the zipper. She wanted to bulldoze the house and leave. But then she'd lose her home. "Janice said Veronica wanted us to find answers in there. There's more to this than tickets and suitcases."

Ivy dropped the tickets into the case. "This is Veronica we're dealing with. If we keep digging, you know we aren't going to like what we find."

"I know." Asia cast her attention to the house. The windows leered at her.

"Besides, does it really matter now?" Ivy closed the other suitcase.

"She's committed a horrible act of some sort. And, like always, she evaded the consequences." Asia clenched her fist.

Ivy crossed her arms, cocked her left hip to the side. "What a major waste of time."

Asia wished she could scream. All those hours spent in therapy trying to forget, only to be thrust back into this madness. The letters, the suitcases, and plane tickets belonging to strangers. The whole scenario reeked of preposterous. No one ever discovered healing in the midst of rotting garbage and secret affairs. And yet, here she was, longing for Ivy to dole out her secrets while they caved to Veronica's bidding.

Ivy clicked her tongue. "What do we do now?"

A voice from deep recesses in Asia chimed in. *Face the past. Save your home. Save yourself.* She breathed deep. "We keep going."

CHAPTER 10

HAVING HER FINGER LODGED in Ivy's vise-grip revealed a strange truth for Asia. Ivy was the only mother figure she had known.

She squirmed for stability on top of the newly polished coffee table. Since they had cleared most of the trash from the living room two days ago, Ivy had insisted they move inside to remove the splinter in Asia's finger. She'd declared the outside was an oven baking her brain.

Ivy tightened her grip. "You dusted this table so much you keep sliding away from me." She bent over Asia's finger. "How did you get a splinter? You haven't touched any wood."

Asia shrieked as Ivy pressed a needle into the soft flesh. "Something in a bag jabbed me."

"I'm never going to get that sliver out if you don't stop jerking away. Get a spine, Asia. It can't possibly hurt that much."

"It wouldn't if you'd quit jabbing me." Asia said between gritted teeth. "Are you sure you sanitized the needle?"

"I used six of your wipes to clean this, ran it under hot water, wiped it down again, and smeared antibacterial ointment over the surface. It's so slippery I can barely hold on."

She bore deeper into the skin. Asia sucked in her breath as Ivy worked the needle under the splinter. In seconds the hair-thin sliver dotted Ivy's fingerprint. "Was that so bad?"

Asia gave a sideways glance as she wiped the spot clean and spread a dollop of antibacterial ointment around the hole left by Ivy's needle. "I need to get a Band-Aid from my car."

"Don't bother. I have a ton of them in my purse." Ivy went to her purse and dug one out. "Here you go."

Asia curled the bandage around her finger and matched the edges before smoothing the flap down. "Since when are you the always-prepared type?"

"I've learned a few things over the years." Ivy put her purse back on the chair, then gave the room a once-over.

Asia readjusted her bandage. Silence swelled and filled the room.

Breathe ... relax ...

She and Ivy inhabited different universes. Ivy ran a business, shared her life with a husband. Her speed in digging out the splinter showed practice. Russ wouldn't sit through such an operation, so Ivy's husband probably wouldn't either. She must have a child. Or many.

Ivy had nothing in common with a special education teacher who lived alone in a rented single-bedroom townhouse. She was accustomed to businesswomen who traveled the country, maybe the world, discussing deals and clients while dressed in fashions that cost more than Asia's biweekly paycheck.

Asia tensed. She was here to face the past and earn the money, not play comparison games with Ivy. In Ivy's estimation, she was nothing more than a poor, desperate failure. Her cheeks warmed. The assessment wasn't far off. "The day's almost over. Why don't we empty that last box you found in the kitchen? We can leave afterward." Her words came as though her teeth were glued together.

Ivy eyed Asia. "Whatever you want." She rose and put her needle in a travel sewing kit.

Asia laid a garbage bag on the floor to protect her bare knees while Ivy ripped the last strips of dried tape off the box. Small pieces of crackled glue dusted the aged cardboard.

The awkward silence morphed into an icy distance between them. Asia's finger pulsed as if ticking off the seconds of quiet until someone initiated conversation.

Breathe ... relax ...

Asia slid on a clean pair of gloves. "What do you think is in there?"

"We're about to find out." Ivy folded the ragged flaps back. The first things out from the box were a stack of old magazines. "More of those celebrity rags." They thudded to the bottom of the trash bag Asia held open.

Next came a plastic bag from a department store. "This company went bankrupt years ago. I read about the debacle in a business journal." Whatever Veronica stored in there bulged through the sides. Ivy held the bag up by the tied handles. "What is this?"

Asia took the bundle. The contents rattled as she inspected the bag. "I'll see what's inside, you keep emptying."

"Part of me wants to save time and dump the whole mess into the trash."

Asia shrieked and the bag dropped to the floor.

"What's the matter?"

"In the bag." Asia pointed at it. If only she could stop staring at the contents, stop shaking *because* of them.

"What did Veronica put in there?" Ivy turned the bag bottom-up and jiggled. A hairless doll's head dropped to the floor, followed by a plastic torso, then arms and legs. Two faded blue eyes came last, plunking on the floor like marbles.

"What is this?" One of the eyeballs rolled to iris-side-up when Ivy brushed it with the toe of her shoe.

"My doll. Christina." Asia stared into the lone, watching eye. "Don't you remember?"

"No."

Asia garlic-knotted her arms across her mid-section. "I was six, you were nine. We came home from school that day. Christina was in the middle of my bed ... dismembered. With her head shaved and her eyes dug out."

Ivy raked her hair from her face. "Oh ..." She nodded. "I remember you screaming, 'Christina's dead. She killed her while I was gone!'"

More images of that day seeped from darkest corners of Asia's mind. Ivy trying to hug her. Asia crawling on the floor, gathering body parts. Trying to reconnect them. Failing. She'd sobbed, thrusting them to Ivy.

"You're ol•er. You can fix her. Please, fix her."

But Ivy couldn't fix Christina. Veronica had cracked the body, ruined the holes so the arms and legs could never reconnect. The lost eyes leered at her from the floor. Asia's six-year-old mind had imagined that Christina silently begged for help.

And then Veronica appeared in the doorway of the bedroom. Asia had run to her, held up the broken pieces. *"Please fix her. Please?"* Tears rolled down her face.

Veronica slapped Christina away. The pieces sailed through the air, clicked with a plastic crash as they careened into the wall. *"You shoul•n't fall in love with things, Asia. They •on't last."*

She pointed to the floor. *"Bring me the pieces. Your dolly can't love you anymore, so we have to throw her away."*

"No." Asia had crumpled to the floor in a heap of tears and throat-ripping screams.

Veronica crouched near her, whispering in her ear. *"Now, Asia."*

But Asia hadn't obeyed. Instead, she hid her face against the floor, pressed so hard the end of her nose bent; her tears pooled on the wood.

"I'll pick up the doll." Ivy had taken a step toward the pieces. But Veronica grabbed the hem of her sweater. "She *has to do it.*"

And then she trained her cold, moccasin visage on Asia. *"Get them. Now,"* she hissed.

Asia scrambled to pick up the pieces. With tear-salted lips, she kissed each limb, then hugged them close to her heart.

Veronica forced Asia to stuff her precious baby in a bag. *"That's my girl,"* Veronica cheered in a sing-song voice.

"I'm sorry, Christina. I'm so sorry," she'd whispered each time a body part fell into the depths of the bag …

"Asia, are you okay?" Ivy's touch on her shoulder snapped Asia back to the present.

"I'm fine." She struggled to clear her head. "Just … finding her … here."

"Do you want to keep cleaning or quit for the day?"

Asia washed her face with a wipe. She inhaled, held two counts, exhaled. Her skin vibrated like the zing of static electricity when you touched metal.

"I must finish this." She said the words aloud, because she was an auditory learner, and things stuck better with her if she heard them.

"Take five." Ivy scooped Christina's pieces into the bag and knotted the top shut. Asia watched through the window as she threw the bag basketball-style into the trash can outside. The load landed with a loud thump.

When she returned, Asia was pulling a piece of clothing from the box.

"What is that?" Ivy said, scowling.

"Your prom dress."

"That's impossible. I never came back after prom."

Ivy touched the soft, filmy fabric, then fingered the satin bow sewn to the waist. "There's no way she could have this."

"Look closer."

Ivy's mouth sagged into an "O" as Asia stood and held the dress up. The long folds of the skirt hung in tattered strips. Threads stuck out from the bodice where faux crystals should have rested. Both shoulder straps dangled. They'd been slashed apart.

"How?"

"This is the first one."

"The first?"

"Veronica found it two weeks before prom. She slashed the skirt, pulled out all the beading."

Ivy grabbed a section of the skirt. The fabric rustled between her fingers. "Asia, I wore *this* dress to prom that night."

"You wore a replacement. I used the money I'd earned working for Mr. Gannet to buy another. Miss Strong still had your measurements and altered the new dress."

Ivy's let the fabric spill free from her grip. "You spent your money on me? Why?"

Asia draped the dress over her arm. She smoothed a wrinkle creasing one of the tattered strips of the skirt. "She wasn't taking prom from you."

Ivy clasped Asia's arm. "I never knew—"

Asia wiggled free. "You didn't need to."

"But who does a thing like that without saying ..."

"You went, she lost. That's what mattered."

Ivy opened her mouth to speak, then stopped. Asia set the dress aside and removed a clear plastic bag from the box. A mass of blonde hair filled it almost to the top.

"I don't believe this." Ivy snatched the bag. "Why would she keep this?"

"It goes with the dress. She was so proud when she chopped off your hair that night."

Ivy crumpled the bag in her hand. "I went from fairy princess with hair flowing down my back to a flapper's bob." Her cheeks reddened.

Asia and Ivy had sprawled across the bed on their stomachs as they thumbed through Veronica's fan mag looking for the perfect prom hairstyle. Veronica came up behind them. They knew she was there, but both sisters had chosen to ignore her. Then, their tormentor had lifted Ivy's long ponytail, stroked the length. "*You have hair like silk, Ivy.*" And before either could react to the words, Veronica yanked hard and sawed away the ponytail with small garden shears.

Ivy had shrieked, grabbed the jagged ends of her hair. Asia, bolder than she should have been, pulled her into the bathroom and locked the door. She worked for three hours, trimming Ivy's hair with cuticle scissors, wiping away her tears, applying her makeup. The final look surpassed the models in the fan mags.

With Ivy ready to leave, Asia picked a fight with Veronica so Ivy could sneak out the back door and meet her date. And then she waited ... she waited on the front step until dawn for a sister who never came back.

"Why would she keep such awful things?"

"Trophies. Reminding us of her favorite moments." Asia folded the dress carefully in the box. The billowy satin and tulle mass hissed as she pressed down to close the flaps. "I'm positive she left far worse than this for us to find."

"Probably." Ivy inclined her head toward the box. "Throw the whole thing in the trash can. Good-bye to bad garbage, or whatever the saying is. I'll lock up behind you."

Asia held the box with an overextended embrace and lifted. "Ivy, get my purse on your way out."

"Got it."

The box rattled down the garbage can then lodged midway. Asia shoved hard but the box stayed put.

Sometimes bad garbage refused to leave no matter how many times you screamed good-bye.

CHAPTER 11

Asia surveyed the space of the living room as Ivy unpacked the takeout bag from a local sub shop. Gone were the mountains of magazines, the heavy coat of dust on the floor and the rotted food. The outside garbage can overflowed with trash and the emptied cans of insect spray necessary to eradicate the hordes of roaches. In a week, she and Ivy had managed to make the room tolerable.

Earlier that morning, Ivy demanded they move the kitchen table to the living room. Asia's query as to why was waved away as Ivy barked for help to push the heavy, wooden table from one room to the other. As soon as the matching ladder-back chairs were placed, Ivy declared she was starving and went in search of lunch.

"So, tell me, why did we need to move the table out here?"

Ivy passed her a tossed salad encased in a clear plastic container. "I wanted to save time and eat in, but when I opened that fridge this morning it smelled like something crawled in there and died. Can't stomach eating in there now."

Asia opened her salad and a pack of plastic silverware. "This room isn't much better, with all those boxes strewn about." Her stomach churned at the thought of eating in this room. The images of the roaches and the smell of the garbage still lingered if only in her imagination. She wasn't certain she could eat here.

Ivy shrugged a shoulder. "Those boxes don't stink like carrion waiting for buzzards. Besides, having the table and chairs out here will make it easier to clean the kitchen. More room for that collection of latex gloves and ten jugs of bleach you bought." She squeezed mustard onto the bread of her sub. "I'm going to buy more after we eat. From what I saw in that fridge, we may need ten *cases* of bleach."

Asia shuddered and laid her plastic fork on an outspread napkin. "Those details could have waited until I finished eating." She pushed her food away. "I can't eat here."

Ivy took a sip from her drink before answering. "I guess we know who gets to tackle the fridge."

As Asia watched Ivy gnaw her sub, she swallowed back a gag and thought of the last time they'd eaten lunch together. Fifteen years ago. She had warmed a can of vegetable soup. Ivy ate a handful of crackers because she didn't want her stomach to look bloated in her prom gown. They'd talked about Ivy's date and how late they'd sleep in the next morning. That was the last time either of them ate at the table.

Ivy finished the last bite of her sandwich. She swallowed quickly, washing everything down with a gurgling sip from the straw in her lemonade. "By the way, Janice Browne texted me earlier. She thinks we need to visit Veronica."

Asia's mouth turned to sawdust. She tried to swallow, but a dry knot in her throat halted the process. "I'm not going to see her."

"Me neither. The hospital wants our contact numbers so they can communicate with us instead of Ms. Browne. They prefer talking to family over lawyers."

Asia's palms moistened.

"You're really going to waste that salad?" Ivy said as Asia tossed her uneaten food in the trash.

"Not that hungry. Tell Janice to give the hospital my number and they can leave me a voicemail or text."

"Got it." Ivy's phone rang and she fished it out of her purse. "We'll continue this once I'm off the phone." She pressed the button and said a quick "I'm here" as she rushed to the far side of the room.

Asia thumbed through texts from Russ while waiting. *Hope all is well. Your place seems so empty and quiet these days. Send me news when you can.*

Asia sent him a thumbs-up emoji. If only she could text herself back home to Tennessee and Russ's steady temper and deep, soothing voice.

Snippets of Ivy's conversation drifted to her ears. "I miss all of you," she said, along with "Mom will be home soon" and "I can see other games" and finally "Put Dad back on the phone ... I love you guys ... hug your brothers for me."

She'd been right; Ivy had a real family. As her sister voiced more goodbyes, Asia tried to focus on the texts to bring Russ closer to Florida. But as she reread his words, her attention shifted to the empty space on her left ring finger.

When Ivy returned to the table, she sported the same caught-in-the-act air as when Asia found her kissing a boy behind the band room in high school. "Family."

Asia paused a moment. "Family comes first."

Ivy scowled, then resumed eating the pickle that came with her sub.

Asia surveyed the room. She should have said Ivy's *new* family came first. The one she left behind in this horrid house never seemed to matter. Especially after prom night.

"Hello?" They both jumped at the male voice that called from outside. A loud knocking on the front door followed.

Ivy wiped her fingers as she gave Asia a knowing look, then deposited her trash in the takeout bag. Another knock sounded.

They rushed to the front window. Nolan Delong stood at the door and waved when he saw them. "Got a minute?"

Asia stepped away but Ivy took another glance outside before joining her.

"What do you think he wants?"

Asia shook her head. "I don't know. But something about him makes me a little nervous."

"Yeah." Ivy looked at Asia and nodded. "Me, too."

CHAPTER 12

Ivy headed for the door. "Again, let me handle him." She strolled past Asia and swung open the door in time to flash her best hostess smile. "Come on in, Nolan. You must be roasting out there. Not that it's a whole lot better in here. The air conditioner can't keep up with this heat."

His cologne entered before he could. Expensive. Spicy, woodsy smell. Masculine.

"We were finishing up our lunch. You're welcome to have a seat."

He strode to the table with his upper torso held in a perfect triangle, shoulders and back straightened, making his light blue silk shirt hang just right on his body. Ivy dealt with men who perfected the same swagger often in her business. The urban hunter posture. Appear relaxed but have every fiber of your being ready to pounce.

Oh, fun. Her favorite kind to deal with.

She'd faced far worse men than Nolan. He was still the little neighbor boy, banned from being their playmate because his mama didn't think she and Asia were good enough. The *right* kind of people.

Ivy didn't fault Mrs. Delong. If her boys made friends with the kids of a psycho, she'd nix the friendship too. Mothers protected their sons.

She offered Nolan a chair, but he waved her off. "No thanks, I'm not staying long."

Sweat dotted his forehead. No one stayed fresh in a Florida summer. Another thing she didn't miss in Seattle.

Ivy took deliberate steps toward Nolan, standing with her feet braced apart and her arms crossed loosely. Rule of business: never let them think you're the least bit put out by the unexpected.

"So, what brings you out here, Nolan?"

"Driving by, saw your cars out front and thought I'd check in with y'all. Heard anymore news about your ...?"

"Veronica?"

Nolan shifted his feet. "Right. Any changes in her condition?"

"None that we know of," Asia answered softly, now standing next to Ivy.

Nolan shifted, giving them his best coaching-from-the-sidelines stance. "Have y'all been by to visit? I assume she's at Lake Memorial."

Ivy glanced at Asia. A red splotch now crept up her neck. Nolan was no slouch. He fired a direct shot in less than five minutes.

Asia seemed to fold inward, as if shielding from grief over Veronica. "I'm not ready to see her ... like that."

Well-played. Sounded heartfelt, garnered sympathy, and let her off the hook. Who could fault Asia for not wanting to see Veronica lying in a hospital at her life's end? Only a cold, heartless jerk, and Nolan couldn't afford to come across that way. Not when he obviously wanted something so badly.

Ivy spoke up. "I don't do well in hospitals. And we've been so busy here. She asked that we get this place cleaned out before she dies. We need to honor that. We don't know how much time she has left."

Nolan's face brightened at her comment. "That's why I came by. My wife works as a nurse at Lake Memorial, in the ICU. Veronica is one of her patients."

Asia's face turned red and Ivy clenched her teeth. The rotten sneak knew all along. He was more informed than they were.

Then why show his cards so early? Ivy searched his face. No traces of smug satisfaction or arrogance over his little victory. Instead, his eyes flickered with the same determination her truck drivers wore after a long haul. He came there on a mission, to finish a job. "My wife told me no one has visited her except her lawyer."

"I believe," Ivy said, allowing her words to come slowly, "that nurses aren't supposed to tell who is and who is not in the hospital.

HIPAA laws and all. So, we'll pretend you never said a word." She winked as deliberately as she had spoken.

Nolan blew out his breath. "You know," he said, now scanning the room's clutter, "I could bring in my guys while you're visiting her, have them sift through things, sort out what's worth saving, throw out the rest. My wife's cousin owns an auction house. She could come in and appraise anything of value, contract with you for an estate sale. Make things simpler."

"And you thought all this up? Just now?" Asia tipped her chin, nailed him with a perfect teacher-catching-a-cheating-student gaze.

Nolan continued. "I buy and flip properties all the time. This situation is second nature to me."

"Why are you so concerned about making things easy on us?" Ivy leaned to the right, sighted down her nose at Nolan. "This is *our* family's business, not yours."

A light flickered in his eyes. "I'm just trying to help out … in the name of old friendships." He smiled, but the smile didn't quite catch. "I wouldn't have passed most of high school without Asia's tutoring. My dad taught me to pay things forward when the opportunity arises."

That was interesting. Ivy rubbed her earlobe, ran a finger around the back of her earring. The only thing "arising" in this meeting was the level of blather dishing from Nolan's mouth. A simple, cheap sympathy card would have covered any debt he owed Asia.

"What's that?" He walked to a box sitting near the middle of the room. Asia had found the carton stuffed behind a dozen empty rice boxes in a kitchen cabinet.

"Just junk." Ivy tugged Asia's sleeve, forcing her to follow Nolan. Though Veronica's things held no value to her, she bristled over the thought of Nolan feeling free to nose around.

He bent over the carton and took a figurine from within. He held up a small replica of the Empire State Building, covered in tarnished silver. "Where'd she get this?"

Ivy frowned. She and Asia opted to leave the box for later, but maybe they should have given the collection a second look. "I don't know. Veronica never said she went to New York."

Nolan flipped the figurine over in his hand. "My mother has one of these. My father brought it back from a trip."

Ivy removed the statue from his fingers with a light jerk. "Veronica probably bought the thing in some junk shop ... or somebody's yard sale." Or perhaps one of the men from her male harem gave the trinket to her as a gift.

She dropped the statue in the box. It landed with a metallic clunk. But Nolan wasn't deterred by Ivy's moxie. He picked up a tarnished spoon with a picture of Niagara Falls inlaid on the handle. "Do you know anything about this?"

Ivy raised her chin. "Does your mother have one of those, too?"

He pressed his lips into a tight line. "I've seen one exactly like it ... somewhere." He replaced the spoon in the box. "Are there any more boxes like this? I could take them to my wife's cousin, let her go through them. You never know, there might be some treasure buried in this old house."

He looked around the room, then squinted as attention rested on the far wall. The floor creaked as he stepped closer. "What is that?" He leaned in closer and inspected the wall's face.

Ivy cringed. Once she and Asia cleared away the mountain peaks of Veronica's old fan mags and boxes, they discovered another strange habit of hers.

On every wall of the living room she'd scratched two words—"Filthy Rags"—over and over, filling up the entire surface area from floor to ceiling. The writing was so small that from a distance the words resembled patterned wallpaper. But standing in the center of the room where Nolan had been revealed the true nature of Veronica's scrawls. She'd used permanent marker to fill in the indentations, so it couldn't be washed off easily. Asia tried scrubbing them clean, but like all the others scars Veronica left behind, they had to fade with time.

At first, the writings gave Ivy the creeps. She'd wondered what devious message Veronica was bent on parlaying. Ignoring the words each day she entered the house took away their sting and she barely noticed them this morning when she and Asia started working.

Nolan navigated the entire room, avoiding the landmines of scattered boxes, scanned the walls and the few spots in the corners where Veronica had cut away the carpet and scribbled the words on the floorboards. He traced one set of words with his fingers, then circled back to her.

"What *is* this?"

Ivy sent Asia a silent plea for backup. With her teaching experience, thinking of an explanation for a person's behavior should be second nature. Instead, Asia stood with her hands outstretched as she mouthed a silent "I don't know" in response.

"It's on every wall," Nolan said as he circled the room. He bent down and scanned the scribbles on the floor. "Did she do this throughout the entire house?"

"This is the only room so far."

"Was there something wrong with her?"

Who was he kidding? He and everyone around Sumter County knew the easy answer to that. But for Asia and herself—no, she was just being Veronica. But how did you explain that?

"She may have been suffering from dementia," Asia said.

Ivy cast a sideways glance at her. Dementia? Nice cover, but so far off the mark. Still, dementia garnered a measure of sympathy even though Veronica deserved nothing short of complete annihilation.

"What do y'all think it means?"

Ivy and Asia shrugged in unison.

"Do you think she went insane?"

Went insane? The more accurate answer screamed that she lived and breathed insanity.

Nolan surveyed the walls, rubbed the back of his neck. "What would make a person go and do this … Does this kind of thing run in your family?"

Nolan had pushed his expensively clad toes over the line. "What kind of question is that?" Ivy planted her hands on her hips. Asia was too polite to call him out for having the gall to say such a thing, but she was not.

He swung around. His eyes almost bugged from the sockets, he held them so wide. The whites bore the pink, irritated lines of a contacts-wearer. Nolan held out his palms. "I'm sorry. I got carried away with the questions." He rubbed his arm, glanced at his watch, scanned the room again, then said, "I've got to get going." With booming steps and legs churning like pistons, he hurried from the room. "I'm sorry. Give me a call if y'all want my help. Have a good rest of your day," he called over his shoulder.

He slammed the front door shut with window-rattling force. Minutes later, he sped away to the sound of his tires crunching lime rock.

"What just happened?" Ivy asked. She made it to the window in time to see Nolan barreling down the highway.

"Veronica happened."

"What was the crack about 'it' runs in the family?"

"Maybe he's worried we're bats-flying-in-the-belfry crazy, too," Asia said. "Nolan always was a bit nervous. The day before an algebra test, or a big football game, he'd get so worked up he'd vomit. You remember how much we scared him the time we told him the story about cannibalistic cows?"

Ivy smirked at the memory. "He started to shake and ran home. We didn't see him for weeks." She chuckled. "Cannibalistic cows? We were a couple of weird kids."

"We were trying to make sense of our real world. It was far worse than anything we could make up."

Her words rang true. "I have never been freaked out by a horror movie, no matter how gory or creepy the scenes. When those things come on the screen, I just zone out until it's over."

Asia shook her head. "I lived one, don't need to watch one."

Poor Asia still lived in their old nightmare. And somehow, she thought Ivy held a secret remedy for overcoming. She needed to stop thinking about the past so much, and instead file those old memories away like she had. Their past held no influence on her life now, except making her determined to be a good wife and mother.

Ivy inclined her head toward the walls. "You think that will scare him off from this place?"

Asia shrugged. "He once got so nervous about a football game he threw up six times before kickoff. But, once the game clock started, he ran onto the field and led the team to their most lopsided victory. Veronica's scribbles threw him, but he wants this house and us gone. He'll be back." She wiped her hands. "We need to get back to work."

"Yes, we should."

Though not clean yet, the room presented less as a horror movie and more a normal house. A normal house with a weird message covering the walls, and who knew what else crammed in Veronica's bedroom, and her and Asia's old room. But those tasks and Nolan Delong would have to wait. In only a few hours, she'd be headed home to Seattle.

They'd decided to take off for a week. But Ivy itched to return, so she could put a period at the end of this nightmare and focus on the tax situation at home. "Hold on ... I'm going to the bathroom."

As she washed her hands, she heard a loud scraping coming from the living room. "Ivy, get out here," Asia called.

"What's the matter?" Ivy rushed out while shaking water droplets from her hands.

Asia stood next to a huge hole dug into the wall. She scrubbed her hands over and over with a wipe. The set of bookshelves originally occupying the spot had been pushed to the side. "While I was waiting for you, I noticed this outline on the wall. At first, I thought there was a crack, but then when I got closer, I saw this." She picked up a piece of drywall from the floor. "This was cut out from the wall. Look inside."

A box filled the space, with crumpled newspapers and Christmas wrapping stuffed around each side.

"What in the world?"

Asia grabbed the piece of drywall. "I can't deal with anything else today." She cast a glance behind her to the other boxes. "Let's cover this back up and fool with it when we come back next week."

Ivy complied, then stepped back once the panel was in place. "Asia? What do you think Nolan really wanted when he came back here today?" She stayed focused on the sealed hole in the wall.

"Probably the same thing he wanted when he first came by." Asia crossed her arms. "Whatever he saw here this time spooked him enough to make him run like a scalded cat."

Ivy swung round, crossing her arms as she did, then joined her sister at the window. "You know what I think?"

"No, but I'm certain you're going to tell me." Asia looked at her side-eyed. Waited.

"I think if there's one thing I know, it's a man playing mist and mirrors with me. Especially when it comes to business." She glanced over her shoulder to the modicum of progress they'd made ... to the boxes and bags yet to be searched, including the one in the newly discovered hole. And to the one that had held such interest for their childhood friend. Her brow raised, her heart raced, ticking off beats as the old metronome on her piano did when the boys set it to top speed. "Asia," she said again, this time in her Mom-will-be-obeyed-voice, "You and I aren't leaving. We're staying here."

"What?" Asia circled on her. "Are you crazy? I've got—"

Ivy ignored her sister's glare. "*You've got to stay,*" she said before Asia could finish. "No way, no how am I leaving this place with Nolan Delong on the prowl, free to break in any time he wants." She sauntered to the box of Veronica's cheap trinkets, yanked the statuette of the Empire State Building from its recesses, then held it up to Asia as if it were State's Exhibit A. "He's after something. I don't know *what,* but I do know that we'd better find it before he does."

CHAPTER 13

Ivy's words landed a gut punch. She couldn't … wouldn't suggest that they stay … *in* Veronica's house …

That would mean sleeping there. Lying in the dark, listening to the old noises, watching the shadows slither across the walls and prowl around the rooms. Shivers stampeded up and down Asia's body.

Breathe … Relax … Breathe …

"I will *not* … stay here … ever." She drew in a deep breath, counted to two. Dug wipes from her pocket and wiped her hands. Twice.

Ivy straightened, put her hands on her hips. "Maybe you didn't catch what I said. I'm not leaving this house open for Nolan Delong to come in and scrounge around for whatever it is he's searching for. I'm going to find it first." She sealed the declaration with a quick nod.

Asia's head spun.

Breathe … Relax … Breathe …

"I have end-of-the-year duties at school—"

Ivy leaned toward Asia. "Do you think I'm staying here for vacation? I'll be away from *both* of my companies. And I'm breaking promises to my boys by missing their baseball games. I won't ever get those days back. You're worried about kids who don't even belong to you. Call your boss and get another substitute teacher. They'll understand. You said this was the end of the school year, so it shouldn't be that hard."

The room swirled. Asia's knees melted to Jell-O. Attempts to inhale or exhale resulted in wheezing squeaks that did nothing but dry her throat. "I have to get out of here." She huffed and headed for the door. If she didn't get breath soon, she'd pass out and end up wallowing in the dust still covering the floor.

Asia shoved the door open and stood on the step.

Breathe ... Relax ... Breathe ...

A hot breeze blew across her cheeks. Sweat dampened her forehead.

This house inhabited her nightmares. In her terrors the walls morphed into ghoulish faces, laughed at her as planks of wood pulled from their nails and bound her in splintery restraints puncturing all exposed skin. Too many nights she'd been awakened by her own screams, panting as her heart launched against her chest.

Ivy now stood behind her. She tapped the middle of Asia's back. "Move over."

Breathe ... Relax ... Breathe ...

Asia slid to the side of the step. "I don't care what Nolan wants. Let him have the whole house."

Ivy took the empty spot next to Asia. "This is just a house, Asia. It isn't going to reach out and bite you. And Veronica is comatose in a hospital twenty miles away."

Asia sucked in a breath. "It's more than that."

"Then what?" Ivy flicked away an ant crawling on her shoe.

"You wouldn't understand."

"Really? I know you don't have a family, so you don't get how much of a sacrifice being away is for me, but I'm willing to make the choice so we can get out of here faster."

Asia took a wipe and washed her face. Twice. Ivy's playing the sacrificing-my-family card pricked at her. Burning and piercing at the same time. She owed her students, too. Shouldn't that count … when that was her greatest commitment? They weren't just someone else's kids …

"Where are we supposed to sleep? I can only imagine what our old room looks like. And there is no way on this green earth that I'm sleeping in Veronica's old room."

Ivy shrugged. "I'll run to Walmart and buy some blow-up mattresses or camping cots. We'll sleep in the living room. We can scrub and mop until this place smells like one of your wipes."

"Sleeping here would be like sleeping at the dump."

Ivy clicked her tongue against her teeth. "The dump doesn't have air conditioning, running water, and electricity. And I guarantee there are fewer germs and vermin here."

"What would we do if Nolan shows up in the middle of the night?"

The corner's of Ivy's mouth curled into a grin. "We could show him your doll and the bag of my hair. That should scare him off. He accused us of being nuts, so we'll prove him right."

"And if he persists?"

"We start telling him more cannibalistic cow stories. Those worked well when we were in elementary school."

Ivy possessed answers for all Nolan-related problems. But what about the evil vibes emanating from the rafters, floorboards, and every single nail in Veronica's house? How would Ivy make those go away?

"Asia, I'm sure you can come up with dozens of arguments why we need to leave. And I'm certain they will be well thought out, reasonable, and filled with truth. But instinct tells me we need to stay here. I'm staying."

Asia hugged herself in a tight embrace. "Why does protecting Veronica's stuff mean so much to you? Is it because of the money?"

Ivy stood and brushed off her shorts. "Nope. I just don't want Nolan nosing around in here or taking something."

She searched Asia's face. "I get that you have horrible memories of this place."

When they were younger, she believed and trusted everything Ivy said. But then Ivy left her behind, and the life she lived became the stuff of her own horror show. "Ivy, I can't—"

"Asia, what I'm going to say may shock you." Ivy pinned Asia with a look that demanded she listen. "I've never spent one moment in this house without you. I *need* you here with me."

The daisy-like tops of milkweed swayed in the yard; they seemed to listen to their conversation, waiting to hear what came next. "Why?"

"Because I always knew you'd keep me safe."

Asia's shoulders slumped forward as mind and body went numb. She couldn't fight this confession. Ivy never lied about her vulnerabilities. She once claimed she'd rather have her fingernails yanked out than admit fear. Ivy was determined to protect this God-forsaken turf and she couldn't leave her to do it alone. "Fine. But you have to follow three conditions."

Ivy arced her right brow. "Like what?"

"First, I won't sleep in our old bedroom. Only the living room. The living room has to be swept clean. Walls, windowsills, and windows must be dusted, scrubbed, then wiped down with antiseptic cleaner. And the floor mopped. Twice. And I won't sleep on the floor. Second, the bathroom must be bleached, scrubbed, and sanitized until there is no mold left anywhere. It needs a new shower curtain, bathmats covering the entire floor, towels, and washcloths."

Ivy huffed. "And your last demand is?"

"I want a nightlight for every outlet, in every room. I refuse to step foot in this house if it's dark. I'll help cover the costs."

Ivy's brows twitched. "Deal. And I'll pay for everything else since staying here was my bright idea."

Asia opened her mouth to protest, but her sister stopped her from going on. "I'm paying. It may send me to the poorhouse, but I am paying. That's the deal." She thrust her hand to Asia.

Asia made Ivy clean her hand before she sealed the deal. "I'll notify the school that I'm not coming back before summer break." Her mind reeled through to-do lists of who to call, what to send via email to the sub to keep instruction and organization flowing in her classroom. She'd also message her paraprofessional with lesson plans. Thank goodness the end-of-the-year assessments and IEP updates were completed the week before she left.

Ivy interrupted. "Great. I'll run to Walmart and get bedding, cots, and pillows plus the other things on the list. You need anything?"

"I brought my own bedding and pillow. I also have a sleeping bag. I just need towels and washcloths."

Ivy gave a thumbs-up. "Great call. I'm not using anything that belonged to *her*." She jerked her head toward the house. "I'll grab paper plates, plastic silverware, and bottled water. I guess we can figure out meals later. We'll eat out tonight."

Ivy collected her purse. "I'll run to the hotel and gather up my things, check out, then head to the store. Go get your stuff and meet me back here."

Asia settled her purse on her shoulder and followed Ivy out the door. A blackbird squawked from its perch on the neighboring fence as Ivy locked the door. This entire plan now advanced at the speed of Ivy, with no brake to pull or means of killing the engine. Asia was being shoved forward with hurricane-force winds.

They went to their rental cars in silence. The bird called again as Asia unlocked the driver-side door. She shuddered, then settled into the car. Instead of purring to life, the engine coughed and sputtered. She leaned back in the seat, then reached forward and tried again. Nothing.

Ivy rolled down her window. "What's going on?"

Asia opened the door and stepped out. "Car won't start. There are no idiot lights on, and nothing indicates a problem. I don't know what's happening. The motor worked fine this morning."

"Try again."

Asia complied. The engine answered with dead silence.

"Lock it up and come with me. We'll swing by your hotel on the way to the store."

Ivy had full control now and a boatload of answers for everything. Asia grabbed her purse and an extra pack of wipes from the glove box before exiting.

An eerie sound caught her ear as she locked the car door. A gust of wind whipped from around the house, carrying the shrill, dissonant notes of a familiar voice.

Welcome home, my girls.

CHAPTER 14

The sun sat low on the horizon. Night loomed as Ivy drove to retrieve Asia's things from her hotel. The buzzing of a lone mosquito hummed near her ear. She swatted the pest away only to have the high-pitched needling begin again as soon as she put her hand down. "Add mosquito spray to the list. I'm not putting up with those airline-sized biters that come out at dusk."

Ivy surveyed the road ahead. "Where are you staying?" she asked, mentally kicking herself for not asking sooner. Why couldn't she break down this wall?

"The Orange Grove Motel."

Ivy jerked at the response. "Are you kidding me?"

"I couldn't afford anything else." Asia squirmed.

"Why on earth are you staying there?"

"Ivy, it's the most economical choice."

"What are you talking about? There are a ton of decent, reasonably priced hotels in—"

"Yes, Ivy, there are. But I didn't know how long we would be here, and those decent hotel rates add up quickly on a teacher's salary."

"Oh." Ivy gave Asia a side-eyed glance. She'd roped herself with crossed arms.

Ivy sighed. She'd engaged mouth before mind and stomped on Asia's feelings. Most times she believed hurt feelings were the other person's problem, but embarrassing her sister was different. For a moment, she'd forgotten Asia was no longer fifteen.

The passenger seat remained silent for at least a half-mile stretch.

Poor Asia. When they were kids, the Orange Grove had been a hangout for trouble. The drug trafficking within the surrounding area screamed "bad idea" on its own. The entire county knew it was a cesspool. And now their circumstances forced Asia to go *there* after dealing with Veronica's chaos all day.

She had to give props to her little sister for keeping herself together.

At Ivy's hotel Asia wordlessly aided in bringing out suitcases and packing up the trunk. She parlayed only necessary directions and agreements as they made their purchases in Walmart. The silence pressed Ivy's nerves as they headed for the Orange Grove. The car's headlights cut through the darkness, illuminated the faded sign for the motel. The bottom left corner was shattered, probably the result of an errant beer bottle being thrown through the front.

Ivy clicked on her turn signal. "We're here."

Asia unbuckled her seatbelt. "I'll get my things and pay for the rest of the week."

A short line of cars exited the hotel parking lot. Ivy waited for them to pass. "I'll cover your room fees, since I forced you out of this little piece of heaven." And then add it to the list of unforeseen costs determined to plague this nasty little venture of Veronica's.

Asia glanced at her. "Ivy, I can't let you do that."

"Why not?"

"I don't like borrowing. You know, 'Neither a borrower nor a lender be.'"

"*Who* said that?"

"Really?"

The last car passed, and the headlights spotlighted the interior of Ivy's car.

"Unbelievable," Asia mumbled.

"Why should I know this?" Ivy navigated into the parking lot and drove around a collection of semis camped for the night.

But Asia said nothing else.

Two women with frazzled hair and tight skirts loitered by a blue *Sumter County Times* box situated by the doors of the office. For their sakes and that of the truckers, Ivy hoped there would be no transactions tonight. Most of her drivers were hard-working family men who respected their families too much to imbibe in the sordid. But it only took one interested man and one available woman to make trouble.

She slowed the car. Denney would be disappointed to know she'd allowed Asia, her blood, to stay here. Not knowing was little excuse. She should have checked with Asia about accommodations. But, from the start, her head had only been focused on her needs. "Where is your room?"

"Around back, number 172."

Ivy parked in an open spot nearest the room. "Get your things, I'll pop the trunk."

Asia left without a word.

She came back with a pillow encased in zippered plastic and a sleeping bag. "May I put these in the back seat?"

Ivy opened the door. Asia laid them on the seat, then went for the rest of her things. Once her suitcase and makeup bag were tucked in with everything else, she returned to the passenger's seat.

Ivy slammed the trunk lid then hopped in the car. "I'll take care of your bill, then we'll grab some supper."

Asia ignored her, her focus instead on the star-peppered sky. Ivy suppressed a grin. Fifteen years since they'd shared a room. This new situation had the potential to get interesting. Or completely unbearable.

She drove to the front office, parked and entered. A woman with a short, gray pixie cut sat behind a counter of cracked and scarred linoleum. "Can I help you?"

Ivy bit back a smirk. Asia had nagged her years ago to never to ask *can* I. This woman's bad grammar alone should have sent Asia running. Maybe that explained her moods in the mornings.

She expressed her desire to pay Asia's bill to the clerk, then waited as the woman retrieved the information from a dinosaur computer. Ivy scanned the tiny lobby, the racks of touristy post cards, many of them yellowed and bent at the edges. She could dress herself in pricey clothes and hobnob with Seattle's finest, but deep down, she'd always be a girl who grew up in the land of huge alligators, two hours from Florida's famed theme parks. The boys loved her tales of swimming in creeks while watching alligators sunning themselves on nearby banks. Those days taught her great life lessons. Don't take your eyes off the things capable of biting you. Look away for even a moment and they'll slip under the surface and ambush you.

Just like her tax troubles. She'd put her focus elsewhere and trusted her controller. And here she was paying Asia's hotel bill, buying all the materials to make life at Veronica's tolerable as though she had a grove of money trees back in Seattle.

With the bill settled, Ivy slid her wallet into her purse and walked back to the car. Asia remained silent, her brows lowered so much her forehead puckered.

Why was she so put out? Ivy had slept in worse places. Everybody had hard-luck times. Going through them stank, but after you survived, you grew the right kind of armor for the next time trouble rolled around. Their childhoods were proof of that and bonded them to each other ... regardless of what Janice M. Browne thought.

They would get through this. Or at least *she* would.

Maybe after this nightmare ended, she and Asia could write a book. *The Joys and Sorrows of Sister-Bonding: How to Live with Your Sibling and Avoid Killing Her.*

Ivy laughed under her breath as she opened her car door. They could follow up with a sequel, *How to Survive a Psychopathic Mother.*

She slid into her seat, positioned her legs under the steering wheel. Asia sat as far away from her as the interior of the front seat allowed, her face turned skyward.

Yes, after this was over, they should write those books together. They'd probably make millions. If they didn't kill each other or end up not speaking for another fifteen years.

"What kind of food are you hungry for? I noticed some fast-food joints on the other side of the interstate."

Asia lifted one shoulder. "I just want a salad."

Ivy pressed the START button. "Fine."

She left the hotel parking lot and swung the car into the road.

They stopped for salads at a restaurant near the interstate. With neither of them speaking, supper took less than twenty minutes. The silence continued in the car.

Ivy figured that normal sisters would have welcomed a slumber party, complete with giggling into the late hours, reminiscing over glasses of wine. But she couldn't have wine and none of their shared memories held anything worth giggling about.

Instead, she and Asia would spend their evening installing nightlights in every outlet of the living room and kitchen, hoping to keep old fears away. Though their childhood bogeyman lay in a hospital, her spirit still inhabited every splinter of the house. And there weren't enough nightlights in the world to keep the evil in Veronica at bay.

CHAPTER 15

Asia pressed her back deeper into the passenger seat with every mile the tires ticked off as they sped down the road. If it were possible, she'd melt into the leather covering the cushions and dissolve her cells into the stuffing buried within. Or maybe break into a thousand pieces and fly away on the night breezes like fluffy dandelion seeds, back to Maryville. She'd do anything at this moment to avoid going back to Veronica's.

Ivy didn't understand what sleeping in that house meant. She'd left, before Veronica brought in a new terror. One that prevented Asia from ever enjoying a full night's sleep again. Ivy didn't know that Asia lived on two or three hours of sleep per night all her adult life. That she never felt safe in the dark until the night Russ came running to check on her the first time her home security system malfunctioned.

She'd never said more than a quick "hey" to him in passing each day, yet he'd come pounding on her door, clad in his winter coat over a t-shirt and thin workout pants two minutes after her alarm went off. Not angry about the midnight disruption, as their other neighbors were, but worried for *her*. He'd stayed hours after, drinking cups of tea as she dealt with the alarm company over the phone. He even aided in reprogramming her system the following day. That next night, for the first time in her adult life, she slept until her alarm clock wailed at five-thirty.

Asia ran her finger along his card in her pocket. She couldn't do this. He wasn't here in Emerson, on the other side of a wall, able to come running.

She clawed the edges of the seat as her heart thuds brought pain behind her breastbone. Her lungs squeezed. The air from the air conditioner vent chilled the sweat dampening her forehead.

Breathe …

Why? So the leftover ghouls in Veronica's house could torment her all night?

Relax …

She could never relax within those walls. That's why she'd run away to Tennessee.

Breathe …

She couldn't breathe here. Not in that house.

Asia dug wipes out and wiped her hands, then face. Twice. She held a clean wipe beneath her nose, sucked in the lemony-orange scent, and prayed.

She jumped at Ivy's nudging her with a pointed elbow. "Wake up. Let's unload and go to bed. I'm exhausted."

Asia tried to speak but her lungs held the air in. She coughed, drew two long breaths, and counted to two before attempting speech again.

Ivy hesitated. "Are you okay?"

"Does it matter?" Asia coughed again.

Ivy unlocked the car doors. "Um … yeah. You seem like you're about to have a come-apart here and I'd rather you didn't. I don't know how quickly 911 comes this far out in the county." She reached across the console and gave Asia a fast pat on the arm. "Like I said before, I need you here. This place still gives me the creeps."

Asia drew in another breath. Moths and beetles flitted in and out of the triangular beams projecting from the car's headlights. They'd left the lights on and the house grimaced at them, reminding her of a squared-off jack-o-lantern. All tricks and no treats.

"Leave the car lights on until we get in the house, will you, Ivy?"

"They're automatic. We've got time to get in before they turn off."

"Good. I don't want to walk across this yard in the dark."

Ivy pushed the button to pop the trunk. "Me, neither. Guess we can do that quick run-and-hop thing like we did when we were younger.

I'll unlock the front door so we can get stuff inside." She high-stepped her way through the weeds then jumped from the ground to the top step.

Funny how old habits resurfaced. She and Ivy had perfected the step-jump when they were in elementary school. During the summers, Veronica never burdened them with curfews. She allowed them to come and go as they pleased, as long as they remained silent when entering the house. They broke the rule only once.

One evening a yellow rat snake had chosen the bottom step to cool its heated scales. Asia had been staring at the strange car parked in the yard and failed to see the slender body stretched across the bottom stair. She stepped down, felt the squishy wriggling beneath her bare feet, then screamed as the snake shot away in an s-shaped dance across the gray sand.

Her screams brought out Veronica's male visitor. He stood shirtless in the doorway and laughed. Veronica leaned over to Asia and whispered in her ear. "You broke my quiet rule. I have half a mind to go trap that snake and put him in your bed, Asia." After that day, she and Ivy high-jumped over the bottom step whenever they returned in the night. No sense playing against fate and risking Veronica's wrath a second time.

A cramp along her arms brought Asia back to the present. She'd looped as many bags as could be lifted on each forearm to hurry progress into the house. Her load banged against her legs as she hurried to the front door.

Ivy opened the door and spun around, knocking into Asia. "Whoa there, pack mule. You'll send us both tumbling if you don't slow down."

Asia swayed, then pushed forward past Ivy into the house. "Sorry."

"What's your hurry?" Ivy followed her in.

Asia dropped the burden of bags on the floor then rubbed the deep ruts left by the plastic handles. "I wanted to get in before the mosquitos ate me alive." And the memories, which seemed to dive-bomb her and draw more blood than the mosquitos.

Ivy shrugged. "It's that time of night." She dug through the bags until she removed a jug of bleach, a new box of reinforced rubber gloves, and a box of copper scrubbers. She thrust them at Asia. "You clean the bathroom and I'll clean up the living room."

Images of furry, black grout on the shower walls and the floor tiles hit Asia. The rust stain in the toilet bowl and the brown ring in the tub added an extra hue of filth to her imaginings. Her tongue curled. The few bites of salad she managed to swallow at supper threatened to make a half-digested reappearance.

She swallowed hard as her blood pulsed in her ears. She'd developed a system to help avoid using Veronica's bathroom. Every time she and Ivy left for lunch, she used the ladies' room at the restaurant they visited, cleaning it multiple times with her own wipes. She cleaned the restroom in her hotel room at The Orange Grove the same way. Both could be brought up to tolerable standards. But Veronica's? "Me? No, I—"

"You trust me to clean it to your standards?" Ivy cocked her hip and crossed her arms.

Asia's head spun. No. A thousand people armed with the greatest industrial cleaners in the world couldn't make that space clean enough for her to wash her hands, much less anything else.

Why had she agreed to this? She had a hotel room. She could escape the hold of this house and get away. Call Russ when she got up the nerve, to give him more than an update via text. And, she had a break from Ivy and the trappings of her perfect life. The Orange Grove may have been one hair better than a hovel, but it provided sanctuary.

A sanctuary now gone. She was trapped in this house again, in the dead of night. She'd promised herself to never return, repeating it over and over years ago when that Greyhound bus took her far away from Veronica's reach.

She drew in two breaths, exhaled, then gathered up the cleaning supplies. Sometimes cleaning messes settled her nerves. "I'll probably be in there all night. Just put my pillow and sleeping bag on the cot." She started for the bathroom, then called to Ivy. "I don't want to sleep anywhere near the windows."

Ivy looked as though she'd eaten something rancid. "Me neither." She motioned across the room. "I'll push the cots up against the far wall. Away from the windows, pointing toward the door. We'll have the best view of the house plus plenty of room to pass by the table and the tarp when we need to."

Asia settled a mask around her nose and mouth, then headed for the bathroom.

CHAPTER 16

Asia sat at the table in the living room, cradling her throbbing head. Her body's clock wasn't accustomed to ticking off life after midnight and her shoulders ached from scrubbing the tiles in the shower. Her inner thigh muscles stabbed from squatting to scrub the floors five times and the toilet bowl six—or had it been seven—times. She lost count somewhere around three o'clock, when Ivy declared the living room was as clean as it would get and she tumbled onto her cot fully clothed. Asia continued cleaning, hoping fatigue would take over and force her into sleep. When she could no longer think straight at five thirty, she showered twice, then curled up in her sleeping bag.

The smell of brewing coffee awakened her. She took her phone from under her pillow and checked the time. Nine fifteen. She'd kept it there in case she needed to use her flashlight app in the dark. She'd also read over Russ's nightly text to her before she fell asleep.

Ivy poked her head through the door. "Coffee's ready and I'm scrambling eggs. Made toast, too. You want some with strawberry jelly or grape? I know you always liked grape best."

Asia stretched and sat up. "When did you get food?"

"I got up at seven. You were still dead to the world, so I showered and ran to the store." She held up a finger. "Picked up eggs, bread, peanut butter, jelly, soup, milk, OJ, and coffee." She held up a second finger. "Went to Walmart for a skillet." Another finger. "And a pot to cook the soup. Figured we could do a regular shopping trip later to pick up other items we'll need." She cocked the edges of her lips into a crooked grin. "I'll let you make the next list."

Lack of sleep left Asia foggy. She wriggled free from her sleeping bag. "You did all that in two hours? Since when were you an early riser?"

Crackling drew Ivy's attention, and she went back into the kitchen. "I have three boys. There is no sleeping in at my house. Mornings, I hit the ground at a full gallop," she called.

Asia rolled up her sleeping bag and packed her pillow into the protective covering. Ivy's morning mania had nothing to do with energetic boys. Frayed nerves had always amped her beyond normal energy levels, no matter what she claimed. After pulling two wipes from a fresh packet, Asia washed her face twice, then her hands.

Daylight calmed the house's evil whispers, but a bone-chilling presence still floated between the walls like heavy morning mist. She drew in a deep breath. Exhaled. Twice.

Ivy bustled through the door, balancing a plate of scrambled eggs and buttered toast on each arm. "Food's ready." Neither eggs nor toast slid from their spots as she set them on the table.

"Wow, you're really good at managing that food. I'm impressed." Asia claimed a chair and sat. She sniffed the aromas wafting from the food. "Smells wonderful." Now that the room was clean, she could entertain eating a meal at the table.

Ivy settled into her own chair across the table. "I've put in a lot of hours and mileage as a waitress." She spread a paper napkin across her lap. "Great job on the bathroom. The shower sparkles." Ivy scooped up a forkful of eggs. "Definitely assigned that job to the right person." She grinned, then ate her bite of eggs.

"You've showered, too?"

"Yep." Ivy scooped another bite of eggs.

Asia took a bite of grape-jelly toast. She glanced around the room. The morning sun shone through the windows, painting shadowed squares on the floor. Too tired to notice last night when she fell into bed, she could now appreciate Ivy's own work in the living room. She worked hard to push the bread down in a fast swallow. "Did you say we had juice?"

Ivy set down her fork and hurried toward the kitchen. "I was so hungry this morning all I thought about was the food." She disappeared behind the door, then scurried out carrying plastic cups of juice and mugs of coffee. She set down one of each for Asia, then herself. "No tip necessary," she said before motioning toward the beds. "Smart move bringing the sleeping bag. Was that in case you had to sleep in your car?"

"No. I always travel with a sleeping bag. I don't sleep on hotel sheets."

Ivy scowled. "What do you have against hotel bedding? What do you sleep on at home, a thousand count sheets?" She took a sip of her coffee.

"No. Hotel bedding is—" Asia shuddered. "—a haven for other people's germs."

Ivy dabbed a napkin at the corner of her mouth. "Oh." She sipped her juice.

They ate in silence. Asia stole glances at Ivy. Though covered with well-applied makeup, Ivy's under-eye bags were tell-tale signs she suffered a sleepless night too.

"This food is great, Ivy. I never thought you'd slow down long enough to learn to cook."

Ivy laid her utensils and napkin on her empty plate. "When you have a great teacher like my husband, Denney, it's not a chore. It's a pleasure."

Of course, Denney would be a perfect cook *and* a perfect husband. Russ was also a fantastic cook. He learned from kitchen duty when he was at the fire station. He offered to teach her some of his recipes once, but she never seemed to make time to learn. Time, past and present, always worked as an enemy against her.

Ivy stacked her utensils on her plate. "When is the tow truck supposed to be here?"

Asia swallowed the last drop of her juice, then answered. "Around ten."

Ivy slid from her chair. "You'd better scoot to the shower. It's five till ten now."

Asia dropped her fork. "*What?*"

Ivy waved then reached for Asia's plate. "Go. I've got the dishes."

Asia ran to gather clothes from her suitcase. Twice she heard a noise, stopped and glanced out the window, fearing the tow truck had arrived. Both times the sounds had resulted from Ivy's cleaning in the kitchen. She grabbed her makeup bag and ran for the bathroom. By the time she showered and emerged from the bath, she heard Ivy call, "Tow truck's here."

Asia stuffed her dirty laundry in a bag, then hurried to the wide-open front door. When they were younger, Ivy forever left that stupid thing ajar. Some of her sister's habits made no sense. Why leave an open invitation to all lizards, snakes, and spiders in Florida?

She tossed her bag under her bed, then passed through the door and slammed it shut behind her. If a snake showed up in the house, Ivy had to deal with the varmint. At the moment, the deal seemed fair and warranted.

Ivy stood in the grass by Asia's car, her hands planted on her hips. The tow truck driver stretched to his full height, towering over her. "That's highway robbery and my sister isn't going to pay it." Ivy cocked her chin at the man as if daring him to take a swipe at her.

The driver adjusted his cap. A hairy skin-roll hung beneath the hem of his shirt and draped over the waistband of his jeans. "Look, *ma'am.*"

Asia quickened her pace. The driver had no idea he was about to experience a sting like stepping into a hornet's nest with bare feet. Her sister spared no bullies, especially when they preyed on the weak. And, in Ivy's personal pecking order, she was still the helpless one.

Ivy pointed in his face. "No, you look. She called the rental agency. They promised a FREE replacement. They said nothing about a sixty-dollar tow fee plus five dollars a mile back to the car lot."

Asia reached the fray and directed Ivy to the front steps. "I've got this."

Ivy glared at the man over Asia's shoulder. "He's trying to cheat you."

Asia gestured to the grassy spot where Ivy stood. "Stay here. I don't need backup."

Ivy's shoulders relaxed and she flashed a half-grin. "Then you go get him, warrior queen." She held her hands as if she were swinging an invisible sword from side to side.

"Oh brother." Asia rubbed her temple. How could two people as opposite as she and Ivy be flesh and blood? Must be like Russ always said, God gave you family, but He let you pick your friends.

She left Ivy to her pretend battle and returned to the driver. He smelled of stale cigarettes, sweat, and motor oil. Asia rubbed a citrus-scented finger beneath her nose. "I'm sorry. I'm the renter of the broken car."

He switched his stubby cigar to the other side of his mouth. "Fine with me. But you still owe me for hook-up and mileage."

Asia squared her shoulders. She'd dealt with angry fathers in her job. This man offered no surprises. Besides, now Ivy would witness that she'd learned to fight for herself.

"Bill at the rental agency said to tell you they will cover all charges. I'll get my phone if you'd like to verify that."

The driver chomped hard on his cigar. "Get it." He hiked up the waist of jeans that looked to be about five wears past a good washing.

Asia nodded, then led Ivy along with her as she headed back into the house. "Stay inside until I'm done."

"But I'll miss the fun of watching you vanquish that jerk with your politeness."

"Watch through the window." Asia closed the door behind them.

They parted as soon as they entered the living room. Asia gathered her phone and rental car papers.

When she walked up, the driver removed his cigar and spat on the ground. He wasn't marking as a male dog might, but his vulgar action meant the same. She stepped around the spot, then held out her phone. The driver took it with grease-blackened fingers.

"I've dialed customer service." She'd have to wipe the thing down with two packs of wipes once the man left.

The entire call took less than a minute. The driver muttered one "yes" and a single "okay" then thrust the phone back at Asia. "I'll be out of here in fifteen minutes, soon as you sign some paperwork for me. Bill said to tell you they're trying to locate a replacement for you. All of the fleet is currently out."

He tromped to his wrecker then brought a single form attached to a battered clipboard. An old blue pen hung from the clip on a frayed piece of twine. "One John Hancock and you're done." He chewed the end of his cigar.

Asia signed quickly. The driver took the clipboard from her. "You're a lot easier to deal with than your twin sister."

Maybe, but her calm didn't reap the same rewards as Ivy's bullheaded personality. "She's not my twin but has many good points."

"If you say so." The driver ambled back to his truck and quickly went to work unraveling the large hook and cable.

Asia side-stepped the marked spot in the grass and headed for the house. Ivy met her at the door. "You handled him well."

Her words caught Asia. Another of Ivy's rare compliments. "Thanks."

Asia slid the folded paperwork for the car in her purse then set to work sanitizing both hands and phone.

Ivy patted her on the shoulder. "I never thought I'd see my quiet little sister work a jerk so well. You've grown up."

Asia shrugged off her touch as she opened a new pack of wipes. "A lot happens in fifteen years. I also learned to drive, cook, balance my checkbook—"

"Got your first kiss?" Ivy wiggled her brows.

"Sort of." Asia threw away the pile of used wipes.

Ivy slid into one of the chairs. "When, where, and from who?"

"From *whom,* and no one you'd know."

A loud knock on the door made them both jump. "Guess he's finished."

Asia opened the door. The driver stood at the bottom step. "Got your car hooked up, so I'm outta here." He turned for his truck without giving Asia time to thank him.

Sweat soaked the back of his shirt. He wiped his face with the tail of the front, exposing rolls of hairy fat in the process.

"Isn't he just a fine figure of manhood?" Ivy rested her chin on Asia's shoulder as they watched him slide into his truck.

Asia dropped her shoulder and stepped away. "Be nice. He did his job." She shut the door as the truck and her rental car clunked down the driveway.

Ivy shrugged. "You're too nice."

Yes, she was. If she and not Ivy had been the stronger one, she'd not be sleeping in this house. She would have kept her self-made promise and refused to leave the safety of her hotel room. The list of things she'd never do would be miles long had she been the strong one. She'd be the one with a husband and children, living in a grand house …

Living … not working every day and night to fight off the ghouls from the past.

Asia shoved the thoughts back. "Speaking of jobs, we'd better get to ours. We still need to tackle our old bedroom. And Veronica's." Then they could go home.

Ivy crossed her arms. "I'd just as soon learn how to run that tow truck."

Asia withdrew two wipes from her pocket and ran each around her hands. "I can think of a million rather-do's right now. But …"

"But …" Ivy bowed and motioned for Asia to lead.

Their steps echoed down the hall. Asia twisted the knob with her gloved hand. "Ready?"

"As I'll ever be."

CHAPTER 17

THE HINGES GROANED AS Asia opened the door to their old room, just as they had fifteen years ago when she ran from this house and Veronica forever. That night she feared what would happen if Veronica heard the noise and barred her escape. Now, she feared what Veronica left for them to find.

"I don't believe this," she whispered from the opened doorway.

"What in the world?" Ivy barreled into the room.

The space stood empty. No furniture. No carpeting. Nothing.

Asia crossed to the closet and opened the door. "Empty."

"Why would she pile up magazines and garbage bags in the rest of the house, but leave this room empty?" Ivy asked.

"Anger? Maybe clearing the room was her way of erasing us because she felt we'd erased her?"

"As if…" Ivy turned toward her. "The door was warped. I'd guess she hasn't been in here for years, maybe since you left."

"When I left, I took my clothes and left everything else behind. She's been in here since then and with a purpose." Asia pointed to the wall that flanked the closet. "Her favorite message is all over the walls, but this time it's written with a red ballpoint pen."

"Unbelievable." Ivy ran her finger along the scribbles.

"I guess she figured out the red wouldn't last as long so she switched to the permanent marker in the other rooms." Asia backed to the middle of the room.

She and Ivy had slept here. Kept their clothes, completed homework, and hid from Veronica's men here. These walls knew none of their secrets; she and Ivy shared those in the clutch of pines that grew in the empty field behind the house. This room watched them grow into young women, but never friends-for-life sisters. Their bedroom was a barracks for two soldiers trapped in combat against a common enemy.

Their own mother.

Their beds had rested against opposite walls, too far from each other for them to sneak in giggles at night. They scooted the beds closer once but returned home from school the next day and found them pushed back to their original spots. They never changed the room again.

There were other memories stuffed between these walls, and Asia had been left behind to face terrors Ivy never knew.

Ivy's voice snapped Asia back to the present. "Where do you live?"

Asia took a pause. Were memories tapping on Ivy's shoulder too? "Maryville, Tennessee." She shuffled her feet. "You?"

"Seattle."

"Wow." Asia could think of no better response. Ivy protected her current life like a politician. Give enough information to answer a question without saying anything of substance. Why was she breaking with her normal operations now?

"Veronica cleaned this room recently." Asia pointed to the corners. "There are some cobwebs, but they aren't big ... haven't been here long."

She touched the toe of her sneaker to the floor. "And the floor isn't too dusty." She rounded to the window. "But she let the window mildew so badly you can't see out. Why?"

Ivy released a long sigh. "I stopped trying to make sense of Veronica ages ago."

Asia slid her hand in her pocket, rubbed the edge of Russ's card. Maybe she spent too much time trying to understand Veronica.

Ivy joined her in the center of the room and pointed at the ceiling. "She removed the light fixture."

Asia shivered. "So this room would always be pitch-black at night."

Ivy tilted her head at the empty hole in the ceiling. "Why?"

"Because you can't see what's coming in the dark." Fingers of black memories clawed their way into Asia's mind. "We need to clean Veronica's room. Now. Before night."

Ivy scowled. "It's not even noon." She looked at the hole where the light fixture once hung. "But, if it's like the rest of this place, the sooner the better."

They left their old room together.

Asia stood by the closed door to Veronica's room. "The last time I went in here was with you." She held Ivy with a level gaze. "You remember?"

"We snuck in to take those drop pearl earrings so I could wear them to prom. I threw those away on prom night." Ivy swept her hand over her shoulder in a mimed toss. "Dropped them into a storm grate somewhere in South Georgia. I hope they're sitting at the bottom of a cesspool."

Asia swallowed hard. Those earrings weren't the only thing Ivy threw away on prom night. "I think I dread this room the most. It's Veronica's sanctum. Who knows what's in there." She checked her pocket. Her fingertips traced the outline of the unopened package of wipes she put there once she showered. And Russ's card.

Ivy arched her brows, then flashed the familiar big-sister smirk. "In a few seconds, we will. After all the welcome home messages Veronica left in the living room, plus the strange suitcases in the bathroom and a box in the wall, what could possibly bother us?" Her voice cracked with the last word. "Ready?"

"Only if you go first."

Ivy placed her hand over her heart. "Your kindness is overwhelming."

"So is your bravery. That's why you get to go first." Asia swept her arm toward the door.

Ivy huffed. "I think I liked you better when you had less gumption."

Asia ran her finger across Russ's card twice. Less gumption made her easier to leave behind. "Let's get this over with."

Ivy wrapped her fingers around the cut-glass knob on Veronica's bedroom door, the only one in the house. When they were little, she and Asia would sit by the door in the morning and wait for the sunbeams streaming from their bedroom window to catch the knob's faceted surface. For a few short minutes a kaleidoscope of reds, yellows, and blues burst through the gloom of their lives while the two sisters huddled together, watching the array of sparkles until the sun moved higher.

Asia brought Ivy back to the moment. "Our own giant, magic diamond. I pretended that if we made a wish when the colors were their brightest, the knob would transport us to some fairy kingdom where our real parents, the loving king and queen, lived."

Ivy locked eyes with Asia. "Seems you were never fast enough with those wishes."

"No. Never."

Ivy opened the door and a dim triangle of light shone into the room. She stepped farther in, then shrieked as Asia bumped into her and raked the toe of her shoe against Ivy's Achilles tendon.

"A little space, please," Ivy said against her clenched teeth.

"Sorry," Asia whispered. "Are you okay?"

"Skin grows back, I guess."

A dusky gray filled the room. The sun cut through a slender space between the drapes at the window. "I'll open the curtains. Could you cut the light on?"

Asia shuffled beside her. "Sure." Her steps clipped across the floor before she flipped the switch. Only one bulb in the light fixture worked, bringing a dull glow into the room.

"I still can't see much." Ivy went to the window and parted the curtains to allow daylight to brighten the room.

Veronica's bed sat tucked against a wall. A rose-patterned comforter was spread smooth across the twin-sized mattress. Pink, ruffled pillows sat arrayed against a white, princess-style headboard.

A pink, filmy curtain attached to a tarnished brass ring in the ceiling cascaded around the bed.

The room was soft and feminine. *Nothing* like Veronica.

A white wooden chest with a vining rose pattern painted on its sides and front stood at the end of the bed. The nightstand next to the bed continued the theme. The scent of rose potpourri that had seen better days filled the room.

Ivy rotated in the middle of the room with her brow furrowed. "This looks like a *little girl's* room."

Standing next to a collection of pink hat boxes stacked largest to smallest, Asia surveyed the room, her jaw slack. "When did she do all this?" She pirouetted to see all of it at once. "It looks like Pepto Bismol took a bath in here."

Ivy noticed something lying under the dresser. "Whatever is …?" She crossed the room, kneeled, and retrieved Veronica's small gardening shovel.

Ivy held the tool aloft. "Why would this be in here? She kept this by the front door to kill snakes."

Asia backed away. Breath squealed from her lungs. "She laughed … she laughed at me … when I-I used it to hit …" She grabbed her middle.

Ivy rushed to the door then heaved the shovel into the hallway. Three loud clanks echoed as the spade hit the floor.

Asia leaned against the wall, sucking wind and counting aloud to two multiple times while Ivy placed her hands on her hips. Doing a needed task would jar Asia from whatever the shovel stirred inside her. "You ready to tackle this room?"

Asia inhaled and exhaled twice. She washed her face with a wipe, then repeated the breathe, exhale, count aloud sequence twice more. She stood straight. "We need gloves." Before Ivy could speak, Asia rushed down the hall to the living room returning with the box of gloves. "Ready." She put on a pair, then passed the box to Ivy.

Ivy slid hers on. "Let's start with this hope chest. What terrible thing could she have put in there?"

Asia smoothed hair from her face. "A dead body, painted pink."

"Oh ha-ha, you're too funny." Ivy lifted the cover of the chest. If Asia were right about the body ... "Oh. My. Gosh." She paused. "You aren't going to believe this. Come look."

Asia held up her gloved palms. "Please tell me I wasn't right."

Ivy waved her over. "It's empty, except for this."

Asia shuffled to the box until she stood a few feet back. Far enough to crane her neck and peer inside the space. "That's insane."

"I know." Ivy surveyed the interior again. The chest remained empty, except for the familiar message covering the sides, bottom, and lid of the chest. Again, written in red ink.

"Nolan might never return if he saw all this."

Ivy snickered. "He'll have to learn that anything associated with Veronica includes a giant side dish of insanity."

Asia's expression darkened. "We're the voices of experience on that one."

Ivy shut the lid of the chest, dusted her hands on her jeans. Too much experience and none worth remembering. They needed to finish this room and get out. Spending time in Veronica's bedroom allowed memories to rush in. Too many of them.

Asia forced off her gloves and cleaned her hands with one of her ever-present wipes. She reminded Ivy of a cat with her constant self-cleaning.

But those lemony fumes and quick-dry cleaners could never wash away the dirty memories trying to reappear in Ivy's mind. Her life held room for Denney and the boys, memories of ballgames, dinners out, Christmases and birthdays. She'd allow no space for the past.

Asia dropped her wipes in a white wicker wastebasket, then pointed to the end of Veronica's bed. "What is that?"

Ivy focused on where Asia pointed. "What?"

"There, between the comforter and the dust ruffle." Asia put on a new pair of gloves, then tugged at a pink envelope until it slipped from the resting place with a soft swoosh. "It's addressed to Veronica, Love D." She blinked toward Ivy. "The same guy from the letters."

"The mushy-gushy ones, or the once-a-month?"

"Once-a-month." Asia squeezed the edges. "No card, but ... something else is in here." She slipped her gloved finger under the flap and tore it open. Asia jiggled until two tickets slipped into her hand.

"They're for a cruise. Seven days in the Caribbean."

Ivy flashed a look of mild shock with a raised brow. "When?"

"June tenth through the sixteenth, 2007. Never used." Asia slid the tickets back in their envelope. "She and *D* must have had a fight and she refused to go." Asia looked up suddenly, her expression set in confusion, as if seeing the walls and floor clearly for the first time. "Of course," she whispered.

"What are you thinking, Asia?" Ivy's pulse kicked into overdrive.

Asia motioned. "Go check her closet."

"For what?"

"Anything expensive."

"Wh—"

"Just do it, Ivy."

Ivy straightened at her tone. If she used the same one with her students, she'd never have behavioral problems. The tone yanked compliance from a person.

She didn't know what she was supposed to be proving with this search. Veronica was never careful with money, bought whatever appealed to her wants or whims. And how did that relate to a pair of discarded cruise tickets from the mysterious and obviously stupid D? She couldn't imagine anyone strong enough to tolerate seven days trapped on a boat in the middle of the Caribbean with Veronica.

The fruity, sweet smell of expensive perfume tickled Ivy's nose as soon as she opened the closet door. She rifled through the clothes. Nothing but off-the-rack jeans, micro-short skirts in varying hues, various blouses and tees. Some were name brand, but nothing too extravagant or interesting.

She slid the clothes to the opposite side of the closet, then stopped at the sight of a long, black cashmere coat, much too heavy for wearing in Florida. Ivy recognized the style without looking at the label. Designer and *trés* expensive. She owned a similar one back home in Seattle.

Three dresses hung behind the coat. A black velvet cocktail dress, a multicolored tweed suit with a modest tailored skirt, and a simple black-and-white sheath dress, expertly cut. All designer. These types of dresses were worn by wives accompanying wealthy husbands to public events where good impressions mattered. And they were all brand new, never worn. The price tags still dangled from the garments' labels with tiny gold safety pins, broadcasting origins from an expensive boutique.

Ivy checked the floor. Beside an array of flats, high-heeled sandals, and one pair of athletic shoes sat six shoeboxes. All designer. She covered her face, blocked out the sight of the loot. "Veronica was some rich man's mistress, wasn't she?"

"Yes. And there's more," Asia said from behind her.

Visions came of Veronica dressed in the black dress as she caressed the arm of the faceless mystery man. Beaming an open brag to all who watched, showing her joy at the time and presents stolen from the clueless wife. The man belonged to another woman, maybe children, a family. And Veronica dared tarnish that with her own desires. She probably laughed at the situation, blamed the wife for not keeping her man satisfied enough to avoid straying.

Ivy clenched her fists. Nothing in life stood more precious than a marriage or a family. "The tickets, these clothes ... more trophies, right? That's why they were never used. She saved them to gloat."

Asia shuffled her feet. "I think so. *But there's more.*"

"Seriously?" Ivy slammed the closet door shut. What *more* could there be? Wasn't finding out Veronica's tawdry habits enough?

"I found something else under the mattress ... a bunch of somethings."

Ivy's shoulders drooped. This was too much.

"Ivy, you've got to see this."

Ivy released a long sigh, then turned. "What ..."

Asia had flipped the mattress to the floor, exposing the surface of the box springs. She pushed the mattress off to the side with her foot, making space for Ivy to take a closer look. “Are you sure you’ve gotten past all this?” she asked as Ivy joined her at the bedside.

Ivy looked at Asia’s discovery. “Not anymore.”

CHAPTER 18

Asia loved the fairy tale of the princess who proved her identity by feeling a tiny pea through twenty stacked mattresses. In the fable she'd found a flower-delicate soul as easily bruised as she. The author understood the world created the strong and the sensitive.

Veronica did not.

Veronica had slept above her collection of stolen affections without conscience, inflicting rather than receiving bruises. Asia thanked God she fell far from Veronica's tree.

"Okay, show me everything." Ivy tapped the floor with the toe of her pointy, red shoe.

Ivy's toe tapping. Guaranteed to arise whenever she had to stand in a long line, listen to a conversation lasting more than five minutes, or wait for her turn to apply makeup in the bathroom mirror. Many times after Ivy left, Asia would swear she'd heard that sound and go searching for her sister, only to have high hopes dashed.

Ivy shifted her stance. "So, what am I looking at?"

"Let's start with these." Asia slid out a stack of documents. "Apparently, Veronica's real name was Debralee Bennet and she was married ... three times."

Ivy's jaw dropped. "Come again?"

"Three." Asia shuffled the certificates to chronological order. "She married an Arthur Conklin in Georgia." She held the certificate up for Ivy's perusal. "Followed by a divorce. Then ..." She slid the certificate and divorce decree to the back. "A year after divorcing Arthur we have Sherman Foreman." Asia dipped her chin. "She married him in

Alabama."

"Sweet home ..."

Asia revealed the next document. "This is where things get interesting."

"Can't wait to hear why."

Asia drew in a breath. "Veronica's final husband."

"And why is he so earth shattering?"

Asia pointed to the date. "He married her two months after her divorce from Sherman." She took a long pause, then began again. "He was African-American. Bernard *Butler*. She married him in Ohio. She had this picture of him attached to the divorce papers." She flipped the photo. "They were married two years."

Ivy mouthed a silent "What?" She raked her hair with her fingers, then snatched the certificate and photo from Asia's grasp and stared as if trying to burn a hole through them. "This guy's obviously not our—we're fair-skinned, blue-eyed-blondes."

Asia pointed to the date on the certificate. "They divorced three years before you were born."

Ivy glanced over the documents, then massaged her forehead. "She was always so prejudiced. I can't count how many times she used the n-word. So why would she marry ... and keep his name?"

Asia shrugged. "No idea."

Ivy tossed the stack on the surface of the bed. "What else is here?" She picked up a faded photo. "This is all scratched up. It looks like some sort of old barn in the background but who are these people with this little girl?"

"I think the two adults ... are our grandparents." Asia curled a finger toward the back of the photo. "There's a date and notation here."

Ivy's mouth fell open. "Grandparents?"

"Turn the picture over." Asia pointed to a message on the yellowed back, written in penmanship no longer taught in schools.

"See? County fair with Debralee. Greenwood, Mississippi. 1964."

Ivy flipped the photo back to the front. "Why do you think these people are our—"

Asia tapped the photo. "Look close at that little girl. It's Veronica."

"But the name change. Debralee Bennet?" Ivy brushed her thumb across the surface. "And why did she scratch out their faces?"

Asia sighed. "Anger. Maybe hatred. That could be why she changed her name to Veronica. She wanted to erase every trace of these people. Like she did in our bedroom."

They studied the photo together, so close they almost knocked heads. What compelled that smiling little girl to deface her parents? And what had made her such a monster later in life?

"Did it bother you that we didn't have grandparents, aunts and uncles, or cousins, like normal people?"

"Sometimes. I'd hear kids talking about staying at their grammy's house, or going fishing with their papaw, and wished I could do that. It would have been fun to grow up with cousins, spend all summer running wild with them, sleeping over at their houses. We missed getting to do any of that."

Asia nodded. "Soon after I settled in Maryville, this sweet older lady in my church asked where my people came from. I changed the subject so I wouldn't have to admit I didn't know."

Ivy's eyes sparkled. "When it's done right, family is pretty wonderful." She held up the photo to Asia. "I'm curious what they were like."

"Me, too. Then again, I'm curious about a lot of things."

Ivy viewed the photo. "Veronica looks like she's maybe five in this picture. That means she must be around sixty. I never knew how old she was."

"Veronica's sixty-four." Asia met Ivy's questioning eyes. "I only know because after she went to sleep one night, I took her wallet to get her birthdate for my college application. The date on her driver's license said July 13, 1956. I never knew if that was right or not. I also studied her signature so I could forge her name."

Her choice to cheat on the application still caused bubbles of guilt. On her graduation day, when the president of the university shook her hand, her knees knocked. She'd hesitated, expecting him to lean in and whisper, "We know what you did to get here" and deny her a diploma.

Ivy passed her hand over the collection. "Is there anything else here?"

"Some old pictures of us from the football games." Asia gathered a collection of jeweler's boxes she'd set aside. "And these. I couldn't venture to guess what all they're worth. You'd know better than I."

Ivy opened them one by one, whistled between her teeth as she held up diamond bracelets, earrings, and necklaces for inspection. "You're right. These aren't department store knockoffs."

She crooked her thumb in the direction of the closet. "Veronica has clothes and shoes in the closet to match these. All designer, tags still on."

"I don't think any of this jewelry ever left the boxes. She hid them under the mattress ... where she slept ..." Asia stopped. No sense in filling in the blanks with Veronica's vulgar habits.

Ivy clicked her tongue. "That's sordid and tacky." She held her hands out, stunned and questioning. "Where did she get those? She never owned a camera."

Asia handed the stack to Ivy. "See for yourself."

Ivy stared at them a moment. "I'm still lost on this."

Asia found the pictures just as confounding. There were seven of them, and Ivy shuffled through them all. Some depicted Ivy in her cheerleading uniform. Others showed Asia in her band uniform playing her flute, giving her speech before the Chamber of Commerce members for a scholarship competition, then her graduation day. They were candid shots, the type proud parents took to remember moments from their child's life. Why Veronica possessed them remained a mystery. She never attended any of the events depicted in the photos.

"These are creepy." Ivy handed the bunch back to Asia. "Did one of her boyfriends take these as part of some sick ... game?"

Asia tucked a stray tendril of hair behind her ear.

Ivy pointed to the photos. "Are these making you nervous?"

"No, why?"

"You did that hair tuck thing."

"It was tickling my face."

"It's okay to admit you're freaked out." She cocked one shoulder. "I am."

This was a new Ivy. One who'd admit a weakness, allow it in others. Marriage and motherhood had softened her, allowed her to grow more in heart.

Asia swallowed back a bitter wave of envy. Ivy ran away and got everything good in life. "They're just pictures, nothing bad or sordid. Why do you think I'm bothered?"

"Normal people put treasured photos in an album. These are trophies, Asia, like everything else she saved. They represented power to her in some way."

What these photos depicted was real life. The normal events most people lived and wanted to remember once their kids left home. Memories to keep the children close to the heart and the bonds strong.

But family bonds meant nothing to Veronica.

"Think about it, Asia. She probably told some sob story to an unsuspecting dad at one of the games, got him to take the pictures, then saved them to gloat over how she manipulated another woman's husband. The only motherly thing she did for us was toilet training. I learned about brushing my teeth and tying my shoes in school and then I taught you those things once you were old enough." Ivy scowled at the photographs. "Whoever took those had value to her, and she *wanted* them found, just like the tickets, the cheap knickknacks in the box in the living room, the suitcases in the bathroom." She pounded her left fist into her palm. "This whole thing has been a scavenger hunt for creepy things leading us in a million different directions."

Asia frowned. "There's nothing left to see in here. But, there's still that box in the wall."

"I tried to forget about *that* box." Ivy checked her watch. "I'm hungry. I'll treat for lunch, and then we can decide what to do after. Let's see if Shelby's is still around. Maybe they serve that Mississippi mud pie you always loved."

And just like that, bossy Ivy stepped in and took control.

Veronica claimed to have left these things behind to make things clear. And, in true Veronica form, she'd created a chowder-thick fog of confusion instead.

Asia slipped off her gloves and threw them in a white wicker basket near the door. She cleaned her hands with a wipe. "Fine. But we have to deal with that box after we eat."

Ivy arched one brow. "Why are you so caught up in that box?"

"I don't think we've found what Nolan wants so badly. And I want to go home."

The corner of Ivy's mouth lifted. "Let's get out of here." She gently grasped Asia by the arm and led her from the room. "I think we finally found a way to get that 'sister-bonding' thing started. Mutual hatred of this place."

Her touch warmed Asia like donning a thick, cozy sweater against a rainy, dig-deep-into-your-bones-cold day. The warmth took its time and spread through like hot tea once swallowed. The feeling still radiated once Ivy let go.

"Ready?" Ivy stood holding the door open. "I'll drive." She jingled her keys.

Just before Asia's fourteenth birthday, Ivy had earned her driver's license and gained Veronica's permission to borrow the car. "To take Asia out for her birthday," she had coaxed Veronica. "To Shelby's." Now, once again …

Ivy's voice sounded over the memory. "Are you going to stand there staring into space or come eat?"

Asia pushed away the memory. "Right behind you," she said before Ivy slammed the door behind them.

"Since I'm treating, we ought to order a full rack of ribs. And those fat fries, too. Take some meat off their bones and put it on ours."

A butterfly fluttered in Asia's stomach. Whether she remembered it or not, Ivy had said the same thing the last time they went to Shelby's.

CHAPTER 19

Ivy twirled the last remnants of sweet tea and ice in her glass. The cubes plinked against the sides like little bells. Not too long ago, she favored drinks without ice. No dilution so she could find the bottom of the glass faster, where the brain-numbing buzzes hid.

The scrape of a fork brought her back to Shelby's. Asia pushed a tomato she'd speared with her fork around her plate. "How long have you lived in Seattle?"

Ivy set her glass down. "Eleven years."

"How did you end up there?"

"Came in on a bus."

Asia raised her brows in question. "On purpose?"

No, purpose had not led her to Seattle. She'd staggered into a bus station in a small town in Kansas whose name she still didn't know. Ivy had thrust wadded singles mixed with handfuls of quarters, dimes, and pennies through the mouse-hole-shaped opening in the ticket window.

"What's the farthest this will take me?" she'd asked as she leaned on the counter for support.

The woman behind the window fingered through the bills and coins. She then clicked her fingers across a computer's keyboard and answered in a soft voice. "Seattle, Washington."

But Asia didn't need to know the tawdry details. "Not really," Ivy told her sister. "Just wanted to be somewhere else at the time."

"And where was that?" Asia slid the tomato into her mouth. Her jaws caved as she worked to chew her food. Ivy had seen those types of hollows before. She assessed Asia's plate. She might have eaten the equivalent of a quarter cup of lettuce and a couple of tomatoes. No wonder her shoulder blades stuck out like tree roots.

"I've been all over. How did you end up in Tennessee?"

"I wanted to live in the mountains."

"I don't remember you liking mountains. I thought you always wanted to live on a beach."

Asia's coloring pinked and she pushed her plate away. "I hate sand." She withdrew another of her ever-present wipes from her pocket. Though her hands were spotless, she scrubbed at them as if she'd been digging in mud muck. When did her sister develop an eating disorder *and* OCD?

Ivy swallowed the ice pebbles. "You're a native Floridian. When did you decide you don't like sand?"

Asia pointed to Ivy's ring. "When did you decide you wanted to get married? You always swore you'd stay single forever."

Ivy rotated her diamond, an inner smile working its way from her heart to her lips. Denney had slipped the ring on her finger in a movie theater, leaned in, and whispered in her ear, "I've waited for you my whole life." He cupped her face in his hands and kissed her, then asked, "Yes?" He kissed her again after she whispered the answer he'd hoped for.

Ivy straightened her ring. "I changed my mind. Apparently, Veronica was a master of that. Three ex-husbands." She rolled her eyes.

Asia forked another tomato. "How could three men be so ..."

"Stupid?" Ivy waved for their server, Destiny, as she checked on a nearby table.

"I was thinking so easily tricked." Asia laid her fork across her plate and tucked her folded napkin under the rim.

Destiny rushed up with their check. Ivy handed over her credit card.

"I'll be right back." Destiny scurried in the direction of the kitchen. When she returned she handed the credit card to Ivy.

"Thanks for coming in, ladies. I hope y'all will come back." She glanced around. "On a day that's not so crazy." Destiny hurried to the kitchen.

Asia unzipped her purse. "I'll get the tip."

Ivy waved her off. "Forget it. I've already figured out the amount on the bill."

"You calculated it that fast? In your head?"

"I'm not an idiot. I can figure twenty percent of a bill."

Asia raised her brows. "I didn't mean anything, just surprised. Math wasn't your strong suit in school."

Ivy shrugged. "I deserved that, after all the times I begged you to do my algebra homework for me."

"And my refusals seemed to have paid off."

"Maybe." Ivy motioned to Asia's leftovers. "You should get a box for that. You have another meal there."

"There's not enough for another meal."

"You barely ate enough to keep a fly alive."

"Is that what you tell your boys?"

No, she never had to tell her boys to eat. They'd come from the womb ravenous. Ivy gave her best listen-to-your-big-sister eye. "It's what I'm telling *you.*"

The zipper on Asia's purse buzzed as she yanked it closed. "I guess the mysterious D was the smartest of the men Veronica collected."

"Why do you think that? He probably allowed her to worm her way between him, his wife, and family. He was just another trophy on her shelf ... or under her mattress. He probably ruined his marriage, ended up divorced."

"How did you manage to be happily married after ... Veronica?" Asia leaned in, as if her whole life depended on the answer and she wanted to hear every syllable that dropped from Ivy's mouth.

"It just worked out." Ivy slid the completed receipt to the edge of the table. This lunch and conversation needed to be over. She put her credit card back in her wallet then dug out her sunglasses and placed them on her head. "I remember that look."

Asia scowled. "What look?"

Ivy scooted her chair back. "The one I got when you were six and asked me why we didn't have a daddy like Nolan had."

She pushed her chair under the table. "I'll tell you the same thing I said then. God works things out in different ways for everyone."

When she was six, Asia answered Ivy's quote with a list of *but whys.* Today she seemed to fold inside of herself. "Thanks for lunch."

"Sure." Ivy headed for the exit. Thankfully both she and Asia had chosen the specials and their tab was small. She opened the glass door adorned with "Shelby's" written in a deep-blue script. What had upset Asia? God worked in his own mysterious ways. They'd both sat in the same Sunday school when the teacher taught that lesson.

Ivy ushered Asia through the door. The blacktop in the parking lot baked her feet through her shoes as they bustled to the car. A gray thunderhead towered in the western sky. Ivy released the door locks with the key fob, then pointed upward. "A storm's brewing. Looks like it's sitting on top of Veronica's."

Asia shaded her face with her hand as she tipped her chin to the clouds. "Veronica's house attracts storms."

"More like hurricanes." Ivy opened her door and entered the car. Asia slid into the passenger side.

As they drove to their old home, indigo clouds bubbled across the sun, dimming the rays. Thunder rumbled in the distance.

Asia positioned the air conditioner vent to blow away from her. "What do you think is in that box?"

"Probably more things like we found under her mattress."

Asia adjusted the vent a second time. "It's like a plotline out of a seedy novel. Tacky and uncouth."

Ivy giggled. "Uncouth? I haven't heard that word in years, China Girl." She drove into the long lane leading to Veronica's house.

"You haven't called me that in I don't know how long."

Ivy parked the car. "I know. It rolled out of my mouth before I even thought about it."

Asia gathered her purse. "You've me called so many different names. But I have to admit, that was my favorite. Made me feel exotic, like I belonged in the Orient rather than here. I never knew how you came up with that one."

Ivy switched off the ignition. "Second grade, when I learned that China was part of the Asian continent. It just seemed to fit."

Unlike Asia, Ivy had found where she belonged the moment she met Denney. Like a lost shelter dog who somehow knows when the right human walks in to take them to a forever home. And like that dog, she'd bare her teeth and fight to protect her rescuer to her last breath.

Asia found a place she liked to live, but anyone could see there were gaping holes in her life.

Ivy shoved the car door open. "What made you move to the mountains?"

"I took the job in Tennessee because it was the farthest one from Florida."

More thunder rumbled overhead. They scurried from the car and huddled shoulder to shoulder on the top step.

Lightning flashed around them and fat raindrops dotted the steps and the backs of their clothes before they rushed inside and slammed the door.

Ivy left this place with a less defined plan than Asia's. Her goal was to be away, without considering how far. "Do you like Tennessee?"

"I do. It's the opposite of everything here. Cooler winters, mountains, streams." Asia brushed her shoes with a wipe. "And no sand."

Ivy ducked slightly as thunder rattled the windows. "Home is where your heart wants to be."

A flash of lightning lit the room. Asia winced as the thunder blasted. "Is Seattle your where you heart is?"

"One hundred percent."

"What do you call this place?"

"If I said what I'd *like* to call this place, I'd owe our family swear jar a dollar."

Asia laughed. "You have a swear jar?"

"Denney's idea. The referee at our oldest son's Little League game made a bad call against his pitching. I colorfully commented, and Denney made me go sit in the car for the rest of the game. The next day this giant pickle jar was on the kitchen counter with 'Swear Jar' written in bright red letters. I have to admit, the idea worked. My boys love pointing out how many dollars I've contributed."

"Why do I get the feeling you are the main contributor to said jar?"

"Not anymore. Bad friendships had rubbed off on me and it took me forever to break the habit."

Asia sent a look that was part compassionate curiosity and part desperation. "Life before Seattle wasn't that great?"

The entire house rattled from a clap of thunder. Ivy set her purse on the nearby table.

A good life and home for her didn't exist until she found Denney and right then she ached for the warmth of his hand closing around hers, the weight of his arm draped across her shoulders or wrapped about her waist.

No, life before Denney brought nothing but pain. Her bad-language habit was the least of her troubles before him. But Asia didn't need to know that.

Another bolt of lightning flashed outside followed by a cannon shot of thunder. Ivy pointed at the wall. "That rotten box isn't going to clean out itself. Let's get busy and throw out whatever tawdry things Veronica saw fit to hide in there."

CHAPTER 20

Asia traced the outline in the wall with a gloved finger. The jagged cut scarred the wall. Fitting. Veronica scarred everything.

A rubbery sound popped behind her. "I now have protected hands." Ivy wiggled her gloved fingers. "Am I cleared for box-opening duty?"

She'd insisted Ivy wear the gloves, in case roaches or a giant rat sprang from the box after the opening. Ivy declared a rat's teeth could slice the thin latex in seconds, but she relented when they both noticed a dead inch-long palmetto bug next to the wall. Asia relished her victory with a private smile once Ivy's back was turned.

Rain pelted the windows. Lighting cracked and thunder continued to boom outside. They were sheltered from the storm, but Asia figured the real threat waited in the box.

"Let's get this over with." Asia yanked the drywall free. Stale air mixed with a mist of dust and crumbling plaster assaulted her nose. "Should we shake it first, to see if there are any bugs or rats in there?"

Ivy put her hands on her hips. "Don't expect me to do it."

Asia stared at the box. "Maybe we should get the shovel and shake it around first?"

Ivy nodded slowly. "Do it."

"You go get it from the hallway."

Ivy held her hands out. "Why do I have to get it?"

"Please get it, Ivy." She whispered around the memory of the shovel dotted with blood.

After an eye roll and another loud sigh, Ivy stomped from the room. "And I'm guessing I get the honor of smacking the box too?"

"You always had better aim."

Ivy brought the shovel. She jabbed the box on both sides. The cardboard stood firm, immovable. Nothing rustled within or crawled from the top. She laid the shovel on the floor. "Well?"

Asia adjusted her gloves. "Grab hold."

They each grasped a corner and heaved. A tingling ache inched across Asia's lower back. She bent her knees, yanked harder as the box inched from the space.

"Is there enough space to empty from here?" Ivy rubbed her shoulder.

"It's too tall. We couldn't get the flaps open inside the hole."

"Let's just forget about what might be in here, seal the thing with duct tape, and haul it to the dump ourselves."

That would solve the immediate problem, and probably stave off a week's worth of worries. But over time, Asia's conscience, fueled by a million what ifs, would tap her like impatient students before Christmas break.

"No. There's a reason Veronica walled this thing in. She's hiding something big in there."

Ivy clicked her tongue against her teeth. "You teachers. Always trying to find deeper meaning in everything. Sometimes people do things because they're nuts."

"Even nuts have their reasons." Asia grasped her corner again.

"Whatever." Ivy hooked her fingers in the opposite corner. "Pull."

The box inched from the makeshift cave with a shushing sound as the cardboard bottom scraped across the living room floor. As soon as the back corners cleared the hole, they stopped.

If Asia hadn't happened to see the cut in the wall while cleaning, she and Ivy would never have known this box existed. Did Veronica want this box to stay hidden? Or did she position those shelves so the cut could be seen and her daughters would be compelled to investigate what dwelled within the wall? The latter seemed to hold the highest probability.

Ivy motioned. "You open it."

"Me?"

"You're the one who needs to find meaning." She crossed her arms to seal her declaration.

Ivy could stand there and act disinterested all she wanted but Asia had seen that sparkle of curiosity in her sister's eyes when they pulled away the piece from the wall. "Shall we count three?"

"Three." Ivy pointed to the flaps.

Asia peeled the cardboard edges back and peered over the edge. Yellowed rags made from old t-shirts and cut in random shapes filled the space.

"Is this packing material or fabric she meant to save?" Ivy rubbed the back of her hand along her jaw.

Veronica's saving dirty rags in such a secret place made no sense. But, with everything else Asia and Ivy had discovered so far, what Veronica hid best presented the most disturbing questions. Asia shuddered. "Good question."

"Let's take them out and we'll see what else is in here." Ivy gathered up a handful and dropped them on the floor behind the box.

"Gross, no. They're covered in brown stains. Knowing Veronica, it could be—"

"Oh brother. My boys have made far worse stains than this just eating their supper. Once you become a mother, you can touch anything."

Asia frowned at her. The way Ivy went on about some things, she seemed to think motherhood had morphed her into some kind of superhero.

Asia drew in a breath. She'd handled crying fits, being punched, scratched, bitten, and students in full-on loss of bodily functions control. Mothers weren't the only ones with superpowers. Teachers developed their own set.

"Look," Ivy said, logic lacing her words, "Whatever stained them has been long dried with no odor." She lifted a rag. "See?" She shoved the cloth toward Asia. The reddish-brown stain was set into the fabric. The only remaining smell was "musty old attic."

Acquiescing to emptying out the rags presented proof to Ivy she wasn't the only strong one now. There was no reason to panic. These stains were old, and all germs had died by now. Asia scooped a clump from the box.

The bottom edge of an extra-large Ziploc bag poked through the ball of rags. She tilted her head for a better view. "What's this?"

"Find something?"

"Not sure." Asia dropped the rags, then picked up the bag. Inside were three official looking documents. She pried the edges open and slid out the papers from within.

"Oh. My. Gosh."

"What's the matter?" Ivy dug more rags from the box.

"These are our birth certificates." Asia shuffled through them. If her heart chose to beat any faster, it would break through her sternum.

She jumped when Ivy leaned toward her. "We weren't hatched, Asia. What's with all the drama? Didn't you need yours to apply for college and such?"

"Yes, but that's not the point. There are *three* of them. Yours—" She laid the paper on the floor between them. "Mine, and ... a little boy born in the years between us." Asia stacked the other two on the first.

"Let me see those." Ivy snatched the certificates from the floor. She wanted to disbelieve what she was being told but knew Asia would never lie about such a thing. The struggle flashed across her face.

She laid the certificates down. "If we had a brother, what happened to him?"

The possibilities were endless, especially with a mother like Veronica. She could have sold him in a fraudulent adoption, placed him in a foster home, or disposed of him in any number of horrible ways. Asia hugged her middle. "I don't want to think about that."

"She wanted us to know." Ivy shuffled the certificates. "He was born in February, after my first birthday in January. Your birthday is in October—"

"April."

Ivy bobbed her head from side to side. "So, he was a little over two years old when you were born."

"Ivy, do you remember another baby in the house?"

Ivy huffed. "I don't remember *you* until you were maybe three or four."

"Do you think she ...?"

Ivy's eyes misted. "I hope not."

Ivy's mind was obviously on her own boys, her heart asking how a mother could just throw a child away. For once in her life, Asia could not recall a verse or idiom to fit this situation.

She looked at the stained rags, her insides quivering. Had Veronica hurt that unknown baby, or had he been adopted by a nice family—a father who gave him a dog for Christmas and watched him play baseball. A mother who cried at his graduation or wedding?

Asia read over her and Ivy's certificates. Veronica's name was typed neatly in the box marked "Mother" along with her age, residence, and occupation. The space marked marital status simply said "single." Another box indicated each of their deliveries as homebirths.

The box next to father noted the same thing on each: "Unknown."

She studied the boy's. Identical answers and no clues to his fate.

The only difference was the names. She and Ivy's were printed neatly on the forms. The boy's read simply *Baby Boy Butler.*

Asia organized the papers together, then ran her finger along the raised state seal on hers, which rested on the top of the stack. "Why do you think she kept us?"

"What?"

"Why did she keep us ... me? She had one of each, why keep me and give up the boy?"

The light in Ivy's eyes flared. "What are you talking about?"

"Veronica had you and the boy when I came along. Why didn't she give me up?"

Ivy's lips parted as if she knew the answer, but she struggled to find the right words. "Who knows what was in her head?"

"Veronica never wanted me, Ivy. She told me all the time." Asia's chest tightened. Her throat squeezed and she fought to keep from gagging.

How many times had her myriad of therapists told her to explore those memories, to face them so she could heal? She'd never allow her sessions to dig that deep. How did you admit to the world that you believed your own mother hated you and was worse than any danger you could conjure in your imagination?

Ivy squatted before Asia. "Hopefully, a nice family took that little boy. Which means there is one less person Veronica tortured."

Asia's heart sprinted while her lungs squeezed.

Breathe ... Relax ... Breathe.

Her streak of attack-free days. She was nearing sixty. Her second milestone. Her longest streak in years. She couldn't ruin her hard work here in Veronica's house over a stranger's birth certificate. And in front of Ivy.

Asia drew in breaths, counted, released, and repeated until her runaway heartbeat slacked. She dug wipes from her pocket and washed her face, inhaled the lemony scent.

Church pews and peace. Safety.

She rubbed her finger along the card in her pocket.

Tennessee ... Home ... *Russ.*

"You okay?" Ivy leaned in closer. "You've lost all color in your face. You want some water?"

Asia acquiesced and Ivy cantered to the kitchen.

Moments later she rushed back. "Drink this before you pass out." She shoved the plastic cup at Asia. "What happened?"

Asia drew a deep breath, counted to two, released. "I'm just tired."

"You have panic attacks, don't you?"

Ivy wasn't just a supermom, she was also a therapist? Asia thrust the cup back to her sister. "Thanks. The storm's let up so the sooner we clear out the box, the sooner we can focus on better things."

Ivy set the cup on the floor behind her. "How long have you been suffering with these attacks? And sniffing the wipes when you get upset?"

"I'm not suffering with some sort of condition. I just get nervous at times." Maybe Miss High-and-Mighty Supermom had a cure for that in her purse along with all those Band-Aids.

Ivy crossed her arms on her chest. "Are you getting help?"

Heated anger crawled up Asia's neck. How dare Ivy stand here and grill her when she was the reason for all of Asia's quirks.

Ivy always thought she knew best. Maybe at her house in Seattle she reigned as an all-knowing hero, but in Veronica's house ...

"I'm fine. Let's do the cleaning."

Ivy stared without blinking. "Whatever. I just hope you're getting help." She went to the box and sank to her knees. "There are a few more rags in here." She lifted a small armful.

Asia joined her and placed the last handful of rags in a pile behind the box. "All that's left is this garbage bag." A heavy-duty, leaf and garden trash type with the top knotted. Asia grunted as she tried to lift it. "This thing weighs a ton."

"I'll help." Ivy grabbed the top. "One ... two ... three."

They both strained as they hauled the load from the box. When they dropped the bag, a thunderous clunk vibrated the floor.

Ivy straightened, stretched. "What in the world could be in there?"

Asia untied the topknot. "Whatever this is, she saw fit to double bag it." She loosened the top of the second bag and spread the opening. "Oh, my..."

Ivy slid next to her. "What now? A skeleton or a collection of dead rats?"

Asia's breath caught in her throat. A collection of dead rats would have been more expected than what lay stacked in the depths of the bag.

Ivy spread the edges wide. "What in the ..."

Asia gained her voice, as she pointed into the depths. "Where on the Lord's green earth did she get *that*?"

CHAPTER 21

"You can't be serious. Count it again." Ivy circled the table until she stubbed her toe on the first of five bowling ball-sized rocks resting on the floor. Veronica had placed them in the bag with the stack of money.

"Done." Asia stripped the gloves from her hands and threw them in the trash.

Every time Asia stopped counting, she changed gloves. When Ivy complained another trip to Walmart was inevitable, Asia launched into a five-minute lecture on the germ-ridden state of US currency. According to her, only miracles kept the money-using population from dying of viruses, bacteria, or some strain of flu that could survive for over forty-eight hours. When she'd finished, Ivy waved her off. She'd changed soiled diapers and was still alive to tell about it.

"How much?" She pointed to the stacks of cash spread across the table.

"I've counted it three times, with the same result." Asia pointed at Ivy. "You've questioned my accuracy every time. If you still doubt me, you take over."

Ivy still struggled to believe their find. How did Veronica get her hands on this much loot?

"Are we going to get in trouble for this?" Asia tugged a wipe from her purse and scrubbed her hands.

"How? We didn't steal it. We found it."

"But if Veronica took it from—"

"She's guilty, not us."

"Shouldn't we notify the sheriff?"

Ivy had to think … but she couldn't. This was … huge. "I don't know."

But Asia's thoughts still whirred. "Can you imagine what the IRS would demand from that?" She sucked in a breath. "We'll be responsible for filling out the tax forms and—"

"Stop. You're going to worry us both to death. No one knows it's here. Nothing will happen."

"What if this is what Nolan was after?"

"He won't know we found it unless *you* tell him."

"But how can we keep it secret? We have to think this through, figure out a plan—"

"Not at this exact minute." Ivy sat at the table and read over the calculations Asia had written on the small, yellow legal pad.

"Your math is immaculate. You want a job as my bookkeeper? I pay well." Or at least she would if the IRS didn't take away her business. And everything else.

Asia slipped her glasses off. "No thanks. I chose teaching for a reason." She cleaned them, then shut them in the case with a loud click.

"Might be fun. We could do some more sister-bonding stuff."

"We'd kill each other by the end of the first week."

Ivy laughed and grabbed a collection of twenties. "I know better than that. You don't want blood on your hands. Literally or figuratively."

Asia smirked. "I'm impressed. You paid attention for more than five seconds in high school English."

"Hush now. You told me to count this and I can't if you keep talking my ear off."

Asia mimed locking her lips.

Ivy tallied the bills, jotted the amount on the pad, then took another stack. Her neck muscles tightened. Counting money for her company never bothered her, but this … she shuddered. Who knew how dirty it was? Literally *and* figuratively.

By the time she finished her thumb tingled and sported a red spot over the swirling print. "You're right. Four hundred and eighty thousand dollars."

Greenish-black smudges covered Ivy's fingertips. Dirty work brought this small fortune to Veronica. And her grime always spilled over on her daughters. Maybe that explained Asia's obsession with clean hands.

"Asia, I need wipes."

She motioned from her spot where she stood staring at the boxes filled with Veronica's trinkets. "In my purse."

Ivy scowled. Asia protected her purse like a spy's attaché case, fussed whenever it was touched or moved unexpectedly. And she wiped the outside constantly.

"Asia, I'd like for you to jump out of the window."

"Um-hmmm." She swiveled around. "What did you just say?"

Ivy grinned. "Welcome back to earth. I need to wipe my hands." She held them palms up.

"Eww." Asia hurried to the kitchen, then emerged with an unopened pack. She retrieved two and handed them to Ivy. They smelled of orange juice mixed with lemon furniture polish.

The gray stains on her thumb and palms required extra scrubbing before Ivy could wash between her fingers. "What had you so spaced out a minute ago?"

"I'm just trying to fit the pieces together."

"Any thoughts?" She tossed the wipes in the garbage. As if Asia would have a clue. Freud himself would have run screaming in fear from Veronica and given up psychology all together.

Asia snapped her fingers. "I think I know where the money in the bag came from."

"Come again?"

"You remember the monthly letters from the mysterious D? I still think he used them to deliver money to Veronica. If he sent her two thousand dollars a month, for twenty years—"

"Hang on a minute, I want to write this down." Ivy lined up the numbers on the pad, scratched quick calculations. "At the end, she'd have four hundred and eighty thousand dollars. Why didn't she spend it?"

"Power. She could hold the cash over his head, maybe threaten blackmail."

"The clothes, the jewelry, and the money. She bled this man like a stuck pig."

Asia gestured at the money lying on the table. "And yet he kept coming back." She scowled. "Why?"

"Veronica and men. They couldn't resist her."

"She had so many sides. Captivating and cunning. She'd listen to every word coming from your mouth as if you were the most profound individual since Gandhi, while simultaneously sizing you up so she could stab you in your weakest spot when it benefitted or entertained her. I don't believe she's ever had any real feelings."

"I know she always seemed entertained by other's misery."

Asia nodded. "Especially when she instigated the misery."

Ivy shifted. "How many times did we watch her twist some guy into believing he was responsible for her cheating on him?"

"If you want the exact number we could go back and count all those letters—"

"I didn't mean *literally*—"

Asia rubbed her arms. "I know, I'm just ..." Her mouth curled in disgust.

"Me too." Ivy saw bands of sunlight striped on the floor, creating a division between light and shadows in the living room. A boundary line, where two opposite forces could not cross each other.

She grabbed another wipe and scrubbed her hands again. "Do you think the money she set aside for us came from this same guy?"

"I don't know. Where would she have found a man with that kind of money?"

Veronica believed the world was hers, and people existed as pieces to use for vicious mind games. The mystery millionaire could have come from anywhere, been someone sniffing around long after they left.

"What do you think we should do with this money? I feel like I need a shower after touching it." Or maybe three or four, anything to wash away the grime from Veronica's money and lifestyle. Yes, Asia's dirty money lecture soaked in a little. But the filth bothering her most couldn't be scrubbed clean by hot water and nice-smelling soap.

Asia put on another pair of gloves. "Let's put the cash back in the bag and hide everything in the wall. We can use tonight to think of a solution."

Ivy stood. "Fine. I'll get the bag and we'll get busy stuffing."

They packed the bills quickly then tied the bag shut and pushed the box into the hole.

"Ivy, would you mind sweeping up the debris on the floor? I won't be able to sleep in here tonight if we don't."

Ivy headed for the kitchen. "I'll get the broom."

"Thanks."

Asia fit the drywall panel into place. She sealed the edges, checked them twice to ensure none of the air from the hole could escape. "Can you see the mark?" she asked as Ivy entered with the broom.

"A little. If you're worried, we can move the bookshelves again." Ivy peeled the gloves from her hands. Her fingers felt dry and crackly as if she'd been digging in the dirt.

Fitting. She'd spent the morning digging in the worst dirt imaginable.

Veronica's.

Ivy swept the last of the dust and plaster bits into a dustpan and dumped the refuse into a nearby trash can. "All done. What's next?"

Asia was gathering clean clothes from her suitcase. "I need a shower. Maybe five."

"Me too. Save me some hot water. It's going to be a while before I feel clean again."

CHAPTER 22

Living alone held advantages.

The hissing sounds from the shower continued in the bathroom. Asia glanced at her watch as she sat on her sleeping bag in the living room. Twenty minutes later than the last time she checked. She clicked her tongue.

After she'd showered earlier, they'd worked through dinner gathering and moving the items from Veronica's bedroom to the tarp in the living room. Neither of them mentioned the money barricaded in the wall. After dinner, they each declared the need for another shower. This time Ivy called dibs for the first.

Breaths of steam curled from under the bathroom door. When Ivy started her bath, the last rays of the evening sun poked above the horizon. Dusk now hovered outside the windows. Night was coming. Why had she agreed to go last? Ivy never left a drop of hot water in the pipes after a shower. At least she wasn't singing.

And as soon as the sun dipped from the sky, the house whispers began. Floors creaked, the air conditioner clicked on, then off. Cooled by the night air, the sunbaked roof snapped an unknown tune. Each noise played a note in the creepy song the walls sang to Asia.

Ivy emerged in a blue terry robe and matching pajamas, toweling her hair as she came to the living room. "Bathroom's all yours."

Asia crumpled the edge of her sleeping bag between her fingers. There were no jobs to lean on tonight, nothing to fill the time before going to sleep. "The bathroom is still steamy. I don't want the humidity to make my hair frizz." She sank deeper into her bag.

Ivy laid her towel on the floor. "I did buy some laundry detergent the other day. I'll do a load of towels and such in the morning and you can add your clothes if you want."

She dug in her makeup bag and produced a clear tube. "The stylist who does my hair uses this." She held the tube up. "Calms my frizz, even on rainy days. You should try some." She squeezed a few dollops in her palm, then slicked her hair back with the gel. The fragrance of fruity coconut wafted in the room.

"No thanks. I've got my own." Asia slipped from her bag. A steamy bathroom was superior to hearing another wonder from Ivy's perfect life.

In the bathroom, she readied the water, tested the temperature. Warm water poured from the faucet, melting away the chill in her fingers. Steam floated around the space, adding to the humidity Ivy left behind. Asia grabbed a washcloth from a shelf by the shower then laid a clean towel by the sink.

She stood on the new bathmat, then stripped off the socks she wore to protect her feet from germs when she wasn't wearing shoes. She tossed the dirtied pair in the trash. Her budget couldn't support designer hair gel like Ivy's *and* a supply of clean socks. Living with protected feet far outranked walking around with silky, smooth hair. Life would be great if she could afford both, but she relied on one salary, not two.

At least the beating rhythm of the shower drowned out the sounds from the house.

After her shower, she sat on her bed and discarded the current pair of socks on the floor. A fresh-out-of-the-bag pair sat on her sleeping bag. Asia wiggled her toes into the ends, adjusting each so the inner hem didn't rake across her toes.

Ivy lay on her bed, her phone to her ear. "I need to hang up now. Love you." She ended her call and motioned to Asia's feet. "You must keep the ladies sock industry in business."

Asia settled into the cocoon of her bag. "Some of the worst germs live on the floor." She removed her pillow from the plastic case.

Ivy set her phone on her bed. "We were designed to fight off germs. Can't worry about every little thing in life. Makes people loony."

Asia socked her pillow, plumping the stuffing into a soft cloud for her head. Worrying over ever-present germs in no way qualified her as loony. The floor groaned beneath where she lay. She jerked at the sound, then checked to see if Ivy had noticed.

Her sister lay on her back, legs crossed at the knee. She bounced her foot in the air. "I can't get the money off my mind." Ivy rolled on her side facing Asia. "Four hundred and eighty thousand dollars. Do you know how we could have lived if she'd used the cash when we were here?"

Cicadas began their buzzing symphony outside. Asia plumped her pillow again. "Not a clue." She'd clipped coupons, watched sale flyers, and rolled loose change to exchange for cash her entire adult life. She threw herself a celebration the day her bank account hit five figures by buying a single chocolate-chocolate chip muffin and only because the bakery had them on sale. Pangs of regret for the splurge hit later. She'd spent the rest of the evening checking her bank account balance to keep calm.

Could she bring herself to celebrate once she paid for her townhouse?

"We could have had food in the house on a regular basis, bought clothes from the mall instead of Walmart." Ivy sprang upright. "We could have had our own shoes, instead of sharing three pairs between us. The first thing I did when I made a little money was buy a pair of shoes."

"Were they designer?" Asia's stomach muscles flinched. She'd never cared about designer labels in her life. A few days with Ivy and her mind flew straight to the irrelevant.

"Lower tier, but yes, they were designer. And I loved them." Ivy fingered a button on her pajama top. "We should split the money. And I'd be fine going seventy-thirty, with you taking the seventy."

How generous of her. Giving her poor little sister the largest chunk of dirty money. "I don't want any of the cash." Every time she spent a cent, she'd think of the pink bedroom and the ill-gotten gifts under Veronica's mattress. There weren't enough wipes in the world to clean the grime from her hands after touching a single one of those bills. "I'm fine financially."

"Then why are you taking the money to clean up this house? What's the difference?"

Asia sat up in her sleeping bag. "Why did you agree?" She could match Ivy in asking-nosy-questions ping-pong.

Ivy scowled but remained quiet. "Did you take it because you're strapped for cash? I know a teacher's salary can only stretch so far."

She'd avoided answering by baiting Asia, which was an old tactic from their preteen years. Asia decided to strike at the dangling lure, then force Ivy to reciprocate. "If you must know, I live in a lovely townhouse in Maryville. My landlord wants to sell it and offered me first chance to purchase. I'm using the check to buy *my* home." She paused, but only for a moment. "Your turn, why did you take the money?" Her words came out close-clipped in a machine-gun cadence.

Ivy held her palms toward Asia. "Calm down. I was just curious." She turned down the bedcovers and slipped between the blankets. "I have some business expenses, and the check would cover them." She squirmed under her covers. "We still have to decide what to do with the money we found in the wall."

Asia nestled into her sleeping bag. "Shouldn't it go back into the estate?"

Ivy rustled in her sheets. "Maybe. I don't want to talk about it anymore. Good night."

Asia yanked the edges of her sleeping bag to her ears. "Night."

Ivy thought she lived a pauper's life. She paid for their meals, the balance at The Orange Grove and the bed Asia now lay in. To Ivy the two hundred and fifty thousand dollars meant the extinguishing of a column of numbers on an account sheet. She could use the money to pay off expenses and then make more money. Nothing in her life was under threat.

The equal footing they once shared had shifted. Life placed them on a seesaw, with Ivy sitting on the heavy end and Asia flailing in the air on the light one. In playground politics, if you were the kid in the air you had two options.

Wait for a friend to sit with you and shift the weight … or jump off.

Asia clenched her fists. She had nowhere to jump and no friend to sit on her end. Unless, of course, she counted Russ.

The house whispered in her ears again. *Ivy has both.*

"Leave me alone," Asia mumbled.

"What?" Ivy propped up on an elbow.

"Nothing."

"Guess it was the house talking then." Ivy rolled over and faced the wall.

If only she might understand …

Breathe … Relax … Breathe …

CHAPTER 23

THE PAST CHOOSES STRANGE ways of sneaking into a person's life. Asia spread the stack of photos from Veronica's bedroom across the table in the living room. Her lack of sleep burned with each sweep of her lids.

She'd been too frightened that the house might attack as soon as she drifted off. Her logical side chided but nothing swayed her childish fears. She prayed, recited favorite literary quotes and Bible verses in her head.

And then her thoughts raced to the photos.

Veronica's faceless parents holding tight to her wrists, not her hands. The large bow hanging askew in Veronica's hair. The photo was the only one they'd found of their mother or their grandparents. And one she'd marred.

At midnight Asia had crept to the box where they'd been stored. She'd gathered the stack then settled at the table to study them, using the light from her cell phone.

Much later, Ivy stirred on her bed, then sat up. "What's the matter? Can't sleep?"

"Insomnia I guess," Asia said. No reason to admit the house wouldn't *allow* her the sweet relief of sleep. She checked the time on her phone. Three o'clock.

When Ivy joined Asia she pointed to the photos. "What's got you so hooked on those things in the middle of the night?"

"It's like there's some clue here, but I can't seem to put the pieces together."

"Add it to the list."

"I did." Asia held up a sheet of paper. "I've been keeping track of all the weird things we've found."

"What? Let me see that." Ivy flipped on a lamp then took the paper. "Neat and organized, but I see no connections."

"There has to be a common thread. The jewelry, the knick-knacks, the money in the box, the letters, and the clothes only point to her being with Mr. D." Asia gestured at the list. "The welcome home balloon, the rotted cake, the hoarding, and the two suitcases have no relation to him. Those were solely for us. Then there's the origin of the money in our checks."

"And?"

"I have no idea."

Ivy gave the list to Asia. "You're doing a great job, Detective Butler."

Asia studied her written words for a moment. "If we could figure out the common denominator between all these things, we'd see the secret she left for us."

Ivy sliced through her hair with her fingernails, leaving large parts along the way. "Veronica was nuts. That's the common denominator."

"She was brilliant, Ivy. We both know that. She intentionally made this a puzzle and when we figure it out—" Asia waited for her sister to finish.

"We win the game."

"It's not about winning." Asia laid the list on the table. She dreamed of waking free, greeting a morning with joy for what new things the day held, not fearing this would be the day the walls crumbled and she snapped.

"Then let's be done. We'll pull the money out of the wall, load the bag into my trunk, and leave the whole lot with Janice. Then, we call Nolan and tell him to give the rest of Veronica's things to his wife's cousin the estate seller."

"You mean quit?"

"Yes. Pack up our little selves and go home."

"What happened to protecting all this from Nolan? And the

contract with Veronica?"

Patches of red colored Ivy's neck. "Let him have the whole, stinking lot. We cleaned the house but can't figure out her secret. So what? We'll collect our checks and go home. She'll never know."

Asia met Ivy head on. "I'll know."

Again Ivy raked back her hair, this time shaking it free so that the parts weren't so visible. "Why does this matter so much to you? You were just talking about wanting to go home."

"Ivy, I want to run away from here as fast as I can. But I can't."

"Why not?"

"Because I have to finish this ... the right way."

Ivy scooted a chair out and sat next to Asia. "How did you get the scars on your wrist?"

Asia jerked her hands under the table. "What?"

Ivy tipped her chin toward Asia. "I noticed them before. The big watch and bracelets you always wear don't really hide them that well."

Had her fellow teachers seen them, her students ... or worse, their parents? Her cheeks burned. Asia wore nothing but long or three-quarter length sleeves to work, then stacked bracelets at her wrists. "They're from an accident." Why had Ivy suddenly decided to go from speak-no-personal-truths to spill-your-guts all in one evening? Or morning? Or whatever time it was? She had to get control. "I'm tired, Ivy. I—"

"I know what causes that kind of scar, Asia. Those scars are no accident. I've seen them before. And they always come in twos. One on each wrist."

Asia pressed her back into the chair. She'd admit nothing else. Ivy could believe whatever she wanted about the scars.

Ivy laid her hands on the tabletop, palms up. "Show me your wrists."

"No."

Ivy took Asia's hands, held firm as she rolled Asia's wrists over, exposing the scars.

Asia struggled against Ivy's grip. "No, I don't want your—"

Ivy released her, then folded her sleeves past her elbow crook and laid her arm next to Asia's. "See? I have my own."

Two angry-red rows wormed their way across her sister's skin. Though she wished to look away, Asia couldn't. "What happened?"

"Heroin." Ivy held up her other arm. Another set of long, red marks. "I was so high once that I took a dare to see how long it would take for me to bleed out." She inclined her head toward the marks. "Did this with a rusty razor blade we used to cut drugs. I don't even remember slicing myself. Later on, a person who was supposed to be my friend told me what happened."

A student Asia had taught bore similar marks on his arm. He'd been knife-sliced on his bicep during a fight with another guy. He wore his shirt sleeves rolled up, showing his scars as a badge of honor.

How one attained their scars made a huge difference in their value.

"I can't imagine the pain. How did you survive?"

"I don't remember. We were in this drug house, and my friend dragged me to the street, then called the police. She ran away when they showed up for fear of being arrested. I woke up in the hospital three days later. My *friend* came up to see me once." Ivy slid her sleeves over the scars. "I never saw her again."

Heroin was one of the more difficult drugs to clean up from, but obviously Ivy had. "How did you get clean?"

Ivy hesitated, then spoke. "Denney. I was fresh out of my *second* round of rehab. I saw an ad for a dishwasher at his family's restaurant. He interviewed me. I had to take a drug test, which I failed."

"How do you fail when you just got out of—?"

"I bought some cheap weed a few hours after my release. I convinced myself it would give me the guts to go get a real job." Her cheeks reddened. "I couldn't face going back to what I did for money *before* rehab."

Asia's heart clenched. "Were you a ..."

"I was twenty years old, all used up, and dead on the inside. I needed money for drugs."

An old memory tapped Asia. Veronica. Standing in the doorway to Asia's bedroom, holding her calculus book, threatening to tear pages from it. Veronica's mouth twisting into a toothy leer. "I gave Ivy beauty and all you got was brains." She ripped out a fistful of pages, then threw the book at Asia. It landed at her feet with a thud. "Let's guess who turns out best?" She tore the pages into confetti, tossed the paper flakes into the air, cackling as the spray rained on Asia.

"How did he help you?"

Ivy rubbed her fingertips across the tabletop. "Denney told me I was too beautiful to be wasted by drugs, loaded me in his car, and took me back to rehab. On the way there, he told me how his family had lost his younger brother. He committed suicide the month before. Self-imposed overdose. Denney said he couldn't stomach seeing another life destroyed by poison."

Ivy rubbed her eyes. "He visited every Saturday until my release."

"He's a gift from heaven, Ivy." A rare gift few drug addicts received. But, of course, Ivy had somehow managed to find him.

Ivy continued. "I know. After I was released again, he gave me a job at his warehouse counting inventory, with one condition. I had to enroll in a program and go to weekly meetings. He sought me out every day to check on my progress." She paused, as if searching for the right words. "Denney listened to *me,* like I mattered. I kept expecting him to make a pass at me, but he didn't. I never met a man like him. It felt so good to be treated like a whole person, not some pretty face or a body." She winked at Asia. "I set my mind on landing him, so I worked my way out of the warehouse and into the front office."

"And into his heart."

Ivy went on. "On our second date, I told him all the terrible things I'd done." She paused. "And you know what he said?"

Asia waited, hung on the silence.

"He put his arms around me ..." Ivy demonstrated by hugging herself. "And told me every caterpillar deserved the chance to become a butterfly."

Ivy twirled her diamond around her finger. "I told him I didn't know *how* to be anything that good. He said he'd be privileged to spend the rest of his life watching me change into the woman he knew I could be." Her face softened. "We married three months later."

Ivy traced lightly over her scars. "I believed I would never get Veronica out of my system. It seemed as if she went all the way to my bones. I think in some way I did this to get rid of her."

Asia's heart dropped. She couldn't count the times she'd sat on her couch, watching old movies that mirrored Ivy's fairytale. A troubled girl saved by the strong, understanding man. Love bloomed and happily-ever-after reigned until the closing credits came.

But never for her.

She was a broken doll on a store's shelf. In the store, she appeared whole and normal, sitting in a box that hid all her imperfections. But once purchased, when the new owner opened the box at home, the dolly's arms and legs would fall off, forcing the buyer to realize they were burdened with something beyond repair. Just like her sweet Christina.

A dolly you couldn't love.

Ivy bore shallow scars a good man overcame. She'd set her mind on landing normal and she succeeded. All because she left Veronica—and Asia—behind.

Asia's chest tightened. *Breathe ... relax ... breathe.* How many times had she watched *The End* flash on the screen after those old movies and held a pillow over her mouth and screamed "Why won't somebody save me?" More than once, she'd thought of Ivy, and the message changed to *why didn't my own sister save me?*

But instead, Ivy now asked the questions. "Why did you want to die, Asia?"

Because dying promised release from the pain of tomorrow. Asia sucked in a deep breath, held to the count of two, then exhaled. Her head buzzed with early ripples of dizziness. "I think we've sister-bonded enough for one night. Let's try to get back to sleep."

Ivy peered at Asia's scars again, then slid her eyes back to meet Asia's. "Maybe so." She switched off the lamp and they crawled in their beds, leaving the photos on the table.

Asia stared at the soft glow of the nightlight anchored in the outlet nearest her cot. Her mind drifted to the moon vines covering the fence behind her townhouse. Given freedom, they grew thick and wild, blotting out everything else around them. But the landscapers trimmed them back weekly. With their pruning, the vines bloomed, sporting pure white flowers that opened at the end of each day and perfumed the night with their sweet fragrance.

Ivy had pruned the past with Denney's help. She found healing in a stock room. Asia ran away to Tennessee hoping to find peace in the pine scent of the mountains. Instead, old memories twined around her brain like those uncut moon vines, choking out any happy thoughts because she couldn't prune them.

The visions of moon vines faded as Ivy's voice called. "What do you think we should do with the money?"

"What?"

"The money. What *should* we do about all that cash?"

"Leave it be for now and get some sleep."

Ivy stretched under her covers. "I don't want to leave anything undone this trip. I promised myself a long time ago to be done with Florida. This is it."

"At least you can count that one as a promise well kept." Asia yanked her sleeping bag to her chin and rolled to face the curtains again.

"What's that supposed to mean?"

Asia squirmed in her cocoon. "Nothing. Go to sleep."

Ivy's sheets snapped as she threw them back. "No. You tell me what you meant."

"I didn't mean anything."

"Yes, you did. You're trying to say I didn't keep my promises. Name one time I didn't keep my word to you."

Asia peeled away the sleeping bag and sat upright. "You can't be serious."

Ivy now stood between their beds, hands on her hips. "I'm dead serious. I'll admit, I did a ton of bad things to you, but not once did I break a promise."

This time Asia flipped on the light, then faced Ivy. "You broke far more than one."

Ivy stepped closer to the bed. "Name one."

Asia drew a deep breath. Then another. "I'll do better than tell you. I'll *show* you."

CHAPTER 24

Silence encased them. Asia's legs buckled, as if bones and muscles melted. The sisters stood inches apart, two opposites locked in a duel.

"Tell me, what promise did I break?" Ivy spoke low, deliberate.

Asia's heart thumped, fueled by a fifteen-year-old mix of rage and unshed tears. "I have to show you, or you won't understand."

"Asia, have you lost your ever-loving mind? It's four in the morning and no time for riddles. Plus, its dark."

Asia kept her sights on Ivy. "We're only going down the hall."

Breathe ...

Ivy crossed her arms. "What are you so bent on showing me?"

"Come in the bedroom."

"I'm not going in Veronica's—"

"Not hers." Asia grabbed Ivy's hand. "Ours." She steered her down the hall, flipping lights as she went.

Relax ...

Stagnant air and the smell of dust rushed at them when Asia opened the door. Glowing checkerboard squares lit the floor as the moonlight sliced through the window. Asia's dreaded spectrals danced, brought to shadowed life by the hall lights. The wires from the missing light fixture hung from the ceiling like black worms.

The bedroom's floor creaked as she dragged Ivy with her. Asia flashed her phone's light toward the far wall, but only for Ivy's sake. She could have found what she sought with her eyes closed.

"Over here." Asia's fingers whispered like silk as she released Ivy. Though the room stood bare of furniture, she pictured her old bed sitting against the wall. And the rectangle of yellow expanding between the door and the jam as a silhouetted figure staggered into the room.

"It happened after you left." She stepped toward the wall. The floorboards groaned beneath her feet, warning, "Stop. Go back. Forget."

The darkness swallowed them. "This is too creepy, Asia. I'm leaving."

"Stay. Please."

"For what?"

"This." Asia shined the light on the wall where a chunk of drywall was missing.

Another scar.

Ivy brushed past her, leaning in to look closer. Her profile stretched in the circle of light. She combed back a shock of hair cascading across her face as she yawned. "Did we do that?"

"*I* did." Asia bounced the words against her clenched teeth.

"What's the story then?" Ivy straightened, massaged her lower back. "This place is aging me."

"You're lucky it's only aging you. This house *killed* a part of me."

Ivy reached forward, traced the pock on the gouged surface. "Don't be so dramatic. How is this evidence I broke a promise?"

Asia struggled with the memory, wanting to just say it outright, but the knot in her throat strangled the words. But it was here. All here. The black figure moving toward her bed, the odor of beer and cigarettes surrounding her. The high-pitched, scratchy voice, speaking slurred words that bore no consonant sounds. Speech didn't matter. She knew what he wanted.

Her body remembered too. The muscles tensed. Fear drummed her heart. Asia clasped her quaking arms around her middle, squeezed tight.

She'd hugged herself that night, too, as she wheezed out sobs because fright choked her cries. Prayed Ivy would come back and save her from the booze-soaked shadow stumbling toward her.

Her lungs deflated. Sweat coated her forehead and cheeks. She teetered on her feet as the spinning merry-go-round sensation swept over her.

Breathe ... breathe ... breathe ...

She couldn't ... *wouldn't* have an attack now. She'd waited fifteen years.

Breathe ...

Asia drew breath. Ivy must learn the truth. She'd share the fear, take away one straw and save the camel's back.

"Remember what you promised me on my eighth birthday?"

Ivy didn't answer for a moment, until, "Same thing I always said, that someday we'd get away from Veronica. I stopped saying it when we were older."

Asia's skin crawled. Ivy missed the sheets being torn from the bed. She missed the goose bumps popping on Asia's arms and legs. Nothing Ivy said or tried to do would erase the memory of sweaty, unwashed male, and the suffocating weight of his body.

Asia aimed the light toward Ivy's face.

"Asia, tell me what promise I broke. I need to go back to sleep."

"Promise to listen?"

"With both ears."

Should she tell her? Tell her of the night Dewitt the Twit's scratchy stubble scraped against the tender skin of her neck. The cold handle of the shovel as she pulled it from the hiding place under her bed. His screams. Blood dripping.

Asia shuddered. Dewitt managed nothing more than a slobbery kiss, planted on her mouth. That's when she kicked him back before smacking him with the shovel. Metallic thuds marked her successful hits. Over and over until Dewitt countered with slurred curses and flailing punches.

She missed only once, rendering the chunk taken out of the wall. Dewitt fell over the side of the bed and lay in a silent heap. Asia knew she'd killed him.

Veronica had giggled as she padded across the room in her bare feet. She clapped her hands. "What a great show." She stroked the scar on the wall. "That's my girl. Never let anyone get the best of you. Just like Mommy says."

Then she squatted by Dewitt, held her fingers against the side of his throat. "Cheer up, sweetie. You got lucky. He's too dumb to die." She stood and nudged him with her toe. Dewitt jiggled, and drew in a whistling breath.

She pointed to him, then to Asia. "This is *your* mess. Get it out of my house. Now." Veronica left the room humming a tuneless song.

Asia had sat alone in the dark, listening to Dewitt's pig-snorts as he slept off his liquor. Long minutes passed. Finally, she turned on the light and looked at him. Sweat mixed with blood beaded on his hair, streamed down his cheeks like rain on glass. Even now she could hear his feet bumping down the front steps as she dragged him outside to his truck, leaving him in a patch of sand to sleep it off. He drove home the next morning, swerving his way down the lane. She never saw him again.

"Go ahead, Asia," Ivy took a step back. Away from the light of the phone, her face became a skull, her eye sockets black holes. "Tell me what I did." Her voice quivered.

Asia braced for the crumbling of the dam and the flood of runaway emotions. Blocked for fifteen years, they would surely tear through her like a high school's football team rips through pep banners at the beginning of every home game.

A rush of electricity exploded within her, spread like wildfire through her veins until her fingertips tingled. The palms of her hands stung. Her nails dug into the tender skin.

For fifteen years, she'd fought against this breach.

Not tonight. Tonight, she'd be free of one her worst memories. Cleansed. Whole.

The inky dark of the room blurred Ivy's movements as she planted her hands on her hips. "Why are you stalling? Get this over with so I can get back to bed."

Asia raised the light to Ivy's face. Her sister always considered herself the tough one. They'd see how tough she really was. The shadowed light from her phone didn't hide the flicker at the corners of Ivy's mouth. Her lips quivered. The skin above them puckered.

Asia moved the light to see Ivy in full view. And saw her own face. As it was in the bus station's bathroom mirror. Filled with hopelessness. Fear. Self-hate.

Scarring pain.

The kind Veronica inflicted. And if Asia uttered another word, told one-fifth of what happened to her, the pain would grow into a scar Ivy would carry forever.

Turning Asia into Veronica.

"I'm tired, Asia." Her sister's voice rose in near anger.

The truth sat wadded in Asia's throat. Her anger with Ivy had been filtered through the mind of an injured fifteen-year-old. Tonight, the filter tore, revealed who Ivy was the night she ran. A terrified child who acted on impulse to get away from horrendous abuse.

Asia shined the light on the wall's scarred surface. Was the lessening of straws on her own back worth the scars she'd inflict on Ivy? *God, I can't do this.*

Breathe ... Relax ... Breathe ...

She pushed past Ivy and headed for the door. "I'm going back to bed."

"But what about ... coming in here? Seeing the proof you just *had* to show me?"

Shadows slid along the walls as Asia hurried down the hall, Ivy's footsteps clomping behind her.

"Asia." Ivy grabbed her by the arm and yanked Asia to a stop. "Why did you want me to see that chunk taken out of the wall?"

Asia wrenched from her grip. "I'm going to bed." Her lungs tightened until she coughed.

"Do you realize how nuts this is?"

"Yes." Asia gasped. Her heart pounded faster ... faster ...

She hurried back to the living room.

Breathe ... breathe ... breathe ...

Asia tumbled onto her bed.

"What is the matter with you?" Ivy plopped onto her own.

Asia panted. "Just go to sleep."

Breathe ... breathe ... breathe ...

She tugged a wipe from a package she'd placed under her pillow and washed her face as Ivy nestled into bed.

Asia washed her face and hands a second time. She drew in breaths, counted to two. Released, then repeated. The pain in her chest swelled. Silence walled around her and Ivy. She couldn't tell Ivy the truth about the mark on the wall. For fifteen years, she'd dreamed of watching shock and remorse fill Ivy's eyes. Fifteen years she'd waited to have her say. And when the time came ...

Ivy broke the barrier of quiet. "Have you ever wanted to change anything about the past, Asia?"

Asia gripped the edge of her sleeping bag. "I wish I could change a lot of things. But I know I can't."

Ivy rustled her feet within her sheets. "Knowing is the easy part. Accepting is what rips your gut until you learn to live with it."

"How did you learn to live with the past, Ivy?"

"Before tonight, I would've said just being determined to get over it. But now ..." After a quiet pause, she rolled over and faced Asia. "What things would you change?"

Asia stared back at her. The pain in her chest eased. "I'd stop being afraid ... and angry at a frightened little girl."

Asia rolled away from Ivy as her ears caught a new sound in the house—silence.

CHAPTER 25

Ivy sat with Asia as they ate lunch at Veronica's table. Neither of them had gone back to sleep after Asia's episode the night before. That morning, they both dragged themselves through showers and skipped breakfast.

Ivy had begged Asia to take a break from the cleaning and go shopping. "I call it 'retail therapy,'" she said. But Asia poked out her chin, then launched into a five-minute explanation of why they shouldn't. Ivy's attention drifted as an ache slashed through her. All three of her boys did the same thing with their chins when revving up to argue.

She'd never noticed any resemblance between Asia and her boys before, but now ... Matteo's nose bore the same bump on the bridge. Marco's wavy hair framed his forehead no matter how he combed his bangs to the side. Asia constantly brushed her own rippling tendrils from her face.

And her sweet baby, Mickey. Always the first to defend the bully's victim or befriend the friendless. How many times had she and Denney been called into the school because Mickey allowed a child to copy his homework? His defense never wavered. The classmate didn't understand the assignment, and he wanted to help. He *neve*r passed an opportunity to help another.

Just like Asia. For ten years, she'd been surrounded by tiny pieces of her sister flowering in her boys. And she'd missed them because she was too stubborn or guilt-blinded to see. Never in sight, never in mind. Never face what she'd done that night after prom. She'd shattered the only security Asia had ever known, taken away the closest thing to a mother she'd had. Her two older boys shrank from her hugs now and wiped off her kisses in public, but deep down, they still needed her. When they were afraid, sick, or worried, they wanted her to sit with them, hug them in private, or fix them a giant glass of chocolate milk that they'd slurp from the squiggly straws won at a fall festival at church.

Asia had needed mothering too. And when Ivy left on prom night ...

The image of the scars on her sister's wrists ... And the unexplained chunk in their bedroom wall.

Cramping spasms ripped through Ivy. No matter if her insides tore apart and started leaking from her body, she would face this. "Asia," she said, keeping her voice steady, "what happened after I left?"

Asia stopped mid-chew. She swallowed hard to clear her mouthful of salad. "Nothing."

Ivy reached across the table and grabbed her wrist. She pointed to the neat row of scars with the other hand. Even in trying to take her life, Asia attempted perfection. "You need to tell me what happened. And I *need* to hear it."

Asia yanked her wrist free. "I told you, an accident—"

"I'm a tough girl, Asia." She lifted her chin. "The truth. Please."

Asia's shoulders drooped. She cleaned her hands with a wipe. Twice. "I sat outside on the steps all night so I could help you sneak back in. The mosquitoes almost ate me alive, but I stayed." She rubbed her arms. "No more cars passed on the highway. The night was pitch black. I shivered, even though it was humid because, after a while, I *knew* you weren't coming back."

"What did Veronica do?" Ivy fisted her hands underneath the table. She wanted the story of the scars, not prom night. But she knew that prom night must be the first step toward them.

"She called me a pathetic dog, waiting for a master who wasn't coming back."

Asia rubbed her finger across the back of her hand. Twice. "She said you never loved me." She focused on the table as if there were answers that she, and she alone, could read. "Why did you leave me?"

"After she cut my hair, I couldn't take being in this house anymore. The photographer at prom approached me at the punch bowl. He asked if I'd ever done any modeling. When I said no, he told me I was a natural, and he could introduce me to people in the business."

Ivy shifted in her chair. "I knew he was lying, but he offered a way out and I grabbed it. He drove me to his apartment in Orlando and got drunk. Then he tried to make a move on me and I slapped him." One shoulder went up in a shrug. "He slapped me back."

She showed her hands, curved her fingers. "I clawed him. Drew blood. He came at me again but tripped over a stool. He was so drunk he just lay there, screaming at me. I took his car keys and drove off. Ran out of gas in Valdosta. I left his car in a ditch on the interstate and hitch-hiked my way out of Georgia. For months I slept in all sorts of places—dirty places—until I ended up in Seattle. You know the rest." She sought her sister's face. "I'm sorry, Asia. I never meant to hurt you. I just didn't think—"

What would Denney think of his butterfly now? As she sat across from her own blood, staring at death lines she'd helped create.

Asia pointed to the tiny scar under her eye. "Veronica threw an iron at me. The tip gouged me. That's what gave me the nerve to leave. I spent the rest of that night in a Greyhound station trying to stop the bleeding because I needed to board the bus without attracting attention."

"Why did she throw an iron at you? She was crazy, yes, but never violent."

"Because I denied her a shining parental moment. I was Valedictorian of my senior class, and I didn't tell her. I didn't even tell her the time or the date of graduation. She found my diploma three weeks later."

Ivy clapped three times. "Good for you. For being valedictorian *and* for leaving. Where did you go?"

"Gainesville. I was accepted for summer admittance at the

university."

"And you never came back?"

"No. I interviewed for the job in Maryville before graduation, then left Gainesville and went to Tennessee. I used money I earned from two part-time jobs to pay for food and a dorm room. Scholarships paid for tuition."

Asia snapped the lid on the plastic container for her salad and tossed the remnants of her lunch in the trash. She cleaned the table, then wiped her hands clean. "You finished?" She pointed to Ivy's leftovers.

Ivy slid the lot to Asia. "You've got a ton of guts."

Asia's brows arced, broadcasting huge surprise at Ivy's compliment. "Me? I don't think so."

"Are you kidding? You survived Veronica. *Alone*. You put yourself through college. You got a job, moved away, and started a new life. Alone. That's gutsy."

"I did what was necessary." Asia dropped Ivy's leftovers into the trash can.

Ivy leaned back in her chair. "Was slicing your wrists necessary?"

Asia's back snapped straight. She twirled around to Ivy. "Why can't you leave that alone?"

"The mark on the wall in our old bedroom and those on your wrists are connected. I want to know how." Ivy knitted her fingers together and laid them on the tabletop.

Asia held her hands out to the side. The bracelets on her left arm slipped below her wrist. "There is nothing to say."

Ivy spied the scars. "You never lied to me, Asia. What is so bad that you'd start now?"

Asia rubbed her arms as if she were standing in arctic air. "I'm not—"

"Yes, you are." Ivy leaped from her chair. It fell over and banged on the wooden floor. She grasped Asia by the shoulders, careful not to dig her nails into her sister's flesh. "Tell me the truth about the wall in our old bedroom and your scars. Please."

Asia looked away but Ivy leaned close, craned her neck until she faced her sister. "You used to tell me things when Veronica wasn't around."

Asia broke from Ivy's hold. "Veronica's *always* around." She reeled and went to the tarp. "We need to get back to cleaning."

Ivy headed for the front door. "Yeah, well, I need some air." As soon as she slipped through to the yard, gnats buzzed, flitting near her nose until she fanned them away. She sat on the top step. The emptiness of the weed-infested yard, the barren field next door and uninhabited new homes up the street closed in on her. She pounded her palm with her fist.

Asia had sat here on prom night, knowing she'd been left behind. And now she believed God had sent them back to Veronica's for a reason.

A blue jay screeched from a perch on the neighboring fence. A flock of white cattle egrets drifted from the sky and landed in the upturned dirt next door. They scoured the patch on long, graceful legs. Their thin beaks tweezed through the mounds of soil like yellow lacquered chopsticks as they searched for bugs.

Ivy walked to the patch of grass trampled flat by the car's tires. She wheeled around, dropped her chin, and faced the house.

There were things in life requiring more than a simple "I'm sorry." Some required a fall-to-your-knees, please-forgive-me kind of sorry. She owed one to both God and her fifteen-year-old sister who spent prom night watching a black, empty road.

She looked to the cloud-dotted sky. "I'm terrible at apologies. But I have to fix this," she said. "Please help."

CHAPTER 26

Asia stepped back from the tarp and surveyed the clothes, jewelry, cruise tickets, and knick-knacks belonging to Veronica. Normal people cleaned their parents' homes and reminisced over the souvenirs of their lives. They enjoyed the opportunity to see their parents as individuals who experienced the pangs of a first love, went on trips to faraway places, and gathered trinkets to mark their life's events. How pitiful that such a tacky, tawdry assortment of items summed up her mother's life ... and her own.

Asia ran her finger along the red scars on her wrists. Two days had passed since Ivy demanded the truth about them. Two college degrees, three Blount County Teacher-of-the-Year awards, and four published textbooks bearing her name would never erase the past lying on the tarp spread across Veronica's living room floor or her wrists.

She fixed her gaze on the nearby wall. *Filthy rags.* What twisted message had Veronica wanted to convey with those two words? The phrase tugged at her memory like a persistent child pulling the hem of Mama's shirt. She'd heard them before, but in a book or the Bible or even Sunday school ... she wasn't certain where.

She googled the phrase. The results popped onto the screen and all from the Bible. She pressed the first entry and read. Isaiah 64:6. *All of us have become like one who is unclean, and all our righteous acts are like filthy rags; we shrivel up like a leaf, and like the wind our sins sweep us away.*

Why would Veronica quote the prophet Isaiah when she had always hated God and dismissed the notion of sin or repentance?

She rubbed her temples. Ivy had gone to retrieve food and more bottled water, leaving her trapped. Like Persephone in the Greek myths, when abducted by Hades.

Asia surveyed the room. She'd always believed this house could have doubled for the lair of Hades.

Ivy burst in the door, shattering the silence of the room as she dropped a case of water on the table. "My phone says it's ninety-two outside." She fanned her face. "And I believe every degree of it."

She dug a bottle from the packaging. "Why are you staring at that junk?"

"Trying to figure why she kept all this."

"She was nuts, that's why."

"It's more than that. There's a story here. One she's determined for us to know."

"I say we toss the whole lot into the garbage and wait for the movie version."

Asia uncapped her water, took a long drink. "I can't stop thinking about this. The answers we're looking for are here, but I can't see them." She squeezed the bottle cap in her palm.

Beside her, Ivy shuffled. "It isn't there, Asia."

"What?"

"What you're looking for isn't on the tarp."

"And what might that be?"

"The secret to finding the peace you are so desperate for."

Ivy passed her hand before the array. "This. Does. Not. Define. You. That—" She pointed directly toward the tarp. "— is *Veronica's* life." She pointed to Asia. "Not yours." Ivy switched to herself. "And not mine." She took Asia's hands, flipped them over, exposing her scarred wrists. "These don't define you either." Ivy tightened her grip as Asia squirmed to break free. "They don't define you, Asia."

The warmth from Ivy's hands spread to Asia's. "Do you want to know why I left?"

Breathe ... Relax ... Breathe ...

Ivy leaned in close enough to hear Asia's breathing. "I left because

I had to. And you were strong enough to survive her ... alone."

Cold sweat chilled Asia's burning forehead. "No ... no ... I—" Words tangled in cottony dryness in her throat. She coughed around a painful lump. "You were the strong one. Not me." She swayed on her feet until she slipped free and rushed to a chair at the table.

Ivy followed, settled across from her. "Right. I was the *big* sister who yelled at that dumb boy who teased you on the bus. And I told off Mr. Dunham when he cheated you out of a grade on a project."

"It was a test," Asia said as she wiped her hands, then breathed in their citrus scent.

Ivy slammed her hands on the table. "Whatever. I rushed into battles for you when I *knew* I would win. Who needs strength for that?"

She pressed her hands together and gestured to Asia. "You fought Veronica all the time. For me. You earned a teaching degree with jobs and scholarships, didn't numb your pain with drugs and alcohol, and remained respectable. If I were smart enough to write a dictionary, I'd put your picture on the page and claim this is the definition of strength. My baby sister, Asia."

Asia drew a shaky breath against the stabbing pain in her chest. Ivy's words sounded good but carried light truths. "I didn't ... I'm so messed up now ... so broken."

Ivy countered. "Yes, you did. You handled her for three years. On your own. I couldn't, probably would have killed myself."

Asia held her wrists up to Ivy. "I failed at that, too."

Ivy balled her hands to fists. "You want to know how I overcame the memories? Mandatory group meetings for addicts. After three stints in rehab, Denney knew I had no coping skills. So, when he asked me to marry him, he had one condition. That I keep going to my meetings. Every Monday night, I trucked to a local church, sat in a circle, and spilled my sad little story before twelve people who couldn't handle their drama any better than I could."

"But you finally cleaned her out of your head, Ivy." Asia blinked back an onslaught of tears. "I've been trying for so long. Nothing works."

Ivy unclenched her fists and rested her chin in one palm. "I wish you could see."

Asia swallowed back more tears. "What can't I see?"

"You're not broken. Dented, but not broken." A tear caught on the corner of Ivy's smile. "I seem stronger because I have bigger attitude and a louder mouth. I'm not."

Asia brushed a tear from her own cheek as she choked back an uncharacteristic giggle. "To me, that made you Ivy."

Ivy crossed her hands on her chest. "I am so—"

Asia held up her hand to stop Ivy. Sorry wasn't what she wanted or needed. "I know." She dried her face with the wipe. "I must look a fright." She retrieved a makeup bag she always kept in her purse and left for the bathroom.

When she returned to the room Ivy waved her over. "Sit down. We need to talk."

Asia slid into the offered chair.

Ivy pressed a button on her phone and swiveled the screen to Asia, displaying a photo of three black-haired, brown-eyed boys beaming as they hugged each other. "These are our boys. That's Marco on the left, Matteo in the middle, and Michael on the right. We call them Marco, Mattie, and Mickey."

Asia looked at the picture. Mickey grinned—the cat who'd feasted on the missing canary—Mattie stuck out his tongue, and Marco clowned at the camera with crossed eyes and fish lips. Mischief crackled around the two bigger boys. They gave Ivy a run of it for sure.

"They're really handsome, Ivy. All that black hair."

"They're like raising three wild monkeys. I asked them to look nice, and this was what I got. Mickey, our youngest, is the calmest of the three."

She scrolled to another photo, showed it to Asia. "That's my husband, Denney."

Asia's mouth popped open. With his square jaw, jet-black hair, and laughing brown eyes, Denney really captured a person's attention. "Oh my," Asia whispered, "He's very …"

Ivy's lips stretched until she resembled the famous Cheshire cat. "Yes, he is."

Asia studied the face of the man who'd given Ivy the sparkling diamond on her left hand along with his pledge to love and cherish her for the rest of their lives, for better or worse.

Asia forced herself to comment. "He has a kind face."

Every inch of Ivy sparkled as she stared at Denney's photo. "Everything about him is kind. And, thankfully, he's tough as nails underneath. Me and my mouth have never fazed him."

Asia shifted in her chair. "That *is* amazing."

"I know. Who knew there was someone out there with enough patience to put up with me?"

"Certainly not me." Asia glanced at the photo again. "But I'm so glad you found him, Ivy. He's one in a million."

Ivy powered off her phone and put it back in her purse. "Now you can go back to that lady at your church and tell her you have people in Seattle. A huge family of Italians."

"But they're *your* family, not mine."

Ivy waved Asia off. "No, ma'am. We both belong to them. As soon as I tell them about you, they're going to be planning your 'Welcome to the Family' dinner. They'll fall in love with you just because you're my sister."

Ivy's conviction was sweet. As a concept, Asia was easy to love. But as flesh and blood ... Once they met her, she'd become the unstable, spinster in-law talked about at family reunions.

Ivy tapped her on the hand. "I'm ready to hear about this mysterious Russ."

Asia's mouth popped open. "Who ... how do you know—?"

"I'm nosy and you leave your phone lying around in conspicuous places. I noticed he texts you every day." Ivy tucked her chin, leaned closer. "Somebody special?"

Asia's stomach fluttered. No. She liked Russ too much as a friend. Unlike Ivy, being coupled with her had no better. Just worse. "No. Just my neighbor. He helps me out with things that need fixing around my townhouse."

Ivy leaned back. "So, he's an old, retired guy who needs to get away from a nagging wife?"

"He's a widower."

"Oh. You help him out by giving him jobs to do."

"Not exactly." Asia's cheeks warmed, as if she'd stepped from shade into morning sun.

Ivy's brows shot up. "Really. Then what is it, exactly?"

Asia hesitated. Sharing Russ with Ivy meant opening a window into her world. Sharing the entire cake of her life, not crumbs and smears of icing. Connecting here, in the present, and not just their shared battles of the past.

In this moment, she *wanted* Ivy in her now and her future.

Her heart happy-thumped against her chest. "Russ isn't an old man. He's my age. His wife died of cancer shortly after they married, and he's been a bachelor for the past eight years."

Ivy crossed her arms on the table. "And?"

"He's a firefighter."

"Is he worthy of a month in a calendar?"

"That's so tacky."

Ivy put up her hands as if surrendering. "It's a valid question."

No, it wasn't. It cheapened Russ, and she suddenly felt obligated to defend his worth. "I think I have a picture of him on my phone. He was trying to teach me how to take a selfie."

As she went for her purse, her blood pounded in her ears. She should stop this. Pull back. Keep Ivy out.

Asia thumbed through her gallery until she found the photo. Pure Russ, with his big grin and hazel-green eyes that glinted with a mixture of charm and humor. She handed her phone to Ivy. "That's him."

Ivy whistled. "Hello Mr. Any-Month-You'd-Like."

"Really? Your husband looks like a model. Or a movie star."

"I'm not lusting. Just appreciating. This man is gorgeous, Asia. Since when did you go for tall, muscled, and light-brown hair?"

She never saw Russ as a type. To her, he was the man who cooked popcorn without salt because she couldn't stand the grit, who took her car in for oil changes because the filth at the garage made her cringe. He wasn't someone to be ogled in a calendar, he was ...

"He's my neighbor." Hopefully that put a period to where Ivy's mind wanted to meander.

But Ivy persisted. "And he obviously likes you—"

Asia put up hands in protest. "We're just friends."

Ivy handed back her phone. "Friends? Any man who texts you daily, offers to fix things around your house, and teach you how to use your phone wants more than friendship." She scowled a moment. "He isn't some sort of sociopath, is he?"

"No. The only reason he's texting so often is because the alarm in my townhouse kept going off. He needed the code for the alarm company and didn't want me to worry about it while I'm here, so he's been sending me updates. He's not some weird stalker. Just a really nice, really gentlemanly guy."

Ivy raised a brow. "Those 'updates' sure come in handy, don't they? Have you considered the possibility of ..."

Asia shook her head so hard it jostled her hair. "He's not looking, and neither am I. We get along together, and we like many of the same things. We're just friends. Really."

"Really good friends, I'd say." Ivy took another look at Russ's photo. "I'm glad you have such a good *neighbor-friend*. If you've got at least one, you'll make out okay."

Asia's mind steered back to her first day of school. She sat on the bus, her knees shaking so hard Ivy threatened to tie them together with her shoelaces. Every time the bus stopped to pick up a child, Asia entertained bolting down the steps and running into the countryside to hide until school was over.

Ivy had shot her best big-sister-knows-all look at Asia. "Just make one good friend today. Then you'll be okay for the rest of the year."

"I want you to be my one good friend," Asia had told her.

Ivy straightened in the seat, squared her shoulders. "I'm your sister. That means I'm your friend for life."

Asia shot back to the present. That's what hurt the most when Ivy left. She'd lost her friend for life. But now, they sat together again, not sharing war stories, but life. At least Ivy was.

Ivy nudged her shoulder. "I'm not joking when I say I think Russ wants more than friendship. He—"

"He doesn't need me in his life. Not like that." Asia turned off her phone. "He's been through enough with his first wife. He needs someone who doesn't come from the scratched and dented shelf."

Ivy pulled out her phone. She touched the pictures of Denney and her boys, then pointed to Russ. "*They* define us, Asia. Not that rotten tarp covered with Veronica's garbage." She swiveled in her chair, faced Asia head-on. "Denney knows me inside and out, but no one will ever know me like you do."

Asia's breath caught in her throat. Without thinking, she'd exposed her scars. "I did this in college. Alone. I sat on a stack of towels so I wouldn't bleed all over the floor in my room. After the RA found me, I spent six weeks on suicide watch in a mental health facility. Lost an entire semester of college. When I recovered, I finished school. With a bachelor's degree, a master's degree ... and wrists covered in scars. These are never going away, Ivy. Not ever."

Shadows crossed Ivy's face. "I wish I had some magic wand to make this all go poof, but I don't." Her lower lip trembled.

"I know." Asia smiled slightly. "Neither of us are any kind of bargain ... but at least we've each got one good friend."

CHAPTER 27

Asia circled the tarp, looking for connections, hints, *anything* to clue into Veronica's intended message. Two days ago, she and Ivy bonded as sisters for a breath of time. They'd shared, cried, and later celebrated with chocolate milkshakes.

Asia slept soundly that night, and the next. The sleep should have cleared her mind, helped her focus on the mystery Veronica wove within the refuse she left behind. But now, after two weeks of cleaning and discovering, all she saw was one woman's trophy case, a testament declaring, "I have the power to hurt and I wield it with glee."

Ivy sat at the table, filing down a broken fingernail. "Any progress?"

Asia went to answer in the negative, but her brain jolted before she could speak. She scanned the tarp one more time ... and then she knew. She scurried around, sorted items into groups, stepped back, then grabbed another armful and made new piles.

The scratching of Ivy's nail file stopped, and she stood. "What?"

Asia stopped, stood back, and pointed to the new display around the bag of money. She spun around, snapped her fingers. "I've got it."

Ivy rushed to her. "You figured it out?"

"It starts with the money. We know that D sent her these letters and money once a month, right?"

"Right."

"Why would a man send money every month?"

"We already guessed this, blackmail for their affair."

"No, there's another reason."

Ivy's blank expression testified that she wasn't following.

"Think, Ivy. Of the two of us, you should get this one."

Ivy huffed. She stayed silent until a spark lit in her and she playfully slapped her forehead. "Child support."

"Right."

Ivy pointed to the tarp. "All of this came from ... from ... our *real* father?"

"Yes. And the photos." Asia motioned to the paternal evidence. "I think he took them."

Ivy squatted for closer inspection of the new array. "Of course. These are candid shots of us, doing things that a parent would want to remember. To be proud of." She stopped to catch her breath. "Our father took these, which means—"

"He lived here." Asia picked up a letter and handed it to Ivy once she stood. "The letters came in envelopes with no stamps or addresses. They were hand-delivered."

"I need some water." Ivy went to the refrigerator and removed two bottles. She offered a bottle to Asia. Condensation trailed down the side like rivers of tears.

Asia's tongue curled in her throat. "No thanks."

"What's wrong?" Ivy took a long drink of water.

"The bottle's all wet." Asia shuddered.

Ivy held up her index finger. "Be right back."

When she rushed back, the bottle was dried and wrapped in paper towels from the kitchen. "No more drips." She winked at Asia as she passed the bottle to her.

Since their talk two days ago, Ivy was again the friend Asia had missed all those years. When they were children, Ivy made her breakfast, helped her dress, and reminded her to brush her teeth. She held Asia when thunder rattled the windows. She'd cried with Asia when Veronica destroyed Christina.

Asia uncapped her water, took a long swig. The liquid chilled her throat and cooled her from the inside out. Those memories escaped her all these years. How many others lay buried, awaiting their turn at reappearing? How different things might have been if she'd remembered more of the good in Ivy and spent less time feeling victimized by her leaving. She'd spent too many years savoring her right to be angry with Ivy because forgiving seemed to say the abandonment was justified. But forgiving didn't erase the wounded teenager nestled deep within her psyche. Still, it lifted a weight, brought relief and restoration. Ivy was back, and she was no longer alone.

"Who do you think our father was?" Ivy tossed her empty water bottle into the box Asia set aside for recycling. "Or is?"

"Hard to say. Physically we're carbon copies of Veronica, so our father could be any man in Sumter or any one of the surrounding counties." Asia set her bottle on the table.

"What if he only traveled here once a month to pay her?"

"I don't think that's how it was." Asia picked up the stack of photos. "There's a certain feeling of… intimacy in these. Gives me the impression he was here. That he knew us somehow."

Asia gathered the photos. A shot of Ivy in her cheerleading uniform rested on the top. "I always thought you and Martina Collins were the best on the squad." She held the photo up to Ivy. "Do you remember which game this was?"

Ivy puzzled over the snapshot. "Not a clue. I can't tell if this was taken at a home or away game. All you can see is me." She took the photo. "I did love cheering at those games. Most of the girls on the squad stayed firmly rooted on my last nerve, though."

"I thought they were your best friends. Y'all ate lunch together every day, went to the mall weekends, even dated the same boys."

Ivy took the photo and dropped it onto the tarp. "I wanted to be popular. Those girls determined who occupied the best places on the social ladder. I charmed them and put up with their nonsense to get what I wanted. Simple high school politics."

The next photo showed Asia in her blue-and-white band uniform. She chuckled as she ran her finger across the image. "Those uniforms were so awful. We looked like little soldiers in cheap polyester. Everybody had heat rashes after the games until it cooled down in

November."

Ivy pointed to the image. "Look at all those medals on your chest. I used to brag to the cheer squad about you always winning at solos and ensembles competition."

Asia turned to her. "You bragged about me to your cheerleader friends?"

"You bet I did. Every time they squawked about you being a band geek, I'd brag how smart you were and how many medals you'd won." She patted Asia's shoulder. "I remember you sounded like a horse with jingle bells on the reins. You were like some decorated war hero."

Asia sifted through the rest of the photos. "Do you want to look at any more of these? I'm not really interested in seeing any of the others."

Ivy peered over her shoulder. "They aren't bad memories. But I'll admit I've got a queasy feeling in my stomach knowing some strange guy was watching me all those years."

"Me too." Along with creeping shivers skittering down her back and the impulse to run to the window and see if the man still watched.

"What if he had other kids?" Incredulity stirred in Ivy's wide-eyed grimace. "We might have gone to school with them, sat next to them." She wrinkled her nose in disgust. "What if we dated our missing brother, accidentally?" She feigned gagging.

Asia wiped her hands. "I never dated anyone here. And I think we would have recognized similarities in another guy."

Ivy cringed. "You hear about this stuff happening all the time. People get married, then find—"

"Stop it. The only place you hear about those things is on sordid talk shows and sleazy magazines." Asia put the photos back on the tarp. "This is driving me crazy."

"It's not a drive, it's a short putt."

"*What?*"

"It's an old golfing joke. Denney uses it on the boys all the time."

Asia mouthed an *okay.*

"I know you're close to putting this together, but maybe we should take a break, go get some sweet tea or lemonade at Shelby's. Anything to get out of this house." Ivy gestured at the door.

"I'll grab my purse. Location breaks help me think. Meet you at the car."

While they headed down the driveway, Asia watched the empty lot next to Veronica's. Mounds of dirt sat piled against the flimsy barbed-wire fence rimming the property. A stack of rocks the size of kickballs lined the fence. Those rocks were the bane of every farmer's existence in this part of Sumter County. They sat hidden beneath the topsoil, out of sight. Mr. Gannet swore they waited there, plotting to shatter chunks from plow blades.

They resembled the ones in the money bag. Those rocks were found predominantly in Veronica's area of the county, which offered one solution to the mystery. She probably swiped hers from the lot next door to savor the satisfaction of taking another's private property.

A tap from Ivy brought Asia back to the present. She bobbed her head toward the lane. A black truck barreled from the highway in a white cloud of limestone dust.

Asia leaned forward. "Nolan."

"Yep." Ivy slid the gearshift into park. He drove alongside them and rolled down his window. Judging by the hard lines around his mouth, the purpose of his visit went beyond friendly.

Ivy powered down the driver's side window. "Hey, Nolan." He'd left the motor running, and Ivy had to yell to be heard over the rattling of his diesel engine.

"My wife just called me. And yeah, I know she's not supposed to. But we all go way back so … Anyway, she wanted you two to know that your … Veronica took a turn for the worse."

"And?" Ivy asked.

"She said the doctors don't expect her to last much longer."

CHAPTER 28

Veronica hovered at death's door. Asia had waited her entire life to hear those words. When she was six, she wished God would take Veronica away and send Ivy and her a new family. A loving family. But God hadn't answered then. Now death had only to claim Veronica.

The news should have brought peace and relief. Instead Asia's gut sat empty, barren of anything other than shock and skepticism. Part of her always believed Veronica would outlive her and Ivy, would be at their funerals to mock and heckle.

The location break to Shelby's had been shattered by Nolan's news. When he finished delivering the message, he backed his truck to 301 and headed in the opposite direction. Without a word, Ivy shoved the rental car in reverse, and they went back to the house.

They lay on their beds silently until Ivy announced she was starving and would track down dinner. She left without asking Asia to ride along.

The silence pressed in around her, triggered her conscience. Should she feel remorse? Honor Veronica's memory somehow? That's what normal people did when a family member passed. Especially a mother. But how did one honor a woman who possessed no redeeming qualities? Asia pressed the heels of her hands into her temples.

After some time, Ivy bustled back into the room as thunder rumbled outside, her hands filled with takeout bags. "Got back just before the rain." A flash of lightning lit up the window.

"How long has it been storming?" Asia wiggled out of her sleeping bag.

"It followed me here. The clouds rolled in as I left the restaurant." Ivy unpacked the bags, set the food on the table. The smell of grilled cheese sandwiches wafted through the room. She held up a handful of napkins. "I asked for extra." She placed a large pile by Asia.

Asia's stomach growled as Ivy reached into the bag and brought out a Styrofoam container. "Hot tomato soup. It's still your favorite, right?"

"Yes." Asia sat at the table.

"I picked up sandwiches, too. Make sure you eat one. I shouldn't have let you skip lunch. You need all the calories you can get."

Asia unwrapped one of the sandwiches while Ivy went for paper plates, then, after Ivy returned, held the sandwich in the air for approval. Ivy winked and passed her a plate before she sat down.

"With the weather coming in, I stopped at the nearest restaurant. Thought soup and sandwiches were good for a night like this."

After Nolan's announcement earlier, *nothing* was suited to a night like this. Asia's mouth had gone desert-dry the moment he shared Veronica's status. The cottony coat still hung on her tongue. But she said, "Good thinking."

Asia lifted the lid from her soup. The steaming red liquid smelled enticing, but her stomach refused to get on board with her nose. She spooned a small mouthful, worked to swallow. Her throat clenched as if she'd sucked in bitter medicine.

Ivy separated the halves of her sandwich, then opened her own soup. "Any new ideas about the father thing?" She stuck a triangular end of the sandwich into the soup, then tapped it against the bowl's rim.

"Nothing." After Nolan's announcement, all thoughts scattered like dried leaves in the wind and she couldn't rake them together.

Ivy swallowed a bite. "What do you think of Nolan's news?"

Asia nibbled from her sandwich. The bread tasted like buttered sawdust and she wondered fleetingly as she chewed if Ivy's way made it better. She swallowed. "I don't know."

"Seems things will be over soon and we can go back home." Ivy dunked her sandwich in her soup again, then took a bite.

Home. The mention of the word brought Asia an instant longing for mountains and the lightning bugs that dotted the nights. She loved when Russ offered to go driving after dark, searching for them. They'd spent hours sitting in his truck watching the light show in a cozy silence.

She shivered. Was it acceptable that she wanted to think on happy memories of home while the woman who brought her into the world lay dying alone in the hospital? "What do you think we should do about Veronica?"

Ivy put down her last bit of sandwich. "Nothing. Things are coming to an end. We'll contact Ms. Browne, have her settle the estate, pay bills ... or whatever."

"That's not what I'm talking about."

"What else is there?"

"Her funeral."

"We'll tell Ms. Browne to handle that too. Maybe you should start a new list."

Asia tried to get another spoonful of soup but found the container empty. She'd eaten the entire awful meal and remembered none of it. "We can't pawn that off on Ms. Browne." She covered the container with the lid.

Ivy dabbed her mouth with a napkin. "Why not? If we hadn't come back, she would have handled it anyway."

"But we did come back. We need to do what's right by Veronica, Ivy."

Ivy wadded her napkin into a ball and dropped it on the table. "Fine. We'll have her cremated."

"Ivy."

"What?"

"That sounds so heartless. And cold."

"*Veronica* was heartless and cold. It suits her." She gathered the trash from her meal and put it in the takeout bag. "On the good side, all that loot stuffed in the hole in the wall will more than cover the expenses."

Asia added her own trash to the bag. "I think we should ask Ms. Browne if Veronica left instructions for her funeral."

"If she did, they're probably morbid and horrible."

"Whatever they are, we need to honor them."

"Why?"

"Because she was our—"

Ivy held up one finger. "Only through biology. I don't think that obligates us to do anything."

"We can't do nothing."

"We'll send flowers." She gathered their trash and dropped the overflowing bag into the garbage.

Asia moved to her sleeping bag and watched the raindrops dotting the window. She pictured a hospital room, the beeping of the monitors, the glint of lights on the tubes and equipment. And Veronica lying in a bed. Alone and dying. What she deserved, after the life she lived.

"Ivy?"

"What?"

"I think we should go see her. Before it's over."

"I think you're nuts." Ivy picked up her phone. "I'm going to see if this weather is supposed to last all night."

Asia rubbed chills from her arms. "It's the right thing to do."

"For daughters of normal mothers."

Asia fell silent. Normal mothers. The types who tucked kids in with stories and protected their babies with mother-bear love. She saw the type at parent nights.

Veronica had done none of these. Ivy was right, normal mothers deserved real funerals.

But what did Veronica deserve?

Asia lay back on her sleeping bag. She rolled over and rubbed her cheek against her pillowcase as Ivy slid her phone in her purse.

"I'm taking a shower and then I think I'll go on to bed. I'm tired."

Asia squirmed. Of course, Ivy could think of going to sleep with a clear conscience. But Asia couldn't. Visions of Veronica lying alone in that hospital room nagged worse than a throbbing tooth.

Never in her life did she remember Veronica voicing fear, acting anxious or worried. She was always a picture of eerie calm in complete control of everything.

But now, machines and hospital personnel ruled her. She lay in a bed, unable to control anything, including her own body. Completely at the mercy of those around her. Like a great dragon who suddenly finds itself dewinged and declawed, captured by the people it once hunted.

Once, when Asia was little, she wondered if monsters got scared. She decided they must, because there was always a bigger one waiting to prey on the smaller.

Every human feared something.

But was Veronica human enough to fear anything?

CHAPTER 29

Asia finger-traced the rim of a Styrofoam cup. Drifting steam curled in ghostly wisps from her hot tea. A half-eaten blueberry bagel lay on a napkin. Her growling stomach presented no match to her swirling brain. She crumpled the bagel into the trash.

Ivy's plate sat empty. "These pancakes are laying like bricks today. I'd complain to the cook if I weren't ... the cook." She'd inhaled five pancakes and two pieces of bacon, all drizzled with maple syrup. And she would probably never gain an ounce. Ivy drained the last of her coffee. "I have an idea about what to do today."

Asia waved away Ivy's offering of a banana. "We have to keep trying to unravel the message behind the clues." Her brain needed a rest. All night her mind had jumped between the unsolved mystery of the house and guilt over not going to the hospital.

Ivy pressed on. "I thought we might do better if we took a day off. Maybe go shopping in Ocala. Or go to the flea market in Webster. There's always Dade Park, you used to love walking the nature trails there, or the battle trail. We could even head over to Mt. Dora for lunch. Ever been to the Windsor Rose Tea Room?"

"No. And I don't want to go."

Ivy cleared away her breakfast dishes and stopped short at the kitchen door. "Let's take the jewelry to a pawn shop, the clothes to a local charity, and throw out the items no one would want. We'll give Ms. Browne the money and the okay to handle the funeral. And go home happy."

Asia leaned forward. "We can't do that."

Ivy's brows lowered. "Why not? We've cleaned out the trash-pit house, found all her little secrets. It's not our fault we can't decipher her twisted clues."

"We have to see this to the end. We're on the edge of finding answers—"

"I don't care who our father is. Never did. Throw out everything, including the money. Then I can go home to my husband and our boys."

"Ivy, we have to finish this, including burying her when the time comes."

The dirty dishes in Ivy's hands shook. A fork slipped from a plate and clattered on the floor. "I owe her nothing, Asia. The only thing she ever did for me was scramble my brain so badly I almost killed myself." She inclined her head at Asia. "And she did the same thing to you." Ivy hurried through the door. The sound of dishes being dropped into the cavernous farmhouse sink echoed to the living room.

When she returned she plopped down at the table. "Don't let that soft heart of yours bleed for her. Go any deeper into this and you'll only get hurt again." She grabbed Asia's hands and flipped them so the scars showed.

Asia slipped free and wiped her hands. "Did you ever stop to consider we might heal if we took control of this?"

"I don't need to heal. I'm. Just. Fine. And, I think the fact that we have connected again will help you. Don't you?"

Asia washed her hands again. "No."

The corners of Ivy's mouth drooped. "Wow. What a sucker punch to the gut."

"I didn't mean being with you won't help. I don't think you're completely over this either."

Ivy straightened in her chair. She squared her shoulders. "What's that supposed to mean?"

"Because even though she's in a coma and dying, you won't face her."

"I'm not afraid. I just don't *want* to."

"She was—*is*—our mother. We should visit before she dies."

"What are you ..." Understanding flamed and Ivy went on. "You mean the honor thing, don't you? We obeyed that commandment by not killing her when we were younger."

"Ivy, what an awful thing to say. Even about Veronica."

"Whatever." Ivy stormed to her purse and dug deep into the main compartment. She stomped to the table and slammed the rental car key and fob on the surface. "There."

Asia drew back from them as if they were a nest of hornets. "What are you doing?"

"Go see her. You want to, right?"

"No."

"Then how are *you* going to honor her without facing her one more time?" Her voice boomed off the walls. "I may not know my literature like you," she said, "but I do remember the hero's victory comes after facing the enemy one last time. What are you aiming to gain by being kind to her at the end?" She marched to the bathroom and stood in the doorway. "At least you'll be in the best place when you have your panic attack." She slammed the door.

Round one of Hurricane Ivy had begun, followed by rattling curtain rings and water flowing in the shower. A half minute later, Ivy opened the door and walked out. "This idea of yours stinks."

She marched to her suitcase and collected clean clothes. She stuffed them under her arm, stomped back to the bathroom, and slammed the door again.

Asia rubbed her temples. Her sister's tantrums should come with a severe storm warning. This was obviously the eye, when a person could get lulled in by the quiet only to be blasted by the more powerful backside of the storm.

Ivy opened the door again. "Didn't you tell me last night that you were on your longest streak without a panic attack? This will push you over the edge. Think of yourself, Asia. She won't know you're there. Stop being over-nice." She jerked her chin then yanked the door shut.

Asia crumpled onto her bed. Ivy was right; her streak was in jeopardy if she went to the hospital and she would have sacrificed her one fragile victory over Veronica.

She pounded her fist against the silky tufts on her sleeping bag. What had she been thinking? Yes, Ivy was not only right, but 100 percent right. She shouldn't go. Just thinking about Veronica for more than a minute brought on knee-knocking panic attacks. Furthermore, going to an ICU in a hospital? A huge, institutional petri dish incubating MRSA and antibiotic-resistant everything.

And the conditions to earn the money didn't dictate visiting Veronica.

But the thoughts continued hounding her.

All night her mind had nagged that mothers should be honored in death, no matter how horrible they had been. Each time she'd talked herself from the idea it swooped around and pecked at her until she relented and made plans to go.

The shower stopped. Asia rose from the bed, snatched the key fob and her purse, then scooted out the door. She possessed no stamina for a second storm front.

She held certain the true source of the persistent urging didn't come from her own mind. The push resembled the one that brought her to Florida.

God was sending her to face Veronica.

Minutes later, she maneuvered onto the highway. Her mind drifted as trees and fences streamed past. She should have taken Ivy's advice. Veronica lay in a coma, wouldn't recognize her presence. This visit *wouldn't* be honoring her. True, but showing up at the hospital absolved Asia of guilt. In essence, the visit was more about her than Veronica and should be abandoned because hypocrisy drove the true motive. She could go back to the house, order flowers, and send them to the room. Colorful blooms demonstrated care. Any florist would attest to that.

Yes, she would turn around, forget the visit, and order flowers.

She slowed to a stop at a traffic light. By now Ivy must be getting dressed and stewing over her leaving. A nearby gas station offered a spacious parking lot with room to turn around. Instead, she pressed the accelerator and merged onto the interstate.

A semi plowed past her; its turbulence rocked the car. Other vehicles zoomed by until she drove alone, and the pack raced ahead of her. Fine and good. She preferred following the speed limit. Lower speeds increased gas mileage and decreased chances of accidents. Plus, her heart rabbit-raced behind her ribs, and pulling over to ward off an attack seemed imminent.

She gripped the steering wheel with sweating palms. *Breathe ... Relax ... Breathe ...*

Asia took the next exit, then slowed as the lane narrowed to a two-lane country road. Pine-covered bumps swelled the landscape. Hills to Floridians, but not so to her Tennessee-seasoned mindset. Cows grazed on some, others bore homes with swing sets out front or flowering gardens dressed in bright summer blooms. Nice, simple little homes far away from everything. Pure Sumter County. The road ended at a stoplight, then merged onto Highway 27.

A blue, rectangular sign stood to her right. She read the words.

Ellis Memorial Hospital 5 Miles.

Veronica's hospital.

Breathe ... Relax ... Breathe ...

CHAPTER 30

Asia stood before the elevator doors in the hospital lobby. Her phone buzzed. She retrieved it and checked the screen. Ivy. Asia pressed the icon, then read the message.

Where are you?

Ivy's text offered a welcomed delay in going to Veronica's floor. Asia surveyed the nearby sitting areas for empty chairs. Of the four to choose from, she picked one with vinyl cushions, far away from the elevator doors.

After wiping the seat and back clean, she sat and answered Ivy's message.

Ellis Memorial. Text you when I'm leaving. Thanks for checking in.

Ivy responded. *Still think this is nuts.*

It is, Asia answered, then shut off her phone.

Ivy failed to understand. Her life thrived like well-tended roses. But Asia's . . .

She slid her phone into her purse. Like the moon vines, a person must prune the bad memories choking the joy from life. If facing Veronica one last time helped her do this, then she could tolerate being a little nuts.

She also needed to find the hospital directory. After a quick perusal of the lobby, she found it by the elevators.

ICU was located on the third floor. She pushed the UP button and waited. Then, once inside the carriage, she scanned the double row of buttons and jabbed at the 3. The car jiggled and moaned as it headed upward. Asia leaned against the back wall for support rather than grasping the handrail. She shuddered to think how many fingers had wrapped around those shiny, silver breeding grounds for every germ living in the hospital.

Asia jumped as soon as the doors opened. White walls with wooden handrails came into view and that "hospital" smell permeated her sinuses. She entered a slender hallway banked by a wide, glass window encasing a nurse's station. Nurses dressed in pastel scrubs bustled about behind the glass. A sign on the wall to the right of the window displayed instructions for visitors on allowed visitation allotments. A buzzer and speaker rested beneath the sign. All visitors were to press the button and wait to be admitted.

Asia's feet rooted to the floor. She could leave without anyone knowing. Ivy would cheer because she'd regained her senses and given up the insane idea of confronting Veronica.

Would Veronica even know she was there?

She'd read about patients in a comatose state and how the deep recesses of their mind remained conscious of things going on around them. One man relayed how he listened to his family say their last goodbyes. He'd mentally screamed to them, tried to tell them not to give up. He shocked his loved ones and doctors when he awoke a few days later.

Yes, somewhere deep within, Veronica would know she was there. And she'd see Asia was the one with enough guts to come and face her. But this wasn't supposed to be about her fortitude. She set her goal to honor her mother. And fulfill the reason for being sent to Florida.

Who was she kidding? This was about trying to close the door on the memories, the images and the fear attached to Veronica. Ivy was right. She was the hero trying to face the enemy one last time, hoping to vanquish her worst foe before death stole away her opportunity.

Wings of fear beat in her stomach as she pressed the call button with her elbow.

The nurse seated at a desk closest to the window looked up, then spoke through a speaker. "May I help you?"

Asia leaned toward the speaker on the wall on her side. "I'm Asia Butler. I'm here to visit Veronica—Veronica Butler."

"One moment." The door buzzed. "You can come in now," the nurse said.

Asia pushed the heavy door open. The typical institutional tile covered the floor, beige colored and speckled with sky-blue dots. Signs matching their hue hung on the wall, inscribed with directions to rooms and reminders to turn off cell phones, but they could have been written in Japanese for all the help they offered. She stared at the words, her mind unable to process any meaning.

A cacophony of noise surrounded her. High- and low-pitched bells and buzzers from the arc of doorways surrounding the circular nurse's station. The voices of nurses and visiting family members blended. A man in blue scrubs pushed a squeaking gurney toward a room.

Men and women entered and exited various rooms. Another man stood nearby, typing on a computer outside a patient's room. Crash carts, unused monitors, IV poles, and carts topped with small laptops lined the walls.

Asia rubbed her arms. One of her students liked to cover her ears when walking through the hallways at school. If she could, Asia would have done the same.

Instead she made her way to the nurse's station. "I'm here to see Veronica Butler."

"Room 413. You'll see her name on the plate outside the room." The nurse glanced at her watch. "You only have about fifteen minutes."

"Okay." As soon as she stepped toward the patient rooms, her body balked. If her feet became any heavier, she'd be stuck standing in the middle of this hallway forever. Soon Veronica's name loomed before her.

Warmth washed over her. Hospitals were supposed to be notoriously cold, but her nerves seemed to be producing their own personal humidity.

Veronica. No more than ten steps away. Asia shuffled toward the nameplate. The symphony of beeps, buzzes, and humming played around her. A male voice floated from the next room, explaining the intricacies of some procedure to family members. Dry, hacking coughs barked from one room. Probably signaled pneumonia, maybe emphysema. A nurse exited the room wearing a mask.

Asia shuddered. She should have asked for a mask. Who knew what germs she inhaled with each breath? If she didn't leave soon, she might join these poor ailing souls.

Run ... Run ... Run ...

But the nameplate with Veronica's name written in black marker loomed. Her lungs tightened.

A young woman with red hair and an elderly woman stooped by age passed by, their arms linked.

"Maybe he's better today, Mimi," the young woman said.

"I keep hoping."

Asia's breath caught in her throat. Everything around her—every sight, every sound, every scent—melded into a hum that echoed until the walls of the corridor spun around her.

Breathe ... Breathe ... Breathe ...

CHAPTER 31

Beyond the doorway, in the gray darkness of a room, lay Veronica.

Asia's lungs constricted; no air flowed. The space around her rolled like lazy waves at the shoreline. She needed to grasp a rail for support, but thoughts of touching any surface brought additional waves of nausea.

Footsteps hurried as a nurse came to her side. The scent of antibacterial gel permeated the air around them. "Are you okay?

"Yes ..." Asia could hardly get the word out.

"Maybe you should sit down in the waiting room." The nurse placed a chilly hand on Asia's arm. "Here, I'll help you."

"No," she panted. "I can't. I—I can't do this."

She read the name neatly printed on the nurse's photo badge hanging from a lanyard. *Nicole.*

"I have to go."

Nicole took her hand. "Are you Asia or Ivy?"

"What?"

"You favor your ... Veronica. I'm ..." Her free hand rested on her chest. "I'm Nolan's wife. He said you and your sister might come by."

Nicole squeezed her hand gently. "I'll go in with you. This place is very overwhelming at first. But it gets easier." She smiled, her entire countenance offering a practiced patience.

Asia backed away. "I can't." She nearly sprinted for the elevator, darting between the computers on their wheeled stands. She hoped the sound of her shoes clicking on the floor didn't disturb the patients, but what could she do? She had to get out, before the listing walls and rolling floor sucked her in. Trapped her here. With Veronica.

She punched the elevator button, again and again. Gasped. Waited. Watching the lighted numbers. The elevator stopped at each floor.

Breathe ...

This was taking too long. She couldn't stay another minute. She pressed the button harder. Pushed and pushed.

Relax ...

The elevator's cable's groaned. Was it breaking down? Dizziness spun her. Dampness soaked her underarms. She searched for the staircase ... no, she shouldn't wander around looking ... that would risk more exposure to germs.

Breathe ...

The arrival bell dinged but the doors remained closed. Asia punched the button. A second ding rang out, but the doors seemed glued together

Panic boiled inside her. She was trapped. What would she do now? She punched the button again ... and again, then she pulled a wipe from her purse, held it to her nose, and inhaled. She pressed the button a final time as pain sliced through her chest and her lungs seized.

She couldn't breathe. A balloon of pain pressed against her ribs.

Breathe ... relax ... breathe ... She would break her streak if the door didn't open soon.

A droplet of sweat trickled down her temple.

The doors rumbled and slid open. Asia staggered inside, colliding with a white-haired woman carrying a plastic grocery bag filled with books. The woman glared, then stepped on Asia's foot as she maneuvered out the doors, which then slid shut behind her. Asia looked at the floor, avoided the stares of the other occupants as the elevator eased downward.

Silent, heavy air seasoned with the breath of those around her, smothered her. She had to get out of there, breathe air not tainted by smells and germs and ...

The numbers ticked down as they neared the first floor. Another chime and the door slid open. She shot from the car. A nearby sign pointed to the exit and she ran to the door. Her knees gave way and she fell, the contents of her purse scattering across the dark-tiled floor.

An elderly gentleman called to her from a nearby check-in desk. "You okay?"

Asia ignored his help and stood. "I'm ... fine."

She grabbed her package of wipes and scrubbed the floor grime from her hands, wallet, sunglasses, and key fob. Twice. She put them back into her purse and cleaned her hands again.

Four wipes were required to clean the length of her capri pants. They were going into the garbage as soon as she got to the house. She'd get Ivy to deposit them while she showered the germs away in the hottest water the shower could produce.

Twice.

Somehow she managed to make it through the lobby doors. They swished closed behind her. Pain cracked in her chest.

Breathe ... breathe ... breathe ... just breathe ...

She hobbled toward the parking garage, pain from her ankle radiating up to her knee. Asia chewed her lip with each step, hoping she didn't draw blood. What a stupid, idiotic idea this was.

Relax ...

Shudders rippled across her back as she stepped out of the heat and into the muggy recesses of the parking garage's first-floor elevator that opened as she approached. Almost as if it had expected her to be there. She pushed the button for the fifth level, then scrubbed her fingertips with a fresh wipe. Thank goodness she'd put a new bottle of antibacterial gel in the car a few days ago. She needed the entire container. Maybe she should stop on the way home for a second bottle to cleanse her hands. And more wipes to scrub away the filth from her fall. There was no three-second rule for hospital floors. Even in the lobby. *Especially* in the lobby.

She'd put Russ's card in her pocket and a corner poked against her leg. She wanted to rub the edge but didn't dare touch it without cleaning her hand. As soon as the doors opened, she stepped out, gritted her teeth against the ache that knifed through her foot. She pointed the key fob at Ivy's car. The flash of head and tail lights became her beacon.

Breathe ... relax ... breathe ...

Asia collapsed into the driver's seat, shut the door, and started the car, allowing the air conditioner to blow hard on her face. After three packages of wipes, she no longer smelled the antiseptic odor of the hospital on her skin. She inhaled the lemony scent of the wipes. The ache in her chest lessened. She drew in a deep breath, held the wipe to her nose again. Counted to two.

Why did this have to be so hard? Colleagues at work, acquaintances at church, they faced nothing like this when a family member died. They grieved, buried their dead, grieved some more, and life went on.

Why was this so difficult?

Because Ivy was right; Veronica brought nothing but pain.

Asia clenched her fists. When would this end? Anger seeded in childhood mushroomed, burning in every inch of her. Why couldn't Veronica *just die?*

This wasn't fair. She bit her lips to block the screams building in her throat.

Die, Veronica.

Asia pummeled the steering wheel. Her pinkies throbbed but she pounded over and over. *Die. Die. Die.*

Footsteps clicked toward a nearby car. Asia took a wipe and washed her face, aware of her audience but not caring. After all, crying in a hospital parking garage was nothing unusual. No one would fault her for red eyes and smeared mascara. But what if they knew the truth? That she sat here, pounding on her steering wheel, wishing her own mother would die?

A car horn blared from somewhere in the garage, the echo startling her. Gas fumes wafted into the interior as another car drove past. Across the way, elevator doors opened and a man and woman stepped out. Spying her, they raised a hand. Asia shivered.

The woman cupped a hand around her mouth. "Are you from

around here?" she asked loudly enough to be heard.

Asia cleared her throat and lowered the window. "I used to be."

"Could you suggest a place to eat nearby?" The woman bent for easier communication but crossed her arms across her middle. "We've been here for over twenty-four hours and we're sick of the hospital food."

Exhaustion clung about her, from her dark-circled eyes to the way she was dressed. She wore no makeup, and her hair was gathered in a no-fuss ponytail. Her husband's scruffy face and mussed hair testified to a lack of sleep.

The woman inclined her head toward the man. "His father's been here for a week. We flew in early yesterday. We don't know this area at all."

Asia hesitated. "I've been gone a long time."

The man took a step closer. "My phone died, and she left hers back in Dad's room. We have no idea where to go. If you can—"

Asia couldn't ignore the woman's pain. Hurt along with love for the man they left back in the hospital shone through. Like a real family. The couple needed more than food. They needed to step away from this cold reality and breathe a little. Asia understood. In her own way, she understood.

She drew a breath before speaking. "If you take a left when you come out of the garage, go about a mile, you'll pass by a mall. There used to be several places to eat around there."

The woman straightened. "Thank you," she said, her face now showing care. "Do you have someone here in the hospital?"

Asia adjusted her seatbelt. "Wish you the best."

The man laced his fingers with the woman's. "Hope all goes well for you, too. Thanks again." As they went away, the man leaned in and kissed the woman's cheek.

Asia slipped the gear to reverse. She was a nice person. Never wanted to hurt anyone. Hated bullies, always supported the underdog. Yet here she sat, in a rental car, wishing her mother would die, while this couple who'd just asked for simple directions no doubt hoped for a better outcome. What kind of person did that? She was supposed to honor her mother, not beg for her demise.

She backed out, then straightened the wheels and put the car in drive as a single thought came to mind: she and Ivy had cleared most of Veronica's poison from their childhood home. Far more labor was required to erase her handiwork from their souls.

CHAPTER 32

Sumter County lay before Asia as she drove home from the hospital. Green, tree-dotted carpets, with various colors of cows and horses spread across the landscape. The kind of place writers celebrated. Virgin countryside trying to resist the bustling push of modernization from developers like Nolan. Retirees from up north streamed here all year, soaking up sunshine and enjoying trees covered in leaves. She'd seen some of them at Shelby's, sporting t-shirts that read "I Love Sumter."

Such a stupid slogan. She'd never celebrate this county. Every blade of grass, each bellowing cow, or graying fencepost rotting in the sun, reminded her of Veronica.

Coming back was a mistake. No matter how hard she cleaned out the house, Veronica remained cemented in her mind. The memories seared into her, never to be washed away. She'd come here with a hopeless cause.

Asia drove through a twisting curve, mindlessly watching the trees go by until a house to the left caught her eye. The two-storied portico with snow-white columns tripped a memory. She checked the rearview mirror. No cars in sight. She made a U-turn and parked in the ditch bordering the front of the property that was Nolan's childhood home. When she was younger, the house was one of the largest in the county, broadcasting the Delong name and status to all who drove by. The grounds still flowered with blankets of multicolored blooms and golf course-perfect grass. Nolan's mother was a noted gardener, and rumor once had it that she'd actually developed and patented a type of rose.

A fountain made from the same rocks that plagued the local farmers sat behind a white picket fence. The structure stretched in a pyramid three rows high. Water spouted from the top and folded over like the branches of a willow.

Asia rolled down the window, listened to the steady hissing as the water flowed. The rocks lay in neat rows, stacked and positioned however needed to keep the base in manicured layers. Her focus trailed to the top row, almost hidden by the spray of the water. She scowled, then leaned farther out the window. "No, she couldn't have …" Asia squinted, adjusted her focus, killed the engine. "There's no way …"

She got out of the car but left her door open. The grass swished around her ankles as she sneaked to the gateposts flanking each side of the driveway. No, her mind hadn't deceived her. She hurried back to the car and grabbed her phone.

Asia watched the front door of the house for signs that anyone noticed her trespassing, but there were none. She crept up the driveway to the edge of the lawn, a few feet from the fountain. Taking the picture would have been much easier had her hands not shook so hard. She took three, ensuring she got the shot she wanted. *Needed.*

The front door opened. A woman in light-pink scrubs stuck her head through the narrow opening. "May I help you?" she asked and Asia ran for the car, then tumbled into the driver's seat, started the engine, and backed into the highway as the woman still watched from the doorway. Hopefully she couldn't see the license plate, wouldn't think to write down the number and call the police. Could the police track a rental car? She pressed the accelerator, checking the rearview mirror for signs of a local police car, then drew in a breath, counted to two, exhaled. Checked the rearview mirror. Twice. Her common sense screamed to stop worrying about a police pursuit, but nerves prodded her to keep checking.

Her heartbeat drummed. At the next stop sign, Asia glanced at the console where her phone lay in its black-screened sleep mode. She'd stumbled on a key piece to Veronica's puzzle. A piece that Ivy needed to see. She squeezed the steering wheel.

Asia drove on until she spied the sign for Shady Brook Park. She took a right into the park's entrance and followed the winding, narrow road to the parking lot, then motored into an empty space covered by a canopy of massive boughs from a nearby water oak. After grabbing her phone, she left the car and walked to the old swimming hole. Tangles of oaks shaded the area when she was a kid, with cypress knees and tufts of thick, bright green weeds rimming the bank. One of the giant oaks she remembered along with the rope swing tied to one of its limbs was now gone. She'd loved that swing.

With trembling fingers, she swiped her phone to life. The last picture of the Delong's fountain greeted her. Asia pressed the text button. Even with fumbling fingers, she managed to send the message.

Heading to house. Have something to show you. You aren't going to believe this.

She pressed send and waited until a jingle announced Ivy's response.

Be still my heart, how will I survive it? A picture of a stack of rocks.

Asia looked back at the gaping space where the tree once stood. When she was young, she'd grabbed hold of the rope, jumped from the safety of the oak's bough, swung in wild arcs, fearless of the tea-colored water below, and let go. Now, she sucked in a deep breath in an involuntary attempt to survive. Inhaled the earthy, metallic scent of the water, the trees, and the sour mud on the bank. Counted two. Texted Ivy. *Be ready.*

Ivy's answer beeped. *Always ready.*

"We'll see," Asia muttered, then got back in the car. Sunlight streaming through the trees danced along the hood of Ivy's rental car as she exited the park and headed for Veronica's. She'd forgotten how she loved *this* little slice of the county. After pulling into the driveway and positioning the car with its nose toward the house, she killed the engine, pushed open the driver's door, and rushed into the living room. Ivy lay on her bed, legs stretched straight, wiggling her feet in time with music playing on her phone. "I hope you're carrying a bag full of burgers and fries with you." She sat up. "And a chocolate milkshake. I'm starving."

Asia took out her phone. "It's only twelve thirty. Why didn't you cook for yourself?"

"I cleaned up breakfast. Now I want some restaurant food since I've been trapped here all morning." She pointed at Asia. "You owe me."

Asia joined Ivy on her bed. "Later. You have to see this." She waved her phone at Ivy. "Take a look at this."

Ivy waved it away. "Not until I eat."

"But this is—"

Ivy pointed to her face. "This is my 'Mom's-done-talking' look."

"But—"

Ivy held up a hand. "Eat first. Then listen." She crossed her arms on her chest.

"Fine." Asia swiped to Google and called the pizza parlor she'd seen near the interstate. "Delivery please." She drew in a deep breath. "One medium cheese pizza and an order of your garlic bread. Also, extra marinara dipping sauce." She gave Veronica's address, then hung up. "Satisfied?"

"You said you hated pizza."

"I said I didn't eat it, not that I hated it."

"What's the difference?"

"The difference is that it can be delivered here, and we can eat and talk in private."

"What's the big secret? No one here cares about anything we have to say."

Asia slid her finger over her phone's screen until the fountain pictures appeared. "This is big. And we need to talk with no other ears around."

CHAPTER 33

IVY NEEDED A WAY to get off this crazy train. Asia's brain seemed to be running on lunatic fumes, about ready to jump the track, and her stomach growled to an almost embarrassing degree. "How long till the pizza gets here?"

Asia checked her watched. "Fifteen minutes."

Ivy motioned to Asia's phone. "Now that I know food is on the way you can blow my mind with your big discovery."

Asia held the phone down where they could both see the screen. "I took this picture today at Nolan's parents' house."

"Why on earth were you at Nolan's? I thought you went to see Veronica."

Asia's cheeks reddened and she kept her face toward the screen so she didn't have to meet Ivy's eyes with her own. "I couldn't do it. Freaked out when I saw her room. I took backroads home to calm my nerves and somehow ended up at Nolan's, where I took *this* picture," she said, pointing.

"You mean to tell me you zoomed right up in their driveway and started taking pictures like some nutball tourist?"

"No. It wasn't like that. I stopped in the ditch in front—"

"Like a stalker."

"No." Asia said through clamped teeth. Now she raised her eyes with a look that said *get your attention off the trip to the hospital an• the pizza delivery and back to the issue at hand.* Ivy wondered if this was a look she often gave her students, one much like her "Mom's-not-playing-now" look. "I can't explain why, but I just wanted to look at the house."

Ivy exhaled through pursed lips. Asia always loved the Delong house.

Once, when Asia couldn't have been more than seven or eight, a hand-drawn picture of the home slipped out of her folder one morning before school. The paper floated feather-light to the floor, picture side up. Naturally Veronica happened to be standing there and picked up the drawing.

Asia's face shaded to ghost white.

Ivy would never forget how the corners of Veronica's mouth curled like leaves dying in too-hot sun. She held the picture up to Asia. "Did you draw this?" she asked, and Asia had stood dead still.

Veronica bent eye level with Asia. She crumpled the picture into a tight ball and threw it into the nearby trash can. She leaned in, nose to nose with her youngest daughter. She spoke in a hissing whisper. "Don't dream about that house, Asia. They'll never welcome you there."

Ivy motioned to the photo on Asia's phone. "The Delong's rock fountain. They've had that for what, forty years? Big surprise."

"Look closer." Asia tapped the screen and enlarged the picture. "At the rocks."

"So what? They're like all the other billions of rocks in Sumter County."

"Look at its construction. Each row has the same number of rocks," Asia pointed to the screen. "Except this top one. See this space between the row and the fall of the water?"

Ivy leaned in, squinted. She saw rocks with water flowing over them. Again, no surprises. "And what am I supposed to be seeing?"

"The space at the top, just beneath the water line. Five rocks are missing."

Ivy took a second look. Now that Asia singled the image out, she did notice extra space. "Maybe they fell off. Water eroded them."

"I saw the fountain close-up, Ivy. I parked in the Delongs' driveway and studied the rocks." Asia held her hands apart, pantomiming a ball shape. "They're about the size of a bowling ball."

Ivy gasped. "The rocks ... in the bag of money."

Asia nodded. "Veronica took them from the Delongs' fountain."

"Makes sense. Veronica always hated Cynthia Delong. She probably took them to irritate her."

"I think there's more to the story than that." Asia got up and retrieved the list she'd been creating on the yellow legal pad. "Let me show you."

Ivy pulled her sister down beside her. "Enlighten me, Madam Detective."

Asia smoothed her list. "Veronica hated Cynthia Delong."

Ivy shrugged. "She hated everybody."

"I believe there was another reason. Jealousy."

"Why would Veronica be jealous of Cynthia Delong?"

A knock sounded at the door. Asia and Ivy both jumped. "Pizza delivery," a muffled voice called.

Ivy rubbed her stomach. "Thank goodness. I'm about to pass out."

Asia took her wallet from her purse. "Does *anything* affect your appetite?"

"Morning sickness."

The delivery man knocked again. Asia hurried and paid their bill then brought the pizza and other items to the table. Aromas of warm crust, parmesan cheese, and buttery garlic wafted between them. Ivy's stomach growled again. Her breakfast digested long ago. She needed calories.

But Asia was onto something. Something big.

She opened the box before Asia could set it down. "Yum." She took a piece from the carton. Long strings of cheese stretched from the pie as she pulled away her slice. "This is fresh." She motioned to Asia. "I know you haven't eaten all day. I want to see you eat at least two slices."

"I'm not hungry." Asia set the pizza box on the tabletop.

"Eat, or I'll stuff slices down you." Ivy gestured toward the kitchen. "I restocked the fridge with bottled water while you were gone. Get me one?"

Asia returned with two bottles. She wiped each with a napkin, then handed one to Ivy.

Ivy sat back in her chair, sent Asia a not-going-to-cooperate eye roll before she spoke. "I know you're having a breakthrough here. But I will not look at another item on that list until you've eaten."

Asia raised her hands to plead. "We can eat and talk."

Ivy squared her shoulders. "Nope. I won't listen to another word until you've eaten. Two pieces." Because her little sister could not afford to skip any more meals.

Asia cleaned her hands then lifted a slice and nibbled on the pointy end.

Silence settled as they ate. Ivy watched her sister down each bite, happy that Asia fell into old habits and allowed herself to be bossed into compliance. When she finished her first slice, she wiped her hands clean. She held them out to Ivy. "All done. Now may I go on?"

"I said *two* slices." Ivy inclined her head toward the pizza box. "Piece number two is waiting."

After much under-the-breath muttering, Asia clomped to the box and took another slice. She mumbled as she plopped in a chair, the only intelligible words being "strength" and "slap her silly."

"I worry about you because I care." Ivy made a heart shape with her fingers over her chest.

Asia narrowed her eyes at her, then dramatically bit into the slice, chewed, and swallowed her final bite before washing the reddish-hued grease from her fingers. Twice. "Right. *Now* may I continue?"

"Go." Ivy took a second slice.

"Veronica hated Cynthia for another reason. I think Bill Delong was her—"

A wad of pizza stuck in Ivy's throat. The glob swelled, cutting off her ability to breathe, gluing itself to her esophagus. She tried swallowing, but the dough stayed. Asia pounded on her back. Coughing and sputtering, Ivy finally forced the dough ball free and spat into a napkin. She downed a mouthful of water. The cold liquid landed in her stomach like lead. She threw the rest of her pizza slice into the garbage.

"*Bill Delong*? ... Why?" Ivy's words came out in a graveled whisper. She tipped the bottle for another drink.

Asia returned to her chair. "Think about it. The rocks came from his fountain. He owned this house. At the time, there were no other neighbors around so he could come and go as he pleased without notice." She shrugged. "For that matter, he could be seen visiting once a month—" She curved her fingers into air quotes. "— to collect rent."

"The clothes and jewelry. He must have cooked the books and hid the money he spent on Veronica from Cynthia."

"He could skim off a little here and there, then use the cash on Veronica. She would have loved the underhanded scheming that went into her gifts."

"Better trophies."

Asia mimed a check in the air. "Exactly."

Ivy closed the pizza box. "Bill Delong." She laid the bag of uneaten garlic bread on top, along with the marinara sauce. "I'll put these in the fridge in a minute." Her appetite had died. If Asia's suspicions held up, Veronica had corrupted one of the most upstanding, well-respected men in the community. She'd wormed her way between Bill Delong, Cynthia, and Nolan. Ivy's gut churned worse than it did after riding the Scrambler at the Washington State Fair. Had Cynthia and Nolan waited at home, wondering where Bill was while he stole time with Veronica? Or worse, did they know what he was doing, and with whom? He'd gone on trips, divided his heart between Nolan, Cynthia, and Veronica when choosing souvenirs to bring home to his loved ones. Souvenirs like the little Empire State Building.

A new revelation cramped Ivy's stomach. If Nolan knew, that would explain his hurry to bulldoze Veronica's house. He wanted to destroy all traces of the woman who'd infiltrated his family.

Asia interrupted her thoughts. "Do you think Cynthia and Nolan know?"

The question hovered in the air, waiting.

Ivy pressed a finger into her temple. "I was just thinking about that. Maybe it wasn't Bill. What about Dewitt the Twit? He hung around like a stray cat. Maybe he was D?"

The mention of Dewitt made Asia wrinkle her nose as if she'd smelled something rotten. "He was too poor to afford all those gifts and chronically jobless. No money to pass on to Veronica."

"You're right. When would he have reason to visit New York City?"

Ivy laced her fingers together into a single fist. She rested her chin on them. "It does make sense." She pointed to the tarp. "You stick Bill Delong in the middle of all those pieces and the puzzle comes together. The house, the money, the clothes, the jewelry, the knick-knacks like the Empire State Building—"

Asia dipped her chin. "And why Nolan's mom had one just like it."

"This is *really* what she wanted when she demanded we clean the house. To drown us in sleazy drama." Ivy raked her hair from her face. A coming headache pulsed in her temples.

"It doesn't explain the suitcases or those pictures of us, though."

"I don't know about those suitcases, but I'm sure she talked Bill Delong into taking the photos. He would have been at those games to watch Nolan play. Another power play. Eating up the thrill of making a man pay attention to her kids instead of his own."

Asia crumpled the final bites of her pizza into her napkin and dropped the remnants into the trash. "Should we talk to Nolan?" she asked as she crossed the room and sat on her bed.

Ivy grabbed her wallet. She slid Nolan's business card from a slot next to her credit cards. She'd almost tossed the card in the garbage, but her business sense stopped her. Never throw away a contact or network opportunity. But that was business. This was *Veronica.*

Ivy looked up as Asia smoothed a tiny wrinkle from her sleeping bag. "What are you thinking, Asia?"

"I don't know ... *should* we tell Nolan?"

Ivy read Nolan's name on his card, neatly printed in black letters to the right of his company logo. "It's not every day you get to walk up to your childhood friend and say, 'Hey your dad and our mom had a thing.'" She looked at Asia. "Whether he knows or not, we don't *have* to tell him that *we* know."

"Maybe it's best we don't."

Ivy's mouth fell open. "*You're* willing to lie?"

Asia bit her lip. "Omit."

Ivy's insides twitched. "That's not like you at all. What's brewing in your head, Asia?"

Asia met Ivy with the same expression she held on prom night, right before she left the bathroom to distract Veronica. A blend of terror and gut-stirring revulsion. "How messy do you think this is going to get?"

Ivy's insides lashed with the same emotions her little sister expressed.

"What do we do, Ivy?"

Ivy thought for a moment, her mom sense and her business sense rising until they joined forces. If they came right out and told Nolan what they knew—what they suspected—then the next steps could be properly taken. If they didn't, the nightmare—Veronica's nightmare—would go on forever. "Clean up this food and get out of this house for a while. Maybe drive to Leesburg and go see a movie. Get to bed early tonight. Then, tomorrow I'll drive us to Nolan's." She put Nolan's card back in the slot. "We're ending this."

CHAPTER 34

Asia stared at the flowers flanking the porch of the Delongs'—and now Nolan's—house. The last time she and Ivy stood together in the Delongs' yard, the visit ended with the sisters running away. Her stomach dropped. Nothing was worse than visiting a place where you weren't welcomed.

When they were younger—she had been only five—Nolan hatched a plan during church. As the choir sang the final stanza of "I Surrender All," and while struggling to compete with the flashes of lightning and thunder outside, Asia watched him pass a note to his mother written in his seven-year-old scribble on the church bulletin. Cynthia read the message, then met her son's upturned face. After a long pause, she agreed. Nolan clasped his hands together prayer-style, mouthed, "Thank you, Mama" and flashed a beaming face to Asia and Ivy.

He'd cajoled Cynthia into giving her and Ivy a ride home to protect them from the storm. While the three of them whispered in the leather-bound back seat of his mother's car, Nolan extended an invitation to come and play at his house the following day.

She and Ivy had risen early that Monday morning. They washed their faces and put on clothes they'd worn after church the day before. Veronica hadn't done the laundry in days and those outfits had the fewest stains. Asia remembered breakfasting on plain toast and flat soda, the only food left in the house other than a box of macaroni. They'd jogged through the phlox-covered ditch along the highway, excitement raising the pitch of their voices as they talked of the fun they could have in Nolan's big house. But the fun died as soon as they reached the edge of the yard. Cynthia Delong stepped out the front door and called to them. "You girls go on back home." She waited, watched from the porch that wrapped around the entire first story of the house.

"Go home or I'll call Mr. Delong." A quick nod of her head emphasized her words.

Nolan had told them once that his mother had won a beauty pageant. Asia's five-year-old self believed him as she watched his mother descend the steps to the yard with her head high and her back straight.

"Nolan can't play with you girls today. Go on, now." She waved her hands as if shooing away two stray dogs.

Asia had grabbed Ivy's hand and taken off at a full run. Mr. Delong scared her. He had the build of an oak tree. Once she and Ivy went to the 7-Eleven to get milk and cereal because, again, there was no food in the house. Nolan and his father were there. Mr. Delong yelled at Nolan for acting squirrelly and dropping a loaf of bread. His deep voice echoed through the entire store, sending shivers from Asia's hair to her toenails.

The thump of door locks brought Asia back to the present. It was time to talk with Nolan.

Ivy stood still, gave the house a once-over. "Never in a million years did I expect to come back here." She glanced around the yard. "It hasn't changed that much. Same color on the outside. Different flowers."

Asia eyed the tidy beds bordering the front of the wraparound porch. They overflowed with billowing red and pink Penta, bordered by dark green liriope. "I wonder what happened to Mrs. Delong's prize-winning roses?" Asia always linked those roses and Cynthia Delong. Without them, the home didn't seem like it belonged to Nolan's mother anymore.

"I decided he wasn't worth my time or effort after his mama chased us off and he didn't even say he was sorry," Ivy said softly. Her voice cracked. She said no more.

"That always bothered me." Asia ran her fingers along the package of wipes tucked in her pocket, then Russ's card.

It had taken her forever to get over Nolan. Being discarded like unwanted trash caused a deep ache in her. She had loved him like she loved Ivy and hoped he would rebel against his parents and come back to them.

But he hadn't.

A hint of their former friendship reared after she'd started tutoring him, when Nolan stopped her on her way to class and held out his recent Algebra test paper. A bright green "B+" emblazoned the top right-hand corner. She'd smiled at him. "I'm proud of you. Well done," she'd said.

Nolan wrapped her in a bear hug and lifted her off the ground. "Thank you, thank you," he whispered in her ear.

And then, as if a switch flipped, he'd let go, and backed away as if she carried the plague. "Sorry. Gotta go." He ran down the sidewalk. Asia trembled. Had the lightning-swift change in his mood come because Nolan knew about Veronica and his father? Or was it nothing more than fear of his friends seeing him hug a less popular girl?

"I hate this, Ivy."

"Me, too. He was our friend once."

"What if we're wrong, and Bill Delong wasn't D?" Asia took a wipe and cleaned both hands. "And what do we do if his mother is here? Can you imagine what she might say about all this?"

"I know what *I'd* say if two women showed up at my house and declared Denney had an affair with their mother and gave her a fortune."

The Delong family had always been revered in Emerson as close-knit and God-fearing. Nolan's father opened doors for his mother, bragged about Cynthia's cooking and green thumb. Bill Delong attended every baseball, basketball, and football game Nolan ever played. He was well known for his kindness. Asia remembered a band concert where she'd played a solo on her flute. When the song ended and the crowd clapped, Nolan's father jumped to his feet and cheered, sparking a standing ovation across the gym. At the time, she dismissed the action as him being kind. But now … She shivered. "Better go ring the bell, before I lose my nerve."

Ivy linked her arm with Asia's. They walked up the steps to the front door. Ivy rang the doorbell. Asia closed her eyes. Drew two breaths.

Please help Nolan remember we were once friends.

CHAPTER 35

THE CHEERY MELODY OF the doorbell failed to soothe the frenzied butterflies in Asia's stomach. Wooziness swamped her, as if she were floating on a raft in choppy water.

Not now. Not here.

Ivy squeezed her arm. "When this is over, we're getting doughnuts. Extra icing and sprinkles. My treat." Ivy tried to pull her face into a playful expression. The worry lines on her forehead killed the effect.

"If his mother's here, we may not make it past the front door."

Ivy reached and pressed the bell again. "Then this worked better than expected."

Staccato footsteps drummed on the other side of the door. Fear gripped Asia, the swirling in her head grew. Perhaps time had softened Cynthia's hatred of them. Nolan was grown and married. What harm could she expect from the two of them?

The door lock clicked open.

Breathe ... Relax ...

Asia rubbed Russ's card. Ivy shifted, stood straight and tall. The knob rotated. The door cracked open. A scent of orange-ginger mixed with maple syrup wafted through the widening space. Chills tickled down Asia's spine like tiny bug's feet. The condemned must feel the same dread as they waited before the guns of a firing squad.

Relax ... breathe ... relax ...

The door swung wide. Nolan's wife stood in the entryway. Of course, she would be there. She lived there. But unlike her previous demeanor at the hospital, this time Nicole scowled. "Good morning."

Her voice rose with more question than greeting. "It's nice to see you again."

Needed words caught against Asia's dry throat. As she coughed to free them, Ivy pointed to her chest. "I'm Ivy."

Nicole hesitated, then spoke. "Nice to meet you. Asia and I met at the hospital."

Ivy released Asia's arm. "We're so sorry for dropping by early and unannounced, but we needed to talk to Nolan. It's urgent."

"Of course. Come on in." Nicole stepped back, ushered them into an open foyer with hallways leading in opposite directions on either side. The morning sun gleamed through the tall windows lining each wall.

"Nolan's finishing breakfast. Y'all go on into his office." She pointed to the hallway on the right. "First door on the left. I'll tell him you're waiting."

Nicole's sandals clapped against the polished wood floor as she left the room.

Asia scanned the room, took in the wood floors, the abstract art painted in dark red and yellow shades hanging on the walls. "I imagined the house looked like this. Except they had a huge stone fireplace with a collie sleeping in front of it."

"I dreamed they had velvet carpeting with matching velvet couches." Ivy tapped Asia's arm. "Let's get this over with. This place creeps me out almost as much as Veronica's."

The interior resembled a magazine layout, but she couldn't escape the atmosphere. Asia shuddered, as the walls seemed to bear invisible eyes bent on following them, judging them. But they weren't out to hurt anyone. They just needed the truth.

The office presented a different aura. The long, red leather couch by the window, the oversized mahogany desk and black leather office chair were meant for use by the Delong men whose height stretched beyond the six-foot mark. Cynthia in all her daintiness would have been swallowed by the burly pieces, and Nicole's willowy frame would look small and out of place if she sat there.

Nowhere in the room was the slightest hint of a lady's touch. Two photographs stood in costly frames on the corner of the desk. A large, framed, sepia-toned map covered the wall nearest the window, and one plant stood in a corner drinking in the light from the outside. Built-in shelves along one wall contained a signed football in a glass case, photographs of Nolan and his father on golf courses, and various civic and business awards. Some bore Bill Delong's name, others belonged to Nolan.

A wooden antique clock with "Cool's Black Leather Oil" in faded red letters circling the face hung on the wall across the room from the map. The steady tick-tock echoed through the room, pounding in Asia's ears.

She drew in a shallow breath.

Relax ... breathe ... relax ...

Her chest tightened. If she didn't train her attention on a sound other than the clock's heartbeat, she'd slide into a full-blown panic attack in a matter of seconds. Asia settled on the couch. The cushions crackled as she leaned back.

"You okay?" Ivy called from across the room. Asia sent her a quick nod. There were spots where the leather cracked and rolled back, exposing the cream-colored threads woven underneath. She ran her finger along one, pressed the edges down.

Veronica's voice spoke from the back of her memory. *Nothing beats a red leather couch.*

Asia jumped to her feet, backed away until she crashed into the wall. The frame surrounding the antique map stabbed her spine, rattled with the contact. She rotated to see, noticed the word printed in the legend at the bottom left corner. Then the plant resting in the corner. A long vine covered in dark-green leaves leaned toward the sunlight as it trailed to the floor.

"Oh no."

She looked back at the map, reread the word, just to make sure she wasn't seeing things.

No. She'd read it correctly.

Her teeth chattered as if she stood in the middle of the Arctic.

Ivy called to her. "You have to see this." She held one of the framed photographs from the desktop.

"Recognize anything?"

Asia focused on the photograph. "It looks just like Veronica's bedroom."

Ivy tapped the photo. "That is Cynthia Delong when she was a little girl. Bill must have told her about this picture and Veronica decided to steal the decorating idea."

"Or Veronica saw it herself." Asia swayed. "I have to get out of here." She started toward the door, lost her footing, and went down on her knees. Ivy dropped the photo onto the rug and rushed to help.

"What's the matter?"

"It's too much. The map, the plant in the corner, the couch ... and that photo."

Ivy searched the room. "What are you talking about?"

Asia sucked in a shallow breath. "The map. Look at it."

Ivy helped Asia up then crossed the room. "It's old." She shrugged. "What am I supposed to be seeing?"

"Look at the corner." Asia pointed a shaking finger at the legend.

Ivy's forehead puckered as she read it. "It's a map of ... *Asia.*"

"Now look at the plant, in the corner by the window."

"We have some just like it in the restaurant. It's English Ivy—" She sucked in a whistling breath as she looked back and forth from the map to the plant. "Oh. No."

Ivy pointed to the couch. "She always said ..."

"There's nothing better than a red leather couch," they said in unison.

"Nolan's the little boy ... our missing brother." Asia started again for the door. "I can't stay here another minute."

Nolan appeared in the doorway. "Good—"

Asia plowed into him, but his sturdy body stopped her progress. He grabbed her by the arms, steadied her. "Asia, are you all right?"

She wrenched free from his grip, then pushed her way past him and ran into the hallway, then the open foyer.

"Asia," Ivy called as she followed.

Asia stopped. A much older, time-stamped Cynthia Delong stood between her and the door.

"What are you doing here?" Cynthia took a step toward Asia, her thin fingers curled into cat claws. "I told you *never* to come back here."

"Mother, it's okay." Nolan's deep voice echoed from the hall.

"Asia." Ivy shoved Nolan out of her way.

Cynthia narrowed her eyes and advanced to Asia. "You don't belong here."

Asia took a step back. "No … no, ma'am, we don't."

Cynthia clawed the air, lunged forward but Asia sidestepped her and ran for the door.

"Asia, *wait,"* Ivy yelled.

But Asia ran for the car. Her straining lungs were closing. If that happened, she'd never make it to the car. She'd die here, surrounded by people who wished she'd never been born. The only one who'd mourn was Ivy.

Ivy.

Ivy stood at the end of the walk, fishing the key fob from her purse. She jingled the keys in her hand. "Let's get out of here."

Asia tried to lift the door handle, but the trembling weakened her hands so that she couldn't grasp the handle. Ivy came and reached around, lifted the latch. "Get in."

Asia slid into the passenger seat. Cold sweat dampened her forehead. She dug two wipes from her pockets and raised them to her nose.

Breathe ... Breathe ... Breathe ...

She drew in a breath, but it was too small. Her lungs demanded more.

One ... two ...

Ivy shook her. "Asia … Asia …" Her voice grew softer with each word. "Asia, don't you dare pass out on me."

Asia's head spun, her chest ached, and her lungs screamed for air.

Breathe ...
"Asia, talk to me. Asia ..."

CHAPTER 36

Ivy jostled Asia hard. "Wake up, Asia. Please."

Her sister's head wobbled as if she were a masterless puppet. "Asia," she screamed in her sister's ear.

No response.

A knock sounded on the window. Nolan stood with his face inches from the glass. "Everything okay?"

Was he insane? Asia was passed out in the passenger's seat. Every single item in Nolan's office had a direct link to her and Asia and proved that Bill Delong ... Ivy pushed the start button as though she were punishing it. No. She wasn't ready to accept what the map on Nolan's wall, the red leather couch, the English Ivy growing strong and healthy, and the photograph she'd found on the desk testified as truth.

Nolan knocked again. "Should I call 9-1-1? Or ... get my wife?" He looked to the front door where his wife stood, her eyes wide.

Ivy clenched her teeth. *She* needed to get Asia to a hospital. "No. You should move before I drive over your toes," she said through gritted teeth. She and Asia must have lost their ever-loving minds to think coming here was a good idea. Ivy pushed the engine's Start button. The engine whirred to life. "Move, Nolan," she said, this time loud enough that he could hear her. She rammed the gearshift into reverse. The tires squealed on the concrete as she backed out, but who cared? She had to get Asia help, get her away from this place.

The car barreled into the path of an oncoming car. The driver honked and swerved to avoid hitting Ivy's rental. She slammed the car into park in the middle of the road. If another driver happened to come their way, they could just go around like the last one. She wasn't going another inch until her heart stopped pounding. She looked back to see Nolan standing in the driveway, waving his arms, and motioning for Ivy to come back to the house. Nicole joined him.

Ivy patted Asia's arm. "Hang on, honey."

She was certain she appeared completely mental sitting in the middle of the road. And she'd sit right there until she was able to make good on her promise. Because she owed Asia for ditching her with Veronica. Payback always cost more than the original offense. Going to the hospital yesterday and then being in Nolan's office today must have jarred Asia until everything inside her head boiled over like overheated marinara sauce.

Ivy spotted a car through the windshield, heading her way. Time to pull herself together with a good, deep breath. She inhaled then blew the air out so hard her cheeks ballooned. Her stomach and head twirled as if she were riding on a roller coaster. The car's engine thunked as she slammed the gearshift into drive in time to move out of the other car's way.

She cast a quick glance at Asia, still slumped in the seat, eyes closed, her skin a ghoulish white. "Please be okay," Ivy whispered.

A horn blared. The grill of an oncoming semi-truck filled the windshield. Ivy yanked the wheel to the right, but it slipped in the grip of her sweaty palms. The car swerved into the ditch. Ivy slammed the brakes and jerked to a stop. She killed the engine. Hysterical giggles bubbled from within and she laughed until tears streamed down her cheeks.

Asia's eyes fluttered to awakening with a glassy-eyed confusion. "What happened?

Ivy leaned her forehead against the steering wheel. "Don't ask. How are you?"

Asia rubbed her head, now dotted with perspiration. "Foggy. And I have a headache. Did I pass out at Nolan's?"

Ivy flopped back against her seat. "In the car."

"And he saw?"

"Oh, yeah."

"Wonderful." Asia blinked several times, glanced around. "Why are we sitting in a ditch?"

"You know those old movies, where they show people meeting a truck head-on and then waking up"— she pointed to the car's floor—"down there?"

Asia closed her eyes, leaned against the headrest. "Will the car still drive?"

"Of course. I'm a great driver and I missed the truck."

Asia turned to look behind them. "There *was* a truck? I thought you were kidding."

"It was real, I missed it, so quit worrying."

Asia cradled her head. "I think I need to be unconscious again."

Although she only rubbed her temples, the action accentuated Asia's natural grace. When walking, eating, or picking up trash, she carried herself with a ballerina's grace. Feminine, quiet strength seasoned with fragility. That must be the quality Hunky Neighbor Russ saw as well.

Ivy could have told Asia how beautiful she was a thousand times, but she'd never accept the compliment. She could never see her own beauty. Denney would have said she had a classic look, like the actresses from the golden age in Hollywood. When had Asia blossomed? Before now, she pictured Asia as the awkward fifteen-year-old who chose books over boys.

Ivy smoothed her hair, checked her reflection in the rearview mirror. No bumps or bruises, but Asia's pasty coloring alarmed her. "I'm taking you to an Urgent Care Center I saw near the interstate." She restarted the engine.

Asia shook her head. "Don't. I just need to get back to the house and lie down."

Ivy rammed the car in gear. "No ma'am. You're getting checked out by a doctor." She revved the engine then drove onto the highway. "And no arguments."

Ivy rubbed her bare arms in the exam room as she waited with Asia. "They could hang meat in here."

Asia shivered on the exam table. She refused any offer of blankets and resisted sitting on the surface until the nurse wiped the blue vinyl clean and covered it with the protective paper that now crackled as Asia squirmed. "What time is it?"

Ivy pointed to a clock on the wall behind Asia. "Almost noon."

"Sorry I've wasted our morning."

Ivy waved her off. "Our morning tanked the moment we entered Nolan's driveway."

"Good thing you're such a skilled driver. Didn't we end up in a ditch the last time I rode with you on that road? You were seventeen, I was fourteen?"

Ivy squirmed. The hard metal seat offered no comfort. "I don't remember that at all." A new thought struck. "Asia, who taught you how to drive?"

A blast of cold air shot from the overhead vent. Asia answered the question with chattering teeth. "Mr. Garner."

"Driver's Ed in summer school?"

Asia dipped her head. "The summer between my junior and senior year. I forged Veronica's signature on the permission slip because she refused to let me take the class. Mr. Garner trusted me, which was sad because I cheated."

Ivy sat straight. "What? You never did a dishonest thing in your life."

"I did. We were required to keep a log of hours driving during the day with adult supervision. I forged her name on every single entry in my log. I'd sneak out to practice after Veronica went to bed. Almost got a ticket when I was teaching myself how to parallel park."

Ivy couldn't imagine any police officer looking into Asia's big-blue-eyed, scared-rabbit expression and accusing her of doing anything unsavory. "Good grief, what happened?"

"I was at the high school, practicing by the curbs in front of the office around two in the morning. They had those giant streetlights rimming the parking lot and I could see well enough to judge my distance. Do you remember Tim Penn's older brother Brian?"

"Barely. Why?"

"He was the cop who saw me driving around. He thought I was loitering. I nearly died when he pulled in with his lights going."

"What did you tell him?"

Asia shrugged. "The truth. I was practicing for my driver's test the next day, and I was so nervous I couldn't sleep. When he asked where Veronica was, I told him I didn't want to wake her up. I apologized, but said I was so nervous I had to practice."

"Did you get the ticket?"

Asia gave her a half-smile. "No. He said from what he'd seen I was a fine driver and told me to go home and quit worrying."

Ivy slipped into silence. Teaching her boys to drive would be an experience. But her first student should have been Asia. "Did you go to prom?"

Asia's cheeks went pink. "It was a complete disaster."

"Did *anything* positive happen in your teenage years?" Ivy asked.

Asia tilted her head to the side. Another half-smile played about her mouth. "There were a few."

"Please tell me one. I need to hear it."

"I won the Chamber of Commerce scholarship. I had to read my essay before the members at their annual ball." Her eyes sparked, enhancing their sapphire hue. "I wrote about how the rough patches in life teach us the greatest lessons. The moment after I spoke my final line, the entire audience erupted in applause. Shot to their feet. They clapped and cheered until the emcee came on stage and told them to sit." Asia paused. "I had delivered the entire speech from memory."

Asia looked toward a large, framed poster of wildflowers—Ivy was sure it was meant to calm patients—as if the applause were sounding in that moment. Her gaze came back to Ivy. "I can still feel the way my stomach flipped. Like a flock of cattle egrets took flight within me. It was one time I felt … valued."

Ivy blinked back tears demanding release. "You were always an awesome writer. You could have written books."

Asia smoothed a crease in the paper. "I have."

"Get out. Novels?"

"No. I've cowritten four English textbooks and developed curriculum guides for special needs students that are being used in several of our schools in Tennessee."

"Asia, you're—"

A doctor breezed into the room carrying an iPad in one beefy hand. He greeted Ivy with a chin-dip, then addressed Asia. "Good news. Your EKG and blood tests came back normal, so we're not dealing with any heart issues. Have you been under a lot of stress lately?"

Ivy grunted, and he turned to face her, his brows swooped together in a fiery fit of disapproval. Ivy tilted her chin and squared her shoulders.

Asia cleared her throat, drawing the doctor's attention back to her. "I struggle with panic attacks." Her cheeks reddened. "I had one this morning and fainted. This has happened to me before."

"Are you on medication?"

"I've been on Prozac, Xanax, and Valium but the side effects were causing more problems than helping. Per my regular doctor's instructions, I'm not taking any meds at this time."

The doctor opened the iPad, typed a few lines, then closed it out before turning back to Asia. "All right then. Make sure to get extra rest today. Call your doctor as soon as you return home. You're clear to go." He gave a slight bow before exiting.

Ivy huffed after the door slammed behind him. "He has the bedside manner of a badger."

Asia slid from the table. "Let's go. I want to lie down for a while."

Ivy stood to help steady Asia while she dressed. "I need a nap myself. Hanging out with you is exhausting." She linked her arm around Asia's waist. "But I'll keep you anyway."

Outside the afternoon blaze beat down on their heads and radiated through the soles of their shoes from the parking lot's blacktop.

Ivy clicked the doors open. "This humidity is awful. When we get back to the house, I'm going to turn the air to arctic blast."

Asia folded into her seat and leaned against the headrest. "I need a shower."

A tap on Asia's window made them both jump, Asia gasping. Nolan stood outside, peering in.

Asia glanced over her shoulder at Ivy who muttered, "That man's habit of popping up at the worst times is beginning to grate on my nerves."

"What do we do now?" Asia asked.

"I'll take care of this." Ivy got out and faced Nolan across the roof of the car. "How did you know we were here?"

Nolan stuffed his hands in his pockets. "I followed you." He glanced toward Asia. "Is she okay?"

"A good nap and she'll be fine."

Nolan shifted his stance. "I need to talk to y'all."

Ivy tapped the roof of the car. Yes, they needed to talk. He also needed to do something about his mother, but then again, the same could be said about her. "Tomorrow. At Veronica's."

Nolan nodded once. "What time?"

"Ten a.m."

"Done."

"Fine." Ivy stooped to get into the driver's seat. Under normal conditions making plans for a meeting brought flutters to her stomach. Few things topped the thrill of presenting a sales pitch or winning over a new client.

But this was no business meeting ... this was *family* business.

When Ivy got back in the car, Asia was checking her makeup in the visor's mirror. "This is going to be quite a conversation. 'Guess what, Nolan? Your family tree just increased by two branches and we're the new twigs.'"

Ivy started the car. "Let's just pray he doesn't decide to go all lumberjack and chop the new branches down."

She backed from the parking space, then glanced in the rearview mirror.

Nolan stood watching them, his hands still buried in his pockets.

CHAPTER 37

Asia once built a fantasy around a classic farmhouse table she'd seen in an antique shop back home in Sevierville. In her dream she sat surrounded by a fictional, faceless husband and other family members. But as she, Ivy, and Nolan sat around Veronica's table, her dream of family crumbled.

Skin-crawling silence surrounded them as they stared at each other, waiting, squirming, hoping someone would speak first. Ivy took a quick swig from her bottled water and slammed it down with the force of a judge gavel-banging to bring a court to order. "We have a lot to cover." She spoke as if they were heads of a corporation meeting to discuss a merger rather than her and Asia's tawdry parentage.

Nolan wove his fingers together and rested his hands on the table. "We do." He split his gaze between them. Then Asia saw a flicker behind the façade he worked hard to uphold.

He'd known all along.

But why not tell them earlier? "When did you find out we were your sisters?"

Ivy jerked to face Asia. "Asia ..."

Nolan's Adam's apple bobbed as he swallowed. "Do you remember the last day we met for tutoring in the library?"

Asia did remember. Nolan never spoke to her again after that day.

He continued. "We were sitting at the table across from Mrs. Blount's office window and I saw our reflection."

Nolan pointed to his head. "We have the same hair ... and chin. Then I realized we had the same eye color. My nose and cheeks are a little different, but …"

Asia looked hard at Nolan, noted the curl of his bangs, the shade of his eyes, the shape of his chin. "Why didn't I see it before?" she asked herself more than anyone else.

Ivy joined in the evaluation. "You're right, Asia. We should've have seen it before now."

Nolan's brows rose. "You didn't know until just now?"

Asia exchanged glances with Ivy, then returned focus to Nolan. "We figured it out yesterday, in your office."

Incredulity flashed in his wide-eyed stare. "She never told you?"

"Veronica never told us *anything*." Asia flexed her fingers, drummed her digits on the tabletop. Twice.

Nolan rubbed the back of his neck. His fingers dug into the skin, massaged the tension she was sure gnarled the muscles. "How did you find out?"

"Veronica left us a trail of clues," Asia said. "If you want to see them, I'll show you."

Nolan looked from her to Ivy.

"She's right. You should see them," Ivy said.

Their newfound brother pushed from the table, then stood in the middle of the empty living room. "Where?"

"Over here on the tarp." Asia gathered the stack of photos and their birth certificates.

She handed them to Nolan. "We found the birth certificates in a box she'd hidden in a hole behind that cut-out in the wall." She noted a vein throbbing at his temple as he studied the photos. "We found those stuffed under the mattress in her bedroom."

He handed her the stack and Asia placed it back on the tarp. Next, Nolan read through the birth certificates. He held them side by side, studied them. "Anything else?" he asked, returning those as well.

Asia set the certificates down, then picked up the letters. "We found these in a garbage bag."

Nolan read through the top three. "He told me about the monthly checks. Mother threatened to divorce him more than once over those, but Dad wouldn't relent. He wanted you and Ivy to be taken care of." He handed the letters back to Asia.

Ivy's steps echoed across the room. "He had a rotten way of showing that."

Nolan rubbed the back of his neck again. "You don't understand. He begged Veronica to let him take y'all. He promised to still send the checks, but she refused."

Asia blinked at the words. Veronica had never acted as if she cared one whit about them, so why hold on when she could have had freedom from motherhood, which she hated, *and* Bill Delong's money?

Nolan shrugged. "She never wanted me."

Asia couldn't help but notice that not a trace of sadness flavored his words. He delivered them as if he were saying a neighbor no longer wanted a used car. Would she or Ivy ever come to speak of Veronica that way?

She set the letters down. "Don't think that Veronica loved *us*. She didn't. Not ever. We were a means to an end for her."

"Well, I do know that Dad wanted you both. But she threatened to expose their affair if he tried to take you." He blew out a breath. "He was *obsessed* with Veronica. She could talk him into all kinds of reckless things." Nolan rubbed his jaw. "That's why there are three of us."

Ivy stood shoulder to shoulder with Asia and squarely in front of Nolan. "If he loved us so much, why didn't he risk public embarrassment to save us? The scandal would have blown over eventually."

Nolan stretched to his full height. He walked to the wall and pointed to Veronica's faded scribbles. "I know what this means."

Veronica's cryptic message— "Filthy Rags"— was one of the few things they couldn't figure out.

"How?" Ivy asked. "How do you know?"

"Because it's an ugly piece of this puzzle."

Asia slid her hand into the pocket of her shorts, rubbed the edge of Russ's card with her thumb, and said, "With Veronica there is no other kind."

CHAPTER 38

Asia watched every step Nolan took as he grabbed a handful of the dirty rags from the box in the wall. "Did you look closely at these?" He held one out for inspection. "These brown stains aren't paint, or rust. They're blood."

Asia's innards tightened as if Veronica herself reached in and twisted them in the same way she'd wring out a washcloth. "Did Veronica ..."

Nolan exhaled loudly. "Their names were—"

"Vernon Dell and Rita Robinson." Ivy rushed to the suitcases, then thrust them toward Nolan. "We found these hidden among some trash in the cabinet beneath the bathroom sink."

"Who were these people?" Asia asked.

"Vernon was an obstetrician in Leesburg. He was a friend of one of Dad's business acquaintances. Rita was a midwife Vernon hired ... and his mistress." Nolan gathered a handful of the rags. "They delivered the three of us here in this house."

Nolan dropped the wad of cloths back to the tarp. Wiped his hands on his hipbones. "These were my dad's old undershirts. Mother used them as cleaning rags and kept them in the garage."

Ivy tucked her hair behind her ear. "How did Veronica get them?"

"Dad paid Vernon and Rita to fill out the birth certificates without listing him as our father. Vernon knew a lawyer who would take care of my adoption and keep it secret." Nolan shuffled his feet. "Mother couldn't have children, so Dad convinced her to take me, so they could have an heir. At the time, she thought I was the product of a onetime lapse in judgment. She didn't know you two were my sisters until the day, back when we were little kids, that I invited you to come over and play. Dad told her the whole truth then."

"And that's why she chased us away," Asia whispered.

Nolan exhaled. "They almost divorced because of you and Ivy. She promised to stay for my sake. But y'all were carbon copies of Veronica. She wanted nothing to do with you." He spoke so softly Asia almost questioned whether she'd heard properly. Then, he kept going. "After Asia was born, Vernon kept demanding more money, threatened exposure if he didn't get it. Dad paid him off and bought plane tickets so they could disappear together."

He paled under his tan. "When Dad told Veronica about the blackmail plan, she laughed. Said everything would be okay." He kicked the pile of rags with the toe of his shoe. "Dad said Veronica came to the house after midnight, covered in blood, claiming she'd solved his problem permanently. He grabbed the shirts, drove Veronica back here, and spent the night cleaning up the evidence."

Realization swamped Asia and she fought against it to speak. "She killed them ... *here?*"

He snatched his foot back, as if the rags suddenly became hot to the touch. "When Dad asked where the bodies were, she laughed, wouldn't tell him. Those rags tied all this together."

After sharing disbelieving looks with Ivy, Asia confronted Nolan. "She killed two people ... and your father never told the police?"

"Dad didn't want her to go to jail and have the two of you forced into foster care."

Ivy crossed her arms. "He had better choices." She stomped to the tarp, picked up the bag of hair and Asia's broken doll, Christina. She thrust them at Nolan. "See this hair? That was mine until Veronica tried to shear me the night of my senior prom." She threw the bag back on the tarp. Next, she dumped Christina's body parts at Nolan's feet. "And this? This was Asia's favorite doll when she was a little girl. Veronica dismembered her and left the remains on Asia's bed." Ivy scooped the parts back into the bag. "That's what our life was like,

Nolan. Every. Single. Day. But you still think we should just give good old Bill a free pass because he *meant* well?"

"No," he said softly. "But both women in his life refused to consider what might make him happy."

"And yet, he still carried on with Veronica after the murders ..." Ivy's words carried the venom of a rattlesnake's bite. She pointed to the bag of hair and Christina. "We found those early on and threw them out. But I went back and dug them out of the trash today because I wanted you to understand what your Dad made Asia and me live through."

Nolan continued. "Veronica was Dad's addiction. He just couldn't let go of her. I believe his guilt ate him alive until it killed him."

Asia squeezed her middle. So, this was it; she and Ivy were the product of obsession on their father's side and psychotic power on their mother's. Her father's addictive personality and her mother's evil narcissism dwelled deep within her, Ivy, and Nolan. Maybe in the marrow of their bones, the mitochondria of their cells. They were connected by blood, in so many ways.

In Nolan she saw her childhood friend, with whom she and Ivy shared their best stories. A lock of his hair stood up from the part, arching across the white line of his scalp. The same thing happened when she cut her own hair short, and no amount of hairspray tamed the errant tendrils.

Would the sins of their parents forever punish their three children?

"He was just a trophy, Nolan," Ivy said. "She never loved him."

Nolan scowled. "A trophy?"

Asia blinked as she gathered her thoughts. "Yes, a trophy." She pointed to the bag of money on the tarp. "Every dollar your dad gave her is in that bag. She never spent a single cent of the cash."

Nolan grew up insulated in a nice home, surrounded by loving parents who went to church, served the community, and pushed him to excel. Learning how hard they worked to spin the web of lies necessary to protect the fragility of his world must have devastated him. All because he noticed a resemblance in the school librarian's office window. In time his wounds had scarred over. Then she and Ivy arrived, raked off the scabs, and the past now bled all over the three of them.

Ivy dropped Christina and the bag of hair on the tarp. "We need to show him her room."

"What's that?" Nolan shoved his hands in his pockets.

"You need to see her bedroom." Ivy gestured toward the hallway. "This way."

They proceeded single file, with Ivy leading. As children they often played follow-the-leader. Nolan protested whenever Ivy's turn came. She added twirls, pirouettes, and fairy dances to her paths. He complained she used too many girly moves. Chances were good that he wasn't going to like this walk either.

Ivy stopped at the door and pressed her back against the wall of the passage. She motioned to the knob. "Go ahead. Asia and I will wait out here."

Nolan lowered his brows. "Why?"

"You'll see." Asia stood by Ivy, slid her feet back to make room for Nolan to pass. He opened the door.

A muscle twitched along his jaw as he stood on the threshold. "I don't believe this." His voice cracked. He stepped into the center of the room.

Asia and Ivy stood together inside the doorway. Asia flipped on the light. "She did this after we left home. We didn't understand at first because this isn't Veronica's style."

"But then I saw the photograph of your mom at your house—" Ivy said.

"And the map of Asia ... the English ivy ... and the couch," Asia added. "That's when we put the pieces together."

Nolan smoothed the errant curl along the part in his hair. It stood back up as soon as he stopped. "I don't understand."

The silence of the house closed around the three of them. Nolan's attention darted about the room, his hands fisting tighter. Veronica's madness had to be unsettling. Asia stepped in. "Bear with me, Nolan.

I'll try to make the situation clear. In your study, we saw the map ... of *Asia.* Then we noticed the plant by the window ... *ivy.*" She pointed to herself. "Asia." She turned her finger toward Ivy. "Ivy."

Nolan swayed. "I need to sit." He bent his knees as if he were thinking of sitting on the floor, but Asia rushed to guide him to the bed. He sat a moment, as if this new information must coagulate before he'd hear more. "Go on."

"The map and the ivy aren't the only evidence. Veronica always told us a red leather couch, like the one in your father's office, was a symbol of luxury. I think in her mind, they were part of her trophy collection. She ... *met* your father in the office." Asia hesitated. She couldn't put words to where her mind wanted to take this.

Ivy broke in. "In other words, Nolan we may have been conceived—"

Nolan held up a hand. "I get the idea. The map was my father's favorite antique. Ivy was his favorite type of plant. He kept cuttings growing all over the house. Always. And the couch was his favorite place to lie down and relax. It's been there forever. As far back as I can remember, anyway."

Asia nodded. "In Veronica's mind, naming us after his things marked him as hers. Another trophy ... a very big one. She must have seen the photograph on one of those visits then decided she wanted Cynthia's childhood bedroom."

Ivy piped in. "Veronica loved antagonizing and intimidating. Our names were like a neon sign, directed solely at your mother."

At the mention of Cynthia, the lines on Nolan's forehead deepened, his jaw tensed. "My mother had a complete breakdown. Dad worked hard to hide her state for a long time. He relocated most of his business into the house when I was in middle school, so he could keep an eye on her. Growing roses helped her to stay calm and lucid."

Nolan leaned his elbows on his knees, knotted his fingers together as a rest for his chin. "I believe keeping all the lies ate her up on the inside, so she let her mind go." He stared ahead, not seeing. "Her body may still be alive, but I lost the woman who was my mother long ago." The dullness persisted. "I still don't understand why Veronica copied the photograph. Mother was a little girl in that picture."

Asia rubbed her arms. "I think I know. Your mom was smiling... happy. Veronica wanted to steal that away too. I'm sure she found a way to make certain your mother knew."

"What kind of person does things like that?"

"Veronica," Asia whispered. "There's no other way to explain it."

As Nolan scanned the room once more, Ivy leaned against the doorframe, fiddling with her wedding rings. The diamonds caught the light, sending prisms along the wall.

Pain etched deep creases in her siblings' faces and, Asia was certain, on hers as well.

This was Veronica's final legacy. She'd built this web of pain to leave behind scars as the ultimate trophies. Fresh scars. They couldn't be erased, thrown away, or destroyed. They would live on long after she died, sealed deep in the memory forever haunting her victims.

Nolan stood before Asia and Ivy, the third point of a triangle none of them had created but whose boundaries they would forever inhabit. "So, what do we do now?"

"Technically, we fulfilled Veronica's wishes," Ivy said, then turned to Asia. "The house is clean. I say we throw everything away and give the money we found back to Nolan."

Nolan raised his hands. "No. It's not mine. Dad meant it for you two."

Ivy shook her head. "I don't need it or want it. Neither does Asia."

Asia thrust her hand into her pocket, rubbed the edges of Russ's card. "We can't throw away four hundred and eighty thousand dollars. Maybe we should find Vernon's and Rita's families. We could send the money to pay them back for their loss."

Ivy drew her head back as if the suggestion were hard to believe. "That was a hundred years ago, Asia. You can't just send complete strangers that much money after all these years."

"They had no family," Nolan said. "Dad hired an investigator to research their background years ago. Vernon and his wife are both dead and had no children. Rita was an only child who lost her parents when she was in her twenties."

"The perfect victims." Ivy's face brightened with the light of an idea. "Why don't we donate it to a children's home? Anonymously."

"You can't do that." Nolan pushed past them and stalked down the hallway.

Ivy glared at his back. "Well, why not?"

CHAPTER 39

Ivy swallowed back burning rage. When they were younger, she and Nolan often clashed; he'd stomp off and pout, then Asia played the peacemaker who tried not to take sides. They weren't going to fall into those roles again. Their gang of three needed to pull together, make decisions and then everyone could go home. She followed Asia and Nolan back to the living room. Her phone beeped as a text came through. She checked the sender.

Denney.

"I need to answer this." She slipped into the kitchen.

Once alone, she skimmed the message. He wondered how she was, if things were winding down. In their last conversation, she'd evaded his questions. Denney pressed until she barked at him and ended the call. She texted him seconds later, begging forgiveness and blaming her attitude on exhaustion.

I know. A smiley face blowing a kiss accompanied his response.

Ivy set her phone on the counter by a loaf of bread. Had Denney meant that he understood her situation, or was he telegraphing that he'd figured out her secrets? She kept dipping into the addict's sack of tricks, lying, misdirecting, and then growling when confronted. And Denney knew them all. She needed to get back to Seattle.

She kneaded a marble-sized knot in her shoulder. When should she tell him about Asia and Nolan? And her tax problems. Not over the phone, for sure, but in person, so she could read his thoughts, expressions, and then be reassured in his arms once her story ended.

She picked up her phone and hurried to the living room. Nolan's voice boomed against the walls. "There's no reason to go to the police about this."

Nolan's cheeks burned blood-red as he wheeled around to Ivy. "Asia is insisting we take the rags, the suitcases, and the money to the sheriff's office and tell them what happened."

Ivy's heart leaped against her ribs. "*What?*" She swooped on Asia. "We can't do that. It's mental."

Asia pinned her with a look broadcasting a clear message: *You're siding with him? Abandoning me ... again.* At least, to Ivy, this was the clear message, and it stabbed straight to her soul. But they couldn't go to the police. Bill Delong was a prominent developer across the state, with strong political connections nationwide. Soon the tales would make their way to the press. To Denney and the boys. Before they could take it back, their story would be a Friday night segment on *20/20.*

Good news strolled to listeners. Bad news galloped.

But Asia was right. Being tied to such people was bad. Covering up for them and possibly going to jail for the act was unthinkable. They had to stand together as sisters.

But at what cost?

"We have to turn this over. We have evidence of a *murder*, Nolan. We know who—"

"No, Asia. We. Won't." Nolan looked at his watch. "I've been here too long." He headed for the door. "I'll call later." He pointed at them. "Don't do anything. I'll be back later this afternoon." The walls shook when he slammed the door behind him.

Ivy went to Asia. "I'm so sorry. I'm so scared I can't think."

Asia was in deep thought, only half listening, if she heard at all. "He's worried about Cynthia. And Nicole and their daughters. He's harbored this a long time. Maybe he's worried about going to jail. But he's wrong."

Ivy sat at the table and took a long drink from her bottled water. "I understand too. This will hurt my family too. Maybe Nolan has a point. Do we need to go to the police? Bill Delong is dead, and Vernon and Rita are long gone. The only person who really knows what happened is in a coma and expected to die any day."

"Ivy, we *have* to make things right." Asia buried her face in her hands. "No wonder Cynthia didn't want us to play with Nolan."

"Maybe he's wrong. Knowing Veronica, she probably skinned a stray cat and spread its blood all over those rags and her car, to scare Bill."

Asia slipped her hands down, peered over her fingertips at Ivy. "Then how did she come to have the suitcases?"

"She could have seen them in a car in the parking lot at the hospital and stolen them."

"Maybe." Asia pointed to the pile of rags. "Any lab in the country could probably test those for DNA."

"You've watched too many crime shows. I don't think DNA lasts that long."

"It can last for years, Ivy. I watched a documentary about it."

Ivy reached across the table, laid her hands over Asia's. "Please drop this idea. Nolan and I have too much to lose."

"Ivy, we *can't* ignore this."

"My brain agrees with you, but my heart and mama-bear instincts want to keep innocents from being hurt."

"I do too, but …"

"How do you think Russ will react? A murderous mom is not the normal baggage a girl carries with her."

Asia's brow furrowed. "Russ wouldn't hold Veronica's actions against me. He isn't that type of person."

Ivy pressed on. "And what about your colleagues at school? Your students … or their parents? Do you think they'd feel comfortable knowing their child sat in the classroom of the daughter of a psychopath?"

Asia got two wipes from her pocket and cleaned her hands. "Psychopath isn't a real term. The condition is called—"

Ivy shoved her hair back from her face. "Who gives a feathered flip what it's called? All the parents will think about is their precious babies being in a room with the daughter of a murderous nutjob. They may even wonder if you could just go off one day. Can you imagine the rush of phone calls to your boss, demanding students be transferred from your class immediately?"

Asia pressed her lips into a thin line. "But ... we *have* to do the right thing."

"For who?"

"Whom," Asia corrected

Ivy pounded the table. "Who, or whom, cares?" She needed to be home. She'd climbed out of Veronica's traps long ago. Yet, now, here she sat, caught in another. She'd worked too hard to keep Veronica, and Sumter County, and this rotten house out of her life. Somehow, she had to get Asia to understand that some things are better left in the past.

But if they stopped, kept the secrets as Bill and Nolan had, she would be allowing Veronica to control her. Again.

Ivy pictured Denney and the boys. How many times had she preached at them to tell the truth, no matter how painful? If she held back what she knew, she'd let them down. If she gave the evidence to the police, they'd see her lies. And let them down.

"No matter what we do, Asia, we lose, and she wins. Just like old times ... *nothing* has changed."

CHAPTER 40

Asia held the rental car's key fob in an iron grip as she skulked around like a teenager trying to sneak out to a forbidden date while her parents slept. But her mind wouldn't rest. Poking and pricking, like a sandspur in a sock, her thoughts had scratched her conscience all night, preventing sleep.

Turn the rags and the suitcases over to the police. It's the right thing to do.

The microwave in the kitchen beeped as Ivy clattered about making breakfast. Asia retrieved Russ's card and rubbed the corners. What would he advise her to do?

She checked the clock on her phone.

Eight thirty a.m.

Police stations remained open around the clock. She could find an officer to talk to or ask for the business card of a detective. *If* Emerson's police department employed detectives.

The kitchen door opened, and Ivy emerged in her robe. "Going somewhere?" She carried a bowl of oatmeal in each hand.

The keys and fob jangled in Asia's hand. Ivy set the oatmeal on the table. "What are you doing?"

Asia drew two deep breaths, counted to two, then exhaled. "She committed murder, Ivy."

"Asia, we spent half the night talking—"

True, but she was done talking. Asia trudged to the front door. "We can't keep this to ourselves."

Ivy followed close on her heels. "Wait," she said, then reached for her phone. She pushed the home button, then held the picture of her boys up for Asia to see. "They're innocent. Why should they be hurt by Veronica's madness? Tell me that."

Asia stepped back, released a slow breath from her lungs. "We can't deny the truth—"

"We don't *know* the truth. Bill Delong repeated what Veronica told him, and we both know she lied as easily as others breathe. No one still standing knows the truth. How can we say what really happened without proof?"

"She killed those people. And you know it to be true."

"But do we know for sure? Nolan said there were no bodies. Just blood in her car."

Breathe ... Relax ... Breathe ...

"I can't live with this rolling around in my head, Ivy. I was awake all night." Asia stood firm. "I cannot go back home with Vernon and Rita's deaths on my conscience. I will lose my mind."

Ivy pointed to the photo. "I can't hurt my boys, Asia. I won't."

"Can you go back home and face them? What would hurt them more? That their mom told the truth, or that she protected evil?"

Ivy stood, staring dead-straight at Asia. All at once, she exhaled loudly as her posture slumped. "Go make us some toast. I'll get dressed. We'll go to the sheriff's office after we eat. Together."

Asia laid the key and fob on the kitchen table. "I'll make coffee, too. Strong and black."

Ivy shifted in her seat. Even if they provided a velvet, overstuffed sofa it would fail to make sitting in a sheriff's office comfortable. Asia sat next to her, scrubbing her hands with her wipes, filling the room with their fake citrus scent.

Ivy nudged Asia. "You know, one of these days you're not going to have any skin left on those fingers."

Asia tossed the wipe into the nearby garbage can. "At least my bare bones will be germ free."

"Wouldn't skeleton hands freak out your students?" Ivy waved a hand before Asia could answer. "Never mind. This place is making me nervous and all I can think of is useless, nonsensical conversation."

Asia sat next to her. "Thanks for coming with me."

"Don't thank me yet. If they make us wait much longer, I'm going to bolt."

Asia scowled. "Again?"

A slow anger simmered its way through Ivy's gut. "I thought we worked past the whole 'abandoning you' thing." Her fingers air quoted.

"That was a cheap blow." Asia breathed in and exhaled. Twice. "I'm sorry. Can't stop thinking about all the ways this can go terribly wrong."

"I stopped counting at a thousand," Ivy said.

Echoing footsteps drew Ivy's attention to a tall, slender man coming toward them. He held out his hand when he stopped before them. "Ladies, I'm Detective Ben Graham."

Ivy took in his salt-and-pepper hair combed into a fade-away style her older boys favored. His face remained void of emotions, a sound tactic that would give away nothing to hardened criminals trying to size up their arresting officer. But she and Asia were the victims here. Ivy shook away the thought. No, she was no one's victim. "I'm Ivy Morelli and this is my sister, Asia Butler."

Asia dipped her head in greeting. "Thank you for meeting with us."

"Let's go in my office where we can talk." Detective Graham motioned to a doorway located across the open waiting room. "Follow me."

Ivy leaned close to Asia's ear. "We could still run out of here."

Asia answered with a side-eye glance. "Not with my conscience still intact."

Ivy fell in step behind Asia. Wouldn't she love to have a sweet little chat with Asia's conscience. But Asia was right. They had to expose their findings in Veronica's house and sever the shackles of her secrets.

Detective Graham directed them to two chairs. He smoothed his tie as he sat on the other side of the standard office desk. His faux leather, swivel chair squeaked as he scooted closer. He rested his arms on the desktop in an "I'm-a-good-listener" pose. Ivy contained the smirk threatening to curl her lips. She'd wager his seen-and-heard-it-all air would change in no less than fifteen minutes into their tales of Veronica. She checked the time on her watch.

Detective Graham pulled a small notepad from under a stack of what Ivy recognized to be unfiled call reports. "Could I have your names, please?"

Ivy spoke first. "Like I said before, I'm Ivy Butler Morelli and this is my sister, Asia Butler."

He jotted the information with a blue Bic pen, the kind purchased in a ten-pack for little to nothing. "I need addresses and phone numbers next, in case I need to get in touch with y'all."

Ivy rattled hers off, then quickly studied the framed pictures and commendations hanging on the walls as Asia gave hers. Outstanding police work plaques hung next to cheaply framed photos of the detective holding stringers filled with bass and smaller fish and the detective with his arms wrapped around a blonde on a lush mountain top.

Detective Graham's voice brought Ivy back to the conversation after Asia gave her Maryville, Tennessee address. "We own a cabin up that way. Go there every summer for a couple of weeks to get away from the humidity and the threat of hurricanes." He tapped the pen against the pad's page. "What kind of work do y'all do?"

Detective Graham seemed intent on making them relaxed. Ivy draped her hand over the end of the armrest on her chair. He was being low-key and friendly. One of the best ways to catch someone off guard was to come across as a puppy when you were really a Rottweiler. Art of Negotiation 101.

She flashed her well-practiced, understated-for-business smile. "I own a shipping company that delivers farm-raised food to restaurants in the Pacific Northwest and I also co-own two Italian restaurants in Seattle with my husband."

"Nice." He finished his comment with a quick nod.

Ivy squeezed the edge of the armrest. He didn't need to purr approval at her. She did not need nor seek his good graces, thank you.

He shifted to Asia. "What do you do in Maryville?"

"I teach a special needs class at Craig High School."

Detective Graham beamed. "Good for you. Such a vital need in schools." His fingers gripped the end of the pen as he wrote the information. He pointed to his laptop. "It says here y'all found some disturbing items in your mother's house, and you're not sure what to do. What'd you find?"

Ivy deferred to Asia. "It's your show."

Asia drew in a deep breath, which she held for a couple of seconds, then exhaled. Ivy tapped her shoe on the tile floor. Hope Detective Graham had patience for this interview. Asia would probably want to wipe her hands two times before she could speak. But Asia had surprised her with a steely calm when she dealt with that tow truck driver.

Asia sat forward, leaving a slice of space between her and the back of the chair. "We found suitcases belonging to a man named Vernon Dell and a woman named Rita Robertson. There were two plane tickets in one of the cases."

Detective Graham nodded while as he wrote. "Did your mother know these people?"

"We've been told ..." Asia sent a help-me-out glance toward her.

Ivy shrugged. Her preference was to say little and keep the lid on all the sordid details. But Asia had opened the proverbial bag for all the cats to stampede their way out. And since there was no way to herd cats, they were now stuck.

Asia went on. "We've been told she did. Our father did, too."

Detective Graham poised his pen. "Mother's name?"

"Veronica Butler."

"And your father's?"

Asia hesitated. Ivy poked her with her elbow as a silent "go on" and Detective Graham took his attention from the notepad but kept his pen … waiting.

Asia lifted her chin and drew in two deep breaths. "Bill Delong."

Detective Graham's brow froze mid-forehead. He blinked. "Come again?"

Ivy leaned back and crossed her legs. "You heard her right, Detective. She said Bill Delong. And, yes. *That* Bill Delong."

She had to give him credit. Other than the locked brow, Detective Graham showed little reaction to their revelation. Ivy glanced at her watch. Thirteen minutes, thirty-seven seconds had passed since she started the countdown.

As the news sank in, the detective's calm countenance wavered for a moment. He lowered his hands to his desktop. He blinked rapidly. "Y'all have any proof of this?"

Ivy leaned forward in her chair. "Yes, sir. A whole houseful of it."

CHAPTER 41

Sweat dribbled down Asia's back in an itchy trail but she couldn't scratch away the sensation. She stood frozen, her arms leaden as she watched the sheriff's men carry out box after box from Veronica's house.

What had she done? Three hours ago, when she and Ivy entered the police station, sharing information about Veronica seemed like the right thing to do. Now that the police had rifled through the house, she wished she could hit rewind and stop them. Detective Graham and every officer involved now saw the evidence of Veronica's tawdry habits, knew the dirty secrets that led to her, Ivy's, and Nolan's births.

Nolan.

She shivered. Ivy had called him as they drove back to the house from the sheriff's office, taking the phone off the car's stereo speakers and onto "private call." Still, at one point, Ivy had held the phone away from her ear to escape the volume of his yelling. He was on his way to the house, he said, as soon as he could "let go," Asia heard him say.

Ivy shuffled up next to Asia. "They just brought out the bag with the money."

"Maybe they'll end up keeping it for evidence and we won't have to worry about what to do with it."

"Makes life easier on us, for sure."

Chills struck Asia's arms as a female officer carried the box of rags down the steps. "Those dirty rags have the largest story to tell, don't they?"

Ivy lifted her hair from the back of her neck and fanned the exposed skin. "We'll see." She released her hair and it fanned across her neck. "In the midst of his tirade, Nolan dropped a little nugget of news."

"Really? What?"

"Apparently, Veronica has improved."

Asia stared silently at Ivy. "Oh. I guess that's good."

Ivy took a hair tie from her pocket and wrapped her blond tendrils into a ponytail. "Is it?"

"It should be."

"There are a lot of things that *should* be good in our life, Asia. But …" She cocked her head to the side.

Asia nodded. "But for Veronica …"

Three officers exited the house carrying the rocks from the Delong's fountain. Another followed carrying the garbage bag filled with the monthly letters from Nolan's dad. *Their dad.*

The chills morphed into crawling creeps. She took two wipes from her pocket and scrubbed her hands. Once. Twice.

Breathe ...

Squealing brakes on the highway stole her attention away from the action in the house. Asia opened Ivy's car and deposited the wipes into the trash bag as Nolan flew up the lane. The afternoon sun glared from his truck's windshield in a blinding ball of light. The wheels dug divots into the sand as he slammed into park. After killing the engine, he leaped from the driver's side and shoved the door shut with a loud thud.

He snatched his sunglasses from his face as he stomped toward Asia and Ivy, shouting, "Why?"

Ivy started to puff up, but Asia grabbed her arm and squeezed. "Stay calm." Ivy nodded, but her countenance from head to toe remained primed to meet Nolan nose to nose.

Nolan cheeks blazed cherry red. "I asked y'all not to do this."

Ivy squared her shoulders. "No, you *told* us. And besides, this is *our* ... Veronica's house and around here, we—" she pointed her thumb toward Asia then back to herself, "make the decisions. And since you never bothered to come back yesterday, we couldn't fill you in on the details."

Nolan pawed the ground with the heels of his boots, flinging loose sand behind him bull-like. "That's not fair and you know it." He raised his brows at Asia. "I expected you to do better."

Ivy charged into his space with face upturned and challenging. "What's that supposed to mean?"

Asia stepped between them, shot both her best teacher-taking-control look first at Nolan, then Ivy. "Let's wait until these men and women are finished. *Then* we can discuss this."

Nolan crossed his arms. "The time for discussion passed when you two decided to go against me."

Asia recalled their last summer together. Nolan had reacted in kind, arms crossed, and bottom lip stuck out so far that a buzzard could have perched on it. "You two always go against me. It isn't fair," he'd complained.

Asia caught his gaze. This situation must not devolve into a two-against-one hissy fit. "*I* went against you. I couldn't live with ignoring the deaths of two people simply because I didn't want my name muddied in a scandal. Those poor souls deserve to rest in peace."

Nolan huffed. "They've been resting for thirty years, Asia."

Asia's jaw dropped. "That is cold, Nolan. We have an obligation to—"

He leaned into her face. "I owe them nothing."

Fear percolated behind the blue of his eyes. Along the years, Nolan apparently learned another fear tactic, that of an anxious dog. Bite first and wait for the opponent to back off.

Ivy inched closer to Asia. "Don't get huffy with her just because you wanted to keep Daddy's dirty little secrets hidden. She did the right thing whether you want to admit it or not."

"It's easy for you to be on her side, Ivy. You can run off to Seattle and pretend none of us exists. Just like last time, right?" Nolan knew what happened. Of course, the entire county knew, had put the truth together when Ivy up and disappeared.

As Asia struggled to hold her back, Ivy wrenched free to stand before Nolan, her forehead even with his collarbone as she glared into his face. "Oh, that's rich of you to talk about pretending like somebody doesn't exist. What did your dear old daddy do to us all those years? Asia and I have every right to expose all this horror because we *lived* through it. Every. Single. Day."

"It still gives you no right to—"

"It gives us *every* right, Nolan," Ivy shouted. Two officers peered from the front door of the house. Detective Graham parted them like curtains and walked down the steps. He crossed the yard to the three newly found siblings. "Everything all right here?" He raised his brows as a father might when confronting his squabbling children. Asia cringed in shame. He probably reckoned they were fighting over the money or other valuables from the house. Or, maybe after seeing Veronica's trove of trophies, he'd gathered the pieces together to see the entire tapestry of their lives.

Nolan and Ivy separated. Asia addressed the detective, trying to be the calm between the two fronts. "We're fine."

"I see." He widened his stance.

Asia shuddered as Detective Graham swiped away perspiration dripping from his hairline. He wiped the wetness on his pants. "Did any of you three know you were related before this?"

Nolan was the first to speak. "I've known since high school. Asia and Ivy just found out yesterday."

Detective Graham shifted his attention to Asia. "Is this true?"

"Yes, sir."

Detective Graham took in the information with a quick nod. "Nolan, did your dad ever mention if Ms. Butler might know what happened to the missing man and woman?"

"She made some outlandish claims, but nothing was ever proven. Dad hired private investigators years ago to look into things but found no new facts." Nolan stood statue-still, showing no signs of nerves over the question, acting as if he'd closed the case and nothing else need be said. This poker face was a new side of Nolan.

The detective pursed his lips, as if ruminating on Nolan's statement. "I need to talk with you about Bill's actions in more detail. Can you come to the station later today?"

Nolan's jaw flexed. "I won't be free until after five."

Detective Graham scratched his arm. "All right. See you then. Call me when you're on your way." He removed a business card from his pocket and handed it to Nolan.

The female officer came to Detective Graham's side. "We've loaded up all the items you tagged. Is there anything else?"

"No."

"We'll take everything to the property room."

"Go." He waved her off and the officer trotted back to the SUV where her colleagues waited. They drove from the yard and disappeared down the lane in a cloud of limestone dust.

Detective Graham remained silent until the car made it to the highway. He presented an outstretched hand to Nolan. "Thank you for your cooperation."

Graham moved his attention to Asia and Ivy, thankfully without extending his sweaty palm. "Thank you, ladies. I may need to ask y'all some more questions once we get a look at the items from the house. Would you be available tomorrow, around eleven?"

"Yes, sir," the sisters answered in unison.

Graham swiveled to Nolan. "See you later, Nolan."

Nolan shoved his hands in his pockets. Asia did the same, running her finger along the edge of Russ's card. She now stood in the eye of the hurricane between Nolan and Ivy. As soon as the detective left, the backside of the storm was coming. Because both were ready to erupt into a rolling boil.

Detective Graham waded through the weeds to his car and was soon traveling on the highway in the same direction as his officers. Ivy launched the first bands of anger. "Anything else you want to say, Nolan?"

He pressed his lips into a thin line. "No. I've said *way* more than I planned." He voiced a few choice words as he pounded through the weeds to his truck.

Asia watched him stalk a few yards away where he rested his hands on his hips, the back of his shirt dotted by sweat. "He's right," she said, keeping her voice low enough that Nolan couldn't hear. "As much as I believe we did the right thing, we don't have to stay here and live through the looks and whisperings once this comes out."

Ivy shrugged one shoulder. "Do you honestly think people didn't know or at least suspect Bill Delong and Veronica were involved? Besides, with all the wailing and protesting about troubles in the country, who gives a flip what happened between two people thirty-some years ago in the county?"

"Nothing has faster feet than a good, juicy scandal." Asia glanced at Nolan, aware that he had heard Ivy's declaration, then looked to her feet. "He's scared. He's been keeping this secret a long time. He made promises to his father. Allowing all this to come out probably feels like a betrayal." She looked at her sister. "You weren't happy with my decision at first either."

"Well, he needs to get over it. Secrets need to come with an expiration date."

Ivy was the last person who should be preaching about secrets. Maybe it was the heat boiling them, or the stress of the day, or the way Ivy tossed her head when she spoke her last that weighed heavily within her. Asia faced her sister head-on. "Do yours?" she asked, this time not caring how her voice carried.

Ivy wrinkled her nose. "Do my what?"

Asia's heart quickened. "Do your secrets come with expiration dates?"

"What are you talking about?"

"Have you told Denney and the boys what happened between us when we were younger?"

Ivy's shoulders drooped. "I promised I would."

"Promised, yes, but with no follow-through."

Ivy's brows slanted together. "What do you know?"

"I work with teenagers. I read body language like others read books. You've been lying to him. I hear it in your voice every time you talk on the phone."

Ivy faced her now, a single bead of sweat trickling from her brow and down the side of her face until it traveled along her jawline. "You get to stand in judgment over me now? Yes, I disagreed with you, but I went with you to the station. And I sat with you during the interview, and I'm standing here now, sweating like a pig, still backing you up. But, like always, you pity *Nolan* because he whined first and loudest."

Asia's temples pulsed. She drew in a breath, counted to two as her heart raced and her palms moistened. For a moment, she'd stopped seeing her sister. Instead, with her blue eyes snapping and her lips curled in anger, Ivy resembled Veronica. Too much.

Breathe ... Relax ... Breathe ...

Nolan turned, then returned to Asia's side. "You're out of line, Ivy."

Ivy shot him a look that would have pummeled concrete. "No one asked for your opinion."

"Which is precisely why we're in this fix. If you two would have kept your mouths shut, we wouldn't be here right now."

The blistering sun cast their shadows together on the ground. Nolan's towered above theirs. His and Ivy's voices blared, reminding her of a billion car horns all honking at once. Asia's heartbeat zoomed and her body swayed as clouds of dizziness ballooned in her head.

She covered her ears.

Breathe ... Relax ... Breathe.

Asia tried to draw a breath, count to two, but her constricting lungs accepted no air. Nausea bubbled in her. And that's when she knew. The moment the plan became all too clear.

This was what Veronica wanted. To push the three of them into a dogfight none would win.

"*Would you both hush up?*"

Nolan and Ivy's arguing ceased in an instant, both turning to look at Asia.

Asia ran into the house. The living room and Veronica's bedroom were strewn with boxes and items discarded by Detective Graham and his officers in their search. The clutter made her heart pound faster. She pushed one of the kitchen chairs to the isolation of her old bedroom.

Asia plopped down next to the window and scanned the barren dirt in the vacant lot next door. If Veronica had been there, she'd have counted the day's events a celebration. She would have probably laughed and clapped at the spectacle of her three children fighting. She loved pitting Asia and Ivy against one another whenever she could. What could top all three of her offspring scratching at each other like roosters in a cockfight?

Or Asia sitting alone in the emptiness of this room, staring out the window, on the verge of a panic attack? For certain, Veronica would have bent over her, leered with her serpentine gaze and pounced. "I taught you better than this. Never allow anyone to see your fears or tears. They make you an irresistible target."

Asia fought to draw a breath. Her head ached. She shoved the window open, tried to inhale fresh air from outside, but it was too arid. Too stale. She tried to focus on the thick green trees lining the field in the distance ... and the line of cottony clouds against the blue sky ... The clumps of rich field dirt that lay ready for Nolan to pour a new foundation, build a new home for someone. The old fence marking a boundary and rocks lined in a row against its side. Anything but Veronica's words.

Breathe ... Relax ... Breathe ...

CHAPTER 42

The sun sat low in the rose-gold sky. While Asia idled alone in her old bedroom, the afternoon melted into evening. Nolan's truck engine had revved hours ago, followed by the screeching of tires as he drove away. Time passed and she'd prayed. Counted. Breathed. Waited. And then ...

The essay.

Written for her AP Language Arts class. Five hundred words relaying lessons learned from the most influential person in her life. Asia spent three days in Miss Parkson's computer lab after school outlining, composing, and editing until the words she'd always kept in her heart gained life and breathed on the pages she typed. She'd based every word on Ivy. Her plan had been to present the final, graded draft to her sister. A way to say thank you and maybe stave off the detachment she sensed between them.

But Veronica found the essay first.

Asia pushed the memory behind those imagined iron doors. She'd come to their old bedroom to get away from Ivy ... and Veronica ... from Nolan ... from the drama. But the memory pressed through the barrier. Tiny, shredded triangles scattered across the floor like paper snow.

Veronica sitting on Asia's bed, leaning back on her hands. Her black t-shirt emblazoned in glittering rhinestones: SUGAR. She'd dipped her chin, sighted down her nose, and locked onto Asia. "I couldn't allow you to hand in that paper. All lies, Asia."

Asia had stood frozen in the doorway. One hundred and fifty of her grade points now lay on the floor between the beds. And she just stood there. Not moving, protesting, or demanding an apology. Her heart's words, created as a present to her sister, lay in the dust on the floor.

Veronica leaned over and blew across the slips of paper. They twirled in the wake of her breath like leaves caught in an autumn breeze.

She'd stood, fixed Asia with her moccasin eyes. "You'd best clean that up before the bus comes." Veronica flicked a piece of the essay from the bridge of her foot. She leaned in close. Her lips brushed the outer rim of Asia's ear as she whispered. "We both know you've learned far more from *me* than Ivy." She stalked to the door on cat-quiet feet. Veronica snapped her fingers and coiled back around. "Forgot why I came in here." Her mouth screwed into a pout. "You missed the bus."

Yet again Veronica caught her in a double trap. No homework and no way to get to school. Except…

A mockingbird's chirp outside the window brought Asia back to the present. She bit her bottom lip to sew in the sobs that so desperately wanted to escape. Corked in her chest, they bulged against her heart. She had been helpless against Veronica. Like a mouse who knows the hunting snake has crawled into its hole and blocked all escape routes.

A touch on her shoulder made her jump and her heart leaped when she saw Veronica's face leering down at her. She sucked in a breath and skittered back.

"Are you okay?" Ivy's voice rang in her ears. "You've been in here for hours. You haven't eaten anything. I'll reheat some leftovers or go get food." Ivy's head tilted in question. "What's going on with you?"

Breathe … relax … breathe …

She took another breath. The inhalation whistled. Her lungs missed the message that a breath had come, screamed for more.

Breathe … Breathe … Breathe …

Now Ivy was beside her, her arms slung around her shoulders. "I'm here … breathe, Asia," she said, reiterating her words, though they sounded as if Ivy stood at the end of a long, dark alley.

"Is this because of our fight? Because, if it is, I'll call Nolan later and apologize, if that's what you want."

Asia nearly doubled over as she gasped for breath.

"Is it about Veronica?" Ivy asked, her voice climbing. "She can't hurt us anymore, Asia. She's not here."

Yes, *she* was. She was *always* there. Slithering in the memories, waiting to strike and poison her mind. Asia trembled. Why didn't Ivy understand? They were all tiny insects who'd been sucked into the vortex of Veronica's sadistic whirlpool. They could swim to the edge but lacked the power to break free to calmer waters. In time, the swift currents would sap their strength and they'd be sucked into the center of Veronica's fury, with nothing left to do but drown.

Asia tried to gather another breath. Her chest burned and her heart marched in a frantic double-step. She clenched her jaw. *Dear Go•, you sent us here. But how are we suppose• to escape Veronica?*

Ivy now folded Asia into a tight embrace and rocked her. Over the din of the panic waves washing over her, a soft melody played. Ivy, singing to her. A lullaby? Asia focused on the sweet pitches. She drew a shallow breath, held for a count of two, and released as Ivy continued. Asia tuned into the melody, pictured Ivy doing this same type of thing with her boys. Something Veronica would have never done with the two of them. Ever.

The pounding of her heart eased.

Her lungs relaxed.

CHAPTER 43

Ivy rubbed Asia's back as her sister relaxed against her. Her boys would nestle like this when they were babies and coming down from a crying spell. "Feeling better?"

Asia drew her first deep breath since Ivy entered the room. "Maybe."

"Do you need me to drive you to the clinic again?"

Asia shrank from Ivy's touch. "No. I'm okay."

"You're drenched in sweat and white as a ghost."

Asia took her ever-present wipes from her pocket and bathed her face, then scrubbed her hands. Twice.

Ivy now sat on the floor at Asia's feet. She bent her knees and hugged them with her arms. "You're scrubbing," she said with a quick smile. "Now I know you've settled down."

Asia slid another set of wipes from her pocket. "Go get another chair. I'm certain Detective Graham's people tromped all sorts of dirt and grime in here."

Ivy rose then brushed the back of her shorts. "Hand me a wipe." She washed each finger, then her palms. "Give me your used ones. I'll toss them for you." As she neared the door, she called over her shoulder, "Come out here and sit with me. I'm calling Denney as soon as I throw these wipes away. I want you there with me … so you can talk with him too."

Asia sat ramrod stiff in her chair. "What? Don't. I wouldn't know what to say."

Ivy leaned against the door frame. "Please, Asia. For me?"

Asia squirmed. "The last time you stood in that spot and asked me to help you it didn't turn out well for me."

She crossed her arms. "My husband isn't Veronica."

"Then why have you lied about me all these years?"

"I love my life, Asia. The money, the companies we own, our house ... I started my own company. It's my baby and I could lose it soon. And I'd get over that and move on. But Denney and the boys ... my family ..."

The corners of her mouth trembled, which only served to infuriate her. "I'm not sacrificing you for them any longer. You're my family too." She'd laid the only olive branch she had before Asia. Now she must wait for acceptance.

"All right," Asia said, then followed Ivy to the front of the house where she tossed the wipes, then sat on her cot while Asia went to her own. "I just need to know ... that you care that I exist."

Ivy opened her mouth to debate that issue, then closed it and dialed Denney. He answered on the second ring. "Hold on, honey, I want to put you on speaker so Asia can hear you as well." She pressed the screen of her phone. "Coming through?"

"Yes." Denney's deep voice rang into the quiet of the room.

Ivy leaned over the phone. She motioned for Asia to move over to her bed. *Ready?* Ivy mouthed and Asia answered with a nod. "Hey, Denney, I want to introduce my sister, Asia, to you." She gestured for Asia to speak.

"Hello?" Her voice made her sound more a girl of fifteen than a woman of thirty.

"Hello," Denney said, and Ivy's stomach fluttered at his friendliness. "Wonderful to meet you."

Asia drew in a breath, held it a moment, then exhaled. "Lovely meeting you as well."

"I see you have an accent as musical as my wife's."

Asia shifted with a smile as her cheeks pinked. "Thank you." She'd have to get used to Denney's compliments. If he were still around to give them. Ivy's heart thumped an extra beat.

"I hope this means you'll be coming to Seattle soon. I'd love to meet you in person."

Ivy nodded. "I'll send you a picture of the two of us after we hang up."

"Love it. How's the cleanup going?"

Ivy squared her shoulders. "It's going. We've cleared out Veronica's house, but we ran into a strange ... side road." Denney remained silent as Ivy tucked her hair behind her ear and kept eye contact with Asia.

"A side road?"

Ivy hesitated. "Yeah. We ... uh ... ran into a big bag of weird."

Asia fiddled in her pocket, then stood.

"Where are you going?" Ivy whispered

Asia removed an empty package from her shorts pocket and waved it in the air.

"What happened?" Denney asked.

Ivy pointed to Asia's cot and mouthed *sit.*

Asia held up an empty packet. "I have to get more wipes from the car."

Ivy's wide eyes testified disbelief of the timing. "Now?"

"Ivy, are you still there?"

"Yes, I'm sorry, we're a little distracted on this end. Hold on."

"Everything okay?"

"Yes, we're fine." She mouthed *go* to Asia with a point of her finger toward the front door.

"Okay, I'm back. So, the weird side road." Within a few sentences Ivy relayed the story of the suitcases then waved when Asia returned inside. "So, yeah ... Detective Graham and three other officers were here most of the morning gathering evidence. It was like those police drama reruns you like to watch after the boys are in bed. Except, none of the police officers were as good-looking."

Denney chuckled. "Must have been a little frightening, dealing with the police."

Asia settled into a chair at the table. She laid the wipes package on top and drew out one cloth.

Ivy continued. "Our …Veronica was an awful person, Denney. We've discovered she did a ton of terrible things."

"Are you two okay?"

"We learned to handle her a long time ago."

She watched Asia, who stopped wiping her hands and gave a slight nod. "I-uh-I need to tell you more, honey."

"I'm listening."

"I haven't been completely honest with you about my sister."

"What do you mean?"

"When I was eighteen, I ran away from home and I left Asia here alone. With Veronica." Ivy hesitated, then sat straight and raised her chin. "I'm the one who broke the relationship. I abandoned her, knowing Veronica would do monstrous things to her. And, until now, I never looked back." She held her breath and waited for him to respond.

"Have you two made up?" Denney asked.

Ivy looked across the room and fifteen years of heartbreak to Asia. "Have we?"

Asia shrugged, then nodded.

Ivy stood to join her sister at the table. Sitting, she said, "Do you remember when you told the boys about the truce between a troop of German and British soldiers on Christmas Day during World War I? They made up for the day, then resumed fighting later. I guess you could say that Asia and I have a similar situation."

"Are you trying to work things out? She's the only blood relative you've got."

Ivy looked across the table to where Asia shot her a knowing glance. "Actually … no, she's not. We found out we have a brother. Veronica and his father …" Ivy's voice trailed away.

"Did you know the guy before this?"

"Yes. He was our best friend when we were in elementary school. But his mother made him stop playing with us when we she found out we were siblings."

"This is a lot to absorb, Ivy."

"There's one more thing." She swallowed. "One of the reasons I agreed to all this is—Denney, my trucking company is in trouble. Big trouble."

Asia's brows arched in surprise. "*What,*" she whispered.

Denney's deep sigh echoed through the phone. "How bad?"

"I owe back taxes. A lot. It's a mess I don't want to get into over the phone. One little glimmer of good news is, the money Veronica offered is enough to cover the amount I owe, but I'm fairly certain there will be other fines involved. Very. Large. Fines."

"I wish you'd told me sooner."

"I know. I'm sorry for not telling you ... for ... lying."

"I don't know why you thought you needed to."

Ivy swallowed the bile that threatened her throat. She drew in a breath, looked at Asia, then back to her phone. "I was afraid I'd lose you and the boys."

Denney went stone quiet. Maybe her worst fears were true. Ivy ran her thumb across the diamond on her engagement ring. Denney had promised to love her forever. Could his forever withstand her lies? Or her lies on top of her lies?

But she shoved the thought away when Denney spoke. "What happens next?"

Next. Implying there would be more between them. This was not an end.

"I don't know. I'm just—I'm just sorry for all of this." Her voice cracked and her body ached. She wanted to push his bangs back from his face, to cook his oatmeal in the morning while he railed about politics. Get back to life and leave Veronica in the past. "I should have trusted you. But I thought—I was afraid of what you'd think of me." She sounded pathetic and weak. Falling prey to her own fears. And what was Denney thinking now? She needed to be in Seattle, where she could throw her arms around his waist and rest her head against the sound of his heartbeat. "Denney, I know this is a big deal. I feel so..." She couldn't find a word that described how she felt.

"No more worries, my little *farfalla.*"

His butterfly. "I've really blown it this time."

Denney's deep voice echoed from the phone. "When you get back, we'll go to dinner. Just the two of us. I want you to text me the details of this tax business, including deadlines. I'll call Paulo first thing in the morning. He and I will get on top of this problem right away. You focus on this thing with Veronica and Asia and ..."

"Nolan," she said, filling in the blank. "Okay. Thank you. Tell the boys I love them and give them hugs."

"Will do. Take care. Again, it was nice meeting you, Asia."

At the mention of her name, Asia's chin notched up. "You too."

"I love you, Ivy. See you soon."

"Love you back."

She ended the call. "Well, that's that. He's mad at me, but ..." Ivy brushed a stray thread from the hem of her shirt.

"How can you say he's mad? He didn't sound that way at all."

"Dinner, just the two of us, is code for we need to hash this problem out away from little listening ears. The boys were in the room."

Asia mouthed *oh.*

"Yes. Oh."

Asia took two wipes from her pocket and worked them around her fingers and palms. "I'm sorry, Ivy, I shouldn't have pushed—"

"Stop. I did this to myself. I lied to his face and told more lies once I got here. I have to answer for that." She pulled her hair into a makeshift ponytail, then let it fall. "We'll work it out. Anyway, things are looking up for you. You're now officially on the Morelli family radar."

"I'm sorry about your tax problems."

Ivy shrugged. "Paulo is our accountant, and Denney's cousin. He'll know what to do next. I trusted the wrong person and now I'm paying for it." She paused. "Or rather, Veronica's paying for some of it."

The cold stare from her sister chilled Ivy.

"What's that look for? You can't be angry with me too."

"I'm not mad at you." Asia balled her hands into fists and pressed them against her forehead. "I'm just so sick and tired of this house, and her nasty trophies, and trying to untangle Veronica's evil from our lives."

Asia shriveled like a morning glory bloom in afternoon sun. Ivy scooted her chair closer to the table, then jumped when Asia pounded the tabletop with both hands. "What are we going to do if the police determine Veronica *did* kill Vernon and Rita?"

"They'll close the case. They can't convict a dead woman."

"And what happens to us?"

"We go on living."

Asia stared dead-straight at Ivy. "You go on living. Nolan goes on living." She crumpled into a ball. "I can't. *She* won't let me."

Ivy reached across the table and grasped Asia's hands. She didn't pull away. "What are you talking about? Think about all you've accomplished. You're using her money to buy your home. That's a good thing."

"All I can think about is *her.*" Asia jerked her hand away. She pointed to her temples. "She's in here, twenty-four hours a day. I want her gone."

Ivy leaned close, rested her arms on the table. "Tell me how to help you."

A tear trailed down Asia's cheek. "No one can help me."

Ivy slammed back against her chair. At home she could put antibacterial ointment or Band-Aids on the boys' hurts. She could fix Denney a cup of coffee and rub his shoulders when he'd had a long day. She'd even discovered homemade brownies and chocolate ice cream with rainbow sprinkles soothed away painful losses at ball games and a lost account at work. But trying to erase the pain Veronica left rooted in Asia went far beyond her bag of healing tricks. "I wish we could rip her out of your head."

Asia lit up. "Maybe we can."

She leaped from her chair and ran to Veronica's bedroom. Seconds later, she held the shovel in her hands. "Do you think you could dig a hole?"

"Right now?" She glanced out the front window. "It's o-dark-thirty."

"Yes. Now. A deep one."

CHAPTER 44

MIRACLES STILL HAPPENED.

The soil shifted as Ivy stomped the edge of the shovel's blade into the ground behind the house. No mosquitoes dive-bombed her. And nothing creepy crawled over her feet. Three flashlights they purchased earlier on their midnight run to an all-night pharmacy provided enough light to fend off worries of chopping off a toe while she shoveled.

Rustling weeds announced Asia's approach. She stopped at the perimeter of the hole, spotlighted Ivy with illumination from her phone. "You look like a prairie dog. Half in the hole, half out."

"Are you complimenting or complaining?"

"Neither. I'm making an observation. I think prairie dogs are cute. And you're probably as dirty as one right now."

"Haven't noticed. Too busy digging." Ivy surveyed the shadowy space around her. "Do you think it's big enough?"

Asia went to the rim, shined her phone's light around the interior of the hole. "Perfect. I can't believe you dug that deep in a couple of hours."

Ivy wiped a droplet of sweat hanging from her hair. "Rage makes for fantastic fuel."

Asia took the packet of wipes from her shorts and handed them to Ivy. The single-minded calm that blanketed Asia once she'd voiced this new plan gave Ivy the creeps. Asia mirrored Veronica too much for Ivy to balk. "Use them all. The pack's jumbo-sized."

"Thanks." Ivy set the shovel on the solid ground, got a wipe, and scrubbed away the grit on her hands and face. A second one cleaned her sweaty neck and down the length of her arms. When she smelled more like artificial citrus fruit than dirt, she decided she was clean.

Asia waited nearby. She'd be useless in helping to get out of the hole, so Ivy sat on the edge and lifted her legs until she could swing them to the grass. Dirt dotted her skin from shins to the tops of her sneakers. She grabbed another wipe. Asia would never stomach her sporting legs resembling a Dalmatian.

Ivy bowed before her sister. "Good enough?"

"I still see smudges." Asia handed her a second pack of wipes. Ivy scrubbed until her skin tingled.

Ivy threw the empty packages into the hole.

They'd made the decision before she started digging to put every last one of Veronica's trophies left by the detectives in the hole. Then burn them.

Ivy agreed as soon as Asia voiced the idea. Burning those trophies served as the final act of cleaning the house. Having them around had stirred feelings she thought she'd filed away long ago and upset the balance she'd worked too hard for. Maybe watching them melt away in a fire of their own starting would aid in Asia's healing.

"Are you ready?"

"All my life," Asia whispered.

They dumped armfuls of Veronica's treasures into the hole. When they were finished, both she and Asia stopped to wipe perspiration from their foreheads. The late-night humidity was another thing she didn't miss about Florida.

"Pass me that lighter fluid," she said, pointing to another of their purchases from the pharmacy. Asia handed her the small can of Zippo. Ivy opened it, squirted the sharp-smelling flammable liquid across the treasures, avoiding the bags of letters, then tossed the empty can on top and retrieved a book of matches from her back pocket—another purchase. "It's gonna get hot around here now," she said, a smirk threatening to raise her lips.

Asia spread two tall kitchen garbage bags across the ground several yards away. "Since when wasn't it? So, we'll sit and watch," she said, "and try not to shiver." Her sarcasm would heal her, Ivy decided. Asia returned to the hole, gathered up the flashlights, then held one so Ivy could see to rip the stem of the match free from the book.

Ivy struck it and a flame sparked to life, then she ignited the entire matchbook. The heat pricked her fingers until she tossed the burning mass onto the bags of letters. Bubbles blistered the sides of the bags, melting them away and exposing the paper within. "Get back," she ordered Asia, then joined her on the kitchen trash bags—close enough to watch but far enough to keep from getting burned.

The paper shriveled and writhed. Embers and ash drifted upward within the smoke. A piece of charred paper caught by the night breeze circled and landed by Ivy's shoes. She ground the glowing ember into the soil. Burning Veronica's leftovers was a good thing. As ash, the letters had worth, they could nourish the soil and bring life, not pain.

They watched the fire, sitting side by side on the garbage bags. Ivy started to circle her knees with her hands, but Asia reached for the wipes in her pocket, and Ivy reached over to stop her. "Talk to me, China Girl," she said, her eyes never leaving the flames that now licked at the night air, crackling like an album on an old phonograph.

"I hate her."

"I did too."

"How did you stop?"

"I haven't."

"I hated you too," she said, her focus also never leaving the flames.

"You had good reason."

"That doesn't make it right. I don't want to hate."

Ivy pulled Asia's hand into her own. She wrapped her fingers around her sister's until they were laced together. They felt warm, alive. "After I left, I forced myself not to think about you." She looked at her sister, the flames reflected on her cheeks. "But then I'd dream about you. And when I woke up, I realized I missed you so much my guts ached, like I had the flu."

Asia turned her face toward her. "Then why didn't you ever come back?"

"Many times, during that first year, I thought about buying a bus ticket and coming back for you." Ivy drew in a deep breath. "Then I'd talk myself out of it. My life was no place for a fifteen-year-old girl. After a while, I got used to staying away."

The fire breathed. Rose again. It had caught hold of something. Perhaps the bags of Veronica's clothes. A popping resonated and Ivy imagined that the heat had exploded the tiny Empire State Building. That the metal of it now folded over and on top of itself. No more ... no more ...

Asia's soft voice mingled with the bursting of the flames. "Veronica let Dewitt the Twit come after me one night."

"Did he ..."

"No. I hit him with the shovel three times. That's what happened to the wall in our bedroom. I missed once."

Ivy's arm slid along Asia's shoulder and she hugged her tight. "You never cease to amaze me."

Asia shifted. "I amaze you? Why?"

"You're so smart. Only you would think ten steps ahead of her and hide a shovel under your bed."

"Surviving was the only way to ... get away from her."

"Exactly." Ivy pointed at Asia. "You," she said, then she pointed to herself. "And me. Survivors."

"I want to be more than that. I want a real life, like yours."

"I didn't do it on my own."

Asia sprang to her feet. "Ivy, I hear ... I think there's a truck turning into the driveway."

The headlights sliced into the dark until they grew bright as a truck barreled around the side of the house. The driver braked and when the door opened, Ivy stood and called out, "Nolan?"

He slammed his door. Marched through the dog fennel. Gone were his designer clothes. Instead he wore a t-shirt and athletic shorts. The white sneakers on his feet glowed in the firelight. "You two have cut ten years off my life." He stormed toward them. "Fifteen people called me about this huge fire on my property. You've terrified every resident within a two-mile radius." He now stood before them and sniffed the air. "Is that butane? And why on God's green earth are y'all making a bonfire at four o'clock in the morning?"

Ivy exchanged glances with Asia. "We're cleaning house," they said in unison.

CHAPTER 45

Ivy waved off Nolan. "Everything's under control, Nolan. The hole is wide and deep enough to keep from burning the yard. Although setting the house on fire did come into our original conversation." Nolan started to speak but Ivy stopped him from going on. "But only for a second. Asia squashed the notion with worrying about being arrested for arson. *We're safe.*"

"Really?" He swung around and pointed at the fire, taffy-stretching toward the stars. "What about all these sparks flying around like lightning bugs? You do realize if just one of them drifted back to the pines this whole place is going up."

"There's little to no breeze tonight. The sparks go up a few feet and then go out. We've been sitting here for a while. Problem free," she finished with a flourish of hand movements.

Nolan bypassed Ivy and went straight to Asia who had returned to her place on the kitchen garbage bag. "You agreed to this?"

Asia looked up. "I proposed the idea."

"I don't believe this. You're supposed to be the sensible one." Nolan raked his fingers through his hair. "Do you have any idea what kind of fine the county charges for illegal burning?"

Ivy shooed him as she settled near her sister. "Who cares? I'll pay, and this—" she cocked her thumb toward the fire "—is worth every penny."

Nolan punched air and muttered a new string of colorful complaints.

Asia tsked from her place on the ground. "Such language from a big brother."

Nolan muttered at her, then motioned. "Move over." He folded his long legs and occupied the spot Asia created for him.

Ivy and Nolan had always battled for power, his desire for control matching hers. He'd once said his parents never argued in front of him. Maybe that's why he always gravitated toward Asia. He preferred the take-time-and-work-things-out-quietly method.

Which irritated Ivy to no end. Why fiddle around with a problem? Denney felt the same way, thankfully. They'd spent many nights hashing things out at full volume, but they never went to bed mad. Her deception about Asia and the tax troubles was the first time in their marriage the sun would rise on a problem stewing between them. There would be many sleepless nights ahead.

The fire crackled and hissed, digesting the last remnants of Veronica's trophies. The top of the pile sank as the middle imploded. The lot fell. A plume of sparks shot into the air, then snuffed as they drifted back into the main body of the fire.

Ivy tapped Nolan's arm. "See, the sparks die right away."

He still sat with legs bent, his hands dangling over his knees. "Great. What are you burning anyway?"

"The trophies," Asia whispered.

"You mean all the stuff on the tarp? The clothes, and that weird doll, the bag of hair ... my—*our* father's letters?"

"*Some* of the letters," Ivy clarified. "The police took most of them. And you don't need to keep calling him 'our father.'" Ivy's knees cramped. She stretched them straight. The fire warmed her ankles. "Asia and I never knew him as anything but *your* daddy."

Her words brought an awkward silence, but Ivy didn't regret saying them. Bill Delong was nothing more than a man in the community she and Asia had known from a distance. He spoke to them when he saw them, but she couldn't remember him ever making any sort of gesture toward them. Other than, maybe, taking the photos for Veronica.

Although maybe it was the fear of Veronica retaliating that kept him from trying harder. Her heart pinched as a new thought came.

Being torn between two families must have ripped his heart in two. He couldn't be a true father to his daughters, only his son.

Well, Bill Delong had certainly done well by Nolan. Ivy's time on the streets taught her how to read a man, and she saw all the right things in Nolan. Loyal, respectful, caring, faithful, hardworking, and willing to commit. For life. But what had he hoped for her and Asia? Was the money for food and clothing? The kinds of extras Nolan had. He had to know how Veronica treated them. How did he justify staying away?

Nolan interrupted her thoughts. "He loved you both."

"You keep saying that, but Asia and I have no proof."

"When he was dying," he said, his gaze never leaving the remnants of the fire, "he could hardly breathe, but he forced himself to talk. His last words were about y'all."

Asia twitched, looked at Nolan. "What did he say?"

"He made me promise to find you and make things right."

Electric pulses of anger surged through Ivy. "Sounds like deathbed guilt to me."

"You're right." Nolan rubbed his hand along his shin, then looked at them both. "He regretted not admitting to the affair and taking the consequences."

A lick of fire swayed in the early morning air. "Why didn't he?" Asia asked.

"Shame. Fear and guilt over hurting my mother, loathing that whatever choice he made would only hurt her more. He knew he was wrong—"

"But he didn't want to live with the consequences," Ivy noted. "Instead, he made Asia and me do it for him."

"He never forgave himself."

"And we're supposed to excuse him?" Ivy stood, then moved closer to the fire. A forced promise of protection and a bag of money were supposed to absolve Bill Delong of the disastrous choices he made in life. She turned back and stood over Nolan. "This promise. Too late. We needed the protection when we were little. Do you have any idea what living with a monster like Veronica did to Asia and me?"

A sudden fireball of rage coursed through her. Asia stood to place her hand on Ivy's back. "Calm down."

Ivy wrenched free. "No, I won't calm down." She gripped Asia's shoulders. "Nolan needs to know, Asia. He needs to know what she did to us ... what his father *allowed* to happen." She pulled Asia in for a crushing embrace. "We have to tell him, Asia. How she let Dewitt—"

Asia pulled back. "Stop it."

"He has to know, Asia." Tears flowed as Ivy begged. "Just one story. One. Then he'll understand why there aren't enough promises from here to infinity to cover what happened to us. Bill Delong's money can't buy off our suffering."

Asia clawed Ivy's arms. "No."

Ivy nestled against Asia's shoulder. Bill Delong should have been forced to bear the responsibility. If he'd been a real man, owned his discretions, Asia would not be wasting away, wiping her hands every few minutes with Wet-Naps, unable to find her own happiness.

"Don't do this to me, Ivy. Please." Asia's tears brushed Ivy's ear. "Don't tell him."

Her anger melted into her as easily as butter in a hot skillet. She squeezed Asia's tiny waist. "I won't ever mention it again," she whispered. Yes, she'd keep Asia's secret. She owed her the favor. And so many more she could never repay.

"Thank you." Asia hugged her tight.

The empty ache flared in Ivy's arms as Asia slipped away to the fireside. Ivy wiped her cheeks with the back of her hand as Nolan joined them near the edge of the cleansing hole. He scratched his head.

"Tell me. Tell me what I need to know."

"It's nothing," Asia replied as she drew a wipe from her pocket and cleaned her hands then drew in a deep breath. Exhaled. Her lips pursed as she repeated the action.

He raised his hands in surrender. "I thought you were set on getting things in the open."

The flames popped. Ivy peered at a blazing face. Christina had slipped to the bottom, the flames now consuming her. Her eye sockets glowed as yellow-orange fingers twined within. The plastic dissolved, stretching her once sweet face into a wild-eyed gremlin whose grimace widened with each lick of the flame. After a few seconds, the face caved, leaving an empty, dripping hole.

Asia sniffed loudly. Nolan stepped around Ivy and went to her, laid his arm across her shoulders. "You brought that doll out to the field once. She had long blonde hair, and a blue dress with little yellow flowers."

This remembrance of Christina brought surprise. In a breath's notice, it seemed he morphed into a different man. He smelled of soap and deodorant, not his usual breath of expensive cologne. A lock of hair curled over his eye, as Asia's did when she wore short bangs. Ivy saw reflections of her and Asia in the shape of Nolan's eyes. The way his cheeks sloped to his jaw. "How could you remember her doll?"

"I don't know. Just flashed through my mind. If you asked me for a description before, I couldn't."

"What else do you remember?" Asia asked.

"The stories. How I thought you and Ivy were twins but so different at the same time. The fun we had. And how y'all never wanted to go home. I thought you were afraid of the bull in Mr. Gannet's field. I never considered it was because of… her."

A light brighter than the glow from the fading bonfire flared in him as a sense of agonizing sorrow burned from within. "I am so sorry. It was right there in front of me." He pulled Asia close to his side, then roped Ivy around the waist with his free arm until he'd bundled them together. "Dad wronged you both. I don't know how you survived."

Ivy broke free while Asia stayed within their brother's embrace. "We had no other choice," she said.

A country song toned from Nolan's truck. "That's Nicole. I was supposed to call her as soon as I got here." He slowly slid his arm from Asia's shoulders. "Be right back." He trotted toward his truck, opened the driver's door, reached into the cab, then stood in the opening, his foot propped on the running board. They watched in silence for a moment as he ducked his head, mumbled into the phone, then rested his hand on the cab's roof. There didn't seem to be a quick end to his call.

Ivy leaned into Asia. "You okay?"

Asia remained silent as they returned to the garbage bags and sat.

Nolan signed off the call. He slammed his truck door and joined them. "Nicole's got the 7-a to 7-p shift today. She's getting ready for work now." He directed his attention to the horizon. "Sun'll be up before we know it." He sat beside Asia, stretching his long legs before the fading flames. "Our girls spent the night with their cousins, won't be back until tomorrow." He crossed his ankles, leaned back on his hands. "Caretaker for my mother will be at the house any minute. So, I told Nicole I'd stay here for a while."

Ivy leaned forward. "Anybody think to bring marshmallows?"

Silence followed her remark she'd hoped would bring at least a chuckle. She sat cross-legged, propped her elbow on her knee, and cupped her chin with her hand. Then, Nolan laughed softly.

Ivy nudged him. "What's so funny?"

"Can you imagine what some high-priced psychiatrist would say about this?" He inclined his head toward the fire.

"We'd tell them the same thing I already told you. We're cleaning house."

"No," he drawled the word for a full three syllables. "This isn't cleaning. This is burning a dragon."

"What do you mean?" Asia asked.

"I haven't thought about this since I was maybe eight or nine. You remember the stories we made up when we were kids? Every time we defeated one of our imaginary dragons, we'd make a stick pile and pretend to burn them. They could never come back and hurt us."

"And as they lay dying, we always told them we forgave them, because they were only being a dragon," Asia whispered.

Ivy recalled the rest of the tale. "And after they were dead, we vowed to never speak of them again. Because dead dragons came back to life if someone held on to their memory." She grunted. "We were smarter than we realized."

Nolan shifted and his knee popped. He rubbed his knee cap. "Old football injury. Blew the entire thing out in college." He squirmed, rolled his shoulders around. "I talked with Detective Graham yesterday."

Asia sat forward. "What did he say?"

"Not much. He asked me what I knew about my father and Veronica. I told him what Dad told me, but that I had no proof of anything until you two found the rags and the money. He said he's certain Veronica murdered Vernon and Rita. But without bodies, he can't prove it." Nolan stood, groaning as he straightened his bad knee.

Asia sprang and ran as if her tail were on fire. "What is she—" Ivy scrambled up, then took off after her, chasing her through the weedy yard. "Asia, what's the matter?"

Asia had reached the car. Had yanked the driver's door open. "Get the keys for me." She slid into the seat. "Now, Ivy."

Her tone jolted Ivy to action. Within the moment, she came back with keys and Asia's purse in hand.

Ivy grabbed the door handle. "Where are you going?"

"Veronica," Asia panted. Her chest heaved as she fought for breath.

"Don't. You *can't.*" Ivy tried to grab Asia's wrist, hold her back.

Nolan called from behind, but she didn't look back. She couldn't. "You're about to have an attack. You'll wreck before you get there."

The keys jingled against the fob as Asia tossed them on the seat. Her breath came in shrill whistles as she gripped the steering wheel. "Shut the door."

Ivy blocked the door. "No. Asia."

But Asia reached around her, grabbed the door handle, and yanked. The door slammed into Ivy. "Asia!"

"Get out of my way," Asia demanded. Her finger found the start button and the car roared awake.

Before Ivy could do anything to stop her, Asia slammed into reverse and sped backward into the lane, the car's door still open. Ivy back-pedaled to avoid being hit.

Asia yanked the door shut.

"Asia, *don't.* Come back," Ivy screamed over the sounds of the car's tires crushing the limerock in the lane.

Nolan half-jogged to Ivy's side. "Where is she going?"

Asia squealed onto the highway and the car's taillights disappeared around the corner.

Ivy rubbed her skin. The ache in her hip where the door crashed into her rose to an intense pain. "I don't understand what happened ..." Maybe Asia had finally snapped. The good Lord knew she'd fought hard. She'd been a tough soldier. Ivy fell against Nolan, laid her hands against his chest, felt the drumming of his heart, pumping blood. The same blood ran through the three of them. "I'm afraid of what she's going to do, Nolan." Ivy grabbed him for support, clawed the fabric of his t-shirt into her palms. "She's going to the hospital. And you're driving me there."

Nolan nodded. "Yes, ma'am."

CHAPTER 46

No. Going. Back.

Asia forced her feet across the dot-flecked hospital tiles. One step … two …

With the exception of left-behind trash from local eateries, the family area down the hall was empty. Beyond the barrier doors, the nurses' station stood to her right. There, two of the personnel concentrated on computer screens and tapped away on keyboards. A few spoke in hushed tones and concentrated only on their conversations. One of them was Nicole, but her back was to Asia and she appeared to be speaking into her phone. She would make an easy approach to Veronica's room. She just had to keep going. One step … two … past the nurses' station.

Until someone spoke her name. She turned to find Nicole behind her. "Nolan just called. Asked me to look for you."

Asia stood, jaws tightly shut. She didn't need looking after. No, instead she was here to stop the torture. "I came to see Veronica."

"I'll take you to her room." If her friendly without being touchy-feely tone was meant to soothe, it failed. She looked back to the station. "I'll be right back, Jancey."

Asia spied a line of dark, windowed rooms. "I forgot which room is hers."

"Come with me." Nicole walked ahead, her soft-soled shoes squishing on the smooth tiled floor. She stopped at the doorway bearing Veronica's nameplate. "There are a few things I need to share with you before you go in."

"I won't run this time." Asia squared her shoulders as Ivy always did, hoping the act would exude strength rather than a cheap guarantee.

"No, this isn't about the last time you visited." Nicole hesitated, then motioned for Asia to follow. "I'll show you."

Asia entered the gloomy recesses of Veronica's room. Stood just beyond the door, taking in the bed and the figure under the blankets. A bedside light's dim beam glinted off the collection of tubes winding their way to an IV pole and the myriad of machines flanking the bed. A monitor beeped in a faint, low tone. "Is that her heartbeat?"

"Yes."

Ivy would be thrilled. She once said the only way they'd ever prove Veronica had a heart was to hook her up to a machine.

"I know all of this is intimidating," Nicole said, "but sometimes seeing helps in the healing process afterward."

"Afterward? Nolan said her condition improved."

Nicole's professional sympathy resurfaced. "Patients like her often get better before they get worse. It's a rally. The 7-p to 7-a nurse just told me; she took a bad turn around four this morning."

The same time she and Ivy began to burn Veronica's trophies. Asia slipped her hand in her pocket in search of Russ's card, then rubbed the surface. It was time to face Veronica. Her feet seemed to miss the floor and press on air as she moved to the bedside. She wavered and the room spun.

Nicole grasped Asia's shoulders and steadied her. "Take a moment," she said. "Breathe." They stood so close their faces almost touched. Nicole studied her with an unprofessional stare. There had to be a measure of curiosity, a wonder of how this stranger, the daughter of her patient, was family. Maybe Nolan discussed Ivy and her in their private moments, told Nicole the kind of mother they'd come from.

Nicole rubbed the small of Asia's back. "Feeling a little more stable?" Her words were coated with genuine concern. Asia pulled from her hold, adjusted her shirt, sending the acrid aroma of the bonfire's smoke wafting around them.

Veronica's trophies ... their nightmare, hers and her sister's, burned to ash. She should run. Jump in the car and squeal her way out of here. But what she wanted and what she must do were two different things. "I'm ready," she said to herself more than anyone else. She walked past Nicole to the bedside. The rail enclosed the bed like a stubby fence at the zoo. Appropriate, since the figure housed inside could be as vicious as a crocodile.

Nicole adjusted an IV. "I like to help families understand what all this equipment does. Helps make things less intimidating."

Asia gave her a side-eyed glance. If only Nicole understood how no machines could be more frightening than the body they kept alive.

While Nicole talked—saying words like ventilator and Foley catheter and nasogastric tube—Asia stared at the rise where Veronica's feet were tucked beneath the sheet. She swept along her legs and stopped at her hips. The sheet barely rose above the surface of the bed. This was not flesh and blood; a skeleton lay beneath the linens. "She's so thin," Asia whispered. The teeth-gnashing, bloodthirsty beast of her nightmares lay still, reduced to a bag of bones.

Nicole slid her hands into the pockets on her scrubs top. "She weighed in the nineties when she arrived. She's lost more since. Cancer causes that."

"She has cancer?"

"Started in her lungs."

"I thought she'd had—we were told she'd had a stroke."

Nicole looked up as she stopped in her ministrations. "She did. But the cancer came first."

"But Veronica never smoked." She would never allow anything as strong as nicotine to have power over her. She was always in charge. Over everything. Everybody.

"Ten to fifteen percent of diagnosed lung cancer occurs in nonsmokers. Two-thirds of those are women."

Asia knitted her fingers together to stop their shaking. Veronica had suffered. She followed the texture of the blanket along Veronica's body. And then she took in the face that had haunted her every day of her life. Veronica's cheeks resembled the dried-apple crafts she'd seen at the Maryville Folk Festival. All angles and hollows, dried to a withered hardness. Her collarbone stood out like the great roots of an oak tree jutting from the ground. Frazzled cords of wiry gray hair twined from her head like slate-colored snakes against the stark white of the pillow.

In elementary school, Asia had drawn her in much the same way for a Mother's Day card. Her teacher shredded the picture before slamming another piece of paper on the desk. "Draw flowers and hearts for your mother," she'd said.

"Medusa still fits you better than hearts and flowers," Asia now whispered.

Nicole's confusion wrinkled her brow. "What was that?"

"How long will she ... before she ..."

"Her doctor usually makes rounds early." She glanced at her watch. "I would expect him any minute now. He'll explain things. I would have ... you know, told Nolan more, but HIPAA laws prevented my saying much. We had to wait."

"Has Nolan told *you* anything?"

Nicole hesitated, clearly weighing how to answer without crossing boundaries. "Yes. I know that you're my sister-in-law. That we're family." She checked a monitor, hiding whether she liked the news. Like the snakes that surrounded Medusa's head, Veronica had sunk her fangs into another victim. Nicole thought she had married into one family tree, only to find out her husband had been conceived by an invasive species that poisoned all the members. That *this woman* was her mother-in-law, God help her.

"Did he tell you that he was our best friend when we were little? Or that he'd been stuck between trying to protect you and your girls and keeping a promise he made to his ... our father?" The "our father" wanted to stay hooked inside, but she forced the words out. Denying the truth wouldn't change the facts. "A very good friend of mine once said God stuck you with your relatives, but he let you pick your friends." She smiled at Nicole. "I'm glad Nolan is my brother. He's a good man."

Nicole dipped her head. "He is."

A knock sounded on the door frame. A small, dark-skinned man with gold, wire-rimmed glasses hurried across the floor. "Hello. I'm Doctor Nurayain." His introductory words came close-clipped, laced with a British accent.

"I'm Asia." She glanced back at the bed. "The youngest daughter."

The doctor gave a compulsory nod, as if it were a mandated practice. "I know this is a difficult time, but it's good you're here … your mother's organs are failing. Shutting down."

"I don't understand. I thought she was improving?"

The doctor continued. "This is very common in patients with conditions like your mother's. They rally, then quickly decline."

Asia looked around as a wild thought came to mind. *Ah, Death … so that's you looming in the room … waiting for your time.* She looked back at Veronica. Her ventilator filled the silence with a steady whoosh-click, whoosh-click. Deep in the recesses of the brain, where humans cannot see with monitors and sensors, did Veronica know her life now faded to black? And, if so, was she afraid?

"Asia," Nicole said, and Asia startled.

"I'm sorry, what?"

Dr. Nurayain smiled as though he understood. "Again, I know this is difficult, but the woman you knew is gone. We ran some tests yesterday." He glanced over his shoulder, then back to Asia. "I've been going over them down the hall. These machines are now doing the work her body cannot."

"What does that mean?"

"The tests indicate that your mother is brain-dead, Miss Butler. There are things we need to discuss …" His words trailed. "At this point—"

"Are you asking me for permission to unplug … the machines?"

He adjusted his glasses. "We cannot make this decision for you nor can I legally advise you, but …"

Asia reminded herself to breathe. "I can't make this decision. Didn't she have a living will?"

"She did not."

Of course she wouldn't. She had probably calculated this moment, a time when she and Ivy would have to make the final decision over her living and dying. "I have to talk to my sister." Asia sought Nicole's face. "And Nolan."

She walked to a chair on legs stronger than she expected them to be.

Dr. Nurayain might find collaborating with death to be a mundane decision, a quick choice. Not for Asia. She doubled over. She'd been asked to do a lot of things in her life ... a lot of things in the last few weeks. But a new fear niggled while the whooshing and beeping of the machines nagged at her. Tapped like impatient fingers on a tabletop. They wanted a decision. The doctor wanted a decision. And maybe ... maybe ... deep in the core of wherever she was, Veronica waited to see if her weakling child would, at last, be strong.

They'd caught every red light ... and now an early morning freight train. "Why do they never cross your path except when you're in a hurry?" Ivy bunched the hem of her shorts into her fingers. The red-and-white crossarms rose with a lack of hurry. The muscles in her neck knotted together. If she didn't relax, her shoulders were going to press into her ears and she'd become the overstressed, no-necked wonder Denney teased her about.

"Go," she said through clenched teeth as the gate wobbled to the final up position.

"I am," Nolan countered as he pressed the gas and drove through the crossing at a polite pace.

"There's no one in front of you," she both whined and barked. "Why are you going so slow?"

"Because the speed limit here is thirty-five and my getting a ticket won't help get us to the hospital any sooner."

Ivy pressed her feet against the floorboard. The train must have been over two hundred cars long. They'd waited for seventeen minutes. She knew because she'd watched time tick away on Nolan's dash clock. The only thing preventing her from pounding the stupid thing was being stuck with the price of the repairs.

Fields still blanketed in the last grips of dusk swept past as Nolan increased his speed. "All right. Barring any other diversions, we should be there shortly. Twenty minutes."

Ivy didn't answer. If she were driving, they'd make it in ten. Her phone buzzed. "It's Asia."

She pressed the talk button. "Where are you?"

"In Veronica's room."

"What? What's going on? Are you all right?"

"I just need you and Nolan here." No doubt Asia was sitting on a chair at the hospital, wrapped into a protective ball and wiping her hands. Ivy switched the phone to her right ear, then poked Nolan's arm. "Go faster. She's at the hospital and needs us there."

Nolan sat straighter in the seat. The truck's engine whined as he pressed the accelerator. "If a cop pulls us over, I'm blaming you."

Ivy flashed a thumbs-up. "Great. I'll pay the ticket if you get one. Just move."

"Where are you?" Asia asked.

"Twenty minutes away."

"I really need you here. Both of you."

"What's the matter?"

Asia hesitated. The garbled words of an announcement played in the background.

"Talk to me, Asia. What's happening?"

"The doctor … he says she's … her organs are shutting down, the machines are the only things keeping her alive, really."

"So, what does that mean?"

Nolan glanced from the road and mouthed *what?*

"They want me to make the choice to let her … die. Unplug her …"

Die.

Ivy had always known Veronica would die. One day. But knowing a truth in your head was far from facing the reality. For fifteen years, she'd worked to forget the woman had ever lived. And soon, she would be gone.

"All right . . . Just tell them yes and let things go their natural way."

"I can't. I don't think it's right for me to do this alone. And you're the oldest."

Ivy cupped her forehead with her hand. "Then I'm giving my consent, and so does Nolan." She ducked her head at Nolan, asked for silent confirmation. He broadcasted a silent but clear response in the soft morning light that filled the truck's cab. *I have no stake in this, don't ask me.* He focused on the road. "Nolan agrees."

"I don't want to be here alone when it happens."

"You want me there with you? Are you in the room?"

"Yes, I told you that."

In the room. Staring at Veronica's dead body. And what would they do there? Reminisce on old times? Laugh and dance and shout hallelujah? Or scream for the world to hear that this woman—this *dead woman*—had torn their lives into shattered pieces. Had left scars from their childhood and created new ones from as far away as a hospital bed. No. If they allowed old memories to surface, they'd both end up in the mental ward. And if she entered that room, she'd be standing inches away from Veronica's dead body.

"Asia, I don't know—"

"Then, I'll do it," Asia said, her voice full of a fire mixed with frustration. Ivy had heard that tone before, of course, but never like this. Something new was being birthed inside of her sister.

The call went dead.

Ivy clamped her phone in her fist. She'd forced her little sister to face Veronica alone. Again.

"Is she okay?" Nolan asked in a low voice.

Ivy stuffed her phone in her purse. "Drive. Faster."

CHAPTER 47

Time paused. The beeps of the monitors, the flow of air blowing from AC ducts and her own breathing melded together as a soft hum in Asia's ears.

"Miss?" Doctor Nurayain's voice called from far away.

"Asia?" Nicole laid her hand on Asia's forearm.

Asia searched Nicole's face. "What am I supposed to say?"

"He wants you to give consent. We'll need to bring in the papers for you to sign."

She'd sign those papers and be the final, and maybe only person, who got the last say with Veronica. "May I have five minutes before you get them?"

The doctor gave a slight bow. "It'll take at least that long *to* get them, but ... of course." He left the room, Nicole right behind him.

Asia shuffled to the bed. She stared down at Veronica's spectral face. Her mother's eyes sank deep into the sockets, as if the muscles gave way and the eyeballs sagged into an empty cavity. Her lids resembled onion skin.

She pulled her wipes from her pocket, removed one, and wiped the bedrail. Twice. Then gripped the cool plastic with both hands. She half expected Veronica's eyes to snap open, pin her with her viperous look. Instead, it was *her* time to talk. And she took it. "Veronica," she said. Then sucked in more breath to support the coming words. "Hello. It's me. Asia."

The ventilator breathed a reply. The heart monitor blipped.

Asia inhaled, wrinkled her nose at the stench of old flesh hovering around Veronica. She leaned close. "For once, *you're* going to listen to *me.*" Volumes of words piled in her mind then, poised to spring from her mouth like sprinters at the starting blocks.

The dam broke. Images flooded over her, memories coming in waves, marching forward with the precision of an ant army. Her nerves tingled. She braced for the coming panic. For the shallow breaths to replace her normal breathing. She searched the bed for the call button, extending a trembling finger toward the white outline of a nurse's head. Memories spun. She was gathering cantaloupes to pay for Ivy's dress. She was arguing with Veronica so Ivy could sneak out for prom. She was preparing her Chamber of Commerce speech, the one she'd practiced for weeks. Ten minutes before she left, Veronica entered her room and dropped a pile of ashes at Asia's feet. "Nice speech, honey. So *fiery*. Shows the world how well I taught you." And later that evening, Asia delivered her speech from memory, legs quaking behind the lectern, so much so she almost dropped to the floor.

But she won the scholarship.

She allowed the memories to play through to their finish until a new truth emerged. The memories were not her enemy. They were simply reminders of each step along a journey God walked with her, bringing her to this moment in time. Through the pain, he'd forged within her strength and wisdom so she could stand in this murky, cheerless room and give Veronica what she needed most.

Forgiveness. Compassion.

Asia smoothed the blanket, tucked the soft fold around Veronica's frail body. New words sprung along with a new voice. A strong voice. "The doctor says you need to go now," Asia said.

She should touch her, hold her hand. Asia reached, but drew back. Blue-gray veins lined the surface. Veronica's yellowed skin appeared so thin even the lightest touch might tear the delicate fabric covering her protruding bones. So, instead, Asia smoothed the lone tendril from Veronica's face. "You taught me well, just like you said. But I survived. And you made me stronger, whether you meant to or not."

She blew out a breath that, she felt certain, had been pent up her entire life. "That is a gift. Thank you." A wall clock swept away the seconds. Tick … tick … tick … Voices mumbled outside the door followed by a knock.

Asia leaned in close, her lips almost touching the curve of Veronica's translucent ear.

"Goodbye, Veronica," she whispered. "Rest in peace."

CHAPTER 48

Thirty years put to rest within the span of thirty minutes. Asia leaned against the back of the padded chair in the hospital chapel. Death's hovering spirit had acted quickly. Less than five minutes after Asia scribbled her name on the form she didn't bother to read, buttons were switched off. Tubes were pulled. Quiet replaced the whooshing and the beeping until *Le Mort* performed his business.

She inhaled the soft scent of lemon from her hands and face. She'd scrubbed every inch of exposed skin as soon as Nicole escorted her from Veronica's room to the chapel, leaving with a promise that when Nolan and Ivy arrived, she'd direct them to where she waited. Asia's legs ached. No wonder, she hadn't slept in over twenty-four hours. Somewhere between the bonfire and Veronica's death, today had melted into tomorrow.

A new day's birth. Her *re*birth. She rubbed her neck. This rebirth felt more a leftover type of death reserved for zombies in a cheap horror movie than what it was.

She smoothed her hair as the soft glow of the chapel lighting faded between her eye slits. Her head slumped to the side, jerking her awake. She stood, wiggled her arms, and stretched. If she stayed in the chair any longer, she'd be sleeping soundly in minutes.

She kneaded her lower back with her fingers. After years of standing in front of students she should possess better endurance. Taking quiet steps in hopes of not disrespecting the room, she noted the chapel's cream-colored walls and dark burgundy carpet. The chairs stood in symmetrical rows. But one chair in the front had slipped out of order. No one else would be unnerved by this, but in straightening the line, her breathing steadied.

She took deliberate steps along the row, stopping at the small diamonds of multicolored light shining on the cushions and the floor. She glanced to the source; the morning sun's rays illuminated a nearby stained-glass window—a kaleidoscope of shapes formed the scene of a sunburst shining over a pure white dove. With a little imagination, she could hear the dove's coo and the whooshing of the feathers. Far different than a life-giving machine.

She spied a small brass plaque attached to the wall beneath the window. Her reader's brain could not resist a chance to absorb wise words.

Given in memory of George Robert Ellis by his beloved family.
June 17, 1976
"But one thing I do, forgetting those things which are behind and reaching forward to those things which are ahead."
Philippians 3:13

Forgetting those things which are behind. She read the words two more times.

Things like broken dolls, ripped essays. A father who chose reputation over responsibility. And a sister who left. They were *all* behind her. Just forget—but this was one thing she wanted but couldn't make herself do.

But there was the other part to the verse: *Reaching forward to those things which are ahead.*

What lay ahead for her?

Her phone buzzed from the recesses of her purse. She fished it from the depths and read the screen. *Russ.* Her stomach fluttered as she pressed the talk icon. "Hey." She sat in a nearby chair.

"Hey there. Haven't heard from you in a bit. Just wanted to check in before I get to the station."

Asia stretched her legs, and in that moment, she longed in a new way to be home in Maryville, sitting on Russ's old, blue couch, speaking face-to-face. "I'm sorry. We've had a ton of things to deal with."

"I figured. How are *you*?"

"I don't know."

"What happened?"

"Veronica died a little while ago."

"I'm so sorry, Asia. I wish I could be there with you."

"Me too." Tears trickled and she dotted them away with her finger. "I don't know what I'm supposed to feel right now." Tremors raked across her. She'd never admitted anything beyond being tired, stressed, or hungry to Russ. And in the midst of all the things happening today, she *wanted* to tell him that her brain numbed, time stopped the minute she entered Veronica's room and that her heart nagged, telling her that she should be sad when she wasn't. More than anything, she wanted to make a memory of sitting in this quiet chapel, talking to him, and for the first time in fifteen years, feeling anchored because he was on the other end of the phone.

"I was with her when she died."

"Was your sister there?"

"No."

"That's rough."

"It wasn't her fault, she was on the way... she just didn't make it in time."

Someday—not now—she'd tell him about the bonfire, about her rushing to the hospital alone and how she'd signed the papers. But in this moment, other words must be shared. "I want to tell you something I should have said long ago."

His truck's door locks clicked in the background. "What's that?"

"Thank you."

"For what?"

"Not thinking I'm crazy."

His slow, deep chuckle seeped through the phone. "You are many things, Asia Butler, but never crazy. And if you were, I'd still like you. A lot."

"Thanks, Russ."

"Hey, I made it to work. May I call you later when I've got a quiet minute?"

"Absolutely. And … thanks for calling. I needed this."

"Asia," he said, then paused, "I'm just so sorry. Take care. Sending prayers. Bye." His end went dead.

Asia slid her phone in her purse, then focused on the yellow, triangular pieces of glass in one of the chapel windows. Grays and blues were supposed to be the calming colors, but today, the yellow called to her as the door to the chapel opened. She didn't turn toward it. She knew who'd come in, knew by instinct. Soft steps padded down the aisle and stopped at the end of the row before Ivy plopped beside her. "Before you say anything, I want to say I'm sorry." She dropped her purse to the chair on her right. "You shouldn't have been stuck with … making that decision … about Veronica. Alone. Again."

Asia met Ivy's gaze. "You don't need to feel guilty."

The corners of Ivy's lips twitched. "We—Nolan and I—left right after you did. We got caught by a million and one red lights and then the longest train in history. Then, there was an accident on the highway. We were stuck in the backup for almost an hour. And then," Ivy's pitch rose, "we get here and they had the entrance to the parking garage blocked off because of a fender bender on the second floor."

"There always seems to be hindrances in our way."

Ivy draped her left arm over the back of the chair then twisted her body so she could face Asia. "The minute I think we're on track, here comes a train to derail our progress." She drew a breath. "How are you?"

"I'm *okay*, Ivy. I think—I think—I was supposed to face this … alone."

Ivy pressed her hand against her lips, her eyes shimmering with tears. She sought Asia's face, bore deep, looking for a way to connect. "We never had a chance. We were soldiers in a war zone, and the only way we bonded was through fighting our common enemy. We had no mother, no father. No one to teach us how to love. We have nothing from our childhoods except shared memories of her terrorizing us and how we stuck together in spite of it." Her bottom lip trembled. "How could a mother treat her children that way?"

"Can a woman forget her nursing child, and not have compassion on the son of her womb?" Asia sought Ivy's face. "That's from—"

"I know where it came from." Ivy grew quiet, sat staring at her hands.

The colors of the window beckoned to Asia. Time, pain, strife all ceased as she watched the dove, suspended within the glass, forever soaring, forever free.

"I'm done, Asia. I don't want to pay for the past anymore. I don't."

The hue of the window's colors changed as the sun must have hid behind a cloud. "Me neither, Ivy. She was who she was, did what she did."

Silence stretched between them until Ivy said, "So, what's next, China Girl?"

Asia rummaged in her purse for a pen and her small notebook. Life required a plan. Death followed suit. "I guess we organize her funeral. Is Marston Fields still in business?"

Ivy crossed her legs. "Do we *have* to do that now?"

Asia exposed her scars. She held them out to Ivy. "We have way too many of these. It's time to push forward. Heal ourselves. Nolan too." She flipped the notebook's cover open. "Should we include him in the funeral plans?"

"No. He already told me he won't come. He said this is between us and Veronica. We were *her* children. And we are sisters."

"We are, and so much more." Asia grasped Ivy's hand in her own and squeezed. "And you are my one good friend."

Ivy raised a brow. "What about Mr. Calendar?"

Asia smiled wide. "Fine. You're one of my *two* good friends."

CHAPTER 49

LET THE DEAD BURY the dead.

If she could have found a ghost willing to bury Veronica, Ivy would have paid him double to avoid standing here alone with Asia, listening to a stranger pray for her mother's soul and passage to the next realm. Or to wherever Death had whisked Veronica when he took her a week ago.

The high-noon sun swamped them in humidity thick enough to slice like bread. Asia stirred the air as she waved the Marston Shields Funeral Home's courtesy fan. The small breeze she mustered rustled the wavy tendrils of hair framing her face.

The funeral director ended his prayer. Ivy wished she could remember the man's name. But she was only half-listening when he introduced himself earlier. He'd ejected from the driver's seat of the black hearse, hurried to shake her and Asia's hands while offering his condolences for their loss. In a single breath, he explained his brief order of service, waved to his assistants to bring Veronica's coffin to the gravesite, then ushered Ivy and Asia to their places. All without appearing pushy, rushed, or unorganized. Such efficiency was rare and sought after in business. And so, in under fifteen minutes, he'd thanked God for his blessings poured out on us all, lamented over Veronica's passing, and prayed for her and Asia's hearts as they faced this difficult time as they moved on. All spoken in a bass voice that rang with a lazy drawl fit for a country song.

Moving on. The best words he'd spoken yet.

Asia nudged Ivy. The funeral director stood before them, hands clasped and waiting for a response.

Ivy shrugged. "Did I miss something?"

"He asked if we wanted to say a few words," Asia said quietly.

The director smoothed a professionally empathetic expression on his face. "Some families find it to be a way toward closure."

The few things she might say would not be appropriate for such a time as this. "No, thank you."

The funeral director nodded. "Take as much time as you want for goodbyes. Leave when you're ready." He showed sincere respect and sympathy as he bowed.

"Thank you for your help during this time. And your understanding," Asia said.

He patted her on the arm. "You take care." He bowed to Ivy. "And you too." He patted her on the hand.

"Thank you. I know this wasn't really the norm."

The director shed his professional demeanor a moment as a thoughtful look came over him. "We're not really here for the dead. Our main job is to aid and comfort the living."

He ambled to the truck where diggers waited under the shade of a distant oak along a back fence.

Metallic clanks sifted through the air. The diggers unloaded their shovels and propped them against the side of their truck. The two men tried to act casual but failed when Ivy glanced their way. One checked his watch, the shovels, and then his watch again. He leaned into the other man, made a quick comment, then rested his back against the truck. Impatience seasoned every move they made. They needed to finish their job.

As did she and Asia.

They stood before the dark casket, adorned with burnished brass handles and trim. It was not the one Veronica picked. When Asia called the funeral home, they told her Veronica had everything prearranged. At their consultation for the service, they discovered the casket Veronica designated was pure white, adorned with tiny pink roses and lined in pink silk.

The minute the director showed them the coffin, she and Asia blurted, "No," in unison. Instead, Veronica was buried in a sedate, polished wood box with cream interior. They also opted to allow the funeral home to write the obituary for the local paper. "She can just pitch a dying duck fit," Ivy mumbled to Asia as they signed the final paperwork.

A glint had sparked in Asia's eyes. "Be careful what you say."

Blue-gray clouds now assembled on the horizon. Low rumbles sounded in the distance. A coolish breeze ruffled the overhanging edges of the funeral tent.

Asia surveyed the sky. "We should go."

"One question first."

"What?"

"What finally killed her?"

"Lung cancer coupled with the stroke. Although, from what Nicole said, the cancer had spread."

Ivy harrumphed. "Lung cancer." She crossed her arms. "I always swore she'd die of pure meanness."

"Did you ever feel like ... she came out in you?" Another rumble of thunder punctuated Asia's question.

"Once. I was in a drug house, and a junkie desperate for a fix stole my stash. To punish him, I took the stash of this horror-movie-demented-type guy and blamed the junkie. I watched them beat each other until they both passed out." She exhaled a long shaky breath. "Took a dozen group meetings, long talks with Denney, and boatloads of repentant prayers to get over that." Ivy twirled her ring around her finger. "What about you?" Long fingers of lightning clawed their way across the distant heavens.

"I did." Thunder almost drowned out Asia's whispered response. "I was a substitute teacher, in an eighth-grade remedial math class. A rough group of students, except for this pale, spindly boy trying hard to fit in. His friends dared him to grab me and—I said ..."

"What did you say?"

A red hue marched upward from Asia's neck to her cheeks. "Little boys beg for a lady's attention. Not men."

Ivy's jaw dropped.

Asia held up her hands. "I know. The poor boy's bottom lip trembled, and he just deflated. His friends laughed so loud the teacher from next door came to shush them. He ran from the class and the principal had to go find him. The second I said it, he looked ... like a gigged fish. A power-rush came over me ... and I loved it. Seconds later my good sense came back. I felt nauseous. That poor boy."

"Did you ever see him again?"

"No. I couldn't make myself go back. Just seeing the school's address made my stomach jumpy."

Clouds boiled above them. Ivy gestured to Veronica's coffin. "Should we be ... crying? Because all I feel right now is relief. Guilt-free relief."

"Me too," Asia whispered. "And I hope it's okay."

A bright flash lit the cemetery. Thunder cannon-boomed around them, shaking the ground. Asia caught Ivy's eye. "This may be the duck fit."

Giggles grabbed the two of them. They huddled together under the tent, shaking, and cackling together as another flash of lightning tore through the area. A gun-shot clap echoed across the graves.

The funeral director hurried to them. "Ladies, I don't mean to rush y'all, but this tent is no place to be in weather like this." He motioned toward their car. "I would feel far less worried with y'all safely tucked in there." His voice spiked to a higher pitch.

"We're done," Ivy said as she wiped away mirth tears. She walked to the coffin. "Goodbye, Veronica." And there it was, the one and only time she'd said goodbye to her mother. And, this time, it was forever.

She tapped Asia. "You ready?"

"I've said my goodbyes."

Ivy dug the key fob and keys from her purse then addressed the funeral director. "Thanks again. I hope we haven't messed up their job too much." She tilted her head toward the diggers.

The funeral director smiled as he ushered them from the tent.

"This is Florida. Comes with the job."

He hurried to the awaiting hearse. A curtain of rain marched through the grave sites as they slid into Ivy's rental car. She started the engine with a push of her finger and the wipers groaned as they swept the windshield. "Looks like this may be a frog-wash."

Asia giggled. "I'd bet you don't come out with that one in Seattle."

Ivy chuckled. "Nope. Takes too much time trying to explain what it means." She reached over and poked Asia's ribs. "That's why I need you to come and visit. We speak the same language."

Drops of rain pelted the windshield and dripped down the glass, draining the humor she'd felt a moment before. She drew in a deep breath, then exhaled. "It's over, Asia. Veronica is gone."

Asia closed her eyes and leaned back. "This was never about that money. The good Lord brought us here so we could let go. And let go we shall." The creases in her forehead and around the corners of her mouth relaxed. "I want to visit Seattle soon. But for now, I want to go home. I miss Tennessee."

"I understand. Where to now?"

Asia kept her eyes closed but pointed toward the windshield. "Forward."

Ivy pulled the gearshift into drive. "I love the way you think, China Girl."

CHAPTER 50

In all the time Asia and Ivy had been in Florida, Janice M. Browne had failed to master the art of being on time. Asia shifted, uncrossed her legs to ease a cramp in her calf muscles. Janice Browne had sucked an hour and twenty minutes from her day. Time she'd scheduled for packing and saying goodbye to Ivy. And Nolan.

Since Veronica's passing thirteen days ago, she, Ivy, and Nolan made certain to spend time talking over the past. And the process had forged a new family relationship. The previous evening, Nolan and Nicole invited them over for dinner. There, she and Ivy were introduced to Nolan's young daughters. Heard "Auntie Asia" and "Auntie Ivy" for the first time from the youngest daughter, Katie. The genes in their family ran strong. Both of Nolan's daughters possessed sapphire-blue eyes and blonde hair. And, like Asia and Ivy, opposite dispositions. The elder daughter, Samantha, clung to Nicole at first, saying little even when spoken to. By bedtime, she'd warmed up some, but still regarded Aunties Asia and Ivy with caution.

The younger Katie bounded onto Ivy's lap at first introductions. She prattled on about kittens, and Auntie Ivy's boys. Her "boy cousins" she called them. Nicole repeatedly told her to get down, but she ignored the command until Nolan intervened and set her down in a different chair. Asia saw a familiar flash in Katie's eyes. The anger of having her will thwarted by another. A cold chill needled down her back.

Katie still resided in early childhood. And Asia remembered from all her child psych classes that the main goal of every child was getting their way. She dismissed the thought and concentrated on getting to know her family better for the rest of the evening.

Nolan married well. A different Nicole from the one at the hospital or the one who'd met them within the walls of her home previously welcomed them now to home and table, inquired about their lives, complimented her and Ivy on their accomplishments and cooed over the pictures of Ivy's boys. She accepted this new normal for her family with open arms. Even Cynthia gave them peace, choosing to stay in her room for the evening and remaining there, even during the meal.

Later, after Nicole had taken the girls upstairs to get ready for bed, Nolan cleared his throat and said, "I heard from our friendly neighborhood detective today. They've done some online, phone, and ground research. Both Vernon Dell and Rita Robertson have been presumed dead for years. Dad's investigator had pulled the information about Vernon and his wife but there had never been a real inquiry into Rita." His shoulders flexed. "Until now. Locals in Leesburg who knew Rita said she left for a work-related trip and simply never returned."

"So, we can still only guess at what happened to them," Asia said.

"Let sleeping dogs lie," Ivy countered.

Now, at the attorney's office, Ivy's chair squeaked as she stretched her arms and yawned. "If she doesn't hurry up, I'm climbing on this table and taking a nap."

Beside her, Nolan drummed his fingers on the arm of his chair. "I have a meeting with the county property appraiser at four today, and I'm supposed to meet with a biologist to go over the results of soil samples on another property I want to buy." He slapped the tabletop. "No time for this."

Janice rushed in then, her arms filled with legal envelopes and files and an insulated thermos. "Cara called in sick, and I'm so behind I'm running into myself coming and going." She sank into her chair with a loud pop. She smoothed her hair, adjusted the red and green bangles hanging on her wrists. She greeted Nolan first. "Good to see you again." She clapped her hands together. "Let me offer my condolences." She focused on Asia and Ivy. "You've been through much these past many weeks," she said as she pulled papers free from a burgundy legal envelope. She extracted her glasses from a case and slid them on her face. Their bright red hue matched her bangle bracelets. "Your mother dictated a letter to be read only to the three of you." Janice passed the copies around the table.

"Another letter?" Asia asked as she took her own copy. What more could Veronica have to say to them?

Janice drew in a breath and gathered up her own copy to read. "My dear children, I spent my life fighting for you. You may not have understood my means, but you benefitted in the ends. My wish was for each of you to find your way and soar among men. I always knew what was best for each of you and made certain those things happened."

Ivy clicked her tongue against her teeth. "I may gag. This is unbelievable."

Janice peered over the rim of her glasses. "I assure you, Ivy, I took this down myself, word for word. This has been certified by the courts."

"I'm not doubting *you,* Ms. Browne. This is vintage Veronica."

Janice raised her brows, then continued reading. "Since I found the traditional legal documents too constricting, I chose to write this letter to my babies as part of my last Will and Testament. I, as always, am of sound mind when writing this. I was not coerced, under duress, or the victim of fraud in creating this document. As you well know, my mind is my own. No one in this universe ever reigned over me. I lived my life well. I have much to leave behind and will die with a conscience free of regrets."

Asia shivered. No regrets. Veronica scarred every human being who had the misfortune of being in contact with her. If she and Ivy tracked down the ex-husbands, she'd be tempted to bet good money all three suffered from PTSD. The old anger should have come. But days after Veronica passed Asia had at last pruned the burden. Standing between Earth and God in the night-cloaked yard at the house, she'd stood with arms outstretched in the moonlight, allowed her mind to drift into the velvet heavens, and made peace with Veronica. No trumpets played, no angels' chorus surrounded her. Instead, stars twinkled like Tennessee lightning bugs. And, somehow in that moment, she let go.

"Excuse me, but I need to stop a minute." Janice's voice cracked. She sipped water from the insulated thermos, cleared her throat, and continued.

"I know you followed my requests. And now you have your answers. They testify to my love for the three of you. Ivy and Asia, the money will benefit you both and make dreams come true. That's all I ever strived for as your mother. The money was a gift from your father, William Bryan Delong. He gave it to me before he died."

Janice stopped to take another sip of water.

Ivy raised her hand in question. "So, let me get this straight. Bill Delong left us the money, but Veronica made us work for it. How is that legal?"

Janice drew a deep breath. "To protect everyone's privacy, he gave Veronica the cash, to hold until she located you. She had me deposit the money in her bank account after Bill died."

Ivy arced one brow. "Did you know about the money she stashed in the wall in her house?"

Janice took a moment to answer. "I handled your father's estate planning and knew he'd given Veronica a substantial amount of money when you and Asia lived at home. I … *suspected* she'd hidden the cash. I agreed to set up the house cleaning deal so you and your sister could find that money."

Ivy clapped her hands together. "And that's why she chose you to do her estate. Keep the secrets in the family. And, that explains your hard-core campaigning for Asia and me to clean the house."

Janice tapped the letter. "There's still more."

She ran her finger over the surface until she found her place and continued reading. "You will handle my estate in the following manner. Bring closure here to our world. You are to set aside from my total estate the sum of five thousand dollars for a party to be held the day previous to the reading of my will. Ms. Browne possesses the list of people you are to invite and the date I wish for this to take place.

They are our blood, my loves. You do not know them because I chose not to expose you to such infected individuals. You will show them that Mommy rose above and strove to do in death what they wouldn't do in life, which was taking action to heal the wounds in our family. Do this for me, my babies. Love, Mommy."

Janice took another drink. "Questions?"

Asia pulled a wipe from her purse and washed her hands.

Love, Mommy. Even in her death, Veronica attempted to twist the world to fit her skewed mindset. She was never anyone's *mommy* … she was a marauding virus. Asia scanned Nolan's and Ivy's faces. "Well, then."

Ivy piped up. "I'm sorry, but I'm lost. Who are we supposed to send these invitations to? And what does she mean about finding closure?"

Asia bit her tongue, repressed the correction of "to whom" dying to escape from her mouth. In the spirit of moving forward, she'd determined to fix personal quirks. Correcting grammar outside of her classroom was one of them.

Janice slipped off her glasses and laid them on Veronica's letter. "Closure—uppercase c—was your mother's birthplace in Louisiana. It was destroyed by a hurricane years ago. We did manage to find some of the people on the list she mentioned. Your family. We have names and addresses for them."

Ivy shoved her copy of the letter back to Janice. "This never ends."

Asia mouthed *it's okay* to her sister.

"No, it's not. There's always another hoop."

Janice broke into their conversation. "The request in this letter and the final settlement of her will are the only matters left as far as her estate is concerned. Her debts, including medical care, have been paid." She inclined her head at Nolan. "Bill Delong saw to that." She paused, scanned their faces. "Which brings me to the last thing I want to cover—the money in the box. I've contacted the sheriff's department and their county attorney on your behalf. We've proven through Bill's letters that it had nothing to do with the possible murders of Vernon and Rita. This cash was part of a contract between Bill and Veronica set in motion years before the alleged murders occurred. Legally, it's Veronica's property and *must be* returned to her estate. Their county attorney is reviewing the details to make certain there is no liability to them and will call for release once that process is finished. Ideally, the estate should get the money back in thirty days." Her head bobbed. Once. Twice, as she laced her fingers together. "Realistically, I believe it will take three to six months for all the paperwork to be completed and documents to be filed. I'll handle all the details of the return and will keep you posted on when we can move to the next stage of the process."

Janice's serious-lawyer expression softened. "In the little time I spent with Veronica she created more drama than any ten clients. She's put the three of you in a terrible position. My best advice is this: avoid putting yourselves through the trauma and hassle of settling this in court or through the state of Florida. Send those invitations, have the party, get the will read, and settle her estate once and for all. Then move on with your lives."

Janice opened one of the files and took out two envelopes. She slid one to Asia, the other to Ivy. "You ladies earned these and both honored Veronica. Well done."

"Thank you, Janice. For everything." Asia ran her thumb across her reward. She'd conquered Veronica's horrid challenge and saved her home. She raised her eyes to find Ivy staring straight at her.

"We did it, China Girl."

Asia smiled. "Yes, we did."

After the meeting, Nolan insisted on taking Asia and Ivy to lunch. Since Shelby's was close, it became the chosen venue. On the way, Asia watched quietly out of the passenger's window while Ivy and Nolan traded work stories. The flat, green fields and clumps of pines and oaks seemed to be dressed in brighter hues this trip. Maybe the recent rains greened them. Or maybe her outlook had brightened.

She'd transplanted her heart in Tennessee. But a fraction of her roots would always remain grounded among the Spanish moss, the alligators, and green pastures of Sumter County, Florida. She'd never pine to wear one of the "I Love Sumter" t-shirts, but she was grateful to God that he saw fit to sprout her life in so beautiful a place. As was true for everywhere, there was good here.

For here in Florida, not Tennessee, she'd been born and reborn. Veronica's death brought calm. The numbing effect wouldn't last, and the pain of the old terrors would rear. But for now, she enjoyed peace.

She touched the scars on her wrists. There were spans of a week, or even a month when she didn't think about them, feel their phantom pain. She'd learn to do the same with the old memories. Prune those vines daily until their blooms sweetened the air in her life.

Nolan directed his truck into the parking lot of Shelby's. An abundance of noontime patrons left no open spaces. He circled the lot twice before landing a spot vacated by a crew of Sumter Electric's linemen.

Destiny waved when they entered together. "Our duo became a trio today."

Ivy pointed to a booth along a far wall. "Is that table open?"

Destiny grabbed a handful of menus and napkin-wrapped silverware. "I need to wipe it down first, but we'll get y'all seated before somebody else comes in." She rolled her eyes. "It's been wild today."

Nolan motioned for Asia and Ivy to go ahead of him. He whispered to Asia as she passed by. "It's always a hair short of absolute chaos in here." His cheeks crinkled and dimpled like Ivy's.

As they ate, years of separation melted through shared stories. Their likes and differences emerged. They were pieces of each other, cast in different molds. Nolan lisped his S's slightly as Ivy did. Ivy shared Asia's dislike for fish. All three detested spicy food due to the resulting heartburn. "We got that from Dad," Nolan commented absently.

Asia and Ivy both stopped, forks in mid-air. Then, as if realizing the impact of his offhand comment, he took a sip of sweet tea and went on. "Look ... I think we shouldn't worry too much about Closure or ... whoever Veronica willed that money you found in the wall to.

It's going to be in police custody for a while, I'd bet."

"They have to release it eventually," Ivy commented around a bite of food. "By all accounts and evidence, he gave it to her legally. Those letters he signed were a binding contract of sorts."

Nolan waved off Ivy's statement. "Yeah, well … y'all can keep playing Veronica's little game or you can take a break and give yourselves time to heal from these last weeks."

Ivy raised her glass of water. "Hear, hear. Time to get back to my family, neglected companies, and the IRS."

Nolan scowled. "The IRS?"

Ivy gave an overexaggerated nod. "Tax trouble. Nothing I can't handle."

Nolan whistled. "Good luck with that."

Asia laid her fork on her empty plate. "The school year ended weeks ago, so I'm officially on summer break."

Nolan wiped his mouth with his napkin. "Let's take a few weeks to relax, then get back together and deal with her final wishes." He then playfully patted his belly. "I'm as full as a tick."

Asia and Ivy both laughed, then Ivy excused herself to the restroom. Nolan took their ticket to the counter to pay, and Asia slipped outside, to soak in a little quiet. She breathed in and tilted her face toward the sky.

Find Closure. By leaving that final request, Veronica denied them exactly what she promised to bring. Twisted what should have been healing and peace-giving into another one of her games.

Just like Ivy had said—vintage Veronica.

The bell on the door to Shelby's jingled as Ivy and Nolan strolled through, trading stories about kids' soccer. Normal, boring, everyday topics. And it was glorious.

Veronica was gone. She couldn't bombard their lives with chaos, hurt, and cruelty any longer *unless* they chose to allow it.

Asia slid her hand into the pocket of her slacks to rub Russ's card. She'd saved her home and hopefully Ivy would save her businesses. And, finally, Nolan could release the burden of keeping their father's secrets. They would follow Veronica's last requests, obey her wishes in her will, and be done.

Forever.

Free.

Game over.

CHAPTER 51

Asia waited while Nolan and Ivy traded goodbyes, believing that few things in life felt better than standing in an airport, knowing you were headed home.

Ivy hugged Nolan about his waist. "Take care of yourself, and don't be a stranger. Call me if any weirdness comes up. I'm always awake."

"I believe you. Have a safe flight." He pulled from her embrace.

He came to Asia. "You have a safe flight too." He draped his arm around her, his hand hanging from her shoulder. His familiar cologne tickled her nose. "I always thought of you as my sister. Take care of yourself. Call me if you need me. Anytime."

"You bet."

He pulled free and smiled down at her. "See you in a month."

"You'll call if you hear anything new about the investigation."

Nolan mocked Ivy with an eye roll. "For the third time, yes."

Ivy stuck her tongue out at him. "Just making sure you listened to your *big* sister."

"Oh, man. This sister thing is going to take some getting used to. I rather liked being an only child." He winked with the old Nolan charm at Asia.

"I need to go. Safe travels, you two. Text me as soon as you land." He waved a final time before weaving through the crowd toward the exits.

Asia and Ivy made their way through security, then claimed a table in the food court to wait for the time when they'd have to separate, go to their respective gates.

Ivy tapped the tabletop. "What should I plan on fixing for Christmas dinner? I was thinking ham would be nice, though Denney's family loves to have lasagna. Maybe we could have both, kind of a Southern-Italian mashup." She gave a look asking for Asia's consent. "What do you think?"

"You're rushing things. Couldn't we just exchange Christmas cards this year?"

Ivy pooh-poohed her answer with a short wave. "You need to think bigger. If we don't push to make it happen this year, it becomes too easy to let it not happen every year." She wiggled her finger toward Asia, then herself. "We're already proof of that."

"Can't argue with that." A passerby made a dramatic step around Asia's chair as he maneuvered past. She scooted closer to the table. "I still think Christmas cards are the best first step."

"Fine. I'll call Nolan and send you a Christmas card. With two round-trip tickets."

"Two?"

Ivy held up two fingers. "Yes, two. For you and Mr. Calendar Guy. We have plenty of space, guest rooms and pull-out couches all over the place. Might as well fill my house with *my* family this year. Denney would love it."

"I only get two weeks for Christmas break—"

"Christmas only lasts *one* day, Asia. Two if you count Christmas Eve." Ivy leaned in close. "And you've got the money. Even after you buy your home." She winked. "And I will have settled with the tax man by then so I'll be ready to celebrate. Who better to share that with than my baby brother and sister?" Ivy grinned.

It all *sounded* good, but Asia wasn't sure. She'd loved spending her Christmases in the mountains. The crisp air, the first dustings of winter's snow. The candle-lit Christmas Eve services at church, the aroma of the pine and cedar branches she and Russ always gathered from the Christmas tree lots and placed around her townhouse. They were the only type of real plant she tolerated in her house because he made sure to debug them before he brought them inside.

The thought of spending the holiday in Ivy's noisy, bustling house, in a faraway city, with strangers ... her heartbeat amped.

Reaching forward ...

"When does your flight leave?" Ivy asked as she pulled a Starbuck's gift card from her wallet.

"Couple of hours. How about yours?"

"Hour and a half, barring any weather delays." She pointed to the coffee shop. "You want anything?"

"No thanks, I'm good."

Ivy put her hands over her heart. "Come on, last chance for me to take care of you."

Asia declined with a silent head shake.

"Be right back ..." Ivy returned with a steaming cup cradled in her hands. She slid into her chair, dumped a packet of sugar into her tall cup. "You'll never guess what I thought of when I was standing in line."

"Can't imagine."

"Remember when we pretended that we were knights on a quest for a golden sword?"

Asia nodded. "We played we were traveling all over England and had to sleep in the woods. I must have gathered a thousand sticks to build fake campfires."

"And Nolan snuck one of his mom's pots out of the house."

Asia giggled. "And we made those awful mud potions in it. Didn't Nolan end up with a rash after that?"

"He was covered in pink spots for days."

"We said he contracted some horrible disease that could only be cured by the dust from a crushed dragon's scale."

Ivy took a tentative sip of her coffee. "You spent days grinding down a piece of the salt licks from Mr. Taylor's cow pasture for the magic powder."

Asia broke into laughter. "And remember how poor Nolan screamed when we rubbed that stuff onto the spots of Calamine lotion his mom spread over him? Can you imagine how badly that must have stung?"

Ivy choked back giggles. "It's no wonder he was so scared all the time. We were flat-out awful to that boy."

Her giggles erupted into high-pitched cackles. Asia laughed so hard her breath ran short. The people sitting around them glanced from their phones and stared. For the first time in her life, she didn't care that she caused a loud commotion. The laughter swept more of Veronica's residue away like the gentle breezes that came days after hurricanes passed.

Ivy whooshed a loud breath. "Coach Mills should have thanked us for toughening that boy up. We had him outnumbered, two sisters to one brother."

"Poor guy can't get a break. Even his children are girls."

Ivy used her napkin to blot her nose. "Those were great times. I had forgotten."

Asia retrieved her own compact, wiped her face dry with a tissue from her purse. "We've spent most of our lives trying to forget all the bad. Let's try a little harder to remember the good. In us … and in Nolan."

"Deal." Ivy reached for Asia's hand, but knocked her coffee cup over instead. A thin stream of brown snaked across the table and dripped in her lap. "Oh brother. Grab me a few more napkins, will you?"

Asia headed for the counter of the closest restaurant. The line of waiting patrons blocked her way to the dispenser. As soon as a hole opened in the sea of bodies, she pulled a palm-full of napkins free and hurried back to Ivy.

"At least this wasn't one of our famous potions." Ivy dabbed at the dots on her brown skirt. "Might have eaten a hole clear through my clothes."

They erupted into gales of laughter again.

Asia maneuvered through the crowd from the baggage claim area in the Knoxville airport, arms filled with her pillow and sleeping bag while also pulling her suitcase behind her. She couldn't believe she'd forgotten to arrange a ride home with the airport shuttle service when she changed her tickets. Now she'd have to waste time walking to the shuttle office and waiting for the next available driver.

Her phone buzzed in her purse. She stopped, rearranged everything to one arm, then answered her phone with her free hand.

Russ.

"Hey. Aren't you at work?"

"Nope. When you texted me that you'd need a ride, I decided to head on over after I knew you'd landed. As it turned out, I had already switched shifts with a buddy last week, so I'm off and today belongs to me."

Asia felt a grin spreading across her face even as confusion set in. She hadn't texted Russ about a ride, of that much she was certain. "Where are you?"

"Circling outside of baggage claim. Get your luggage, walk out, and you'll see me." He paused. "Eventually."

As if timed by God, the moment Asia stepped into the warm rush of Tennessee air, Russ's truck rolled to the curb in front of her. He parked, then jumped out of the driver's side, and jogged toward her. He smiled broadly as he took the handle of her large suitcase. "Welcome home."

"Hey, I don't remember texting you ..." she said as they loaded her luggage into the backseat of the cab. Russ opened the front door for her, and she climbed in as his fingertips guided her at the elbow. "When did you get this text—" she asked, stopping when realization dawned. The spilled coffee. When she fetched the napkins, Ivy must have snuck her phone from her purse and sent the message.

Life at the speed of Ivy. Again.

Russ slammed the door behind her, then headed toward the driver's side while she checked her phone. Yep. There it was, the text she didn't send from her phone.

Russ opened his door and climbed in, then pulled the gearshift to Drive. "Have you had lunch?"

"Not yet."

"Then I'm buying. What are you hungry for?"

"Didn't you say you bought a new grill while I was gone?"

His brows raised, bringing a mischievous sparkle all about him. "Yes, ma'am, I did. We'll need to stop by Carver's for meat on the way home, though."

Home. She liked the sound of it.

"That's okay." Asia laid her purse on her bedding, then stretched her legs under the dash. She'd been wedged between two men on the flight home and they'd taken every inch of leg space in their row. Her legs and ankles remained immovable for two hours. She had practically hobbled down the jetway from the plane.

She leaned her head against the seatback as soon as they cleared the Knoxville city limits. In a short while she'd see her beloved mountains.

"So how was it? Really?" Russ asked. His friends-but-open-to-more gaze was welcoming, assuring her that he *wanted* to know.

"It was … eventful. I cleaned Veronica from her house and mostly from my head, reconnected with my sister, discovered our best friend from childhood was really our brother, and attended the shortest funeral service in history."

Russ whistled. "Wow. That's some deep stuff," he said softly. "Anytime you want to talk …"

"I know. And I will."

He stretched his hand across to hers. He gave a gentle squeeze before allowing his hand to linger over hers. She laid her other hand on his. "I'm glad you're here," she said. "I missed you."

"Me too." He pulled his hand free. "Unfortunately, I need this to drive." He gave her a sideways glance. "You know, I like the thought of being missed."

The scalloped foothills sped by as the steeper incline of the road led to their taller brethren in the Smokies. The trees tucked together on the mountainsides looked like woolly, green congregations of sheep. She'd come back to this flock, a member who'd walked to the edge of the cliff, and would have surely gone over if not for the Shepherd's guidance.

Asia powered her window down and inhaled the piney scents.

She was home.
And she could breathe.

Topics and Discussion Questions for Book Clubs

1. The main theme of *Fresh Scars* is forgiveness. By the end of the book, Asia forgives Ivy, Nolan, and Veronica for the pain they caused her in the past. If you were in the same situation, what would it take for you to forgive them? Have you had experiences in your life where extreme forgiveness was necessary? What were the circumstances? How did it work out?

2. Veronica never expressed remorse for how she treated her children. Do you think Asia, Ivy, and Nolan needed that? Why or why not?

3. Ivy claimed Asia was much stronger than she, though their outward behavior would not suggest that. Do you agree? How was Asia stronger, and why?

4. Ivy was terrified that Denney would leave her if he knew she abandoned Asia as a teenager. Do you believe her fears were warranted? What in her past would make her believe this when experience demonstrated that Denney was devoted to her?

5. Both sisters dealt with the painful pasts in different ways. Ivy became an addict and Asia suffered with OCD and eventually attempted suicide. Both tried to run away from the pain. What in their personalities made them choose such drastically different methods of running away? If Ivy had not left home first, do you think their relationship as sisters would have survived? Would Ivy have still become a businesswoman and Asia a special needs teacher? What would they have done instead?

6. When she finally confronts Veronica, Asia gives her credit for making her stronger. Do you agree this is true, or do you think Asia was wrong to thank her? Why?

7. What are some ways a person can work to move beyond a painful past? Even if they aren't affected as deeply as Asia and Ivy, should they try to forgive or just forget? What do you think is the better choice, and why?

8. Asia and Ivy both dealt with pain from Veronica's abusive nature. Why do you think Asia needed to be the one to confront Veronica on her death bed? Do you believe she was truly able to forgive or was she just numbed to the pain because of the circumstances of Veronica's death?

9. Often in a story, the setting becomes another character. Did you find this to be true in the book? How did it come alive to you?

10. This story deals with aspects and difficulties in living with mental illness. In Asia's case, she had a diagnosable disorder. Do you think Veronica was mentally ill or evil? Do you believe she was born this way or suffered a trauma that caused her behavior?

11. Why do you think Veronica hid her trophies in such strange places? Why not have them prominently displayed?

12. Janice Browne suspected that Veronica had hidden Bill's money in the house but didn't disclose that to Asia and Ivy at the beginning. Should she have been more up front, or did she handle this appropriately?

13. From the beginning of the story, Asia believed God was sending her back to Florida to face Ivy and Veronica. This terrorizes her because she cannot see why he would do this. Do you believe God puts us in tough situations to help us work through something? Why do you think he would work this way instead of making his motives clearer and our situation easier?

14. Asia states that "sometimes bad garbage refuses to leave no matter how many times we scream goodbye." What kind of bad garbage is the most difficult to remove from life? Why? What are some ways that we can get help to rid ourselves of it?

15. At the end, Asia states she is home, and she can breathe. Many of us have a special place where we feel we can breathe. What is your special place? Why?